I0655461

INTERCEPTOR

Anatomy of a Broken Arrow

Michael Nixon

ISBN   978-0-9938619-0-1

Published by:
Broadmead Designs
880 Dalewood Lane
Victoria, BC   V8X 5G6
(250) 744-2850

Book design: bookdesign.ca
Printed in USA

Thanks to Don Nixon and John Cucheran
for their inspiration and "goodly gen"

CHAPTER ONE

Friday 4:45 PM 2145 GMT

'Make way gents, make way…, coming through.'

Flight Lieutenant Duckwalker Jones, Royal Canadian Air Force, forced his way through a maze of blue sweaty humanity and cigarette smoke in an attempt to extract himself from the surge of patrons bellying up to the bar in the Snake Pit of the Officers' Mess on a late Friday afternoon. Standing at five foot five, it was tough for him to see and be seen, but his small-man instincts honed from years of experience gave him the upper hand when he attacked and retreated from crowded bars.

This afternoon he'd frequented the bar several times, finally finding the table he'd been looking for.

When one got the view of Duckwalker Jones in motion, one couldn't turn one's eyes away. In conjunction with his small stature, he walked with a strange gait that could only be compared to a duck's waddle.

This unique characterization was coupled with a baby face that sported a pair of oversized aviator sunglasses that he only changed for clear lenses when he flew. His specially designed dark visor took care of the light by day. At night he flew by the illumination from the iridescent gold of his instrument panel and radarscope.

Few knew the cause of his eye damage, and fewer still had ever seen him without aviator glasses on. Women, intrigued by what lay behind them, were putty in his hands once he'd removed his shades. He could only satisfy their curiosity in the dark, so his glasses became his sleight of hand that even the chastest women couldn't resist.

Being 'a bachelor by trade and choice,' as he referred to himself, and the best radar interceptor-navigator in the Air Force, the RCAF had, due to sensitive incidents, posted him to a job that kept him on the move and isolated him at air bases only long enough to satisfy his combat skills. The overriding reason for his forced separation was to keep him away from wives whose husbands were away on some course or other. Orders were to 'get him the hell out as fast as humanly possible.'

Duckwalker had a particular liking for mature women. A lost love had cast a spell he couldn't break, and the search for her anti-potion sent him into dangerous territory. The problem that he and the Royal Canadian Air Force shared was that the women he socialized with the most were mostly senior officers' wives, who provided too many targets of opportunity. If a Saturday dance at the Officers' Mess was scheduled, the officer commanding had orders to conjure up any excuse to get him as far away from base as possible. His R-211 personal evaluations had two dubious entries. Tonight was TGIF Friday and he was amongst only men.

He deflected questioning glances and double- takes as the throng parted for a better view of him. His sunglasses defined him facially but it was his unorthodox walk that was worth the ticket to the sideshow. His nickname, supposedly

Michael Nixon

unknown to him, lived up to his strange gait. More than once he'd overheard, 'That's Duckwalker Jones.'

To counterbalance these imperfections, Mother Nature had bestowed a baby face that would keep him seemingly young forever, a blond crew cut and, if one had the misfortune to catch him in the buff, a disproportionally large penis.

To those who knew of him, the cause of his strange walk and wearing sunglasses, even in the crowded confines of an Officers' Mess on a late Friday afternoon, was cause for speculation.

Wherever he appeared, rumors abounded about how he got that way. More than once he had to stare down an asshole who'd imbibed a little too much, and had made him the butt of a joke. What was most unusual about him was that when he spoke of his childhood, he bragged of competing at a high level in hockey and swimming. The image of a squawking duck slicing through the water was understandable, but Duckwalker on ice skates was another matter.

Born from years of life-changing social scrutiny, he'd developed the hardened shell of a cripple, and with an acceptance that "this is the way it's always going to be," he nurtured the image of a man of mystery. The stares and hushed gossip when he first appeared on scene was by now a scar that had healed to the point of disappearance.

By a nasty turn of fate, he was baptized Dwayne Wellington Jones, his parents failing to give an explanation of where or how his Christian names originated. In high school and flight training he'd paid dearly for his handle, and had resorted to fistfights more than once to enhance his stature. Then he was a respectable five foot eight and clear of eye. Now, he was three inches shorter and was light sensitive to anything brighter than a struck match.

When he was invited to rejoin the Air Force in 1950, the anonymity gained from the passage of time and his changed image gave him the chance for a name change. From then on, he insisted he be called 'D.W.'

As he weaved through the crowd, he noticed that most blatant stares came from newly-minted flying officers barely out of their teens. Others he knew were WWII veterans called back to service. These were his type. With jackets and ties off, sleeves rolled up and, alternating drinks with drags from cigarettes, the din of conversation harked him back to every mess he'd frequented during the war. Then it was 'drink up boys, for tomorrow we die.'

And they did. He was lucky. He'd seen it all before. He'd seen them all before. It was a different war now. These were the new warriors, pilots and navigators trained to fly one of the most advanced fighter interceptors in the world, Canada's homegrown, designed and built interceptor, the Mark 3 CF-100 Canuck.

Duckwalker had been part of the interceptor's radar design. Its success or failure depended on him getting data from simulated combat situations. Stealth and surprise made for startling discoveries.

'Make way gents, make way. Coming through.' Grasping a bottle of beer and a shot glass in each hand held on high, he weaved through the crowd, sideswiped the billiard table then sat at a table where conversations in various stages of intensity, mixed with flaying arms and flattened palms, were in progress. Table-flying.

His spare whiskey and beer caught the attention of a stout balding man fingering an empty glass and looking forlornly towards the crowded bar. The offer of a shot and a chaser pulled him away from a boisterous conversation that he gathered was with his navigator.

Within seconds Duckwalker was into his usual self-directed conversation. His standard technique was to have others question his sudden appearance on base, then ask him what skullduggery he was up to. As with Cyrano de Bergerac's nose, Duckwalker's sunglasses and waddle were off-limits.

'Who the hell are you, and what the fuck are you doing here?' The now empty shot glass and chaser belied his new drinking buddy's flying experience. His smile erased any impression of sarcasm or menace, just a good set of teeth and a creased bald pate.

'D.W.'s the name, 'Standards' the game…, you?'

Duckwalker knew that his drinking partner was Doc Hunter, the second person to eject from a CF-100 and live. He'd been flying solo during his training at North Bay when he was forced to abandon what had been a perfectly good airplane. To date, no navigator had successfully escaped from the back seat of a CF-100 and as a 'back-seater' he had doubts whether Martin-Baker could save his day when the time came. Duckwalker thrust out his right hand to give a firm handshake.

'Doc Hunter, 440 Squadron, front seat. Good to meet you.' He slid a cigarette between chapped lips and offered his pack. 'So you're one of the guys the GCI boys have been moaning about. Who you with? Who's your driver? Maybe I know him.'

Duckwalker's navigator wings on his tunic were the give-away. He sat in the back seat and it irked him that he'd once worn pilot's wings. He was powerless to allude to it. You couldn't wear one set above another, so his current wings were all he could display. It was his cross to bear, but that was yesterday and didn't count here and now.

Duckwalker craned to find his pilot, but he'd disappeared into the mêlée.

'I'm flying with Lou Fender for now. Standards have a couple of guys to ferry me around.'

A braggart, thought Doc. "Little guy." He put a name and face together.

'Lou Fender! Caterpillar Fender!' He slapped his knee and guffawed. 'You got yourself a decent driver there, that's for sure. Just make sure you're up-to-date on current ejection procedures. With Lou Fender you just never know. I bailed out once, and I don't want to do it again. He's done it what, four times? Then there was the bucking bronco through the trees. How he ever came through that one with his skin I'll never know. The man's a legend.' He snapped his Zippo, took a breath and a deep drag.

'So what's Standards doing here all of a sudden and why on a weekend? And why are you on standby in this fucking weather? Didn't your boss check the weather before he sent you here? When I landed today I noticed a strange crew name on the ready board, and asked the flight commander what gives. He said a Standards crew from somewhere was going to man the fort for a day or two to watch some exercise with the GCI radar site at Mont Apica. Are you it?'

Duckwalker was obliged to stay tight-lipped, to a point.

The skullduggery he was up to had to do as much with the squadron's readiness as the GCI radar site's ability to detect incoming threats and scramble a couple of interceptors.

'We're it.'

From the standby crew's readiness to the quality of the coffee, it was on the weekend that the base was most apt to let its guard down. This particular information he wasn't about to divulge, but not wanting to be elitist, expounded on what he could.

———•—•———

Every airliner off-course coming from Europe or any unidentified blip that appeared on the radar screens of the long-range Ground Control Intercept radar sites scrambled the ready-crew from the closest Canadian interceptor base. Every scramble had its glitches and gremlins, and it was Standards' job to discover and fix the problems.

A post-war engineering degree at MIT in advanced electronics qualified Duckwalker for his job, and his re-enlistment caused the Air Force to welcome him with open arms and instantly promote him to flight lieutenant. There was no officer refresher course, no marching, no bed checks, and no inspections. The Royal Canadian Air Force needed Duckwalker Jones.

Duckwalker felt that the theory, weapon system, personnel, and technology would work, and with tweaking, would work well. It was the aircraft, the interceptor itself, which he questioned.

Each Mark 3 CF-100 that came off the production line was different from the one before, making it difficult to evaluate its performance. Would it live up to its billing as a reliable all-weather day or night interceptor, or wouldn't it? Was it ready to shoot down Russian bombers if they attacked, or wasn't it? Was Canada going to rely on their southern neighbor to protect them, or weren't they? The political ramifications of the program's success were incalculable. Canadian sovereignty was at stake.

He'd recently run two newly-formed squadrons of Mark 3's through the gauntlet, and the experiences gave him doubt. This weekend they were to vet 440, a reactivated squadron at RCAF Station Bagotville, Québec, 'The Protector of the Saguenay' as the Latin on the squadron crest translated. The squadron of Mark 3 CF-100's, backed by a squadron of F-86 Sabre day-fighters, were all that protected eastern Canada from whatever the Russians may send their way.

This weekend, a sneak attack exercise from a 'friendly' would be 440's target. Except for the Standards crew, nobody on base knew when it would happen or where the threat originated. He deflected this information by turning to the topic of an upcoming event that wasn't confidential.

'The Yanks are flying a squadron of B-36's back from England sometime this weekend, and they're going to play war. We're hoping to pick up some information on how their interceptors perform. It's an imaginary war of course. Gun-camera film and radar recordings will determine the outcome.'

Duckwalker wasn't divulging anything Doc didn't already know. That afternoon, half the squadron had practiced pursuit-curve attacks on an unsuspecting airliner en route from England to Montréal. The chatter between the radar sites at Mont Apica and Goose Bay fueled the scuttlebutt. That wasn't the reason he and Lou Fender were there that weekend, but his drinking companion didn't need to know that. He continued.

'The B-36's are coming in over Labrador and the Gulf of St. Lawrence. American Starfires and their new Scorpions from Presque Isle will attack when they start their descent over New Brunswick. Easy pickings. All we get to see are contrails on their descent to Loring in Maine. Our GCI radar site at Gander will be Johnny Canuck's only involvement in this exercise. The Yanks don't have much confidence in their northern brothers. Goose Bay's on stand-down and the American base at Stephenville in Newfoundland is on full alert. Standards wants us in the air when the GCI boys are in action and the bombers are over our turf. They're coming in single file, and they're using their most up-to-date evasion techniques to avoid inter-ception. Their Starfires use the same radar as our CF-100's, so we'll see how well it works. If their own interceptors can't touch them, we've got a problem.'

Doc offered a cigarette and lit both off a battered Zippo. Duckwalker took a deep drag and chugged the remnants of his beer.

'As you know, the B-36 can fly at over 40,000 feet and, with the size of its wing at that altitude, it's more maneu-verable than a fighter. The Canuck will stall on nearly every maneuver at that altitude. Presque Isle is going to see what kind of damage they can do when they try to steal for home over New Brunswick.'

The jovial look on Doc's face turned to concern.

'That lumbering ox is more maneuverable at altitude

than a Canuck? Say it isn't so. I hope the fucking Russians haven't anything that can fly that high, or we're screwed.'

'Has anyone on 440 flown against one?' Duckwalker inquired.

Doc craned his head and pointed to a dark mustachioed flying officer, sporting ribbons on an open battle dress.

'Don over there is our gunnery officer. He and his navigator are writing attack specs on the "36." They've done about a half-dozen intercepts on them. They were setups at lower altitudes so it wasn't like he caught them with their jockstraps off. He flew bombers in the war, and knows about chaff dispersion and bomber evasion tactics.' Duckwalker noted the name. He'd had no experience flying against the giant B-36 and as the current benchmark for bomber development, he'd need to get up to speed.

'Don says the fuckers are so big that he was breaking away 300 yards further out than he should, yet he thought they were going to collide. Says it's something to do with scale.'

'Three hundred yards loses you a lot of punch when all you've got are 50-caliber machine guns,' Duckwalker replied, referring to the CF-100's armament housed in the belly-pack beneath the cockpit. The gun-camera films showed he hadn't had any success. The word from the Yanks' intelligence was that the bomber's gunners shot him down on every pass.

It was Doc's turn to offer a tidbit. 'The hush-hush boys say their radar-controlled 20-millimeter cannons can get you at a thousand yards. Then maybe that's what they want the Russians to think. Haven't you seen his gun-camera films? Are they doing a setup for you?'

Duckwalker shrugged the shrug of a dim bulb. The ruse had worked. He'd seen the films less than a day after each encounter, but this was information best left quiet. He shook his head.

'No, they're not doing a setup for us this time. It's an all-American show.' It was time to go. 'Great meeting you Doc. Where's the bog? I've got to take a piss.'

As abruptly as he arrived, Duckwalker shook hands and headed back into the herd, scanning gaps in the crowd for his pilot. Lou Fender needs to have a chat with this Don fellow, he thought, and he, his navigator. First-hand experience trumped gun-camera films. Standards needed to know how the CF-100 felt, how it performed, how it responded. His ruse with Doc Hunter had become a serious topic for another time.

After his urinal break, Duckwalker headed off to find his pilot. They'd flown in from Ottawa that afternoon, and while en route, his pilot had little to say. He'd met Lou Fender at a Standards briefing the day before, and had beers with him at the mess at Uplands that evening. All he'd been able to glean from him was that he was a re-tread, a bachelor, and dull.

Problems with the APG-33 radar grounded them until mid-afternoon and when they strapped in and fired up there wasn't the usual front and back seat banter.

'Not a team player,' he noted. 'Not good.'

During their flight to Bagotville, the autumn sun had cast long shadows over the brilliant reds and yellows of the Québec countryside, heightening hills and deepening valleys. The benign air mass they flew through contrasted sharply with the towering frontal system approaching from the southeast. The cumulus buildup climbed to over 35,000 feet giving an illusion that they were flying towards the Himalayas at sunset. At Met briefing they'd been ordered to divert to their alternate if the storm beat them there.

The weather pattern was unusual for early October. A dry Arctic air mass had walled off the remnants of a late summer hurricane that had torn up the East Coast of the United States. The storm was intensifying and lingering over the Maritimes and southeast Québec like a nagging head cold. The advancing thunderstorm and deepening twilight was a harbinger of a bumpy approach and landing.

'We're in for a quiet weekend if this shit sticks to the wall,' Duckwalker commented as they'd bounced and weaved on their GCA approach. A grunt of acknowledgement confirmed his suspicions. Lou Fender was a man of few words.

Duckwalker empathized with pilots, and he sensed they knew that he understood the workings of the front seat more than the usual navigator. He was renowned for enduring sustained high-G and violent maneuvers with little reaction. It was unnatural for someone hunched over a radarscope, at night and with no reference to the horizon, not to react with nausea or vertigo, but there was no whipping off the oxygen mask and puking into the bag for Duckwalker Jones.

'Make way gents, make way.' He squirmed through a throng, further compressed by the arrival of the Sabre pilots. 'Let the jousting begin, you jalloonies, and may the best knight win,' he cried to a crowd that never heard a word. The differing aircraft had never been based together so the mixing of CF-100 crews and Sabre pilots was rare.

Michael Nixon

Each aircraft had its own role as a fighter: the CF-100 being a day and night all-weather interceptor and the Sabre an agile dog-fighting day-fighter. The Sabre was proven in battle in Korea but had no value against an opponent in cloud, at night and at high altitude.

Duckwalker had no time for the ribbing about the CF-100's lack of speed and maneuverability, so he avoided contact. His objective was to intercept Lou Fender, and let him know as tactfully as possible that he was the boss. Being a navigator and somebody who outranked him, it wasn't going to be easy.

He spied a house phone and decided to scratch an itch. Cupping the ear and mouthpiece he barked in his CO voice. 'Give me the ready room.'

"Instant response, very good," he thought, a mental tick mark filled a box on his checklist.

'This is Flight Lieutenant Jones. I want one of the standby aircraft equipped with tip tanks and fueled on a half hour's notice. Is there a JATO pack and team here? Good. Keep them handy, just in case.'

He rang off, took a drag, a swig, and adjusted his glasses. Suddenly, a brilliant strobe from a lightning flash shot down from the foyer and he flinched in pain.

CHAPTER 2

F lying Officer Lou Fender sat alone in the darkened lounge of the Officers' Mess, nursing a rum and coke and nervously fingering a cigarette. The din from the Snake Pit below and the boisterous parade of arrivals for Friday night festivities was all too familiar. His life had become a metronome of Friday nights, alone, drunk, and melancholy. There was no wife, no family, no home, no friends; just an endless parade of strange faces that he would meet, converse with, and discard. Lou Fender was an ejected cartridge that had hit the ground too many times.

It seemed to him that every Officers' Mess in the Air Force had been built from the same set of blueprints. The "Snake Pit" was a half level below, and the dining room a half level above, with the foyer and the lounge in between. The sameness of this environment, wherever he was, only enhanced the repetitions of what had become the dreariness of his life.

Mess life was boring, barrack life was boring, and worst, flying had become boring. Flying was his life, and if it lost its allure, he knew that all that remained was the ticking clock of loneliness. Companionship, if one could call it that, manifested itself only in a crowd, but, like the beehive buzz emanating from below, something that he'd once embraced had become superficial, and he had withdrawn into a deeper melancholy than ever experienced.

Lou Fender considered himself the last 'stick-and-rudder' man in the Air Force, and it depressed him. Everything depressed Lou Fender: his job, his divorce, his drinking, Ottawa, the onset of winter, the four-eyed gimp he was shackled to for the weekend, and of course the main reason, the one that started the drinking to begin with, the one known only to him—RANGOON!

Lou Fender was not your standard fighter pilot inasmuch as Captain Smith of the Titanic was not your standard sea captain. Both were very experienced, but both became dangerous when social pressure came in conflict with good practice. In a two-year period during the war, and in the five years Lou had served since his re-enlistment, he'd bailed out of aircraft three times, and ejected once. That didn't count the P-51 Mustang fighter he'd pancaked into the trees on Vancouver Island, resulting in the purple scar that ran diagonally from his right forehead and down his left cheek.

His scar was amplified to a Lon Chaney intensity by his penetrating heavy-lidded brown eyes that evoked a fierceness which, when he wished, could deflect anyone from making overtures of conversation. Women, attracted by his repulsive beauty, rarely approached him for fear of falling under his spell. Erect in stature and with a commanding voice, he had, during boot camp, distinguished himself as a no-nonsense cadet who was singled out to call the parade orders that he directed with a master-at-arms authority.

None of his crashes were attributed to pilot error, but with four flying-machines augured into Mother Earth and one chain-sawed through a grove of fir trees, one had to have doubts. The silk caterpillars in his shaving kit presented by the parachute packers after each successful bail-out were required to be displayed under his campaign ribbons, but he was loath to wear them. One maybe; four, never!

Still a flying officer at 31, he had more flying time than anyone his age in the Air Force but the entries in his logbook were the only measure of him. Since his conversion to CF-100's, he felt the sickening disappointment of one who senses one is on a descent from the loftiest point of one's career.

The airplane he was flying lacked all the attributes he'd expected from the cutting edge in aviation. It wasn't nearly as fast or maneuverable as the ones he'd graduated from; worse, it required a crew of two. Constant breath intakes and wheezing exhales from the cold, moist confines of two oxygen masks was irritating enough, but the idle banter from the stranger sitting behind him felt like fingernails scraping on a chalkboard.

With his escalator rise from Mustangs to Vampires to Sabres, he'd finally become the fighter pilot he'd expected to be: alone and answering to nobody. Why a first-class driver, relegated to an obscure Air Force department was taxiing a back-seater to godforsaken places like this was the price he'd paid for his past. He couldn't avoid the irritant while aloft, but he sure as hell could on the ground.

Lou Fender was meant to fly in an era when seat-of-the-pants skill and exceptional eyesight were all that was needed for a fighter pilot to win in an aerial dogfight. He figured he'd get his chance when he was selected as a pilot in 1943, but he was too late for the big show in Europe, and he'd ended up instructing on the Prairies. A posting to Burma in mid-1945 fueled his expectations of seeing combat against the Japanese, but all he did for four months was ferry twin engine Beaufighters and escort transports to drop sites. He amassed a fortune in twin-engine time, but it was instructing on Harvard trainers that was the most valuable to him.

It taught him to fly.

He'd figured that to be a great fighter pilot one had to be a great aerobatic pilot, and the one thing the Harvard could do best was aerobatics. He perfected them to such a degree that the base commander insisted he perform at air shows and recruiting drives across the Prairies. To an aerobatic pilot, the prairie expanse was most enticing.

He planted two Harvards into Alberta gumbo, and each time he and his student had lived to tell the maintenance officer to go fuck his hat badge. The transition to flying twin-engine Beaufighters raised his hope of getting into action, but with the war in Europe winding down and despite a request for combat duty, he ended up in the Far East, relegated to transport escort work and ferrying aircraft to demarcation ports for shipment. At least he could say he'd been there.

After the war, the only flying jobs came from airline and transport companies, but the four-engine boys swept them up so he was forced go bush flying in the north. In the summer he flew single-engine floats, and when it froze, he switched them for skis. His medical-evacuation flights and 'get there and back at any cost' bravado enhanced his reputation with the locals, but his cavalier attitude of pushing weather didn't sit well with the Department of Transportation, and he was grounded twice. He fell in love with a nurse in Yellowknife, but when she learned of his flying reputation she dumped him for a mining engineer. The solace of the only bar in Yellowknife and the light deprivation of the Arctic winter produced a melancholy that made him borderline suicidal. Alone and friendless, he'd resigned himself to the life of a monk.

An Air Force transport unexpectedly arrived in Yellowknife on a black, blustery, winter afternoon, and with it came a missing piece of the puzzle from his past.

Pete Rylander sauntered into the bar, hung up his great-coat, and gasped.

'Lou Fender, you old fart, as I live and breathe! What the hell are you doing here?'

Lou had been hangar-flying with the bartender, nursing a fourth Scotch and chaser, when the familiar voice and reflection in the bar mirror sobered him in an instant. He turned and greeted the only pilot he'd been close enough to call a flying buddy. He focused on dark piercing eyes and an angelic face that he recognized as having spent too much time in the Arctic.

'What the hell am I doing here?' he responded with a laugh. 'What the hell are you doing here?' They shook hands and with an uncharacteristic show of affection Lou escorted Pete to a table. They ordered drinks and got down to the business of catching up.

'Lou Fender, I've been looking for you since Vancouver. How long has it been?'

Lou had put Rylander on his best lost-and-forgotten list and the shadow of their past made him uncomfortable.

Pete did or did not know of 'the incident' and Lou was not about to query him on it.

'It's been two years,' Pete remarked. 'I never thought I'd meet you in a godforsaken place like this. I never thanked you for what you did to improve my flying skill. Those mock attacks and evasion techniques and tight formation flying on those escort and delivery flights made me a decent pilot. You're the reason I'm still at it.'

Pete Rylander had been a below-average pilot. Out of a sense of duty, Lou had taken him under his wing with hopes of keeping him from ending up in the jungle. Flying did not come naturally to Pete Rylander, and how he'd ended up in a war zone was questionable. His survival would have been poor at best if he'd ever ended up in real combat.

They'd spent the last months of the war in the same outfit and returned to Canada by ship in late November, 1945. They'd shared booze, women, and flying, and except for 'the incident,' Pete knew more about Lou Fender than anybody alive. They'd lost touch and Lou never expected to see Pete again, especially wearing an RCAF officer's uniform.

'What brings you here, Pete?' He passed his pack and lit his Zippo.

'I'm the copilot of the North Star that came in this afternoon. We're ferrying shit around the Territories, and some of the guys on board are working on the Northwest staging route, whatever the fuck that means. They're going to build some radar stations further north. I keep hearing the words "DEW Line." I sit in the right-hand seat, and take over when the captain takes a shit.'

'That answers the immediate question, you asshole.

What I want to know is how the hell did you get back in the Air Force? I thought you were discharged like me.'

'Never happened, old boy. I just kept pounding on the desk and begging them to let me stay in. They said the only officers they were keeping had to have a degree, so I dangled my Pharmacist Assistant diploma in front of them. They said 'good enough,' and here I am, still a flying officer but you got to start somewhere. That two-year course I took before I joined up really paid off. I was never going back to school to be a bloody pharmacist anyway. I just liked playing with chemistry sets. They needed guys with multi-engine time and two's the same as four. Said that if I were a good boy I'd make captain in five years and they'd give me a Permanent Commission. What's your story?'

Lou filled Pete in on his obscure and checkered career as a bush pilot. They drank and reminisced into the night and when the bartender rang last call, they bundled up and staggered to the hangar where Lou and his Norseman were housed.

'It's not much but it's home,' he muttered with an inflection of shame. 'You see, nothing's changed: a bunk, a bog, and an airplane, only it's colder and the pay's better. At least we had the security of two engines. If the old radial quits, there better be a lake close or I'm in the trees. Weather's the real killer. The Met reports are never accurate. You're better off asking one of the elders what his instincts say. I've flown more trips dead reckoning than I care to remember. More seat-of-the-pants flying than stick and rudder, and by seat of the pants, I mean shit your pants, if you get my drift.' His tone was that of a beaten man.

Pete gazed around the meagre bedroom. On the walls

hung a few hero photos and a large map of Burma; the past, nothing spoke of the future.

'Look Lou, they're taking guys back into the Air Force who've got multi-engine time. A couple of eggheads on the plane were talking about a new twin-engine jet they're designing at A.V. Roe in Toronto. It's going to be an interceptor or something. They don't have the cost to train you and you're young enough to give them a few years. You'd be perfect. Check things out. You could fly circles around me. You never know, you might bounce me from out of the sun again…..or maybe I'll bounce you.' He clicked bottles and took a hefty swig.

Lou sensed something greater in his comment.

'They're looking for tired blood are they? Well the blood of this ol' bird has been pretty well drained. I'll give it some thought though.'

In the morning, Pete disappeared into the black of the Arctic winter. Lou watched with envy as the aircraft's anti-collision lights disappeared into northern lights, and he knew events in his life needed a change, or his days were numbered.

Acting on Pete's advice, a month after a visit to the recruiting center in Edmonton found him on a train to Centralia, Ontario, for an officers' refresher course and the security of a Short Service Commission. Three months later, he was instructing on Harvards at Penhold.

His flying skills returned and he formed a three-plane aerobatic team made up of bachelor instructors that he named the "Yellow Perils." On weekends they barnstormed, drank, and screwed their way across the Prairies.

Lou met Francine and fell in love for the second time,

but their childless marriage lasted only two years, and he was shattered when she filed for divorce. Her excuse for the failure was that he was always away on course or flitting about the country, but the scar from the Mustang crash mirrored in her eyes reflected the perils of the wife of a pilot, especially one who had a history of tangling with Mother Earth. He brooded over his loss with an alcohol-fueled ferocity that, until a flight surgeon recognized the seriousness of his problem, had nearly gotten him discharged from the RCAF.

With counseling, his drinking became less self-medicating and, tempered by the fear of a lost Air Force career, it became less of an issue as the challenge of flying faster and more complicated aircraft became his drug of choice. By 1951 he'd graduated to jets. With the advent of the Korean War, he volunteered for exchange duty to fly with the Americans and fight MiGs over Korea, but his requests for transfer were turned down, and he ended up the flight commander of an auxiliary squadron in Montréal.

Caterpillars number three and four came at the expense of a de Havilland Vampire and an F-86 Sabre. On both occasions, he experienced engine flameouts that he was unable to get re-lit. His escape from the Vampire, a jet equipped without an ejection seat, was harrowing. He'd been trained to crawl over the wing and push off to save from being sliced in half by its boom tail, but the slipstream was too strong and he ended up hitting it with his feet, breaking an ankle and losing both flying boots. He landed in a lake, so their loss was his savior.

The F-86 Sabre was equipped with an ejection seat, and once he'd blown the canopy and squeezed the triggers, the explosive kick in the ass, automatic seat separation and opening of the parachute left him dangling over the Ontario countryside.

'Never again!' he swore as he crashed through frozen spruce. 'Never again.'

Except for the GCA approach in Bagotville, and the idle banter from the four-eyed waddling dwarf in the back seat, the flight from Ottawa had been at best an okay start to an interesting weekend exercise. He'd heard his navigator could take stress without complaining and, except for a solo trip he'd taken at the CF-100 conversion course, he'd never had the opportunity to push the aircraft.

The navigator, or whatever the hell they were called, was always the limiting factor. Pursuit-curve attacks could be extremely stressful, and it was not uncommon to go from zero to 6 G's in less than a second. If the navigator blacked out at the wrong time, it wrecked the intercept, or at worst, wrecked your whole day.

With his head in the scope and no reference to the horizon, the navigator could go out cold for several seconds, and, coming to, not know what the hell had happened. The engineering orders dictated the flight parameters of the CF-100, but what could it really take at night in the worst crud God could produce and intercept the enemy? That was the billion-dollar question, the question Lou Fender needed answered. That was his job, his mandate.

The B-36 intrusion exercise from England was out of their bailiwick, but to be in the air at the same time Goose Bay GCI site was in the thick of the foray had its merits.

A practice scramble using one of 440's ready aircraft on a B-25 out of Chatham was to be their target setup and it would have been interesting to see how the four-eyed gimp handled it.

He was different than any navigator he'd flown with. He'd sensed it the first time they strapped in and fired up. Rumor had it that he was involved in the development of the lead collision course radar for the rocket-equipped Mark 4 CF-100. It was his image that spooked him. What were the waddle and glasses all about and how the hell did he rate Flight Lieutenant?

Lou finished his drink and, not wanting to fight his way through a herd of boisterous aircrew for a refill, buttoned his battle dress and slipped his wedgie hat into his belt. A brilliant flash of lightning followed by a peal of thunder heralded the advancing front. The airbase was definitely on stand-down. A mandatory return to Ottawa by Monday noon was all that was written on his dance card. The gimp was right; they'd be sitting on their butts all weekend. The thought of having to hang around a strange Air Force base without getting airborne made him queasy. Boredom meant booze, and booze meant trouble.

The bulletin board advertised the Saturday afternoon matinee as an Audie Murphy western for the kids, and he'd seen the evening movie. The notice board also heralded a dance on Saturday evening. Normally he avoided such events, but with nothing to do, decided to attend. He'd brought along casual wear and fresh underwear. Dress code was not an issue.

He emerged from the shadow of the lounge into the foyer and was about to go up to the dining room, when he was enveloped by a blast of cold air and driving rain. Two wet, squealing, and slightly tipsy women busted through the front door and desperately grasped for him. They giggled with delight, and he scolded them with a gentleman's authority.

'Ladies, ladies, ladies! Now let's behave like ladies.'

With a statue's rigidity he restored their balance and, turning his attention to the young woman gripping his right arm, stared into soft grateful eyes and a smile that produced deep symmetrical dimples. In the snap of time that it takes for a parachute to open once the rip-cord has been pulled, Lou Fender fell in love with Darlene Muncie.

CHAPTER 3

Friday 6:00 PM 2300 GMT

Darlene Muncie had been chasing a phantom pilot from British Columbia to New Brunswick and all Air Force bases in between. The ticket for her Odyssey came via attributes of being bilingual and possessing a university degree in education. Having once met a pilot at a cadet graduation dance at Moose Jaw, resulting in a one-night stand, she'd vowed to hunt the bastard down and get revenge. What her revenge would be once her quarry had been cornered was still undecided.

Her problem was, she couldn't remember his name and he'd disappeared into one of twenty air bases across Canada. By good fortune, the Department of National Defence supplied her with unfettered mobility via a recruiting drive. When she graduated from university she was hired as a roving substitute teacher, taking her to the far reaches of Canada. There, she could hunt to her heart's content.

She grew up in St. Boniface, Manitoba and had Métis in her blood, accounting for olive skin and exotic eyes. With a narrow waist and wide hips, she wore the classic styles of the day that she shopped for while passing through Montréal and Toronto on her cross-country travels. Short-cropped hair capped her high forehead, and a slim neck enhanced her medium height.

She'd gone into the lion's den when she'd taken up her mission. Over a three-year period, she'd perfected a shield that she only let down in moments of extreme intimacy. The mention of the word lesbian at TGIF had more than once been muttered by some unfortunate would-be suitor whose pursuit-curve attack on her had resulted in a botched intercept.

Darlene was surviving a nomad's life in a man's world, but after three years of hunting, she'd lost focus on her mission and was tiring of the chase. Her quest had become blurred, and at times she couldn't remember what her quarry's face looked like. That bothered her the most.

Her appointments rarely lasted more than one semester, and the parade of new faces in classrooms and at the mess were taxing her to a point that alcohol was starting to direct her lifestyle. She was given the housing and mess privileges of an officer and would have rated a salute had she worn a uniform. As it was, she got them anyway.

More than once, she'd overstayed her welcome at mess dances and dinners, but seeing that half the crowd was worse off than her, was none the wiser. She was never around long enough to cause gossip or scandal. At worst, she turned heads or was the object of gossip from women and lusting speculation of men. When tippled, she could hold court with men and women equally, joking and kibitzing with the same ease she had with her brothers and sisters.

'Ladies, ladies, ladies, now let's behave like ladies.' Darlene grasped for a crooked arm perfectly positioned for the tipsy teacher about to end up on her butt. A voice like one she'd never heard got her attention, a voice that said man, not boy.

Then she saw the scar.

Instinctively, she thrust up her left hand and caressed the length of it. Without thinking and with empathy long unused, blurted out.

'How awful! How'd you get that?'

'Darlene! Ferme la bouche,' her partner scolded. 'You've had a few drinkies. We have a gentleman here. Listen to him and act like a lady.'

Darlene couldn't take her eyes off the scar, and she stroked it again. Lou felt a firmer touch and saw moisture soften her eyes.

'No really! How did you get it?' Lou had never been sideswiped by such a brazen approach: after a few drinks maybe, but not in the foyer, and certainly not without a formal introduction. She'd put it out there so she deserved an answer.

'It involved a gun sight, a Douglas fir, and me. The three of us came together.'

Darlene smiled. 'A threesome, huh? Was it good for you?'

Lou's heart jumped to his throat, choking off a reply. How could he top that? Darlene's partner disengaged herself from his left arm and pulled her away.

'Off to the ladies' room for you, young lady.' With the authority of a scolding parent, she nodded thanks to Lou and directed Darlene from the foyer.

Lou froze, transfixed. A flash of lightning jolted him

from a daze. He shook his head. Stunned and slightly bewildered he headed upstairs to the dining room.

'Holy shit!' he swore under his breath. 'Holy shit!' He'd gazed into her eyes for less than ten seconds, yet he knew his future was hers.

'What the fuck just happened?'

He opted for fish and chips and sat facing the door. He was early for dinner and had command of the room. She'd arrive sooner or later, and he'd positioned himself like a goalie cutting off the shooter's angle.

With heart-pounding expectation, Lou picked at his food and checked the doorway.

Suddenly, a deformed apparition appeared and his heart sank.

Waddling into the room and grinning under a pair of aviator sunglasses came Duckwalker Jones. With his hands on his hips he scanned the room, then made a beeline in his direction.

'Fuck,' Lou muttered. 'The prick beat her here.'

'We need to talk.' Duckwalker hung his jacket on the back of a chair and went to get supper. Lou was trapped, and had the distinct impression that the dwarf was going to grill the shit out of him. He was in no mood for it. Darlene was on his mind.

Duckwalker returned, balancing coffee, fish and chips, and a bowl of chowder. Lou suspected that the better part of an hour was going to be pissed away if he let the conversation get out of control. He saw his reflection in the navigator's sunglasses and curbed an urge to walk away. He didn't look so good himself.

Duckwalker knew he was about to ruffle feathers with his decision to have the long-range tip tanks installed.

'I ordered tip tanks installed on one of the standby aircraft. I couldn't find you to talk it over.' He saw an instant squint in his pilot's hooded eyes. 'If we do happen to get away tomorrow, our alternate might be socked in. I want lots of gas. I read that the Americans discovered the F-80 had better speed, range, and endurance when they put tip tanks on it. Lessened wing-tip drag, vortices they call it. Then again it's not something you don't already know about, you being a pilot and all. Like they say, nothing's more worthless to a pilot than the fuel in the bowser back at base, the runway behind, and the air above.'

Lou was dumbfounded. He was the captain. That order was his alone. The idea was good and his dissertation on the aerodynamic benefits of extra range and endurance was by the book, but how did he know about the flight parameters of the aircraft? What else had he got up his sleeve?

"First, I take a shot in the nuts from a princess, now an uppercut from a frog," he thought. "Two punches from two strangers in ten minutes." He pushed away from the table and gathered his cool.

'Very good squire, but we won't be seeing any action this weekend.' He pointed skyward. 'The light and drum show that just moved overhead is only the leading edge of the weather system. We'll be lucky to get back to Ottawa by Monday. You don't want to be bouncing in your straps in the back seat do you? Remember the Tuesday briefing. Why they sent us here in the first place is beyond me. By the way, the next time you tinker with my airplane, watch out! You might outrank me but I'm the captain. Capisce?' Conversation complete, Lou rose, buttoned his tunic and left.

'I think that went well,' he muttered through gritted teeth as he descended the stairs. 'Very well indeed.'

———·•·———

'No more martinis for you, Cherie,' Josette scolded. 'Not tonight anyway.' The drinks they'd imbibed in the barracks a half an hour earlier hit them with a wallop by the time they beat the rain to the mess. If they piled on any more they'd be gossip fodder for next week's TGIF.

Josette Gerard was a forty-three-year-old nursing sister from Hull who ran the base hospital. A career nurse, she'd risen to the rank of squadron leader and she'd done everything from lancing carbuncles to piecing together the remains of some unfortunate aviator destined for a mortuary somewhere in Canada. One of them had been the only man she'd ever loved.

She was the ideal French Canadian, 'La Belle Fermière.' That was the consensus of those who were unfortunate not to have received her charms. Those who did never kissed and told, not because they were gentlemen - though she only dated gentlemen – but because they never wished to divulge the map of her that they felt only they possessed.

She'd yearned for children, but having been raised Catholic and without a husband, she was forced to live the life of a virgin who garnered sexual satisfaction in ways that skirted around actually having sex. As long as it didn't go in, she wasn't going to purgatory. Nobody ever saw Josette Gerard without a genuine smile of satisfaction pasted on her perfect peasant's face. A satisfied nurse was a complete nurse.

She made a final adjustment to her hair and turned to Darlene. 'Let's get some food. I don't know about you but martinis on an empty stomach make me stupid.'

Arm-in-arm, with heels clicking on terrazzo at double time, they ascended to the dining room.

Lou passed them on the staircase, tipping a hat that wasn't there and getting double salutes in return. He fixated on Darlene for the millisecond she offered, and it freshened the vision of her.

Her look expressed coyness and a hint of shame, and the apologetic glance over her shoulder as they brushed past conveyed a 'come-hither later' invitation for a proper introduction. He headed to the Snake Pit for a drink and to find a pilot to talk to. He had to get the girl out of his head.

Lou hadn't been affected with this amount of silliness since he'd courted Francine. He stopped by the bulletin board and discovered that the Saturday dance was a Sadie Hawkins affair. No social dalliance for him and he decided to use the next day to recuperate from the hangover he was about to induce.

———•◦•———

Duckwalker's radar zeroed in on Josette the instant she and Darlene entered the dining room. They queued for the buffet and he soaked in her every move. From the ultra-secret confines of those who were in the know, an unsubstantiated report had zeroed in on Josette Gerard. They were rumors, but rumors started somewhere. A friend at

DND had access to her personnel records. This trip was to be a reconnaissance only, but the quick in and out had become an extended stay, so he changed tactics. There was more time for the approach, and certainly enough time for the kill.

He unabashedly focused on her, shielding his eyes and peeking over the rims of his glasses when she happened to look his way. He nibbled his food, smoked, and nursed a cold cup of coffee while he eyed her. He could tell they were speaking French, and the animation, gestures, and passion in her delivery stirred him. He had a soft spot for French Canadian women, especially one who wore her hair high in a French roll, had big tits, and sported the latest style of eyewear.

Of all the advice he'd ever been given, be it about his immaturity or bravado, he cherished advice offered by older women. When it was time to make a lifestyle change and the opportunity arose, he solicited advice from the wives of senior officers and women of means. If they wanted to screw, that was okay, too.

Women ran the Air Force, or so a CO's wife had told him. His oily approach on her using the sunglasses routine had gotten him into trouble. He was fortunate to leave his new-found ally satisfied enough to convince her husband to leave him alone. He'd never crossed a woman and vowed he never would.

When the women left, Duckwalker waited long enough so as to not appear a stalker. He exited the dining room, pausing at the top of the stairs to see which direction the ladies had taken. He went down to the foyer and peeked into the lounge, where he discovered the two women sitting with Lou Fender.

'You fucking bastard,' he moaned. 'How the hell did you get to them so fast?' With that he snapped an about-turn and headed for the Snake Pit to lick his wounds.

The married officers had headed home for dinner, and the crowd had thinned to a point that he could stand at the bar and carry on a conversation. No sooner had he struck up one, that he was beckoned by Lou to join him at the other end of the bar. He excused himself, and sidled up to Lou.

'What's up doc?'

'I've got a dilemma: two women, three drinks. The drinks aren't the problem. I need a wingman to take care of one of the ladies. If you can remove her from the scene, so much the better. She might be a little old but I can tell that if you play your cards right she's yours for the taking. See if you can get her to take you to the Sadie Hawkins dance tomorrow night. She drinks martinis.'

Duckwalker's brain lit up like a pinball machine.

'Bullshit luck trumps all.' He toasted himself. 'Bullshit luck trumps all.'

With a drink in each hand, Lou marched and Duckwalker waddled back to the lounge.

'Let the games begin.'

Michael Nixon

Major Lincoln F. Crisp, United States Air Force, had finally put in the last piece of the puzzle that he'd locked into the furthest reaches of a mind that was bent on mass destruction. He was going to be flying home from England for the last time, and knew he'd never reach his destination. With the certainty of success for his year-long plan and the finality of his life balancing each other, he felt calm and focused.

Major Crisp was the aircraft commander of the largest destructive flying machine ever built, the B-36 Peacemaker, and he was going to use it for what it was designed to do.

Major Crisp was not in his right mind. Since the discovery of his wife's secret, he had gone through a metamorphosis that had turned him inside out. The hawk had become the dove, and the altar boy had become a killer. Soon, one death would result in the death of thousands.

The oath he'd sworn on his wife's grave was only one day away from fulfillment. He'd crash a nuclear-laden bomber into a friendly city and show the world the effects of nuclear proliferation. The crash wouldn't cause a full-blown nuclear explosion from the bomb, only a dirty blast, scattering radioactive material over a wide swath. The effects of the radioactive material's long-term damage were insignificant, compared to the short-term shock effect. A year of planning and manipulating had him in England, the jumping-off point for his final mission.

He lay on his bunk, recalling the weather charts of the North American approaches. A large stalled cyclonic low-pressure system approaching southern Québec made for a great decoy. He'd use the weather as an added weapon to his arsenal. It completed the puzzle.

Exercise 'Trashcan' was a mission hidden inside a mission. His aircraft was mixed into a squadron of B-36's returning from England to Loring Air Force Base in upper Maine. The joint military exercise with the British Royal Air Force had been a marginal success, and the squadron was set to take off at intervals over the next twelve hours. What the flock didn't know was that his aircraft was a 'boomer.' The rest of the squadron carried dummy weapons for weight and fuel calculations, but he carried the real thing.

He'd ferried a new atomic bomb over, and he was taking an old model home. Under the supervision of the weapons officer, the plutonium bomb would be loaded into his aircraft in the morning, and the ground crew would be finished fueling by the time the aircrew gathered under the B-36's wing in the afternoon.

Major Crisp was the most trusted B-36 pilot in the wing. He'd been vetted by every agency in Washington and had flown bombers since 1943. His discovery that his wife was a deep-cover Soviet agent sent him on an insane journey that still had no end point. The target he'd choose would be selected when the circumstances said it was so.

To protect his future and the integrity of the Strategic

Air Command, Major Crisp had murdered his wife and got away with it. The ensuing guilt had him paying penance through a grand scheme, fueled by self-loathing. The House Un-American Activities hearings and the nuclear detonations by both sides of the Iron Curtain found him reassessing some of his most ingrained, core beliefs. His wife was a commie; he loved his wife. Within a year of her death, he'd reached the zenith of a plan he couldn't improve on. He would show the world its future.

Major Crisp was the aircraft commander of the most potent offensive weapon the world had then ever known; an aircraft that could fly intercontinental without refueling and deliver two nuclear bombs with impunity.

'Getting home is another matter,' he'd lecture. 'But that's what makes the game interesting.'

Six massive piston engines and four jet engines could take the B-36 to over 45,000 feet. Few fighters could reach it. The 'Aluminum Overcast' as it was referred to as 'six turning four burning' frustrated interceptor crews as their contrails passed overhead.

Major Crisp's plan was simple: disable the crew in the forward compartment, put the aircraft on autopilot for a bomb release over the target of choice, then blow his brains out. That was the crazy part of the plan. The real plan was to make the devastation appear to be accidental. He wouldn't be construed as crazy; he'd be seen as a hero who did his best to save his aircraft and crew.

It didn't take long for the simple plan to become infested with gremlins. He was coming home as a Trojan Horse. His ace in the hole was that he planned his flight track to take him in over a vast, unprotected area of Canada. He'd penetrated Canadian airspace on numerous occasions, and his plan was to program the autopilot to his target of choice while over Québec.

The unusual weather pattern over Québec completed the plan more by accident than design, and as he smoked in the dark he visualized the swirling lines of the isobars over eastern North America that he'd studied at Met briefing. The massive cyclonic pattern would send him anti-clockwise over Québec, shooting him towards one of four targets. He'd fly above the storm, using the upper wind patterns to speed him up, slingshotting him to the target he'd programmed into the autopilot. Takeoff time was eight hours away. He popped two sleeping pills and took a swig of Jack Daniels. Major Crisp needed sleep.

Lincoln Frederick Crisp was as East Coast as they come. Lanky in stature, he had the air of one who could shoot baskets from anywhere on the court, and be nonchalant that they all went in. At thirty-four, the widower Crisp became the most eligible bachelor on base but he avoided social events that involved scheming women. Since her death, he'd never wavered from a vow of celibacy.

After the nightmare of disposing of his wife, Lincoln had himself posted to Loring Air Force Base. He was promised a promotion to colonel and a B-36 squadron to command, but he was unenthusiastic about either. All he wanted was to eat lobster, hunt moose, and fly. He'd returned home.

Lincoln had been raised on the ragged coast of Maine near Padre Island, and he'd spent summers working a family-owned dairy farm in Québec where he'd learned the twang of Canadian French. A Trojan Horse speaking gibberish was sure to fuck up the airwaves when the action got heavy. Each aspect of the plan was so outlandish it had to succeed.

Once his aircraft had 'disappeared' over Canada he would rid himself of the forward crew. Everything depended on their simultaneous death, and if someone smelled a rat he had a pistol with a full clip. He'd kill them off and keep one bullet for himself. Keeping the crew in the rear compartment alive, ignorant, and isolated was the key to his defence.

If the Air Force figured out what he was up to, they'd send everything they had to intercept him. The rear gunners were trained against curve-pursuit attacks, and if he was successfully intercepted, the twin 20-millimeter cannons in each turret were enough to keep the hounds at bay. He'd reconciled his plan had the earmarks of a great aerial battle culminating in a world-shattering disaster.

It didn't take long to discover that things could go wrong with the plan, much of which relied on the disposal of the bomber's forward crew. It wasn't until he read the confidential report on the 1953 discovery of a missing B-36 in northern British Columbia that his plan finally came together.

It was thought that the B-36 had crashed into the ocean off the Queen Charlotte Islands after it had jettisoned its Mark IV atomic bomb. That was in 1950. The discovery of the wreck three years later had the Strategic Air Command dealing with its first nightmare scenario: a "Broken Arrow."

The bomber had crashed into a mountain and was in relatively good shape, considering the angle of the impact. Crash investigators recovered sensitive equipment and destroyed what wasn't salvageable, covering up secrets they thought had lain at the bottom of the ocean. The crew had bailed out and most had survived. Major Crisp determined that if he were able to duplicate the same scenario over a populated area, his plan would be complete.

His takeoff time was seven hours away and sleep was coming frighteningly slow. Then again, maybe one's final hours were meant to go that way. His thoughts were all over the place, and when he slept, his nightmare became reality. The Benzedrine would come later.

Duckwalker kept the agreement he'd made with Lou in the Snake Pit, and within minutes of their introductions, he spirited Josette to the darkest reach of the lounge. When she refused a cigarette, he sheepishly stashed his pack and vowed to brush his teeth. While she teased her martini, he took a hunter's look. Behind dark glasses one could broaden the sweep of the radar beam.

The closer he got, the younger she looked, and the heat from her exuberance, from their introductory handshake to escorting her to his lair, drew him in. Sincerity radiated from her every movement and the softness of her sincerity began to intoxicate him.

'D.W. What's D.W. stand for?' His hair prickled.

'They're the first letters of two names I wasn't old enough to choose, so they don't exist.'

'You won't tell me your name? How ridiculous. And why do you wear sunglasses all the time? I noticed you in the dining room and thought it was strange that a man would make himself so conspicuous. Don't you find that people stare at you? And what about the way you walk? I'm a nurse, and I've seen just about every recruit breaking in a pair of shoes on a drill square but I've never seen anyone walk like you.'

Caught off guard, he was forced to address the glasses and deformity at the same time, forcing him to short-circuit the conversation.

'I can't talk about either one.' Josette was aghast.

'You're the most ridiculous man I've ever met. You won't tell me your name, why you wear those silly glasses, and you won't tell me why you walk so funny. And I mean funny.'

She spoke with a strong accent, more Parisian than French Canadian. He couldn't tell if she was serious or joking. Her look said she was serious and he shriveled into his chair like a snail that had been doused with salt. It had been a long time since he'd felt the pain of humiliation. Sympathy was not going to be had from this nurse.

'If I told you that I was sworn to secrecy and that I've received personal injury compensation for what happened to me, would that suffice?' He let his question hang.

'If I disclose the reason for my appearance and it gets back to the powers that be, yours truly will pay a very high price. Very high indeed.' He paused to allow his explanation to sink in, then followed up with his tried-and-true bait.

'As for my glasses, all I can reveal is that I don't wear them to bed. I'm definitely not sensitive to the dark.'

Josette sensed he was more of a player than a freak. He handled himself with whatever poise and dignity he could muster, and she sensed him a brat; but brats don't wear two stripes and live in secrecy.

'How old are you Flight Lieutenant D.W. Jones?'

'Thirty-one.'

'That's thirty-one, Ma-am. Remember, you're addressing a senior officer.'

'I apologize, Ma-am, but you were introduced as Josette. I didn't catch your last name or your rank.'

'That was lack of manners on your friend's part. Surely he told you that I was a senior officer. No? And my last name is Gerard. I also wish to apologize. I handled myself too informally. I have to look out for Darlene. She gets silly when she drinks.' She looked to Lou and Darlene who were in deep conversation. 'What can you tell me about Flying Officer Fender?'

'To be truthful Ma-am, I've flown with him for only a couple of hours and had a few beers. I can't say I've ever had a decent conversation with him. I know for a fact that he's a bit of a loner and a man of few words. He's supposed to be a hot pilot, though you wouldn't know it by the number of times he's bailed out. He has the silhouette of the Grim Reaper painted on his crash helmet, if that tells you anything about him.'

'He seems quite taken with my friend. They bumped into each other about an hour ago and now they're like kids at a malt shop. I hope he's not a heartbreaker. She's very vulnerable.' Duckwalker wasn't in the mood to talk about other peoples' affairs.

'Personally Ma-am, I don't know a thing about him, but from what I understand, he's nicknamed "the Caterpillar." I refer to him as "the Undertaker." Doesn't he strike you that way?'

'What about the scar?'

'He rode a Mustang through the trees.'

'He what?'

'That's an airplane. Let him tell you about it.' He was pissed off that her attention had reverted to "the Undertaker." He'd put his own handle on him; he looked like one, spoke like one, and acted like one. He'd never flown with a hearse driver. Who buries the undertaker, he wondered, as he was snapped back to reality by a generous glimpse of cleavage.

The itch in Josette's nurse's curiosity needed a scratch. Her challenge was to confront him with a perfect diagnosis of his afflictions. If that didn't work, there was always her back-up plan.

'D.W., or whatever you call yourself, I want you to dance with me...... Play "My Foolish Heart" from the juke box. B12. It's free.'

Duckwalker choked back the gulp of somebody who realizes he is in over his head. He hadn't been tested with such concentrated social severity since 'the incident.' She was probing him at ease, and he felt defeat. Time for retreat and call it a day; time for small talk and gentlemanly behavior until one could extract oneself. No sharp one-liners, no hidden meanings, no fun.

Older women jousted the best. The hunt was the fun, but once you pulled the trigger, it became work. Every now and then there was 'the one' but they were usually married to someone who could roast your nuts at a mess dinner, and everyone there would feast on them with gusto.

He escorted her to the floor, and with each step tried to override stabbing nerves to his hips. They coupled and Josette drew him in, moving her right hand up his spine from tailbone to neck, searching for clues. The glasses would come later; for now his legs and spine were the focus of her assessment.

Duckwalker forced his way to five foot six, but the pain was too severe and Josette felt him recoil. The sweep of her fingers up his spine stirred him. Separated nerves from long ago seemed to connect. Some things you can control, some things you can't.

He didn't know what to think. Red flags flashed. She was too smart. The women he was used to were horny, delighted in holding an axe over his head in the form of their husbands' rank. Josette was smart, secure, and single, and had the mysticism of a Mother Superior who didn't wear panties.

He bounced his head off her breast four times before realizing that he was leading. He'd heard that stutterers could sing beautifully, and as the dance progressed he rose to his full height and felt no pain. His reflection in a mirror signaled it was just his imagination.

'I see you wear glasses,' he commented, 'and wear them well, I must say. My compliments on your choice of frames. They're so subtle they're not there.'

He drew her in but she resisted. She was going to do the assessing, not him. His mental assessment would come later.

She'd finished probing, and after escorting him to their seats begged a visit to the ladies' room. There'd be no follow-up dance. No use humiliating the guy any more than she had to. He'd done the best he could.

She went to the basics for her initial assessment. When he stood erect he was in pain; duck walk, no pain. The biggest surprise came from the assessment of his spine. Except for a minor scar near his pelvis, all bones and connectors were in the right place. His problem didn't originate with orthopedics. Her assessment became complete when she discovered that he had a well-controlled large penis. The bump and grind portions of their dance and his subtle penis-deflection move as he escorted her to her chair made her grab for her martini. Could his endowment be part of his problem?

———•·•———

Lou couldn't believe his good fortune. First the girls corner him in the lounge, pleading for forgiveness, and then he runs into the waddler at the bar. Before he could say 'Geronimo' he was alone with the only person on earth he cared about. They sat across a coffee table for an awkward minute.

'You've got to tell me how you got that scar. What on earth happened?' She reached over and stroked its gristly ridge. 'I've never met a pilot who crashed an airplane and walked away.'

She was right on with that, he thought. He didn't know any survivors either.

'What was going through your mind the second before you got this? It must have been horrible.'

It wasn't horrible at all, Lou thought. She had the guts to ask the question, so she deserves a reply.

In the spring of 1950, Lou was transferred to RCAF Station Sea Island in Vancouver, instructing on Mustangs and Vampires at an auxiliary squadron. Flying the Mustang with its massive engine, bone-shaking roar, and tricky rudder contrasted with the Vampire's smooth lines and soulful moan.

A gunnery range had been set up off-shore at Comox on Vancouver Island, and throughout the summer he flew daily trips to observe his students and lead them through attacks when the effects of ground rush and geysers of water had them pulling up too early. The targets had been set out in the strait and the plumes of water from the 50-caliber machine guns were disconcerting.

'I want to see salt on air coolers when you land,' he'd chided at debriefing.

'Trouble began on my return to base,' he recalled. 'The engine quit for no apparent reason. I'm over Parksville, and one moment everything is hunky-dory, and the next moment the engine is sputtering and snapping like an old steam donkey. The fuel gauges said I had more than enough fuel to get back to Vancouver. I wasted 5,000 feet trying to get the engine started, and by the time I realized things weren't working out, I was too low to bail out. I tightened my straps, turned everything off, slid back the canopy, picked two of the largest Douglas firs in front of me and flew between them. And that was what was going through my head. End of story.'

'End of the story!' Darlene exclaimed. 'More like the start of the story! What happened next? You crashed an airplane into the trees, for God's sake! What happened next?'

Lou had never recounted those moments to anyone, not even the flight surgeon who'd asked all kinds of questions. The seconds before, during, and after impact were his alone. There was no way he could ever convey his mental experience.

'Time expands in your last moments. That's all I can really say. I thought my life would flash before my eyes but it was nothing like that. I knew I was in for an experience I'd only do once, so I just relaxed and let things happen. I've bailed out a couple of times but this was different. My time had run out. I hit my face on the gun sight when the trees sheared off my wings. I never lost consciousness. The fuselage and I torpedoed through the trees, not in a straight line.'

He paused and cracked a package of cigarettes.

'I was upside down when we stopped. I remember staring at a stream of blood flowing to the ground. I unstrapped, hit the release buckle on my parachute, and fell into a bed of Western Sword ferns. They got me out a couple of hours later. Needless to say, I was just about dead from lack of blood.' She declined a cigarette and as he flicked his lighter, she exclaimed.

'Fire! Didn't you cause a forest fire? What about the gasoline? You said you had fuel. There must have been gasoline all over the place!'

'The tanks were dry. The fuel gauges were snafu. There was a small fire from oil leaking from the engine, but I put it out with my blood.' He grinned and pointed to his scar.

'That's how they found me. I flew over the crash site a couple of weeks later and I couldn't pick out where I went in 'til I spotted the sheared-off fir trees. If the tanks had been a quarter full, yours truly would now have a Douglas fir growing out through this eye socket.' Lou pointed and laughed. It had been a long time since he'd said anything frivolous.

'How grotesque. You pilots have a morbid sense of humor. I've never found out why. You use your flying bravado for gain but lose half of it with remarks like that. I happen to like the living skull I'm looking at.' She shook her head in mock disgust. 'So, you were off the hook with regards to the rather abrupt meeting you and your fuselage had with Mother Earth. The Air Force didn't drum you out of the corps for destroying their valuable property. Didn't break your sword for your ineptness and all that jazz?'

'The fuel gauges were still intact. They read a quarter full. If I'd burned to a crisp, they'd have concluded I was scared to bail out for a third time.'

'Two in a row? You've done this sort of thing before?'

'A couple of times.'

'Have you had any further mishaps since this?' Her hand brushed his cheek and he recoiled slightly. Familiarity was not something Lou Fender was used to.

'A couple!' Darlene threw her hands in the air and fell back into her chair.

'You're a dangerous man to be around, Louis Fender. Should I be wearing a parachute when I'm around you?'

Lou was caught in the moment; should he attack, bail out, or crash?

A flashback took him to Rangoon, recalling a safety poster on the wall of a ready room. It showed an airplane busting through trees with the pilot standing on the wing, the caption reading: 'Procrastination and Indecision Are Dangerous.' He was the subject.

He'd never thought himself a procrastinator; never indecisive, just someone who, 'til that moment, realized that life-changing opportunities come at the strangest time and place. Darlene Muncie was pulling off his shroud.

Lou had never recovered from the loss of Francine. She was a prairie cowgirl through and through: strong enough to tell the man she loved to fuck off, and mean it. No family; no love. An airplane and a bottle became his life. He cursed his loss, and the further he withdrew, the better he liked it. Alcohol became a crutch, until his self control and a large bite of a reality sandwich put him on the straight and narrow. Now here he was, fifteen minutes after an introduction to a complete stranger, yapping like he'd been shot up with sodium pentothal.

'Miss Muncie, you have an advantage on me. You obviously have some magic in you to get me running on like this. If we were in a dogfight, you'd be positioned above me and in the sun. I'm at your mercy.' The resonance of his voice had been her first impression of him.

'Ladies, ladies, ladies! Now let's behave like ladies!' It resonated with her now. It was intoxicating. She'd found a man who showed pain through the inflection in his voice.

Darlene had been stalked by every young-buck pilot and navigator in the Air Force. She was that beautiful. She taught school by day and hunted by night, if you called living in a lesbian-infested barracks the lair of a man-hunter. She'd stared into the pleading eyes of desperate men wishing to bed her, but none of their eyes matched the eyes of her target.

The frightening thing about what drove her was that, except for his eyes, she had no remembrance of the night. She remembered arriving at the Officers' Mess at seven o'clock with a busload of university students, and she remembered leaving in a snowstorm at two o'clock in the morning. What happened in between needed to be known.

The university she attended had provided the girls, and the Air Force took care of everything else. A notice for the dance was posted in the dormitory, a bus arrived at six, and off they went. Return time was determined by the success of the round-up and weather.

The driver fought a headwind to Moose Jaw, and commented to the chaperone that a hefty blizzard was coming in, but she had a date with a flying instructor and he was ordered to drive on. They were greeted in the foyer by the messing officer, and within minutes had been escorted throughout the lounge. Drinks were offered, the band warmed up, and the dance began. She didn't recall the couple sharing the coffee table, only that the men talked nothing but flying and that she was introduced to martinis. After that, nothing.

She was discovered wandering toward the guardhouse as the bus was leaving. She quizzed anyone she knew about the events of her evening, but there was little response. Two women thought they saw her on the dance floor early in the evening. Then she'd simply disappeared.

The bus stopped at a diner at the east end of Moose Jaw to let the storm pass, and there she discovered that something terrible had happened to her. The trip to Regina was a blur of tears under her parka. She was no longer a virgin. Six weeks later, she discovered she was pregnant. A botched abortion sent her on her quest.

'Lou, will you be my date for a Sadie Hawkins dance tomorrow night? It'll be a lot of fun. I'll put together an outfit for you. Please say yes. Please, please!' Lou, mesmerized by her eyes and moist lips, couldn't resist.

'Miss Muncie, it would be an honor.'

Josette approached with Duckwalker in tow. Darlene sprang to her feet. 'Let's all go to the dance tomorrow. Lou's already agreed. Please, Josette. We haven't been to a dance with proper dates, ever.'

Lou looked to Darlene; Duckwalker looked to Josette. They all looked at each other. Four nods followed.

'Well people, shall we adjourn to the Snake Pit for a nightcap?' Lou was in no mood to let the night end.

'Let the games begin.' Duckwalker muttered as he took up the rear. With Josette's bottom dead ahead and below eye level, he waddled behind, counting each of her steps by the rise and fall of her derriere.

CHAPTER 6

Friday 10:30 PM 0330 GMT

Pete Rylander sat in the damp ready room at RCAF Station Chatham, New Brunswick, hoping he wouldn't get scrambled. He'd ended up at the bottom of the combat ladder, roaming Canada as a moving target. Day or night, he'd fly into the nastiest weather, tempting some greenhorn interceptor pilot on standby to come and find him. Sometimes they caught him; most of the time they didn't.

The weather pattern over Southern Québec had intensified as the front pounded into the high-pressure area stalled over Hudson Bay. If the eye of the storm passed over Bagotville there'd be clear weather for a couple of hours and, as he suspected, perfect timing for his attack. Pete's boss, who he referred to as "The Voice from Ottawa" was more than likely at his desk scheming while he spent hours of boredom waiting for his call.

Pete Rylander flew a twin-engine B-25 Mitchell bomber that did everything from spraying for mosquitoes to simulating a Russian bomber penetrating North American airspace. He lived on call and had developed the responsiveness of Pavlov's dog. His aircraft was WWII vintage, but in short-range situations, it had the speed and maneuverability of the Russian bombers. The aircraft was large enough to live in and fast enough to get out of town when the need came. He'd screwed more women in a B-25 than any man alive.

The windstorm that had hammered them for two days was abating. Trees had been uprooted and creeks had overflowed all the while he waited for the phone to ring.

Rylander had flown the jungle, the Arctic, and the Prairies. He'd flown in every type of crappy weather across Canada, but for him, the worst weather of all was in the Maritimes. There was never stability, and if it was decent, the fog became so dense you didn't need to light a cigarette to have a smoke.

Being the target in simulated combat had its advantages. Every exercise had unique characteristics. The permutations and combinations of day, night, weather, altitude, and skill level made it exciting. Best of all, there was always an escape route.

He'd sneak in at tree-top level under the radar then pop up like a jack-in-the-box causing Chinese fire drills at the GCI radar sites and the ready rooms.

With its onboard radar and ground control vectoring from the radar sites, the interceptor had the advantage, but Pete had been shown a few tricks by the man he was about to encounter. Lou Fender had finally popped up on his radar screen. The best flyer he'd ever known was going to get caught with his knickers down.

The phone rang, and it was The Voice from Ottawa. After a few niceties and a brief business report, The Voice spelled out his orders.

'The eye of the low is going to pass over Bagotville tomorrow. Find your way up there, and give them a scare.

The weather's iffy at best but it will be to your advantage if you can sneak through.'

Pete assured him that he'd flown in worse weather, and that his crew was ready for action. The sneak that he was had already made his move. He'd called the orderly officer at Bagotville an hour before and received the information he needed. He'd pass on the information and get a gold star.

'They've got a regular crew and a couple of Standards guys on standby, Sir. The base is on stand-down because of the weather, but that shouldn't stop them from scrambling a couple of jets. The thing's supposed to be an all-weather interceptor, for God's sake!' The Voice thanked him with a promise of beers at the mess when he got back.

He'd already planned the attack route. A close scrutiny of the current weather map on the bulletin board told the tale, and from it he drew a battle plan. He'd developed a sixth sense about weather, and always used it to his advantage. The route he'd planned had greatest stealth for the lowest risk. The Voice demanded the order of battle.

'I'm going up the Saguenay River Valley at low level, Sir. No Laurentians to dodge. I've got a guy in the nose and a copilot with great eyesight. I shouldn't run into any coureurs des bois.' He sensed that The Voice was hanging on his every word.

'The low-pressure area is moving in a stable direction, so I'll be able to sneak in and out of the weather front and give them some real all-weather practice. Could be fun. I've never had a weather pattern this strong to play with.'

'Thank the hurricane for that. When you've finished humiliating them, I want you to fly up the Gulf of St. Lawrence on Sunday and record everything you can from the B-36's heading for Loring Air Force Base in Maine. Your navigator will get their IFF/SIF frequencies once you've finished working the 440 boys over. I've made sure Bagtown has fuel and oil for you. You'll be loitering, so check your range and endurance charts. I don't care if you have to land with empty tanks. I want everything you can pick up.'

'Yes Sir! When do you want the wheels in the well? We've been at the ready for two days and we're a little thrashed. I've got twenty hours of pole time ahead of me. Can we have a little nap before the festivities?'

'Takeoff's at 0700. Good hunting.'

Good hunting. What war was he fighting? We play games, not war.

Pete Rylander was a skirt-chasing addict with guide-dog skills. He'd flown countless tons of supplies during the construction of the DEW Line and was in awe of the dollars being spent to protect North America from a phantom enemy. He'd flown the Arctic long enough to know that a factor as small as an unknown wind strength or direction could dry out a fuel tank. He couldn't see how the Russians could fly over the Canadian Arctic, penetrate North American airspace, then set up to bomb a target somewhere in the United States. Then where the hell were they supposed to go? The whole system was as obsolete as the airplane he flew.

He fought a headwind out to the aircraft and banged on the fuselage. 'Okay you jalloonies, we fly at 0700. Sleep wherever, but be here by 0630. This fucker better be fueled and ready to fly when I get here.' He headed back to the ready room for a shower and a couch. When he didn't dream, he could sleep on an ant's nest.

His quail-like existence as an object of prey hid a camouflaged hunter in deep cover. A pair of penetrating eyes that evoked reptilian fear and angelic beauty dominated his slight, effeminate face. Without his rapier stare and altar-boy piety, he would never have survived his life in Cabbagetown, Toronto. Girls sought him out because he could kiss and jive and boys sought him for his devious mind. No angel had ever been given powers through stare alone.

After his parents were killed in a hotel fire, he'd been raised by spinster aunts who subjected him to every feminine quirk he could handle. He left the coop after matriculation and studied pharmacy at Ryerson College for two years, but when he volunteered for service, his specialty wasn't needed for the war effort. Further testing shunted him into the British Commonwealth Air Training Plan as a pilot.

When he was re-coursed halfway through basic flight training he knew he wasn't a great flyer. Getting the boot from pilot training got you transferred into air-gunnery or radio-operator school, but that type of flying was not for him. The program coddled him, and after much tutorage, awarded him wings and the copilot's seat flying Catalina patrol aircraft out of Tofino on Vancouver Island, looking for Japanese subs and fire balloons. He flew in conditions that no sensible sailor would drop anchor in. His fascination with weather systems and instrument flying gave him a proficiency that he swore allowed him to smell the glide slope and feel the beam.

He craved combat, but not for the right reasons. Political arm wrestling and an uncle high in the Liberal Party got him transferred to a multi-role fighter squadron in Burma, flying twin-engine Beaufighters. With considerable instruction and a few hairy moments, he became certified.

He arrived in Burma in time for its liberation and an enemy gone from its skies. Over a two-month period he ferried aircraft over endless miles of jungle and plain, dodging weather and navigating to destinations on a monotonous horizon. To alleviate the boredom, he'd played war games with fellow pilots, utilizing mock dogfights and formation aerobatics that scared the shit out of him. He became more comfortable in the air after he teamed up with Lou Fender, a fellow Canadian who taunted and pushed him to excellence with tight maneuvers and spontaneous aerobatics.

At first Lou's behavior intimidated him and Pete responded to his taunts with disdain. After he found out that Lou had been an instructor, he took him seriously, accepting his superiority with respect and friendship.

They flew, drank, and whored together until the day Lou returned from an escort trip a different man.

Where once he'd felt Lou a buddy, he now felt him cold and reclusive. He'd inquired about what had happened on that particular flight but was told that it was between him and "that bastard Wilding," and to never ask again. Pete's suspicions of what had happened to Lou in the air that day were only partially confirmed when they shipped to Canada together. Lou became more distant and sullen and when they arrived in Vancouver on Thanksgiving, they had parting drinks and promised to stay in touch. Whenever the opportunity arose, Pete inquired after him, but the country had swallowed up Lou Fender. A DOT report on an incident in Yellowknife ran him to earth.

When he bumped into Lou in Yellowknife, the changes in him were apparent. The enthusiasm in his voice had changed to defeat, and the new-found heaviness of his eyebrows hooded eyes that hid a great lie. He'd become a heavy drinker, and from Pete's observation, his outlook for him was bleak. Lou's ranting while asleep on board ship during their trip back to Canada seemed to have everything to do with his condition.

'Coward and murderer' had more than once been shouted in the dark of their stateroom and Squadron Leader Wilding's name had been blurted out often.

Lou's re-enlistment had been affirmed when Pete recognized his voice when requesting an altimeter setting during a UHF homing and let-down into Winnipeg. From there, he researched the type of flying he was up to, and was willing to wait for the opportunity to make good a promise. After chasing him around Canada for six months, the time for their rendezvous in the sky had finally come.

Rumor had it Lou Fender was an Avro test pilot wearing a flying officer's stripe. That was the mystery about him. A.V. Roe test pilots certified the aircraft for squadron use, but the factory never got to see how it performed in the field. It was not uncommon for Standards crews to be referred to as SCABS.

Pete was at the opposite end of the combat food chain. He'd applied for inclusion into the CF-100 program, but had been turned down, the rejection of his application coming via flattery from his superior officer on his flying record and experience.

'We're going to be flying propeller aircraft for the next twenty years. Who's going to pass on your skills? How many thousand hours have you got? Ten, twelve? How many weather systems have you flown through? How many emergencies have you walked away from? How many aircraft have you saved? You're one of the most experienced multi-engine drivers we've got. We're indebted to you. You'll be rewarded when the time comes.'

The smoke blown up his ass placated him, and the hunter in him was offered a trap line that would sate a lust for innocence and stormy nights.

As a start-up, he flew CF-100 navigator students out of North Bay, chauffeuring them in B-25's equipped with the CF-100 radar, performing intercepts on practice targets and pilots on solo trips. When a CF-100 crew was chosen, they would spend their first flights as a team flying in the B-25.

Pete relinquished the captain's seat while they struggled with their first attempts to familiarize themselves with the three-dimensional joust of hunter and prey. His initial envy of the student pilots gave way to respect when after a few hours they handled the B-25 like a fighter. Three or four hours later, they would disappear and a fresh team would arrive. Monotony had him pleading for a change. Eventually it was payoff time.

'Congratulations Rylander, you've been promoted to flight lieutenant.'

Pete was standing at attention before his superior's desk, expecting a dressing down. He'd been pushing crews harder and harder; too hard maybe, but his job had become hyp-notically boring, and he'd demanded tighter parameters of them to sate a newfound craving for perfection.

'Sir?'

'Congratulations, Flight Lieutenant Rylander, your pro-motion is well deserved!'

'Thank you, Sir. This comes as a complete surprise.' Pete felt heady and slightly aghast.

'The surprise comes with a price. We've got a posting for you. Your taxi driver days are over.' The CO leaned back in his chair and stared at a model of a Beaufighter. 'You flew these in the Far East, didn't you? Ended up in Rangoon at war's end.'

'Yes Sir! I've got almost seven hundred hours on them. Good airplane. I never saw any action, but I learned to fly multi-engines. Those sleeve-valve Hercules burned a lot of oil, but they were sure reliable. The last thing I wanted was to end up in the jungle. We flew solo most of the time, so companionship was at a premium.'

'I flew them in England. Night-fighters.'

'I understand you had four confirmed kills and a whole bunch of probables, Sir. Well done.'

'I had a good radar operator. Teamwork is everything, which brings me to the reason you're here. I want you to put a crack crew together. Find a low-time B-25 that we can put the latest CF-100 radar, IFF/SIF, et cetera. Load it up with whatever makes it show up like a B-50 or a B-36 on a GCI radar scope. We don't have the Americans' jamming equipment, but we do have a mountain of aluminum chaff stashed somewhere. The aircrews you've been babysitting for the last four months are now in the field. We need to see how they and the GCI sites respond to you popping up from out of nowhere.'

He gestured with a flat hand thrusting skyward. His Operations pin and chest of ribbons spoke of his past. He offered Pete a cigarette, flicked his lighter, and asked him to be seated.

Pete contemplated the combative potential of the B-25. Its wartime exploits as a bomber and ground-attacker were legendary. Add an electronic component to the mix, and you had a machine capable of going in harm's way. The hottest flying he'd done with twin engines had been during the war. The B-25, though not as maneuverable as the aircraft he'd flown, would be a more potent weapon. The electronic age could elevate his three-dimensional mind to a higher level. It was rudimentary, but at least it was a form of combat. The reward at the end of his tenure might still be the front seat of a CF-100.

'Can I have a couple of 50-caliber machine guns mounted in the nose, Sir? If it's reality you want, shouldn't we have the capability of taking out the threat?' He meant it more as a joke, but a nod of approval confirmed his request. Machine guns! What else could he ask for? While he thought of anything he'd overlooked, The Voice got down to specifics.

'You're to operate as a target for the GCI sites and CF-100 squadrons. Day-fighter and auxiliary squadrons aren't involved. Secrecy of your location is important, and you'll be at a state of readiness at all times. You'll be flying in crud most of the time, so make sure you take along your long johns. No married men on your crew. Tell me who you want and we'll do our best to get them. You'll get orders from me alone. Communication will be by telephone. I'll tell you where to go and when to fly. Surprise is the key to the success of the program. If the defence system we're spending billions on doesn't work, we want to know why, we want to know how to fix it, and have it fixed fast.'

While his marching orders were spelled out, Pete focused on the pros and cons of the immediate future. The liability, living out of a suitcase for at least a year in hostile weather, God knows where across Canada. The asset, flying a souped-up B-25, a magician's cape that would allow him to disappear whenever there was a change in the weather or a young lady comes looking. A means of escape had been his method of evasion since his first sexual encounter. His mobility would cover his tracks like fresh fallen snow, allowing him to hunt new territory undetected.

By now he'd spent six months on the job, had yet to experience winter and, except for a couple of air shows, hadn't had any leave. He phoned the tower for a wake-up call, rolled his sleeping bag on the couch, placed the telephone on the coffee table, turned out the lights, fantasized about a nursing student in Edmonton, and fell off to sleep. Tomorrow his encounter with the master would erase eight years of doubt, and make him a rich man.

CHAPTER 7

Lou and Duckwalker escorted the ladies to the Snake Pit. Hangers-on at the bar backed by smokers nursing nightcaps deflected them to a table in a quiet corner. Conversations tuned in and out as they passed by.

'There I was,' started every sentence.

'There I was at 30,000, pulling four and a half G's, and my navigator says he needs to puke. What are you going to do?'

Conversation faded in and out.

'There I was on final turn, and my airspeed indicator says I'm 20 knots above the stall, and my navigator's says we're only five. Who do I believe? It turns out his was right.'

They took drink orders and headed to the bar. The crowd had thinned, and the din had subsided to a point where one could carry on quiet conversation. Lou was feeling uncomfortable, and while they waited for the bartender to mix their cocktails, he needed to talk.

'Look D.W., or whatever you call yourself, I've got something good going on here, so don't fuck it up. I like this girl, so don't horn in.' Duckwalker took this as an insult. With his sunglasses forced into Lou's chin and the snarl of a guard dog, he responded.

'Listen here, Flying Officer Fender. I performed my part

of the bargain. I shall act the gentleman and pretend not to have heard your bullshit. When you get the opportunity, an apology would put you in good standing. By the way, I have no interest in Darlene. Much too young for me.'

With that, he grabbed his drinks and waddled to the table.

The women chatted while the men smoked and drank in silence. Lou was out of his comfort zone, and he felt the frustration of a buck in rut singling out a doe. He couldn't take his eyes off Darlene. She chatted, sipped her martini, flashed her eyes at him, and laughed when Josette joked. The cross-table banter offered chances to interject with the odd anecdote, but mostly he sat silent, fascinated at the ease with which she cast her spell over him.

'Am I addressing Flying Officer Fender?' A tall soft-spoken officer wearing an orderly officer's armband bent into the conversation. Lou nodded and confirmed his identity.

'I'm Fred Malone, the orderly officer. I need to speak to you on an urgent matter.'

They shook hands and moved out of earshot.

'The CO's ordered you to the Operations Center. I'm not to leave here without you.'

'The CO wants to see me? What's up?' Fred Malone beckoned him further away and spoke in a loud whisper.

'I can tell you what I know. About an hour ago, I got a call from some guy in Chatham looking for information. Your name came up a couple of times. I didn't think much about it until I figured it must be someone you knew, or how the hell would he know you were here. Aren't you guys supposed to sneak around? I reported it to the operations officer, he phoned someone, and here I am.'

Lou lit a cigarette and contemplated his next move. He knew who the inquirer was, and why he was in Chatham.

'Let me say goodnight to the ladies. I can't just suddenly disappear.'

He returned to the table, said goodnight and departed. Bewildered stares followed him as he was escorted from the mess, Duckwalker the most bewildered of all.

'What was that all that about?' Darlene questioned. 'Is he in trouble or something? Do you know what's going on, Josette?'

'Je ne sais pas,' she shrugged.

Duckwalker ran the permutations and combinations of scenarios. He sensed that they'd be flying at dawn. Eight hours bottle to throttle, he reminded himself. He checked his watch and there was time for one more drink and an excuse for Lou's departure. Using wits honed from years of extracting himself from similar situations, he called on an old standby.

'I think he's having family problems. He mentioned that his mother was ill. I hope the orderly officer wasn't bringing bad news. He didn't look too concerned when he bid us "goodnight," but I don't think he's the type who shows emotion.'

His lie was met with a degree of acceptance, and he headed to the bar to freshen their drinks. For the next half hour, he was the center of attraction, keeping flying the last topic on the agenda. When Darlene broached the subject of his wearing sunglasses inside the mess, Josette deflected the conversation.

'Darlene has a thing for eyes. I don't know why, but she says she'll know her man when she sees his eyes. Can you give us a peek what's behind your mask? Your face hasn't a blemish on it, so I know you're not disfigured. Are you a vampire, or a creature that only comes out at night?'

With that, he turned from the glare of a wall sconce and lifted his glasses. Both women twisted in their seats, craning for the briefest glimpse, and saw eyes that didn't seem quite human, yet when gazed deeply into, looked all too human.

———·•·———

Lou marched into the Operations Center in step with the orderly officer. A squadron leader, phone in hand, sat with his back to two senior officers who Lou figured were the base's commanding officer and Squadron Leader Carson, 440's officer commanding. Lou stood to attention, saluted, and removed his hat. He saw anger in the CO's eyes, received a half-hearted salute in return, and was ordered to 'stand at ease.'

'Who the hell do you know who flies a B-25 that's currently sitting on the flight line at Chatham? We're on stand-down with the remnants of a fucking hurricane pounding us, then you show up. From what I've just been informed, nobody's supposed to know you're here. I didn't really know you were here. It's obvious the secret's out. Who the fuck are these guys, and why are you the center of attraction?'

Lou realized that the CO had been deliberately left out of the picture, and that he had the nasty job of explaining the charade to him. Diplomacy was the key.

'They're the opposite of us, Sir. We're not on the same team. We don't even work for the same department, but we're after the same results. Standards is an observer corps. We ride along and evaluate. When you get scrambled, we get scrambled. We use one of your aircraft, and we check off a whole lot of little boxes. The aircraft at Chatham plays a combat role. I take it you haven't encountered them before?

Irritated by the unexpected Friday night rigmarole, the CO was in no mood to have his authority challenged. A flying officer questioning a group captain on Intelligence matters was out of protocol, but Lou Fender had had no choice. The CO had been caught with his pants down and somebody would have to pay. Lou's association with the phantom from Chatham had put the base commander's head on the block, and he was clearly agitated.

'I see one of our ready aircraft's been fitted with tip tanks and there was a request for a JATO pack. I understand the tip tanks, but JATO rockets? Are you expecting the runway to be unserviceable?'

As the aircraft commander, Lou made the uncomfortable decision to take responsibility for his navigator usurping his authority.

'The tip tanks are weather related, Sir. Who knows where our alternate will be if the base goes below GCA limits after we take off. As for JATO, I check every squadron to see if they've got jet-assisted-take-off capability. Part of our check sheet.' The CO filled a mug from a bubbling percolator and resumed his rant.

'440 Squadron's just been reactivated, for Christ's sake! The base is on stand-down because of a goddamn hurricane, and some asshole in Ottawa is going to throw crap like this at me. I was told not to expect this sort of thing 'til late winter, even in the spring. You suddenly show up, and now I've got this shit to deal with. They knew the hurricane was heading this way before they sent you here. When I find out who the asshole in Ottawa is that put me in this fucking room at midnight on a Friday when they know we're on stand-down, I'm having a chat with the AOC.' He took a swig of coffee and shook his head in disgust. 'What say you, Flying Officer Fender?'

'I don't think it's a coincidence that I'm here, Sir. I'm pretty sure the guy flying the B-25 is Pete Rylander, call sign 'Badger Two.' We were in Burma together at the end of the war. I don't know who he takes his orders from, but his job is to turn up at the damndest times from out of nowhere to test the readiness of CF-100 squadrons. Weather means nothing to him. This is the first time a Standards team's been challenged. I sensed something was up when they ordered us here. The weather is his cover.'

'Why would he ask specifically about you?'

'I don't know, but for some reason he thinks he owes me one. I'll find out when the time comes. It goes back a long way. The last time I saw him was eight years ago, and I was in civvies.'

'What equipment has he got?'

'He flies a modified B-25 that's got the latest electronics on board, including an advanced version of the radar the two ready aircraft out on the tarmac are equipped with. If it had a couple of machine guns in the nose it would be almost as lethal. More than likely, they've got a top-notch radar navigator. Pete's no great flyer, but he taught me how to push weather.'

The squadron commander interjected with a question Lou was not prepared for.

'When are they going to hit us?'

Lou thought long and hard then moved to the bulletin board to study the weather map. A giant 'O' with an 'L' in the middle, surrounded by even concentric isobars sat off to the southeast of the base, and he could see that it was heading in their direction. He slid his finger from the center of the Low in the direction the storm was moving. He traced a hypothetical route from Chatham. The plan of attack was obvious.

'The bugger is going to use the eye of the storm to get us up. He'll break through the front here and pop up somewhere south of Chicoutimi. The sky over the base will be clear as a bell for an hour or so. If he takes a photo of the two ready aircraft sitting on the ramp it could be embarrassing.'

Everyone focused on the map.

'When can we expect to be scrambled?'

'I figure Mont Apica GCI will pick him up around noon. That's when the eye passes through here.' The operations officer hung up the phone and turned to the group.

'A certain Flight Lieutenant Rylander is presently bunked down, so we can take a breather. Their aircraft's been fueled, and they're supposed to be in the air at seven. That gives us a good head start. Shall we formulate a battle plan now, Sir, or wait 'til morning?' The CO lit a cigarette and turned to Lou.

'I'd like to hear what Standards has to say. All intelligence we've gained so far has come from Flying Officer Fender. Without him, I'd be snug as a bug in a rug, oblivious to the fact that some fucking asshole in Ottawa wants to make the CO of this base and Flying Officer Fender look bad. Once again, what say you Flying Officer Fender—how should we stack the deck?' Lou asked permission to smoke, passed his pack and lighter around, and waited for everyone to light up.

'I'd keep the standby rotation the same, Sir. Whoever is on tomorrow is the crew that will do the intercept. My navigator's the best in the business, so we'll be handy if we're needed. I don't want to be involved in the intercept; that's not my mandate. We're here to observe, but if we can help shove a stick up this guy's ass, so much the better.'

'Where's your navigator now?'

'He's at the mess, Sir. He's had a few.' The CO turned to the orderly officer.

'Malone, have Flying Officer Fender's navigator escorted here.' Lou saw a red flag and interjected.

'I think it would be best if I went, Sir. He's a bit eccentric, and we were accompanying two ladies, one of whom is the base's chief nursing sister. It might seem a little obvious that something's afoot, and I wouldn't wish to alarm them.'

With a sloppy salute from the CO, Lou headed back to the mess to give Duckwalker the news. They were going flying on Saturday.

Josette had only seen owl-like pupils as large as Duckwalker's when she'd applied relaxing drops to patients' eyes for retina exams. His irises were nonexistent, and the contrast between the blackness of his huge pupils and the unblemished whites of his eyes hypnotized her like a swaying cobra. He dropped his glasses, and like Dracula caught in a shaft of sunlight, shielded his face with his arm.

'Sorry ladies, that's all I can take.' Josette was bewildered.

'How can they let you fly? I've done enough aircrew medicals to know you can't fly with eyes like that. The sun would blind you.' Her concern was genuine.

'I wear clear glasses and a special visor when I fly in daylight. I have no problems at night. Think of me as a bat. With regard to my flying status, let's just say that the Air Force pays me well for my skills. Now no more questions, ladies.'

They turned to greet their lost companion.

Lou sauntered to the table and sat down as if nothing had happened. There'd be potential questions, and he'd rehearsed every answer; every answer except the question from Darlene.

'How's your mother?' Startled, he looked to Darlene then Duckwalker.

'My apologies, Lou, I'm afraid I mentioned that your mother was ill.' A nod that signaled 'go with it' sent Lou on a convoluted story that when it came time for him to extract Duckwalker, nobody knew if his mother was dead or alive.

'Ladies, it is with great sadness that Flight Lieutenant Jones and I must hit the sack. Tomorrow we may have to slip the surly bonds of earth. We'll escort you to your barracks, or you may allow us to freshen your drinks. Either way we must bid you goodnight.'

The ladies declined the escort but insisted on solidifying plans for the following evening. Lou and Duckwalker exchanged furtive glances while the women wasted time on plans that had little chance of fruition. Lou pulled

Duckwalker's nose out of Josette's cleavage with a hard tug, and escorted him into the storm.

'You're on your way to the Operations Center,' he screamed over the wind. 'If you're drunk, you've got five minutes to sober up.'

'What the hell's going on?' he yelled back, waddling in quick time to keep pace with Lou. 'You leave me with two women, a bar bill, and whole lot of questions. I had to come up with that lame-brain explanation that, as you can see, didn't hold water.' They buffeted against driving rain.

'The CO wants to brief us. Some asshole with a vendetta is going to scramble a 440 crew in the middle of the storm and we're going along to watch the festivities. When we've finished the briefing, it's back to barracks for shut-eye and ready to fly by nine. By the way, the CO's balls are in a vice. Show me what you can do.'

The briefing was short and concise. Aided by Duckwalker's electronic and tactical skills, they laid out the plan of attack. The CO offered his staff car to deliver them to barracks. The standby crew, recently roused and escorted by the orderly officer, passed them in the hangar.

'You've been busy tonight, Malone,' Lou commented in passing. 'There's not going to be any sleep for you this weekend.'

CHAPTER 8

Saturday 0:30 AM 0530 GMT

Major Crisp spent a restless night fighting demons and guilt. Her story always ended same: grey, blue, and white in death, a sheet pulled down to her breasts, her hair knotted with dried blood, vacant eyes squinting into the glare of the ceiling lamp of the morgue. His problem was solved, and as he fixated on her death-mask, he ticked off the first line of the checklist. He'd killed his wife to save his career. What sort of damage she'd caused to America could only be speculated. How much information had he inadvertently passed on to her prior to the discovery of the secret compartment? As dawn broke, he needed to play the memory tape of their life together for the last time.

Their whirlwind love affair was legendary—decorated military pilot marries beautiful physics major. He borrowed a friend's Beech Staggerwing private airplane, and for three weeks they flew and honeymooned around the country. Soon, the routines of a SAC bomber pilot and a university professor diverged, and their relationship became one of sex and farewells. While he flew B-50 reconnaissance missions along the Iron Curtain during the Berlin Airlift, she finished her thesis at Los Alamos. While he was on the B-36 conversion course, she was lecturing at MIT. Thanksgiving, Christmas, and summers in Maine and

Québec filled the blanks that had become the only substance of their marriage.

The giveaway that Alana was not who he thought she was came by accident when he discovered documents stamped TOP SECRET stashed inside the back of her makeup vanity table in their bedroom. His cufflink had slipped to the floor and bounced underneath. After a quick look, he returned the documents, and made himself appear none the wiser.

The vanity, since destroyed, had supposedly been an heirloom willed by an aunt, and Alana insisted that it stay in her bedroom. On later inspection, he discovered a foreshortened drawer that concealed the compartment. He knew she'd dealt with secure documents and was involved with sensitive material, but he was bewildered as to why she brought the documents home and seemingly never openly studied them.

As his suspicions grew, he discovered the ugly side of living with a four-sided lie. She had split into two persons and so had he. When they made love, it was impossible to tell which combination had come together. Over a three-month period, he checked the amount of material arriving and leaving.

His curiosity frustrated him. The dossiers were sealed, and with their trademark red stamp of TOP SECRET, his imagination had them heading in the direction of the Soviet Union. To a rising star in the Strategic Air Command, his situation became intolerable.

Lincoln kept mum about his predicament, honing the skills of a spy through trial and error. Chance encounters with her associates in public or at social functions had him vetting them by means of acquaintances at the CIA and FBI. His research unearthed nothing damning, and his frustration grew at not being able to plug the leak. After an intolerable three-week period where he saw bundles arrive and leave daily, he concluded that the only way to get rid of the problem was to get rid of his wife. Sixteen-hour training missions to Alaska and the North Pole gave him the time and space to plan his salvation.

Lincoln the bomber pilot and Lincoln the husband of a Soviet spy never crossed paths. He fought the temptation of challenging her political beliefs. She'd alluded to an association with the Democratic Party and never made issue of his membership in the Republican Party. Her lack of any family had him researching a family tree that was nonexistent. During their courtship, she'd revealed she'd been the only child of academic parents who'd been killed in a political demonstration while visiting Germany in the late Thirties. Hefty insurance policies had secured her a residence in an exclusive girls' school in Massachusetts, and academic skills gave her qualifications to enter MIT. Love made him oblivious to the rest of her past.

Alana never suspected her own murder. Lincoln took pride in the fact that the spy he loved had created a spy she loved. The deeper he dug her grave, the more elusive and forbidding she became, fueling him with murderous passion in bed and supreme confidence in the cockpit. The B-36 became his sanctuary, and it was there the final step in his murder plan solidified.

He'd been cruising into the northern lights over Hudson Bay when he put the final touches together. The beauty of the plan was that if each attempt to kill her failed, she would never be the wiser. The Beechcraft Staggerwing, their magic carpet on their honeymoon, became the plan's centerpiece. The owner had been posted to Loring Air Force Base in Maine, leaving it for Lincoln's use if he promised to keep it in flying condition. With it came a murder weapon.

———•◦•———

Flashes of lightning and claps of thunder kept Lou from any semblance of sleep. He wanted to fly alert and refreshed, but that wasn't about to happen. The tap-tap on the door had him up in an instant. He slipped on his underwear, checked his watch and moved to the door.

'Who is it?'

'It's me. It's Darlene.'

Lou opened the door a crack. Darlene, tipsy and soaked to the skin, leaned into the door and slipped by. No umbrella, no raincoat; a slippery seal sliding onshore.

'I hope I'm not being too forward,' she pouted. 'I had to find the orderly officer to get your address. May I sit down?' Without waiting for the answer she faced him, disrobed, snuggled between the still warm sheets, and slipped off her underwear.

Lou was aghast.

He picked up the damp clothes, laid them over the heating register, sat on the bed, and lit a cigarette. The situation had become one of emotion, not cool pilot reasoning, and he felt uncomfortable and inadequate. He gazed into the eyes that he'd fallen in love with.

'Have you any idea what you're getting yourself into, Miss Muncie?' He paused, rewinding his recording tape.

'I'm a sad miserable man who was discarded by a wife who loved me, and ignored by an Air Force that's tried to kill me.'

Darlene pulled the sheet to her chin and nodded agreement. 'I know what I'm getting into, Louis Fender. I saw it when I looked into your beautiful eyes. Then there was your scar.' She reached for him but he shied away.

'No, you don't. You have no idea who I am or what my life is all about. My track record has me dead within a year. We met, what, eight hours ago?'

His comment was meant to put on the brake, but all it succeeded in doing was have her open the sheets to invite him in. He stubbed his cigarette and slipped beside her. They adjusted positions, touched, and readjusted, sensing the awkwardness that came with a first encounter. She broke the silence with a throaty whisper.

'I've been waiting for you Lou Fender. I've been to nearly every Air Force base across Canada hunting for a man who caused me wrong. He was a pilot. I've been searching for him for five years but I know I'm never going to find him. For all I know, he could be dead.' She paused to let her disclosure sink in.

'I've never told this to any man. I met the bastard at the Officers' Mess in Moose Jaw. He drugged and took advantage of me. He made me pregnant at a time in my life when I couldn't take on the responsibility of bringing up a child. The decision to have an abortion was mine alone. I was forced to seek one through illicit means, and it didn't go well. I may not be able to bear children. The only thing I remember about him were his eyes.' Tears welled and she dabbed them with the sheet.

'Three months ago, I decided to give up the chase and get on with my life. Bagotville is my last teaching job for the good old Air Force. I'm going back to Winnipeg to teach at a Métis school; I've wasted too much time looking for revenge. When I ran into you in the lobby and heard your voice and felt your strength, I knew my vendetta was finally over. Your eyes and voice erased all memory of him. Then I saw your scar. I want you more than I've ever wanted a man. Please don't send me away.'

Lou felt a stirring. He wanted to take her then but he knew a rushed attack ended in failure. He'd had few women since his divorce and the affairs had become embarrassing failures. He kissed her neck. She explored for his penis and was about to take it in her mouth when he gently pushed her away.

'You have to slow down. I'm not used to this sort of thing.'

Lou let her release her grip and she rolled on top of him, flattening her breasts against his chest. They were face-to-face, breath-to-breath, and his penis hardened to bursting. It was not a time for conversation. He lifted her by her waist, sat her on his face, smelled muskiness, then drove his tongue between the plumped lips of her vagina, suffocating him in sweet wetness.

She bucked and moaned with each variation in the cadence of his tongue, reaching back with her right hand, playing with his penis that exploded in an ejaculation that left him breathless and limp.

She crawled off him, sucked the remnants of his orgasm, and mixed their juices with a kiss that told him everything he needed to know. Whispering endearments, she kissed the length his scar and toyed with his flaccid penis.

For the next hour, he made love with intensity that he'd never known. Like a drug addict in need to relive the first hit, Darlene had finally found the man who bested the 'bastard from Moose Jaw.'

Lou dozed while she caressed him with the backs of her fingers, sending him to places he'd never imagined. To a pilot, that place could only be heaven, and for the first time since Rangoon, Lou Fender was at peace.

Duckwalker was on the horns of a dilemma. He'd been ordered to fly in the morning, and he needed what Josette Gerard had to offer. She'd slipped him her card at their departing, and it burned a hole in his pocket. While they waited for the CO's staff car to transport them to their barracks, he and Lou had had a debrief in the hangar. Lou had been taken aback by the events that had transpired with the CO.

When they arrived at the Operations Center, Duckwalker became the focus of attention. The CO was forthright in his demands, but Duckwalker counteracted them as he laid on his expertise. Lou sat back, smoked, and watched a snake-oil salesman at work. He'd never seen such a brazen use of little rank. Within fifteen minutes, a battle plan was agreed to.

Lou's silence during the briefing had Duckwalker concerned.

'You didn't have much to say.'

'You seem to know what you're talking about. I'm just a

student of the game. I'm just the driver remember? By the way, you seem to know as much about the front seat as I do. Is there something you haven't told me?'

'Negatron. I'm a student of the game, too. As you probably gathered, my credentials give me a different rank in different situations. When I was addressing the CO in there, I was a wing commander. When I'm bouncing around in the back seat of a CF-100, I'm just a flying officer. That's a big spread. I live the life of an academic who happens to love flying in extreme conditions and in whatever forms it takes, especially in combat-type situations.'

The staff car stopped at the entrance to their barracks.

'Goodnight, Lou, let's hope the weatherman and your buddy in Chatham have a war of their own before they get here.' With that, he was out into the storm.

The instant he closed the door to his room, Duckwalker snatched the card from his breast pocket. S/L J.M. Gerard, BSc. RN. Written under it in ballpoint pen: 'BB10 Rm. 205 tonight.'

Like an addict sensing a hit, he swooned at the possibilities. A fuck before flying always charged his combatant's batteries.

He changed into his flying suit, grabbed his flight satchel, pulled the peak of his Yankees baseball cap over his glasses, and as fast as the fastest duck could waddle, waddled down the rain-swept street looking for barrack block #10.

Josette answered the door in Betty Page lingerie, her glasses the giveaway to her disguise. Her hair hung to each shoulder, and a white negligee revealed a hint of pubic hair under sheer panties. She turned off the light, came to him in the dark, and whispered.

'Take off your glasses.'

L incoln rose at seven and went through his ablutions with the care and detail of a well-paid mortician. His eyes were bloodshot from lack of sleep, and his reflection didn't show the look of a man about to change history. He felt his breast pocket for the pills. At the first sign of fatigue, Benzedrine would carry the day.

Last shower, last shave, last zippering of the flying suit that had been his skin for eight years. Fresh and faded crests adorned it like travel stickers on a steamer trunk. He stuffed maps and checklists into worn pockets and headed to the mess. Met briefing was at eight, so he had time to enjoy a last breakfast. Everything was now last this, and last that.

'Major Crisp! Come join us.' Lincoln had scoped out a quiet table but accepted the invitation on protocol. Arnie Stonehawker and Stan 'what's his name,' his copilot and navigator, rose as he approached. Stan's cockpit was on the lower deck and chances were Lincoln wouldn't have been able to pick him out of a police line-up. He'd flown a few trips with Arnie "the Kraut" but knew nothing about Stan other than that he was green. He'd asked for an inexperienced navigator and they had delivered.

'Lieutenants.' He bowed slightly and laid his tray beside

his copilot. 'We've met, Lieutenant, but I'm afraid your last name escapes me. With a crew of fifteen, you must find that understandable.'

'Gidley, Sir. It's my first trip over. Thank you for the opportunity to fly with you. I understand you've made a dozen trips here.'

'That sounds about right, though I'd rather be up at the North Pole. Summer and winter have such divergent qualities there. Have you been stationed at Loring very long?'

'Two months out of flight school, Sir, and one of them was leave. This was my first trip to England. You could tell by my screw up on the way over that I'm a little rusty. I'll do better on the way home. The scuttlebutt is, we're simulating a bomber stream attack on the States, and the interceptor boys are going to try and target us. That might be a little too much for me to handle, Sir.'

'I'll send Lieutenant Stonehawker downstairs to help you when we're at altitude and things have stabilized. I might run my own little test on you along the way. Looks like we might be in for some unusual weather on the way back.' He unlatched the tiniest wink at Lieutenant Gidley. "Salt the mine," he thought.

'Lieutenant Stonehawker, I'll see you and Lieutenant Gidley at Met briefing; full crew briefing is at eleven.' With that, Major Lincoln Crisp smiled his first smile of satisfaction since he looked down at Alana's vacant eyes and bloodied scalp. Another tick mark etched itself into one more box in the checklist in his mind.

By 1950, Carswell Air Force Base in Texas had become the hub of the Strategic Air Command. It was there that Lincoln converted from the B-29 to the monstrous B-36.

His flying skill and dedication to duty led to a promotion from captain to major, and with further training he became the chief flying instructor.

With her top-secret security clearance and credentials, Alana was offered a post in the nuclear armament section on base, and for a week a month she was seconded to Los Alamos, New Mexico. It was while he was stationed at Carswell that Lincoln made the discovery that started him on the path that turned him into a killer.

Once he'd exposed Alana, Lincoln's urgency to kill her was fueled by his fear of discovery, his love of the Service, and his spiritual rebirth as a liberal. The McCarthy witch-hunts and his ever-increasing exposure to the precipice of nuclear war conflicted with his love of flying and a twisted love for her. The idea that his lover led a double life charged his loins. While he was training to drop atomic bombs on the USSR, she was helping the Russians build their own. He burned his Republican Party card and vowed that her death would be for a greater good.

Lincoln's unfettered access to the speedy Beech Staggerwing allowed him to visit Alana on weekends. He'd depart Carswell at 5 o'clock Friday, refuel in Amarillo, and she'd pick him up at the airport in Santa Fe at ten. From there it was a late dinner in a mesquite-scented bistro followed by a midnight swim at their motor hotel. The rest of the weekend was hers to plan. At 5 on Sunday, they'd kiss goodbye and head in opposite directions. When she returned from Los Alamos, the secret compartment would once again become packed with dossiers.

Lincoln sat at the rear of the darkened Met briefing room, studying the progress of the storm as it advanced in the direction of southern Québec. His plan was still intact, and the monotony of the Met officer's briefing replayed the tape of the weekend in New Mexico that was sending him on his crusade.

When he landed in Santa Fe that Friday, he had no idea he'd return to Carswell with her.

As he taxied to the ramp and shut the aircraft down, he saw her sitting up on the driver's seat of a convertible coupe, cheerfully waving. He grabbed his weekend bag and two sets of chocks from the rear seat and exited the aircraft. Alana bounded to him, greeting with her usual embrace, and after a brief comment about the trip Lincoln chocked the wheels.

'Damned hand brake's busted,' he commented. 'What's up for tomorrow?'

'Tomorrow, my sweet, we're driving to Albuquerque to meet a couple of associates for lunch and shop for china. I've fallen in love with the colors of the southwest. There's a jazz club I think you'll like. I've booked a room at a motor lodge.'

Saturdays were workdays for Alana, and he'd had enough of her 'associates.' There was never a pilot in the lot, and with the one-sided conversation revolving around nuclear proliferation and left-leaning politics, he'd end up getting drunk. His bitterness at the thought of a wasted weekend fueled his anger.

'Next time I come, you're going to have your bag packed and I'm flying you to Sedona and the Grand Canyon for a three-day holiday. I've only seen the Canyon from 30,000 feet. With this here little sweetheart I'll fly you through it.'

He patted the wing, then arm-in-arm, escorted her to the car.

'Could we fly to Las Vegas and stay at the Flamingo? They have entertainment reviews. Could we see a show?'

'You bet your boots we can, but you'll have to set aside three full days. No associates, no work, just me, the Staggerwing, and the Southwest. Wait 'til you see the colors around Sedona, reds and greens like nowhere else. There's supposed to be a spiritual vortex of some sort there. They have a landing strip, so we can refuel and have lunch.'

Lincoln and Alana spent the late evening dining at their favorite bistro. During dinner, he suggested that the trip to Albuquerque could be accomplished faster if they flew down and rented a car.

'We'll have breakfast there, and more time to shop. The weather's perfect, and if your associates stay 'til Sunday, you can ride back with them, if you like. With favorable winds, I could probably fly home direct from there. Anyway, it will give you some practice for the Vegas trip. What do you say?'

'I say, Lincoln Crisp, is there anything you won't do to go flying?'

They drove to the airport at sunrise, put the top up on the convertible, and walked the tarmac to the Beech. Along the way, he explained the sequence she'd go through to remove the chocks. 'Sorry to put you through this sweet-heart, but the damn hand brake's snafu, so you'll have to help me. Just remember what I told you and you'll do fine.'

Lincoln fired up the radial, went through his pre-taxi check, then signaled Alana to remove the chocks and get in. She rounded the lower wing, fought the prop-wash getting in, and rubbed her stinging eyes.

Once she was strapped in he gave her a thumbs up.

'Good job sweetheart; I'll make a ground-pounder out of you yet.' She put on her headset, positioned her mike, and screamed back.

'I don't think I want to be a ground-pounder. I don't think I like it.' But he'd overridden the intercom to talk to the tower.

'Santa Fe Ground Control, this is red Beech Staggerwing Mike Yankee Mike requesting taxi instructions for VFR to Albuquerque.'

The day went as prescribed. They ate breakfast in Albuquerque at eight thirty and finished the evening at a jazz bar, lunch meeting and shopping in between. A midnight swim followed by a subtle slide into bed had him wondering if something else was up. She was more skilled in the clandestine world, and he wondered if she had a counterattack in the works. She was up to something, and the longer he lay beside her, he felt the repulsive force of two north poles of a magnet trying to come together.

Suddenly, he felt a trap door opening and he felt himself falling through a plane. Once through, he knew their life together was over. He stared into the dark with 'Saint James Infirmary' and plans of murder bouncing in his head like a pinball refusing to drop.

With a jolt, the pinball machine went TILT.

'Linc, do you think we're ready to talk about having a family?'

He bolted upright, snapped on the bedside lamp, and faced her nose-to-nose.

'Where the hell did that come from?' He'd never figured on children, now or in their future. What she'd suddenly presented was preposterous. The cool pilot did not keep his cool.

'I'm fucking speechless!'

He grabbed for a cigarette and went to the chaise lounge. She pulled the duvet to her throat and sat up. He smoked half a cigarette, waiting for her to reply, butted it, and thrust his face into his hands. She spoke in a whisper.

'We've never had the chance to plan about having a family. I'm here and you're there, then I'm there and you're here. I'm going to be twenty-eight next November, and if we're going to have a kid, we're going to have to start soon.'

Lincoln was dumbfounded. The traitor was planning a family at the same time she was giving away the nation's secrets at the same time he was planning her murder. He shook his head in disbelief, grabbed his pack of cigarettes and flicked his Zippo.

'Whew! I can't believe what I'm hearing. Is this something you've been thinking about for a while? Because this is a big fucking surprise to me. What about your profession? What about your career?'

'I can keep doing what I do and still have a child.'

'Bullshit! And what about me? When I get a squadron you'll have to quit and become a full-time housewife and mother in some isolated air base. Do you want that? For Christ's sake, keep your profession, and let's keep things the way they are. In two months I'm going to end up at Loring. You'd be miserable up there. As it stands, I'm in favor of the status quo.'

'Loring is close to MIT. I can do my research there. We

can buy a home in Boston and you could fly down with Malcolm's Staggerwing whenever you wanted. Isn't that where he's stationed? With those thirty-hour trips to the North Pole, I'm going to be alone most of the time. When you get home, you sleep for twelve hours anyway. Sure I'll be taking care of a kid, but for me that's only a part-time profession. You know I'd be a good mother. I'm sorry I had to hit you with this right now, but it's something that's been gnawing at me. Can we talk about it tomorrow?'

Lincoln butted his cigarette, turned out the light and returned to bed. He stared into the dark, contemplating the added urgency to his plan. He was not about to murder a mother with child.

The Met officer snapped on the lights, jolting Lincoln out of his reverie. He returned to the mess for a coffee and a crap, then headed to his barracks to collect his gear. He was about to enter the building when an out-of-breath Arnie Stonehawker caught up to him.

'There's bad news, Sir. The loading of the bomb has been delayed. There's a problem with two latches in the bomb bay. Something's not lining up. They're scavenging parts from another aircraft, but the repairs won't be finished 'til five this afternoon. Then they have to load the bomb. We won't be able to get away until sometime this evening.'

Lincoln curbed his anger with clenched fists and curled toes.

'Thank you, Lieutenant. Tell the crew to relax until supper, then have them assemble at the aircraft around seven. If there's any change in the status, I'll be at my quarters. I understand you are a Lutheran. We might make it to Loring in time for church.'

Duckwalker was in his element. His strengths came into play in the dark. He'd reduced his instincts to scent and feel, sensuality taught by mature women. Josette unveiled her body and gave herself to his touch. With his glasses removed, it felt as though a veil had been pulled from his face. She guided him to the bed where her lips explored his face with light kisses.

He explored her from hairline to toes with his fingers, her scent directing him to points of pleasure. The slow steady probing from his lips and tongue signaled to her that he was a man whose lovemaking wasn't based on the need to penetrate, and that satisfaction gave yield to several orgasms. As with the others, she was able to tell a story that was guaranteed to keep her virtue intact.

'I was engaged to be married many years ago,' she whispered. 'My fiancé was a flying instructor, and he was killed trying to save his airplane. He could have bailed out, but he chose to be a hero. He chose wrong. He was in contact with the tower until he hit the ground. He ended up a dead hero, but then, isn't that what you flyers want? To end up dead.' She rolled on top of him, face to face.

'I was the only nurse on duty when they brought his remains to the hospital and it was me who prepared him for shipment home. I accompanied him on the train and attended the funeral. Since then, I've never had a man inside me. I satisfy myself in my own fashion.' With that she slid down and took him in her mouth.

With each change in position, she subtly explored his spine and buttocks. The dance floor had provided only a cursory exploration of his lower body, and there he was in the upright position, his own weight a factor. Her explorations of him during their lovemaking would finalize her assessment. She rode him face-to-face, rubbing her pelvis hard against his, looking for reaction. With each thrust, there was no resistance or indication of pain. Her assessment disclosed no orthopedic abnormality or previous fractures. That left her with one diagnosis.

'Do you have nerve damage in your lower spine?'

'What would make you think that?'

'I'm an experienced nurse. From what I can tell, you've never broken any bones in your back or pelvis. That means you must have nerve damage. It's the reason you have an unorthodox mobility. It must be very challenging for you. Am I right? I've been honest with you about my past; maybe you can be honest with me. Medical confidentiality is a part of our profession. I'm a nurse for heaven's sake!'

Duckwalker had buried his secret for so long that the utterance of his next words seemed to come from someone he'd known long ago and far away. He paused long enough to have second thoughts, but there was to be no second thoughts.

'Your probing was very subtle. Don't think I didn't feel you having fun, but I've been inspected from pillar to post. You're not telling me anything new.'

He paused long enough to assure himself that she wouldn't divulge a secret that could cause him financial ruin. It was time to go for it.

'Ten years ago I was a pilot. I did half a tour on bombers in England just as the war ended and I volunteered for something dangerous, so I could remain in England. I had an ulterior motive and sex was the driving force.'

'Are your glasses and unorthodox walk connected? You owe me at least an answer to that.'

'Yes.'

'You must want to talk to somebody about it. Who better than a nurse? Your secret is safe with me. Tell me what happened.' Duckwalker lit a cigarette and exhaled into the dark.

'An experiment went bad. Really bad.'

It was time to come clean and embrace the past.

'Josette Gerard, may I introduce myself. My name is Dwayne Wellington Jones, the human dummy.'

Flying Officer Dwayne Jones RCAF read the advertisement in the Operations Center and decided then and there that he was the man they were looking for. 'Must be a pilot with combat experience; must be single; may be seconded from any British Commonwealth Air Force; danger pay remuneration. Apply Martin-Baker, Higher Denham, Buckinghamshire, England.'

He ripped the advertisement from the board and headed to the squadron commander's office. He'd finished half a tour flying Lancaster bombers and was waiting to get shipped home for demobilization. Canada would have to wait. A job in England would give him time to finally bed Doris Kemper.

Happy to save the cost of his trip home, the Air Force

released him, and he decided to apply in person. If he didn't get the job, he'd have to pay his own way back to Canada.

The vetting process by his potential employer was held at a hangar in a recently disbanded air base at Higher Denham. After a week of technical and physical testing, Dwayne was shortlisted to a group of five. When he was escorted into the boardroom for a final interview, he had no idea what he was signing on for.

The boardroom had been arranged in the abandoned Operations Center, and he sat before five serious gentlemen whose demeanor was that of former senior military officers uncomfortable in tweeds and hunting jackets, smoking pipes and cigarettes. The chairman wasted no time coming to the point.

'Flying Officer Jones, we wish to employ your services.' Dwayne sucked in a lungful of smoky air, then pursed his lips as he slowly exhaled. Doris Kemper was his for the taking. He smiled in satisfaction and sat back in his chair.

'May I smoke, Sir?' Three board members offered cigarettes.

'I'll get right to the point,' the chairman continued. 'The job we want you for is top secret. For now, you're at a bit of a disadvantage, but when the time comes, you'll be told everything. If you accept our proposition, we'll make you an important part of a select team. We can say for certain that your profile is exactly what we're looking for. Your physique, size, and flying skill make you an exceptional test subject for our program.' He paused long enough for Dwayne to click his lighter, take a drag, then let the statement sink in.

'Any questions so far?'

'You advertised for a pilot, Sir. Am I going to be flying?

Your advertisement said there'd be danger pay. I assumed it must have something to do with flying. Dangerous flying.'

The board members smiled and nodded in unison.

'Oh, you'll be spending a great deal of time in the air. And yes, there's an element of danger in what you'll be doing. You'll need a couple more weeks of training and assessment before we can divulge our program to you and negotiate your value to us, liability and all that. We'll provide a lawyer to give you counsel. Secrecy has its cost, what? We can leave you for a couple of minutes to settle your thoughts if you wish, or you can give us your answer now.'

Dwayne added his assets and subtracted his liabilities. Money, women, and flying could not be trumped, and the aspect of a project veiled in total secrecy gave him a gambler's rush. He had to see the hidden hand.

'I'm in. I'm your man.'

For the next two weeks he was subjected to aerobatics, calisthenics, and psychological prodding by doctors who asked ridiculous questions, and said 'hmmm' after every reply. He rode the centrifuge at the Institute of Aviation Medicine, practiced parachute landings from a hundred-foot tower at a nearby army base, and did calisthenics and weight training at a makeshift gymnasium. Three others who'd been shortlisted soon became one.

Alan Rattenbury, an Australian Spitfire pilot who'd lost his poke in a crap game and was leery of going home broke was now Dwayne's only competition. They were isolated from each other during off-hours, and eyed each other with wariness when their paths crossed. Similar in stature and stamina, they competed at every level and discipline, trying to best the other.

Dwayne had no inkling of what lay ahead but was resigned, win or lose, to following the program to its fruition. As a pilot, he understood the aerobatic and centrifuge, but the emphasis on parachute training had him bewildered and more than a little concerned.

'How fucking dangerous is this fucking job going to be?' he'd asked many a technician who'd offered conversation. The reply was always the same.

'Don't know what you're talking about, Sir. I'm just here doing my job and making sure you're fit as a fiddle.'

He impressed the medical team with his ability to sustain high G and not succumb to vertigo during aerobatics. He was small, tough, intelligent, and daring: the perfect guinea pig. Martin-Baker's secret department had found its man.

As his training progressed he sensed that the value of his body was increasing at a greater rate than the value of his mind. At night, he was isolated in an abandoned barrack block, chaperoned by an elderly batman who delivered his supper and breakfast and attended to whatever needs he had.

'Will that be all for now, Sir?' was the signal that he wished to depart to an adjacent suite, and leave Dwayne to his thoughts and whatever reading material he'd been able to scrounge. He felt that even his very isolation was monitored and graded.

Clues to what the establishment was all about were few. He overheard the word 'ejection' in passing conversations and when once questioned its meaning, was rebuked. 'Haven't a clue what you're talking about, Sir, but if it is some kind of code word for something, then let's keep it hush-hush anyway, what?'

After four and half weeks of torture, he was reconvened with his employers to get his marching orders. He'd ascertained that his value to the secret project was the value of his life and limb, and that value had to be compensated for. Armed with youthful bravado and the determination of a prairie farmer negotiating an insurance policy on the next year's crop, he'd presented his case.

'Gentlemen, with consultation I wish to present my terms and conditions. Since there were no terms of reference, I could only make certain assumptions.' As well as a generous salary, Dwayne had designed an insurance policy to protect him and his family if he was maimed or killed in whatever endeavor he was about to partake in. The parachute training and high-stress flying had spooked him, and he knew for certain that what lay ahead had the potential of being life altering.

A week prior, he'd been woken by the scream of a jet aircraft arriving in the dark, and as he watched the anti-collision lights disappear into a gated hangar, he surmised it was a Gloster Meteor integral to the program. For the next seven nights, men and equipment arriving and departing in the dead of night fueled his curiosity. The permutations and combinations of what was going on teased his imagination with a myriad of differing scenarios as to what the program was about. Armed with a scheme that his imagination and sleuthing generated, he laid out his proposal.

'Gentlemen, if whatever the hell you want me to do disables or kills me, you have to compensate me for my loss, or my family's for theirs. Whatever it is, it stinks of something with an unusually high degree of risk and danger. One doesn't spend a month looping, rolling, and jumping off parachute towers without coming to some kind of conclusion. Am I right?' The board members looked to each other, and nodded to the chairman in unison. The time had come to open up and come clean.

The chairman rose from behind the table and went to a teacart. The cookies were the giveaway.

"Nobody gets cookies if they're being fired," he thought. He was in. The chairman pushed the cart to him and slid his chair opposite him.

'Then let's have tea and talk.'

Dwayne felt in control and pressed his advantage.

'First we talk terms.'

The agreement to his demands came at the expense of a non-disclosure clause that had grave financial consequences if he ever disclosed the secret program. Once the contract was signed and notarized, the price he'd pay for his remuneration was finally spelled out.

'Martin-Baker is in the process of signing a lucrative contract with His Majesty's Government for a device that enables an airman to be automatically thrown clear of a disabled aircraft and parachute to safety. The device is called an "ejection seat." The Germans used them with limited success in the Me 262. You've been selected to be our first live subject.' Dwayne bolted upright, his teacup rattling and his sphincter clenching a cushion button.

'You want me to be a dummy, a live dummy, a guinea pig! Jesus Christ, why not use a dead dummy, a real dummy? Sounds to me it's what I'm going to end up anyway, a fucking dead dummy!' He took a deep breath and attempted to soften his tone.

'You want to shoot me out of a perfectly good airplane and hope I'm still alive when I end up on terra firma.' He set his rattling teacup on the cart and fumbled for a cigarette. The aerobatics, the parachute training, and the centrifuge now made sense. Not wanting to show fear, he composed himself with a heavy drag from his cigarette and waited for the chairman to respond. Time to listen.

'We're the secret side of the company. While the other side trains with dummies to placate the Government's contract inspectors, we're going to try and leapfrog them with the real thing. You're the real thing. A dummy can't tell us how it feels, what human sensations there are, what physical and psychological trauma results.'

Duckwalker's ears pricked up. The program's content said one thing, but his voice inflection said quite another.

'You say you're going to try and leapfrog. Your tone says it doesn't sound like you've much confidence in its success. That concerns me.'

'We have enough confidence and certainty that we know we won't have to pay your price if we fail.'

'What if I walk out of here right now? Tell you to go fuck yourselves.'

'We'll make sure you keep your mouth shut. I understand you haven't a ticket home. I'm sure we can make your life here in England uncomfortable if you were stupid enough to let the cat out of the bag, so to speak. Group Captain Stoval, who's next in line if Flying Officer Jones decides he wishes to work elsewhere?' A folder was opened, and Alan Rattenbury's name and credentials were spelled out.

The chairman poured Dwayne a fresh cup and offered the cookies. He took gingerbread, snapped it for crispness and reflected on the value of his skin, his salary, and Doris Kemper. The chairman broke the silence.

'We want you to be our man. We've met your price. Will you meet ours? We asked you once before and we'll ask you once again. Are you in or are you out?' Resigned to fate, Dwayne grinned and nodded.

'Gentlemen, you've hired yourself a dummy.'

He was introduced to a technology he'd never dreamed of. He felt a winner's pride that he was involved in the cutting edge of flight, and the fact that he was at the tip of the spear elevated his personal worth to a level he felt he may never eclipse. When he sat in the working model of an ejection seat for the first time, he knew he'd made the right choice. Man and machine fitted, for above all, it was a machine.

The cockpit of the bomber he'd flown had an escape hatch that was, at best, fifty-fifty if one had time to bail out once the decision was made and the aircraft hadn't already blown up. This system gave one certainty of life when the battle with gravity was lost.

His future depended on the success of the secret program. A leapfrog had its pitfalls. When one failed to make a successful leap, one usually crashed spectacularly. To secure his future well-being, he became pro-active in the engineering and physiological aspects of the program and his farm-boy savvy had him liaising with engineers and parachute makers like they were seed salesmen.

Riding the centrifuge, jumping off the parachute tower, and flying in the backseat of the partially converted jet fighter became routine. The company had purchased an early version Gloster Meteor fighter jet, and was in the process of modifying it to a two-seat configuration with a full canopy, the rear seat area engineered to accept the ejection seat to be tested. Until the modification was fully complete, Dwayne was given a week's leave.

Doris Kemper had reluctantly agreed to meet him at the Foxborough Arms Pub in London.

Doris Kemper was the frustration of his life. His obsession with her beauty and intelligence drove him to distraction and his only reason for partaking in the field of human experimentation was to finally bed her. He'd met her the first time in London while on leave from his new base at Skipton and he continued to correspond and rendezvous with her while he went on operations. They'd met for brief encounters and, except for the thrill of hand-holding and the brush of her fingers, she'd been as elusive as a German night-fighter.

With a sailor's wife's skill, she'd taken him to the point of no return, and pushed him back more times than he wished to count. Tea and marmite sandwiches, at the half-way point between London and Skipton, became the staple of his bewildering love affair. He was in love with a woman twenty years his senior who was married to a British naval officer. Since their final encounter four months previously, he'd read that her husband's ship had been torpedoed off Gibraltar. He didn't know if her husband was dead or alive, but he suspected the latter. With a wizard's glee, he recognized the consequences of how a German torpedo had given him the advantage. A widow was easy prey.

Dwayne Wellington Jones had consoled many widows, but this widow was the reason he'd decided stay in England and put his ass on the line. Armed with brat-like charm, youthful bravado and a larger than normal bulge under his belt, he was targeted by older women while in his teens. In Saskatoon, he'd been seduced by the wife of a railway engineer and had never looked back. He'd figured that he represented a lost love from their youth or a last chance to have meaningful sex with a well-endowed young male rabbit. Mostly they liked to 'kiss' it; either way, he learned what making love was all about. Passing himself off as a virgin, his well-disguised skills of fumbling inexperience had middle-aged women mothering him. His problem with Doris was that he'd stalked her. None of his experience came into play.

The Foxborough pub was operated to serve Canadians overseas, and it was a magnet for British women hoping to hook a Canadian and immigrate to Canada. For a Canadian to say that one had never been there was like saying that one had never been overseas. Dwayne made his pilgrimage while on leave granted to all aircrew before they went on operations, one last chance to experience the joys of life before meeting the Grim Reaper.

He'd finished the heavy bomber conversion course in Scotland, and was given a week's leave before having to report to Skipton and begin flying operations. He'd planned two nights in London and five days taking a slow route north. He'd heard there were a few Joneses up country that were related, and it was a sure bet for a cheap bed and a breakfast. Nobody turned away a lonely Canadian second cousin, especially a baby-faced pilot with a good chance of never seeing his homeland again.

The Foxborough was near Madame Tussauds Waxworks, and he heard it before he found it. He scoped the boisterous interior, saw no empty tables, and ordered a Guinness at the bar; a beer and meal in one.

'A pound not spent is a pound in the pocket.'

She'd been there. He'd caught her eye, and there the left turn in his life began. Fair-haired and expressive, her Merle Oberon eyes darted his way twice and on return of gaze dropped coyly to her chin.

He'd found his target.

He grabbed his beer and was about to make a move on her when she abruptly donned a wide-brimmed hat, bade her companions goodbye, and headed outside. He paid up, drained the glass and, not wishing to appear a common masher, sauntered slowly out the door.

He followed her for several blocks. The length of her stride and erect stature gave her a cheetah-like gait, and he hustled to keep up and not look like a hyena sniffing for carrion. She stopped at a bakery, bought a meat pie, and after tracking her for a further five minutes, she entered the lobby of a posh three-storey apartment.

He moved to the opposite side of the street to wait for a darkened window to show sudden light, but after ten minutes he realized that all the windows were blacked out. He was hunting prairie white-tail at sunset and he'd lost the advantage. "Time and tide wait for no man," and after a half hour in the dark, hoping for her to emerge, he returned to the pub to pick up her trail.

'I'm Dwayne Jones. May I buy the table a drink?' The group that his prey had been drinking with had not disbanded, and he was offered the empty seat. Her seat. He learned that Doris Kemper was the childless wife of a career naval officer. She lived alone and she hadn't set eyes on her husband for two years.

'She's here every day at five for a Guinness.' They had something in common.

After a day of sightseeing and pub-crawling, he returned to the Foxborough and set up his blind. When she arrived, he felt the stirring in his loins that manifested itself with the advent of high G when he flew, especially when the stranger was the most beautiful woman he'd ever set eyes on.

She joined the two corporals he'd met the day before, and was pleased he'd meet her via an introduction. Formality was the British way. He made his move.

'Hi ladies, may I buy you all a pint, or some spirits?' He addressed the plainer of the two and set himself up to play his most genteel persona.

'I must say I enjoyed myself last night. You were all such good sports.' After his showing of the night before, he was now a hail-fellow well met, and the girls invited him to entertain them with stories of the Canadian west. He complimented them on their spit and polish, then turned his attention to the reason why he was there.

'And who, may I ask, is this beautiful woman?'

'Flying Officer Jones, may I introduce Doris Kemper. Doris is my aunt.'

Dwayne feigned shock.

'I see the resemblance, but I would have assumed sisters.'

The girls twittered at his corny compliment and he looked into eyes that said 'lonely.' He took drink orders, and at the bar he parsed her every motion, imagining her nakedness and touch.

Much to the delight of the corporals, Dwayne focused most of his attention on Doris. 'My aunt hasn't seen her husband for a long time. He's in the navy.'

'You must be very lonely Doris. Do you have family for support? Children? Parents, brothers and sisters?' He played his act to perfection, and with skill at manipulating the conversation and scheduling drinks he was able to keep her there well into the evening. The more she spoke, the more she gestured, the more she moved, the more he was wrapped in the cocoon she was unknowingly spinning around his brain.

'I have to go. It's very late, and I've taken advantage of your generosity and wit.' She swept her hat from the table, and as she rose he grabbed for his hat and volunteered to walk her home.

'It's very late, and who knows who's lurking in the dark.'

'That would be wonderful.' With that they bade the two corporals goodbye, and all agreed that they must meet again someday.

She slipped her arm through his, synchronized her step to match his shorter stature and tightened her grip. She guided him along the darkened streets with a steady gliding pace, following the same course he'd followed her on the night before. The closer he got to her flat, the more his heart rate quickened, and as they made the final turn down her street, he couldn't hold his thoughts back any further. He stopped and faced her.

'Doris, you are the most beautiful, intelligent woman I've ever met. I saw you last night and I had to meet you. I find you intoxicating. I have to see you again. I know you're married and there's an age and cultural difference, but I don't see why we can't be friends. You're alone and so am I. Once I'm on operations, my chances of completing a tour are pretty slim. I sure could use a little mothering along the way.'

After much pleading and playing sympathy cards to perfection, she agreed to meet him in a town on the railway line halfway between Skipton and London.

'There'll be no shenanigans, young squire. We'll meet, play tourist, have tea, then say goodbye. I've been married to the navy for fifteen years and I'm still virtuous. A baby-faced Canuck won't change all that.' She shook her head and scolded him with a half dozen "tsk, tsk, tsks." 'I'm old enough to be your mother. A brat like you deserves a good thrashing with a cane.'

A rendezvous at the halfway point played into his hands. Day trips while on operations were a doable thing and the advantage of secrecy would keep the rest of the hounds at bay.

Doris Kemper had British schoolgirl innocence and the body of Diana the huntress. 'Diana' had become her codeword and he'd envisioned her drawing her bow, driving an arrow through his heart, then weeping over his lifeless youth. Her skill on the national grass hockey team twenty years prior had given her catlike silkiness with every motion, and an aristocratic sophistication when she spoke. She'd become an obsession, and a return to Canada without consummating his fantasy would have left a hole in his life.

Over a period of three months, they'd met half a dozen times at a tearoom two blocks from the railway station and there they'd planned their day. At lunch he'd attempted to impress her with his derring-dos as an intrepid aviator who was only one mission from never seeing her again, but she would have none of it.

'You'll have to do better than that, young squire,' she'd admonished him. 'Remember, I lived in London during the blitz. The brave ones were the people who didn't know whether they'd be alive in the morning. You can fight back. They couldn't.'

He'd write, she'd reply, and they'd rendezvous. A half-dozen meetings got him a kiss goodbye, and his hand up her thigh in a smoky theatre. She touched him once during a Noel Coward film and the sensation took him to near orgasm. Three weeks before VE Day he'd diverted to London due to battle damage, and after pleading to see her, she agreed to let him stay the night.

'The war's coming to an end. I need to see you one more time. You've meant so much to me. More than you'll ever know. After every mission, the first thing I do is check my mail, even before I debrief.' After a silence that made his heart pound faster than the twenty-minute battle he'd just won against a Junkers 88 night-fighter, she replied.

'There'll be no hanky-panky. My husband could turn up at any moment and I don't want him to get any wrong ideas. Remember, I'm a navy wife.'

But there had been shenanigans that night. That's where he now stood. The next day he flew the patched-up

Lancaster back to Skipton, and found out that his war was over. Two days later, he read the advertisement on the bulletin board.

Duckwalker paused for a piss and a cigarette, and when he snuggled back into bed, Josette propped herself on her elbow demanding he continue his story. His affliction, the reason she'd asked the question, hadn't been remotely touched upon.

'What happened that night in London? What happened when you saw her again? What's she got to do with the way you walk funny and wear sunglasses all the time?'

'You have to know that I've never told a soul what I'm telling you now. She's got everything to do with what I am, what I do, and how I think.'

'How can that be so?'

'When I was twenty, women of a certain age and style directed my life: middle-aged women, women your age. I'm over thirty now and the women I'm attracted to are still the same. You are it. Everything about you fits in the mold. I can't help it. Every woman I've been with since Doris I've judged against her and I can't change the trend. When I reach forty I'll be able to make it an even match. What worries me is that when I'm sixty-five I'll still be pursuing forty-year old women, still using her as the benchmark.'

'Forget about that for now. Get back to your story.'

The Foxborough had traded its boisterous Canadian patrons for boisterous British patrons back from the war. Uniforms had become tweed suits and skirts. Dwayne found Doris sitting in an alcove and her nervous smile of recognition signaled everything, and nothing.

It had been two months since their farewell kiss.

'You look marvelous, Diana,' was all he could blurt out.

'I'm not Diana; that has to stop.' She bit her lip. 'I shouldn't be seeing you. What we did, I did, was wrong.' She looked down with shame.

"She got to the point too early," Dwayne thought, as he was taken aback.

'Diana, Doris, all I can say is that it was the most wonderful night of my life. You anointed me with a potion that only you can remove.' It was corny but he meant it.

'Don't be silly. You still have your youth and your future. I've aged ten years since we said goodbye. Our time together made me feel young again. When we almost made love that last night, when fifteen years of honesty, virtue, and self-discipline were nearly thrown away, I realized I was dishonoring my marriage vows. I wasn't sad when I said goodbye.' She fetched a handkerchief from her sleeve.

'My husband isn't coming home. He was lost at sea. A month before the end of the bloody war and his ship is torpedoed! Can you believe that? He fought in every theatre and gets torpedoed coming home.' Tears welled. Dwayne grabbed for her hand but she pulled away and dabbed her eyes. He'd never seen her cry.

'The only reason I agreed to see you again is that I haven't a husband, a marriage, or a future, especially with you. I needed closure. I toyed with you that last night. I teased and toyed with you all the time… and I liked it. I was a young woman being courted by a baby-faced pilot who carried my colors into combat. How flattered I was; how noble you were. How innocent you were. We were opposite ends of a piece of string that wanted to make a knot.' She paused and looked into his bewildered eyes.

'I want you to come home with me. Now! I want you to make love to me…. I want you to make love to me, and then I want you to leave my life forever.'

Duckwalker choked and wiped tears. 'Christ, this is harder than I thought!' Josette stroked his cheek.

'A week later she was dead.'

'Dead?'

'Suicide. I experienced love in the most extraordinary way with the most extraordinary woman, and then she kills herself; fucking kills herself. She takes a bath and slits her wrists. With that she was gone. A week later, I got a photograph in the mail. It was from her. It was a picture of the two of us walking down a sidewalk. I never saw her take the ticket from the sidewalk photographer.'

'What was written on the back changed me forever. Diana was the woman I fell in love with. Doris was the woman who killed herself.'

'How did you find out?'

'She was true to her word. It was our last time together. I left the next day, and we never spoke again. Her niece found the picture and managed to track me down. I was devastated. I got a death wish, and pushed the chairman to get the program moving faster, and we know what happened. This.' He thrust forked fingers toward his eyes then ran them down to his hips.

'That's why she had everything to do with my miserable afflictions. Does that answer your question?'

'It's a start, but I'm more interested in what caused your physical affliction, not your sexual obsession, which by the way might just be an Oedipus complex. But I'm not in the business of psychiatry. I'm a nurse. The damage to your body is what intrigues me.'

'Remember, this is virgin ground for me. I buried this aspect of my life so deep that I have to put my thoughts in proper order to recall all the details. This happened over nine years ago. I'm a different man now.'

'In some ways, you're definitely not. Doris Kemper is responsible for that.'

'If you want to hear the rest of the story, it's on the pro-vision you won't interrupt me.'

Dwayne made his first parachute jump from a beat-up Halifax that had been used to drop agents into France. After half a dozen exits using a static line, he insisted on making delayed jumps from higher and higher altitudes.

While in freefall, he oriented his body into differing configurations, simulating an unconscious pilot relying on a barometric opening device to keep him from turfing in. Technicians and packers focused skyward with binoculars grasped by white knuckles, gleaning first-hand accounts of how the straps and canopy responded to various body posi-tions when the parachute opened. Movies filmed in slow motion had the audience in horror. If the parachute failed to open, they'd know the reason why.

More than once, the ground observers' sphincters tight-ened to knots as he delayed opening his parachute closer and closer to the ground. The last jump before his first live ejection, he became so tantalized by the effect of ground rush that he got only three swings under the canopy before hitting the ground.

'That was a little tight, wasn't it, Sir? The boss isn't going to be too happy if you turf in. They've a lot invested in you. You'll be pushing up daisies, and we'll be the ones getting shit.' Dwayne gathered his parachute, and had a lit cigarette thrust between his pursed lips.

'We won't always have the luxury of bailing out at a nice safe altitude, Harry. If this ejection device is going to work, the parachute, straps, and the canopy have to work at low level, too. At low level, the poor bastard won't have time or space to open his chute manually.' He grinned and winked.

'I'm willing to bet that one day people will be doing this for sport.'

He made three simulated ground ejections using the latest seat attached to a sixty-foot vertical rail. Dressed in full flying gear and strapped in, he was subjected to ever-increasing kicks in the butt as he was shot skyward by varying explosive charges.

With modifications to the Meteor completed, the program went into high gear. Concealed in the hangar, the aircraft swarmed with engineers, technicians, and machinists installing the electronics, ejection seat and modified canopy.

The rear section of the canopy over the test subject was designed to disengage at the moment the seat triggering was activated, and several glitches in the circuitry delayed the first test fire. After three months of isolation and secrecy, he was ready to make the first attempt.

The final briefing before the big day was the harbinger of disaster. The chairman and his henchmen once again convened to throw shit his way.

'Flying Officer Jones, we need to bring you up-to-date on the progress of the firing mechanism we will use to propel the seat from the aircraft. You were aware from the beginning that our program was the secret side of a two-pronged test program. Now we can tell you why.'

Dwayne lit a cigarette and braced for the unexpected. He'd heard through scuttlebutt that the other program was well behind them, and that their test aircraft had nearly crashed when the seat and dummy failed to totally clear the tail. "At least they'd tried a live firing," he thought. The secret project hadn't got nearly so far yet the first test was to be with him. "I'm a fucking dummy in more ways than one!" he moaned to himself.

The chairman continued,

'You experienced three ground-ejection simulations. From that, we've been able to calculate the amount of force needed to blast you out and away. What we haven't told you is that we won't be using that particular type of charge to boot you out, so to speak. What we're going to use is a rocket-type propellant.'

'What the hell is a rocket propellant?'

'Instead of a single explosion, like that of a shotgun firing its pellets, the rocket seat is meant to burn for several seconds and transport you further away from the aircraft, and allow for escapes at lower altitudes. We've been engineering and testing the rocket system up in Scotland, and we're having nearly a one hundred percent success in the duration of the propellant burn and the amount of thrust produced.'

'As we said at the beginning of our association, we want to leapfrog the simpler but less desirable approach. As it stands right now, the only success the other side is having is well above 2,000 feet above ground, and at best they're only fifty-fifty. And that's using a mannequin.'

Dwayne controlled his anger. He was going to be riding a rocket, not a popgun.

'I'm riding a fucking rocket seat. Why in hell didn't you let me know about this sooner?'

'Would it have made any difference? With you, I think not…. Anyway, we weren't certain the system would work. When it came time to sign you up, we were satisfied that the system was foolproof. It's much easier to control a rocket than an explosive device…. Then there's the ability of the rocket seat to actually gain the occupant higher altitude before seat-separation. We've seen the films of you free falling. You even commented to the parachute boys that low-level ejection is a thing of the future. I don't necessarily agree about the sport aspect. Then again, who knows about the future?'

Dwayne lit another cigarette and let out a deep exhale. The time had come.

'The first test run went by the book until the moment of truth. I strapped in, we took off, and then the shit hit the fan.'

'Shit hit the fan?'

'Things went sideways, then downhill. Fast!

'We set up the run at 5,000 feet, so the cameras and the ground observers could get a decent look-see. Two Spitfire chase planes escorted us. We selected 250 knots as the ideal airspeed. Needless to say, my heart rate increased dramatically as the moment came to squeeze the triggers on the seat. Much like it's doing now.'

Josette sensed his anxiety. His heart rate, breath, and perspiration were of someone stepping to the edge of a precipice. She wanted to soothe him but she needed to be there in the cockpit with him.

'They called a countdown over the radio. When it hit zero and I squeezed the triggers, nothing happened.'

'Nothing happened?'

'Nothing happened. It took five minutes to discover a popped circuit breaker. We set up another run, and when the moment of truth came, all hell broke loose.'

Duckwalker paused and rubbed tears. He was naked without glasses.

'I wouldn't be the same. I remember squeezing the triggers, but that's all I remember. Everything after that came from film and the crash inspection. Things happened so fast that the ground observers couldn't agree on anything.'

'Crash inspection! Did you crash?'

'I didn't, but the aircraft did. The pilot was killed. He didn't have an ejection seat.'

Film and the crash investigation laid out the sequence of events. The instant the count hit zero, Dwayne initiated the ejection sequence by squeezing triggers beside each knee. The rear section of the canopy, meant to break away before the rocket lit, failed. The subsequent firing of the rocket inside the confines of the cockpit blew off both front and rear canopies, ejecting Dwayne in a pinwheel trajectory, clearing the aircraft's tail by a foot. The aircraft nosed over and crashed into a field. Film confirmed that the pilot directed the aircraft away from the built-up area of the base.

'The drogue chute, meant to stabilize my trajectory, wrapped around me and I didn't separate from the seat; but apparently I was cognizant of what was happening, because

I managed to free myself from it and pull the ripcord. My parachute opened and I hit the ground. One more second, and I'd be pushing up daisies.'

'How did you manage to do it?'

'When the chestnuts on the ground become a point of reference, you're close to Mother Earth. Training and instinct took over. I saved myself. The crazy thing is I have no memory of the impact.'

'You have an ejection seat now, don't you?'

'Would you believe it's made by the same company? Martin-Baker! Because of my eye damage they designed the seat so you have to pull a blind over your face to activate the sequence.'

'That's what caused your eye problems?'

'The flash from the rocket blinded me for two months. My eyes only work in the dark. My pupils are in a permanent wide-open position. It's like staring at a continuous flashbulb.'

'What about your stature, your unorthodox walk? That crazy name they call you. What caused that?'

'I hit the ground in a sitting position. My butt took the brunt. I wish I'd broken my tailbone or pelvis. If I had, I wouldn't be trying to suppress a constant urge to poop. That's the only way I can describe it.'

'What an awful sensation! Can't you take drugs?'

'Not and fly. When I walk the way I walk, the sensation disappears. It was murder on the dance floor.'

'What happened after? How did you get to here?'

The first to reach Dwayne expected to find a lifeless body under the parachute canopy. Lying in a fetal position with a death grip on the D-ring of the ripcord, was the still-breathing test-subject, and as the shroud was pulled away, he screamed as a blowtorch of light seared his retinas.

The ten minutes he waited for the meat-wagon to get on scene felt like hours, and he reconciled he'd be a blind cripple forever. Blood oozed from his eyes and he defecated. The ride to the infirmary in the meat-wagon transpired in a morphine haze.

In an attempt to cover the company's involvement with their living liability, he was shunted from hospital to clinic to rehabilitation center, existing in darkened rooms and suffering the indignity of wanting to constantly sit on the toilet. Eventually, he found the balance that would allow him mobility and sight.

After three months of isolation, the chairman of Martin-Baker visited him for the purpose of bestowing his remuneration and discharge.

'We've cancelled the rocket program completely. We pushed the technology too far, and two of you paid the price. One man dead and one man crippled. We are truly sorry. Your rehabilitation cost and payout per our contract have been settled. Your lawyer will fill you in on where your money resides.'

'You signed a confidentiality agreement, and we will hold you to it. If you ever divulge the program and what happened to you, we will take steps to ruin you physically and financially. As of this moment, you are not part of Martin-Baker's history.'

'What about the other side of the program you referred to? What happened with it?'

'We eventually had success with the simpler method by using an explosive charge. Because of you, we eliminated the rear canopy on the other test aircraft, and we redesigned the seat's triggering device.'

'We've designed an overhead ring that pulls a blind over the airman's face to protect the eyes from wind blast. One only has to pull down on the ring and the canopy and seat leave the aircraft in sequence. We wouldn't have made those kinds of decisions if we'd used a dummy. You've been very valuable to us.'

Dwayne felt little satisfaction in his contribution.

'We hope your financial position gives you the opportunity to get on with your life. When I leave this room we will hopefully have no further contact. Thank you and good luck.' He paused at the door.

'By the way, we signed the contract with His Majesty's government. You'll be hearing about Martin-Baker for a long time to come.'

'I returned to Canada at Christmas of '45. I'd developed an interest in electronics and applied to MIT in Boston. I could afford the best. Four years later, I had degree in electrical engineering specializing in the new field of computers. They're used in the radar I helped develop. When things got hot in Korea, the Air Force came calling and my specialty meshed into their new interceptors' radar and weapon system. And here I am. I still have a few bucks left in the bank. I'm a cripple who can still do mostly what I want. Sitting in the backseat, telling the pilot where to go; that's my cross to bear.'

'I understand there's nothing you can do about the problem of your sight,' Josette replied. 'You're lucky you can see at all. It's your strange walk that there might be a cure for.

They're making huge strides in spinal rejuvenation. Can't they medicate you for now, so you can stand more erect?'

'I need to fly. Drugs won't let me do that. Now no more questions. I've divulged too much. I have to fly in the morning. I can sleep here or return to barracks.'

'I see you brought your kit. You were confident. I can't turn you out into a stormy night. Junior officers should not be seen leaving a female senior officer's quarters at three in the morning, especially the housemistress's lair. I want you out of here by seven.'

'Thank you, Ma'am.'

'Good night, Duckwalker Jones.'

He curled into her and kissed her shoulder. 'You're the first person who's said that to my face. With your accent, you make it sound noble. Maybe I'll make it my call sign.'

With that, he nestled up to Josette's right breast and proceeded to nuzzle himself to sleep.

<hr />

Lou bolted upright from a troubled sleep. He hadn't woken from the nightmare for nearly a year. Happiness was the trigger. It was always the trigger. It had been that way with Francine. It was the reason why he shunned any emotional involvement with women. As long as misery ruled his life, his cowardice was buried in a secure safe.

'What is it? What's wrong? You've been twitching and perspiring ever since you went to sleep.' Darlene had been resting on an elbow, wondering if she should wake him.

'It was just a dream. You know, a nightmare. It's nothing.'

'Your heart's pounding.' She stroked his forehead. 'You're wet. Let me get a cool face cloth.' She slipped on his jacket and lit the bathroom light, her silhouette reaching for him on the wall.

He studied her, parsing each motion, marveling at the grace of her neck, her legs, and her derriere.

'You're a beautiful woman, Miss Muncie. I might make Bagotville a weekend destination.' She snapped off the light and with strokes of endearment, attempted to cleanse his troubled mind. She disrobed and straddled him to his ribcage. She touched his forehead then drew her finger to her heart.

'I will be here for you. You must be there for me. When you give me what's inside that beautiful head of yours, I will give you my heart.' She kissed his scar, reached behind, and gently squeezed his penis.

'Now, what's wrong with this little gentleman? We'll have to do something about this, won't we?'

Darlene slipped into the storm at 4 AM. Lou promised to call her after he'd debriefed from the flight. His promise to accompany her to the Sadie Hawkins dance was reconfirmed and she made rudimentary measurements of his torso for his outfit.

'When the rest of the girls see you, I'm going to have to bid pretty high.'

'Just make sure you're the one who gets me, Miss Muncie.'

'How much do you think you're worth, Louis Fender?'

'Let's just say that I'll cover for the highest bidder if you can't come up with the dough.'

CHAPTER 11

Saturday 7:30 AM 1230 GMT

Pete Rylander didn't get the B-25's chocks pulled until nine fifteen. A soft tire and Dan Lacey's diarrhea had seen to that.

'Sorry Pete! I just had to sample those survival rations. We better report them to supply. They can't have some poor bastard living on them in the bush if they don't supply a gross of ass-wipe to go along with them.'

They were climbing out of Chatham and had been in cloud from the moment they'd raised the flaps and turned west to rendezvous with the confluence of the St. Lawrence and Saguenay Rivers. The overwhelming roar and vibration from the Wright Cyclone engines at climb power enveloped the cockpit. One never flew with a hang-over in a B-25.

'Give me a heading to Tadoussac, Dan.' He'd level off at 8,000 feet. No need to go higher. Their trick was to appear as a private aircraft proceeding without a flight plan. The GCI site would ignore then forget them once they'd descended under their radar. He had a full load of fuel, the propellers were biting cool moist air, and he was in his comfort zone. Lou Fender was about to find out that the student had become the master.

He leveled off, tuned the engines, trimmed the aircraft, and passed control to Fred Archer, a recent graduate of the Royal Military College and a more recent wings graduate from Moose Jaw. A pair of glasses had him sitting in the copilot's seat, and unless they changed the rules, there he'd stay. He'd be a squadron leader by the time he was thirty, and the thrill of skulking around in a World War II bomber would only be an anecdote at a mess dinner.

Pete had requested an over-achieving copilot who could fly and keep his head out of the cockpit, and was rewarded with Fred. As long as his glasses didn't fog up, he was an owl. He was surprised at the recommendation of Fred by Badger One, The Voice from Ottawa, until he found out that he was his nephew. He'd gotten Fred drunk shortly after the crew was put together, and a small dose of his elixir had him disclosing his true mission. Feeding information back to Ottawa was his 'raison d'être.' Pete made sure hangovers were kept to a minimum.

He closed his eyes and concentrated on the throb of the engines. He felt a difference. He pulled back his earphones and was greeted by a jackhammer pounding in each ear.

'Add 30 RPM to the starboard engine, Fred. Either that or it's running rich. Check the cylinder-head temperature. That'll be a good indicator.' He pressed his headphones back over his ears like suction cups and the numbing vibration from the engines blanked out their din. At this rate, he'd be deaf by forty.

He felt the empty vial in his breast pocket and contemplated his problem. He was out of chloral hydrate, and his prospects of finding a pharmacy in the next two weeks were poor. He'd never run dry, and without the potion, he had little hope of satisfying his habit. He was scheduled to be in Ottawa for the Officers' Mess Halloween party, and had heard that a contingent of newly-minted Air Force nurses were to be in attendance. He courted every mess officer in his trap line with copious quantities of 'hoot and holler' and planned his dance card accordingly.

At pharmacy school he'd been introduced to the effects of the drug when mixed with alcohol, and from day one he'd relied on it to feed his habit. His tactic had never changed: pick out the target, a naïve and inexperienced drinker, squirt chloral hydrate into her drink, then lead the lamb to the slaughter.

Various compartments in the B-25 had been his lair. An erased memory, teamed with a magic carpet and gypsy life-style, offered range to ply his devious obsession. There'd been a couple of mishaps along the way, but he'd been able to wiggle his way out by using Cabbagetown savvy. An unsubstantiated rumor of a young woman's suicide in Winnipeg added guilt, but that was years behind him. To date, he'd never been accused of any wrongdoing, and he intended to keep it that way.

Now, he was hunting game of a higher order. Lou Fender was his target. Pete intended to close a passage in his life he thought would never happen. He and Wilding would finally put Rangoon to rest.

Meeting Lou in Yellowknife had been no accident. He had disappeared into the hinterland, but his DOT records had been easily accessible. Wing Commander Wilding had seen to that. It was only a matter of time before Pete had a layover in Yellowknife and there were few bars to scour. He'd feigned surprise when they'd met but it was all an act.

Getting Lou to re-enlist got Wilding off his back in the short term.

Pete knew Lou Fender's secret. Their stateroom on board ship during the trip to Canada was the theatre of its disclosure. His nightmares exposed a murderer and a coward. He'd never challenged him on what he'd overheard, but an abrupt change of character and descent into the hollow man he'd become was the last evidence he needed to solve the mystery. His charade with Lou in Yellowknife had seen to that.

It went back to the summer of 1945 at Rangoon.

Two Japanese aircraft that Lou had been escorting to Rangoon never arrived. His ranting while asleep revealed that he'd shot them down, and a cover-up with Wilding had ensued. Pete hadn't followed up the chain of command for fear of reprisal, but he could silence the executioner. The 50-caliber machine guns mounted in the nose had been test-fired in flight days before.

'We need to see if the vibration from the recoil affects the radar,' he'd explained. 'The Mark 4 has rockets as well as guns, and we don't want vibration blowing tubes in the radar.'

It was a good cover.

Wilding had re-recruited Pete when he'd immigrated to Canada from Britain shortly after the end of the war. Pete held the poke, and with the poke came power. Lou Fender was the fly in the soup and Pete's reward would come when he disposed of him.

Pete returned to the situation at hand. They were flying west to the confluence of the St. Lawrence and Saguenay Rivers. Fred hadn't waivered more than fifty feet in altitude.

Every copilot who'd flown with him wanted to impress and Fred Archer was no different.

'We've got a pretty good-looking headwind building, Pete.' Dan called from his radar consul. 'Our groundspeed has dropped 30 knots in the last fifteen minutes. With this weather pattern it's only going to get worse. Do you want to add power?'

Pete made calculations on his E6B computer and revised the plan. The eye of the storm dictated the order of battle. When they crossed the St. Lawrence, he'd take the Mitchell down to an altitude he felt safe, then head up the Saguenay River Valley towards Lake Saint-Jean. If he could break through the front into the eye of the storm at the right time, he'd catch the two ready aircraft on the ground and satisfy The Voice in Ottawa. Further, if he were to entice them into the air and lure them into combat, so much the better. Working for two masters was like being a Venetian prostitute, working both sides of the canal without a gondola. He tapped Fred on the shoulder.

'Good work Fred. I have control.' It was time to go to war. He'd set the stage to shoot down Lou Fender and get Wilding out of his life.

———•◦•———

Duckwalker entered the dining room in time to see Lou turn his back. No eye contact meant no conversation; they'd breakfast alone. The Saturday morning cooks jumped to, and he custom-ordered a prairie farmer's breakfast.

He still couldn't believe he'd made his secret known. He'd held it for nine years. There was relief in purging, and he felt the better for it. The weekend had produced more than he'd bargained for.

Josette had not bested Doris, but it didn't matter. There was something else. There was sharing, something he'd never done. A beautiful nurse had broken him free. He ate like a farmer heading to the field, smoked like a steam engine working uphill, and drank three cups of coffee before heading in step with Lou Fender to Met briefing.

A bespectacled meteorologist, who'd been flown in to observe the storm passage, tapped his watch as they sat down. Strange weather patterns sprung up the strangest bedfellows. The 440 standby crew and a helicopter pilot were in attendance, and when the lights switched off, swirls of cigarette smoke jumped into the beam.

With a gurgling clearing of his throat the Met briefer stepped into the spotlight. 'Gentlemen, we have a very interesting set of weather circumstances, unlike anything I've seen in my thirty-year career. In an hour or so, we will be bathed in sunlight and soothed by calm winds. In three hours, all hell is going to break loose.' He swept a pointer to the weather map on the screen, jolting Lou and Duckwalker from their traditional Met briefing nod-off.

'Gentlemen, as you can see, the center of the low is going to be moving directly over us. The weather at the trailing edge is going to be as intense as the front that's been moving through for the last twelve hours. There will be lots of vertical cloud, lots of hail, and lots of icing, especially icing. So stay away from low-level flying. Questions?'

He paused and fired up a long-stem pipe, giving his audience time to soak in the information.

'Questions?' He blew smoke into the projector's beam and squinted at his unseen audience.

'There's an intruder aircraft coming in from Chatham,' Lou piped. 'He's attempting to catch the base with its pants down, take pictures and show the five of us sitting here that we can't do the job we've been trained to do. Any suggestions?'

The Met briefer stared like a deer in the headlights, searching for the origin of the question, then sucked his pipe long enough to get his audience's attention.

'At altitude, turbulence is your real enemy. Check your gust-loading figures. Clear air and sunshine don't necessarily make for stable air, so the eye of the storm may not be as benign as it looks. If you get into—and I for one would not like to do so—the actual storm, the cloud so to speak, you could get torn apart. Questions?'

'This guy's going to have to come in at low level, or we'll be in the air for an hour by the time he gets within a hundred miles of here,' Duckwalker noted. 'He'd be a sitting duck. The GCI site at Mont Apica will have picked him up by the time he breaks through the cloud top.'

'As I said, at lower altitudes icing is the main problem, that and turbulence, especially over mountainous terrain.

'Then he's going to get the shit kicked out of him if he tries that.'

Duckwalker waited for his statement to register. 'If he's smart, he'll come up the Saguenay River Valley. He'll have icing maybe, but turbulence, I think not. It'd be interesting to know what the water temperature of the river is. Large bodies of water and weird weather can make for severe icing and hail, and we all know what kind of problems that causes. I think he's in for a shitload of icing.' He turned and whispered to Lou.

'This is going to be interesting. Let's talk.'

They adjourned to the Operations Center and met the standby crew. Duckwalker recognized the dark, mustachioed pilot who Doc Hunter had pointed out the night before.

'Don, isn't it?

'That's correct Sir, but you have me at a disadvantage. Your face is familiar. Did we meet during the war? I did a tour on Halifaxes at Skipton-on-Swale in '44. And you would be?'

Duckwalker, unable to respond to Don's query about Skipton, introduced himself. Don introduced John, his navigator, and they pulled Lou into the pack to brief them on their upcoming mission. Duckwalker digressed.

'Last night, I was informed by a certain Doc Hunter that you've been involved in a number of B-36 interceptions. I'd like to hear about them sometime. In the meantime, Lou has a few words to say about the adversary that will most likely scramble us in the next couple of hours. That stuff you heard us talking about at Met briefing wasn't bullshit.'

'There's an exercise on?'

'That's why we're here. We want to see how well 440 responds to a fire drill.' He went over to the communal coffee percolator and with a smile, winked at the sergeant behind the counter. 'The first thing we look for is the freshness of the coffee.'

For the next hour they probed for any weakness in the squadron's readiness. They performed their 'walk around' of the two ready aircraft, peeking into wheel-wells and testing control surfaces for excess play. Lou took particular interest in the tip tanks of their aircraft. He'd never flown with them on, and he took note to study the engineering orders and fuel transference on them when he returned to the operations room. He tested their attachment. Everything was solid.

The CF-100 was a large aircraft for a fighter. Except it wasn't really a fighter. It was an interceptor, and as such didn't need the maneuverability and speed range that was needed in a dogfight. The Sabre had the advantage in daylight, but it couldn't touch a CF-100 at night or in cloud.

Circular intakes fed jet engines that hugged each side of the fuselage, and a smooth round fiberglass cone housed the radar dish in the nose. They remotely opened the canopy and climbed the ladder to their cockpits, looking for anything that justified a nasty report. The red-flagged ejection-seat pins were all in place, and the parachute and safety harnesses were neatly separated for quick, easy access.

Lou checked the fuel tanks and connections of the yellow motorized generators that supplied auxiliary power to the aircraft for start-up. Satisfied, he nodded his approval. Duckwalker indicated 'thumbs up' and they returned to the ready room. The aircraft were ready to fly.

Josette waited for Darlene's return and the single set of heel clicks on the terrazzo in the hallway indicated she was alone. She slipped a greatcoat over her negligee and tiptoed down the hall to Darlene's room. She was anxious to know if her suspicions were correct. She inserted her key, hung her coat, and stole softly to the side of the bed. She awakened Darlene with a kiss on the neck and they embraced. In their intimate moments they spoke in French.

'Is he the one? Is he the one with the eyes?'

'No!'

'What is he then? What is he to you? You just met him, and you're smitten.'

'What is he then? I could ask you the same question. What about Flight Lieutenant Jones? Two can play at this game.'

Josette was caught. Men and women had the same allure. The young man had offered more than a pistil to whatever orifice she needed stimulated.

'I was interested in his peculiarities, that's all. It was the nurse in me. I wanted to find out why he looked and walked so strangely.'

'I heard him leave just a while ago. You must have been doing more than giving him a physical. Your negligee wasn't something you just put on for me.'

Josette and Darlene had been lovers for six months. Their bond was the reason Darlene had signed on for another term of teaching. Josette's liaison with the young man had evolved out of nursing curiosity and the results had been very satisfactory. Mind and body had been sated.

'Darling Darlene, you've always known I was bisexual. It was for your sake that I was using him as a diversion. When I saw the look on your face when we ran into Flying Officer Fender in the lobby I thought he was the man you were looking for. Those eyes, that scar.'

'I never said he had a scar, and his eyes were like

that silent movie actor. The one who died young, the swashbuckler.'

'Valentino! Rudolph Valentino?'

'That's him. He had Rudolph Valentino eyes.

CHAPTER 12

Lincoln hustled to his room in the barracks to reprogram the plan that had been thrown a glitch. When it came to weather, timing was everything. The delay meant that the weather pattern he'd planned to use in his attack path over Canada had changed by almost eight hours.

The Met officer hadn't sufficient information to speculate what path the low-pressure system over Québec would take eight hours hence, and he reminded the voice from the back of the darkened briefing room that the weather over Québec would in no way affect a great Polar route from England to Maine.

Lincoln felt sheepish at the question, but nodded to his navigator with a look that said, 'this might be on the exam exercise on the return trip.' Gidley quickly focused on the weather pattern over the Gulf of St. Lawrence, and scribbled on his kneepad. 'Fair warning' he thought. 'The boss is up to something.'

Lincoln checked back into the room he'd departed only hours before. The bed had been stripped, and he darkened the room with a snap of the Venetian blind. Comfort came when he came 'back into the dark.' He disrobed, lit a Marlboro, and lay on the bare mattress. The atmosphere of his last sleep would have all the attributes of a prison cell. The only thing missing were the bars on the windows. Then again, if things went badly, that's where he could end up.

"No fucking way," he thought to himself. "If I start thinking that way, everything will get fucked up. The plan is sound. When I hit Labrador, I may have to make some minor adjustments. That's all."

With each inhalation, the glow from his cigarette lit the screen on the ceiling that the night before had played out the final day of Alana's life. The last chapter had been lost to sleep. To some degree, a final recollection, alone and in a neutral environment, was preferable to one at 40,000 feet. He remembered the week that they'd last spent together at the farm.

He masturbated, fantasizing about the time she teased him in the barn at the farm in Québec about his French-Canadian twang. He'd been teaching her basic French without realizing that she was quite fluent in it. When he twigged on, 'the roll-in the-hay' that followed was now the subject of his fantasy. When he climaxed, the bliss turned to horror when her death mask suddenly flashed onto the ceiling.

He closed his eyes and remembered the moment he woke up in the motor hotel in Albuquerque with Alana sitting on a chaise lounge, smoking a cigarette.

'When did you start smoking?'

'I've smoked for years, usually when you weren't around. I hid it well. You never knew, never suspected?'

He sensed frost in the air.

'Obviously I didn't. And when I think of all the times we could have had a smoke together. Lost opportunities, and all that.' He lit a Marlboro and headed to the bathroom. He sat on the toilet, smoking and conjuring. No, he hadn't suspected. There was no scent, no breath, no stain, and no withdrawals. And what about the family thing? Had the spy in each of them become their dominant persona?

'The plan starts now,' he muttered. 'No turning back, no regrets.' He finished his ablutions, dressed in the outfit she'd bought for him the day before, packed up, and headed to the airport for breakfast and the flight to Santa Fe.

The freeze was still on at breakfast. They ate at the airport diner in silence. Every now and then, each would attempt to start the conversation, but to no avail. Lincoln sensed that the issue was to do with the kid, or lack thereof. He had no answer for her, because the answer was NO. Her 'out of the blue' family question had him reeling. When the plates were cleared and their coffee cups had been topped up, he broached the topic.

'Sweetheart, I don't want us to fight. We've never been very good at it.'

'I only asked. It wasn't an ultimatum or anything.'

'It was just your tone, the way you presented it. And I must say your timing seemed a little inappropriate.'

'When is it an appropriate time for God's sake? I'm here, you're there, I'm coming, you're going. Didn't you ever want to have a family with me?'

Lincoln passed her a cigarette, lit both with shaking hands and paused to frame an answer.

'No darling, I didn't. From the moment we met, the subject has never arisen, and until last night, never spoken of.

I always assumed that our careers were of greater importance. You really threw me a curve last night. I didn't sleep a wink.'

'If it's any consolation, I didn't sleep a wink either.'

'You used the word "ultimatum." Where did you pull that from? The mention of the word "ultimatum" has its connotations. How long has this child thing been banging around in that clever head of yours? And are you giving me an ultimatum—no family, no marriage, no Alana, no Lincoln?'

Alana took a sip of coffee and a deep drag from her cigarette. He knew the answer.

'I guess I'm making it an ultimatum. I didn't plan to deal with this issue, or have this conversation here and now, but maybe it's for the best. I don't think you're in love with me.'

A chill rippled down his spine. Divorce was not something a career officer wanted on his record. Colonels and generals had strong marriages. She'd backed him into a corner.

'Darling, of course I love you. What would make you say such an outlandish thing?'

'If you were in love with me, having a child would be the natural thing to do. I was waiting for you to bring up the subject. Obviously, I would have waited 'til hell freezes over for that to happen.'

They finished their coffee and cigarettes in silence. The freeze had become more intense. Lincoln paid the bill, and they walked into the rising sun to the aircraft in silence. Lincoln's heart pounded with anticipation. They strapped in, and Lincoln went through the start-up procedure and pre-taxi checks. He was about to request taxi instructions when he realized that the aircraft was still chocked.

'I'm sorry sweetheart, but you're going have to get out and pull out the chocks.'

'Can't you do it? I was really nervous yesterday.'

'The hand brake's broken. If you can't help I'll have to shut down and you'll still have to do what you did yesterday. I'll throttle back when you get out so you'll be able to open your door easily. You can do it. Just keep your eyes on me.'

He helped her undo her straps and prompted her to exit. Her movements were timid and as she approached the nose of the aircraft, she looked to him for guidance. He motioned her with hand signals and she bent down and pulled out the left chock. With the sun in her eyes, she turned and proceeded to the right wheel.

The instant her back was to the spinning propeller Lincoln added power, canting the aircraft on the chocked right wheel, catching Alana unaware. With a sudden 'WHACK,' the propeller caught the back of her head, spewing brain matter and blood over the canopy.

She collapsed under the whirling propeller, and he knew she was dead. With a pounding heart, he shut down the engine and screamed into the mike.

'Ground control, this is Red Beech Staggerwing Mike Yankee Mike! There's been an accident here! Send an ambulance immediately. My wife just walked into the propeller!'

He exited the cockpit and crawled under the wing to her body. She stared at him with eyes that never moved. A wailing fire engine and security guard were first to the scene and he was cradling her and weeping when the ambulance arrived a quarter of an hour later.

He spent an hour alone with her in the morgue. 'I'm sorry darling but you gave me no choice,' was all he kept muttering to himself. Through a request from the pathologist and out of morbid guilt, he donated several of her organs to the local university.

That afternoon, the FAA interviewed him for two hours. The issue of the broken parking brake was front and center to their investigation, but the fact that an experienced Air Force bomber pilot was as much a victim as his wife led them to conclude that her death was the result of flicker vertigo from the sun on the spinning propeller. He'd rehearsed his story to perfection, taking the FAA inspectors on a second-by-second recounting of what had happened.

'For some reason, she went against everything I taught her,' he'd explained. 'She pulled out the port chock, stood up, swayed a couple of times, and backed into the propeller. Next thing I knew, I was holding her in my arms. Somewhere in between I saw the windshield go red. The rest was a complete blur. Obviously, I shut the aircraft down and called for help. That's all I remember.'

Faking shock was an easy act. What he didn't mention was that he'd canted the aircraft back to its original position the moment he'd exited the cockpit.

'And as for the sun, I park facing west when I can. Who wants to get into a hot cockpit in the morning?'

Flicker vertigo was caused when one stared into a slow turning propeller with a low sun as a backdrop. It hadn't caused her death, but it was a perfect alibi. He'd gotten her on the first attempt. The plan had worked to perfection. The morning before in Santa Fe had been a practice run and he'd picked up a few pointers; but to pull it off the way he had was divine providence.

There was to be no inquest. The propeller was filed down, and he was entrusted to take her body to Carswell. He'd never figured on being her hearse driver. She was placed in a body bag filled with ice, and strapped into the backseat. Throughout the flight, he spoke to her with endearments and apologetic banter, sometimes laughing, sometimes crying. It was a hell of a start to a new journey.

Lincoln lay naked. He was physically, mentally, and emotionally numb. Self-induced Novocain controlled everything, and that everything was nothing. He began to shiver and he wrapped himself in a fetal position and began to cry. Her murder was only half the horror. The real horror started with the telephone call from Washington a week after her funeral.

'Major Crisp, we wish to meet with you regarding significant events concerning your wife. I'll be flying in on an FBI aircraft tomorrow, so I'll leave it up to you to get the pertinent clearances. You may wish to engage a lawyer.' For the next twenty hours Lincoln never ate, drank or slept. His first bout of the 'Novocain.'

The following afternoon, he and his lawyer were ushered into a boardroom festooned with model aircraft and autographed hero shots. Photographs of Chuck Yeager and William Bridgeman waved at him as he entered. Each team sat facing the other across a thick glass table balanced on a machined-out radial engine. 'Nothing hidden under the table here,' quipped Lincoln as he reached across to shake hands with Mutt and Jeff.

After the introductions, Lincoln's lawyer was, 'due to sensitive security and personal issues,' asked to leave the proceedings, but be on-hand if needed. Lincoln nodded approval. It was one against two. He calmed himself with a cigarette, concealing a shaking lighter with a twist of the body. Then came the shock of his life.

'Major Crisp, the FBI is very saddened by the death of your wife and child. She did a great service to this country.'

'CHILD!' He exclaimed. His shocked expression became their shocked expressions.

No words uttered to Lincoln had more relevance on the potential course of modern history. He gagged and fought off a faint and his temples thumped like a tom-tom. He took a deep drag and coughed up smoke and saliva. The two FBI agents looked as stunned as he.

'Major Crisp, you had no idea your wife was pregnant?' They stared at each other in embarrassment. 'I apologize, Sir. From the pathologist's report, she was a fair way along. We just assumed.'

'If I didn't know she was pregnant, how the hell did you know she was pregnant? What the fuck's going on here? How is the FBI involved with my wife?' His feigned bewilderment was his only cover.

What came next was the greatest shock of all.

'Your wife, Alana Crisp, or "Phoenix" as we knew her, has operated as a covert double agent for the FBI and the CIA for several years. Her position in the nuclear scientific community gave her access to sensitive information. We recruited her as a university freshman and we kept her "asleep" so to speak for number of years. Her left-wing leanings, which were quite false by the way, and her student radicalism made her ripe for her potential use as a double agent. We conjured up a minor sex scandal regarding her and a female roommate, fed it to the Russians, and they found a way to blackmail her and bring her over. Imagine what would have happened to your career if your CO received some rather compromising photos of her. Goodbye Air Force. You know she had no living relatives?' Lincoln nodded and lit another cigarette, needing to slow down, the quicksand enveloping him.

'Her background, character, and brilliance made her one of the best we ever had. Her mandate was to give the Soviet Union disinformation on our nuclear weapons program, especially about the H-Bomb, stuff that was plausible but not really possible. The energy they'll expend on the follow-up was meant to slow them down. We sensed that they were on to her a month or so ago, so we decided to pull her out.'

'I can say for certain that giving away secret information is far more difficult and dangerous than gathering it. She was our top agent, and when an agent dies and we have access to the body, we have an autopsy performed. The cause of her death was obvious, but we had to know about her general health. It wasn't like her to walk into a whirling propeller. The pathologist's report indicated no drugs or alcohol, but it definitely indicated that she was pregnant. Add in the flicker vertigo to possible morning sickness, and anything can happen. I'm very sorry we had to break it this way. You're obviously upset. We can adjourn for a few moments if you wish.'

The speaker was a blur and Lincoln swooned again. He was in disbelief. The more they spoke of her the more he scrambled what they were saying. The night before her murder she'd alluded to having children. She already knew she was pregnant. If she was getting out of the trade, why hadn't she told him? Why hadn't she come clean about everything? Maybe he just hadn't listened.

He had the security clearance to handle that type of information. She knew that. She had to share some of the blame for her death. His head was swirling with questions only he could answer.

Major Lincoln Crisp, husband and lover, was quaking in his boots. Lincoln Crisp the killer demanded to take control. Then, as quickly as his nervous reactions started, they stopped. He was back in control.

'Gentlemen, this is so shocking that I may have experienced a lapse in self control. From out of the blue, you tell me that my wife was not who I thought she was, and that she was carrying a child I knew nothing about.'

The magnitude of his miscalculated evil overwhelmed him, and he began to shake. 'I not only killed my wife, a hero to this country, but I also killed a child she was nurturing for our future. What must you think of me?' Tears welled and he turned his head away.

'Major, we're not here to cast judgment on you. Her death was a tragic accident. We're here to offer you this medal and to express our condolences. The effort she put in will be of use for years to come. Tell me something, did you ever suspect her?'

'Never!'

Few mourners attended her funeral. It was held on base

at the Protestant chapel, and those who signed the book of condolence were either squadron mates or faces he recognized from her past. The two men in dark suits who arrived late and left early and didn't sign the book were now sitting across the table.

Her funeral was a closed-coffin affair. Her body was to be shipped to Washington, D.C. for burial. Her head had bled out so thoroughly that no amount of embalming fluid or makeup could put realism back into her face. Through her will, he was surprised to discover she had purchased a plot in a well-to-do cemetery, and that she had left to him a sizeable estate.

He saw her face for the last time when he was given ten minutes of privacy with her after the service. In direct violation of everything he believed in, he raised the lid of her coffin and kissed her cold blue lips.

'Je t'aime, je t'aime,' he murmured and wept.

Lincoln was unaware of the changes that had overcome him. The lean man became leaner, loved ones were shelved, and mutual friends vanished in the social mix that was military life. Single men did not mix well in the social hierarchy of a military base. He was unable to see his reflection in the eyes of others, and he withdrew into melancholy and remorse.

There was no conceivable way he would touch another woman again. The face that kissed him would always be hers. Then there was the child, their child. He'd done the calculations and was satisfied that it was his. The barn in Québec had seen to that.

How could he have miscalculated? He was smarter than that. He'd had no faith; that was it. If he'd had faith, he'd have sought spiritual guidance, instead of taking a warrior's stance. He'd never miscalculated on such a grand scale, yet no one was the wiser. It gave him power. Three weeks after his encounter with Mutt and Jeff, the nucleus of the plan germinated 40,000 feet over Baffin Island.

The vastness of the Arctic, with the combination of the northern lights or a sun that never set, and the vibrancy of the B-36 at altitude put him above it all. He was at the top of the world, waiting for Armageddon, yet all he could think about was his repentance and how he would atone for his evil. When he turned south for home, he'd added details to some portion or other of his grand plan.

It wasn't until he was called before his superiors to receive news of his promotion that he realized her murder was part of a grander scheme.

Major, "soon to be Colonel," Lincoln Crisp was made the officer commanding of a B-36 squadron that secretly ferried nuclear weapons between the United States and Great Britain.

Loring Air Force Base was the northern-most Strategic Air Command Bomber base on the East Coast of the United States. Hewed out of the Maine bush in the late 1940's and only miles from the New Brunswick border of Canada, it was designed to operate a hundred B-36 'Peacemaker' bombers. Nearby was the East Coast's nuclear arsenal, protected by squadrons of Nike ground-to-air guided missiles. Presque Isle Air Force Base, only miles away, provided interceptor protection. By population, Maine had more firepower per person than anywhere on earth.

Once there, Lincoln profited from the solitude of moose hunts in the fall, visits to the farm in Québec, and flights to the coast in the Staggerwing to pick up lobster for the mess. The hen house from the Officers' Mess attempted to fix him up with a number of female officers and the widow of an interceptor pilot from Presque Isle, but he resisted all temptation of fraternization. His history became gossip, and the buzz from the hive drove him to distraction.

Everything became clear when the plan for his redemption fell into place. Alana and the child's death would be vindicated through an act of historical significance. Their mutual field of nuclear creativity and deliverance could be used simultaneously to warn mankind of the potential dangers of nuclear proliferation. A nuclear 'accident' in America would change everything.

That's how he'd set things up. He'd make it look like an accident, like something had gone so wrong with the latest in fail-safe technology that America, or the world for that matter, couldn't protect itself. Nuclear disarmament would have to follow. With each phase of the plan completed, he grew ever less remorseful, and he took salvation in the exchange of his one horrendous deed for another.

His shivering abated and he felt at peace. No more reminiscing, no more self-loathing. He'd never relive the past again. From this moment on, his focus was on the mission and the mission alone. He sang as he showered, and his reflection in the mirror was that of a confident leader, an explorer and a warrior about to win a great battle. He gave himself a smile and a 'thumbs-up,' picked up his kit, and headed to the Operations Center to get things moving. He was in command of all faculties and he needed to show it. He was Major Lincoln Crisp, United States Air Force, and he was in control.

Michael Nixon

P ete Rylander had flown in every weather pattern that Canada, Burma, and God Almighty had created, but the weather just thrown at him had him transfixed and scared. The change in their status started too quickly to diagnose well. When it came to weather, it came on its own terms and never lost. He'd beaten it by bullshit luck and had scoffed on those few occasions when he'd thought he'd mastered it, but that was very rare. He knew weather, but he'd never seen conditions that spelled doom quicker than what had been thrown at him in the last minute.

He'd handed the controls to the copilot for the descent over the St. Lawrence River, and he'd done okay. The best way to see what kind of balls a rookie had was to throw him into the fire and see if he could put himself out. Instrument letdowns in turbulent cloud at low level were a great equalizer. Pete kept a wary eye on the vertical speed indicator and altimeter. For the moment everything seemed all right.

They broke through the cloud base at 1,200 feet, and were greeted by wind-spun waves advancing from the north shore of the Gulf of St. Lawrence.

'Holy fuck Dan!' Pete exclaimed. 'We're standing still.'

'Don't let the illusion fool you, Cappy. The waves are twenty footers. Crest to crest, they're 400 feet. That freighter up ahead will give you a better sense of scale. We've been slowed down by a pretty decent head wind, but with a little more power and the confines of the Saguenay River Valley, we should make it to Bagotville the same time that the eye of the storm is supposed pass through. Just like you planned. We'll catch those fuckers on the ground with their fingers up their asses. So how about it Cappy, can you give me a little more gas? Say ten more knots.'

Pete nodded to Fred who added enough power to satisfy the navigator and the fuel flow indicators.

The fortunes of chance make widows of even the wariest pilot.

They'd descended to 500 feet and bounced across the Gulf and into the mouth of the river. The wave action lessened as they approached the north shore, but the cloud layer had dropped so low that the entrance to the river only appeared at the last second.

'How the hell did you hit dead-on, Dan? That was damn fine navigating.'

'It's this Hughes APG-40 radar we've been outfitted with. I can see the ground in the scope well enough to discern the difference between land and water. Your job up there is to keep us from running into the hills on each side of the river. They're near-vertical. I'll keep you posted if I see any sailboats coming up. Just joking, of course.' Pete tapped Fred on the shoulder. Time to take back his aircraft.

'I have control.'

Pounding upriver at wave-top height under the overcast was a new experience. This was not the broad expanse of the Mackenzie River where it was flatter than piss on a plate. Sensing something amiss, Pete pressed his face to the windshield, looking for the telltale sign of his greatest dread: ice!

Jake Brown positioned his nose inches from the Plexiglas. His eyes swept what horizon he could discern. His eyesight, photographic skill, and love of firearms made him the perfect tip of the arrow. He operated the cameras and machine guns and kept a lookout for impediments to flight. Observation carried greatest weight when it came to decision-making in flight.

He didn't take his responsibilities lightly. On more than one occasion, he'd spotted what neither pilots saw, saving the day. Radio towers not shown on aviation charts were the greatest threat. His application to Officer Candidate School and flight training was currently heading through channels. Flight Lieutenant Rylander's R-211 personal appraisal had him a shoo-in. The Captain had introduced him to airmanship he never knew existed, and though he was the lowest-ranked member of the crew, he was treated with pagan reverence for saving their skins.

He sat in the bombardier's seat with the breeches of the twin 50-caliber machine guns at his right hip. He'd checked the ammo feeding trays prior to takeoff. The Captain had requested ammo, explaining 'one never knows when game is in season.' Vibration-testing on the radar's vacuum tubes was the true reason.

Pete banked to port as they entered the river valley. Fred commented on the old trading-post town of Tadoussac as it passed under the starboard engine.

'At one time it was the center of commerce for the whole of Canada. It's the oldest surviving French settlement in the Americas.'

As if to say 'keep your eyes straight ahead,' Pete grunted an acknowledgement. He leveled off from the bank and trimmed the aircraft nose up on the control column. He released the control column, and saw a rise in the altimeter and vertical speed indicator. When one flew at low level, it was important to have a dead man's switch.

'OK Jake, our lives are in your hands,' Pete barked over the intercom. 'I hope you cleaned the Plexiglas because it's going to get a little dicey up ahead.'

'Vinegar, soap and water, Sir, just like momma used. And I hope you meant dicey and not icy.' Jake checked the defroster blower switch, focused the nozzle to the center pane, and pressed his face to the Perspex lens close enough to not let his breath cloud his view.

Jake Brown knew about lenses. Technical training in aerial photography eclipsed his skill as an observer and machine gunner. Pete had recruited him from the aerial mapping section of the Northwest Staging Route where they'd flown sorties. Pete admired the clarity of detail in photographs he'd taken at different altitudes and light conditions. His night-flight photographs exposed under the northern lights had been published in an American photography magazine.

Jake operated two movie cameras: one in the belly and one in the nose. After each attack and subsequent aerial engagement, the film canisters were flown to a lab in Ottawa. He'd hand the canisters to the operations officer, and he'd never see them again. It was frustrating to never see the fruits of his labor.

He remarked that the films were either used as the

dictate of a grand defensive scheme or a weapon in a vendetta. But that was speculation.

Dan Lacey sat below and to the rear of the pilots' compartment. The two Loran units that had been the latest in navigation technology two years before were now hidden by a bank of metal frames dominated by rows of glowing tubes; this culminated in a compact space dominated by Dan, strapped into a static Martin-Baker ejection seat and hunched over his radarscope. The cockpit had been arranged in the configuration of the navigator's cockpit of the Mark 4 CF-100.

Dan, still queasy from the effects of the tainted rations, couldn't believe the moving picture on his radarscope. Before him was the broad reach of the river valley with the banks jagged as a whipsaw.

'Pete, if you get into cloud and you don't want to climb out, I can give you a pretty good idea of where to go. This machine is fucking jazzy.'

'Better be more than just pretty good. We're in a fjord. I can't rely on "just pretty good." If we hit cloud any lower than this, I'm going to climb out. Mont Apica GCI will pick us up, and we'll become the prey. Let's not let that happen.'

'You mean the great clag beater is admitting defeat? That's not the intrepid birdman we've all come to know and love.'

He'd flown with Pete for six months and respected his judgment, but a great flyer wasn't necessarily a great pilot. More than once, Pete had sphincters biting washers with casual approaches to unusual situations, but when it came to weather, nobody could touch him.

Dan was not a navigator of the old school, best with

a chronometer, sextant, starry sky, and a steady platform. The electronic age had changed all that. He loved working with onboard radar but an inability to handle the confines and stress subjected to the navigator in the back seat of a CF-100 caused him to rethink his career. He'd been selected as a CF-100 navigator early in the program, but a penchant for airsickness shunted him to a slower, more sedate, flying machine.

He'd graduated from university with a degree in electrical engineering. No designing television sets or clock radios. He was recruited into the RCAF, and after completing Central Officers' School was shunted into the CF-100 program. Things went sideways when his afflictions emerged, and he was about to request a medical discharge when he was asked by Pete to fly with him. The enticing aspect of the offer revolved around the use of the 'lead attack' radar earmarked for the new Mark 4. He would be the first to test its use and reliability, and although his 'office' would be in the belly of a medium bomber he felt comfortable in his space. The fact that the aircraft was noisy, antiquated, and cold didn't bother him, the difference being that it was not the least bit aerobatic. His cockpit resembled Professor Frankenstein's laboratory with a few touches of his own. There was a coziness about it that gave him full comfort when he strapped in.

The radar dish was situated on the leading edge of the right wing, and he'd attempted to soundproof and insulate his compartment by stuffing anything from engine heating blankets to sleeping bags between him and the engines. The Captain abused his space on occasions when he exercised his authority, luring inquisitive young women into its confines for 'the thrill of a lifetime.'

'If I asked you once, Pete, I've asked you a thousand times, air out and roll up the sleeping bags after your late night trysts. My compartment is not your private whorehouse.'

At an air show in Winnipeg, he'd had enough, and in frustration had draped the sleeping bags and used condoms over his control column and throttles. Thereafter, the neutral ground of the tunnel to the bomb-aimer's compartment became his lair. Jake Brown knew it was only a matter of time before his sanctuary would be violated.

The crew agreed that the Captain had the gift. How he convinced his conquests to leave their panties dangling from the access ladder as a token of their esteem enhanced his stature. Pete Rylander never went home empty-handed.

The B-25 was off-limits to anyone but the Captain. If there was uncertainty whether it was occupied or not, Jake Brown would get the call from Pete and it was his job to inform the rest of the crew that the "bedroom" on the tarmac was off-limits for the night. It was unnerving to be bedded down in the cool of the fuselage on a hot summer night and be woken up by a pounding on the aircraft's skin.

'Sorry Sir, but the Captain says he told you he was going to need the aircraft tonight, told you to get a room in the barracks.' The response from the interior was always the same.

'Listen here, Sergeant Brown! You tell that asshole to go fuck his hat badge.'

'Can't do that Sir; he's my ticket to the big leagues. The least he could do is let us in on his secret.'

Pete's secret resided in his breast pocket. Any hint of

his indiscretions would have the Air Force dismissing him, and the courts sending him to prison. A game to him was rape in the eyes of the law, but after ten years of practicing sleight of hand, he didn't see it that way. Habits were hard to break. There'd never been any hint of a police follow-up to his crimes, because there had been no complaints. There had been no complaints because there'd been no memory. The pharmacist in him had devised an expertise at administering his elixir in various doses, adjusting it ever so slightly for his prey's weight and desirability. The evil-ness of his actions was lost in the game.

Not suffering the consequences of getting caught had become as stimulating as the control he wielded. Once he'd 'slipped her a Mickey' the hunt was over, the thrill was gone, but the smell and confines of the aircraft when the deed was happening became more intoxicating than the act itself.

Cutting the prey from the herd and whisking her to his lair was the easy part of the operation. Finding a way to skulk into the night without leaving scat became his specialty.

'Would you like to see inside my bomber?' loosened panties like no other opening line.

'Oh could I?'

'Let's have another drink.'

He never culled from the same location twice, but there were only so many Air Force bases to go around. If he happened to run into former prey, thought of discovery fueled his hunger. His memory had faded on the early con-quests, and on occasion he'd been stared down by a look of confused recognition. Then it was time to beat a hasty retreat and 'disappear' himself.

The Officers' Mess had been his primary hunting ground. The training bases on the prairies where student pilots and navigators held dances and graduation ceremonies were his preferred trap line. Student nurses and university undergraduates provided grist for the mill, and every six weeks any one of a dozen bases went through the ritual of sending cadets and newly-minted officers to the next level of training, providing him with an inexhaustible supply of fresh game.

His copilot snapped him out of a daze.

'We're icing up!' Pete had noticed a slight sheen on the windshield and had adjusted the flexible heating pipe, but the sheen had persisted.

'Thanks Fred, good eyes. Sergeant Brown, what's the poop from your end? Can you still see clearly?'

'I'm getting a little blurring, but my defroster is taking care of it for now.'

'Let me know if there's any change. I have a funny feeling that icing conditions might be a little more acute than our Met briefer anticipated.' The Met briefing that morning hadn't been more than a visit by the Met officer to reaffirm what everybody knew. The low-pressure system was moving northwest, but the conditions they were presently encountering hadn't been mentioned.

'Something's weird, Jake. At this altitude and temperature, there shouldn't be ice.' Pete activated the de-icing boots on the wings and checked the pitot heat switch. A clogged pitot tube made the airspeed indictor inoperative.

He had a bad feeling.

'Okay you guys, let me know if there's a change in visibility.' The mission had been thrown a curve but he still had two strikes left. Weather always fucked up his ideal world. That's why he loved it.

He focused on every instrument, planning. There was something about this operation that transcended everything. Wilding's plan had evolved over years of patience and frustration. All Pete was required to do to get his share of the money was to kill Lou Fender. That's what the weekend was all about: Rangoon! He did a final instrument check, and nodded to Fred.

'You have control, Fred. I'll keep a lookout.'

The first time Pete climbed into the copilot's seat of a Catalina flying boat, he'd wilted under the uncertainty of what the Air Force had feared. He wasn't up to their standard. If he hadn't been subjected to the weather patterns of Canada's West Coast, he'd never have developed his unique skill of flying blind.

The temperature and relative humidity were the same then as they were now. Then, it had ended in near disaster. They'd made it back to base at Tofino only because he'd picked out the shoreline of Long Beach before the sea fog had taken everything down to zero-zero.

They'd confronted similar conditions then that they were encountering now: weather conditions that could confound even the most intrepid aircrew. A basic compass heading and an altimeter were all that was needed. "Turn east and hope to find the shoreline before you find a mountain." Eyeballs had superseded instrumentation.

Pete was struck by an overwhelming sense of déjà vu and fear.

'Something's not right, Fred. I've flown in weather on the West Coast similar to this, but I can't figure the element that's missing.'

'Captain, I think we might have a problem.' Jake's transmission had an inflection in its urgency that sent a chill down Pete's spine.

'I don't know about you, Captain, but I'm blurring up down here. The heater on the Plexiglas isn't keeping up with what's happening outside. I can't see anything up ahead.'

Pete needed the navigator.

'Dan, are we OK? I don't want to have to climb out of here and fuck up the day if I don't have to. Can we continue as planned or do we have to give ourselves away? It's up to you.'

'Captain, as long as we know how fast and high we're flying I can keep us on course using the radar, but if you sense any fluctuations in airspeed or altitude, all bets are off.'

The two pilots nodded to each other in understanding. The urgency of the situation quickened heart rates and tightened sphincters. Pete readjusted his seat and placed his feet on the rudder pedals. He needed to connect with the aircraft. He ran his gaze across the instrument panel and squinted into the windshield. As his instinct told him that something was about to bite him in the ass, a torrent of rain exploded against the windshield.

Jake set off the alarm. 'Holy shit Captain, there's a fire hose blasting me. I can't see a fucking thing!'

Fred tapped Pete on the shoulder, then pointed to the

airspeed indicator. The fluctuations of the dial meant one thing.

'The pitot tube's freezing over, Pete. If we're into freezing rain, we'll ice up for sure.'

Pete was concerned with more than the icing of the pitot tube. The pitot heater would take care of that. If the static vent for the altimeter and vertical speed indicator froze over, they'd be in worse shape. With three primary instruments unserviceable, they'd be unable to fly on instruments, and if they couldn't fly on instruments the icing would become exacerbated. Either way, the mission was doomed. He fine-tuned the reference aircraft on the attitude indicator and admitted defeat.

'Pilot to crew, we're getting the fuck out of here.'

With that he advanced the throttles and ascended into cloud.

CHAPTER 14

SCRAMBLE!

L ou and Duckwalker stared at each other in disbelief.

'Too soon,' Lou exclaimed. 'Either they've slipped us a Mickey, or something's wrong.'

Duckwalker knew it was the latter.

'They're getting the shit kicked out of them, Lou. Like I said at Met briefing, the river's done them in.' He winked at John. 'Let's rub a little salt in their wound.'

With their flying suits peeled back and boots at the ready, and estimating a two-hour wait before the call to action, they'd relaxed into easy chairs with coffee and cigarettes.

'Don's the squadron's gunnery officer, Lou. While we're waiting, why don't we get him and John to brief us on their experiences intercepting B-36's?'

They'd conversed for only a half an hour when they were jolted by the cry of the operations officer.

'Mont Apica's picked up a bogey north of Tadoussac. It's our man. Time to scramble, boys!'

They suited up and ran to the aircraft as the ground crews fired up the APUs. They climbed into cockpits that came alive with snapped switches and twisted dials. Lou fired up the engines and called for taxi clearance. He nodded to Don to take the lead, added power, and both aircraft taxied to the active runway.

'These guys seem to know what they're doing,' Duckwalker remarked as the canopy slid shut. He made a note on his kneepad, unhinged the radarscope from its stowed position, shielded his eyes, exchanged glasses, and lowered his visor. The hum of the inverters and the cadence of their breathing were interrupted by the tower confirming Mont Apica's call sign and frequency.

'Rhubarb One and Rhubarb Two, be advised that the weather to the east will begin to clear forty miles out. Scabbard advises to contact them once you've passed through a thousand. You're cleared for takeoff.'

They lined up in echelon right and with returned salutes, advanced their throttles and released brakes. They'd stay in formation through the takeoff and climb into the storm. Once at altitude, Rhubarb One would break off to perform the intercept while they watched the proceedings using their own radar.

Lou stuck to Don, watching for any reaction to sudden wind shifts, but halfway through the takeoff run he lost concentration and they nearly collided.

'Holy shit! That was close.' Duckwalker muttered to himself. 'I've got to watch out for this guy or he's going to get me killed.'

A crosswind had both aircraft crabbing to port as they broke ground and were enveloped in cloud and rain, bouncing and shifting in turbulence. The near collision on the runway had Lou spooked, and he tucked in to Rhubarb One as close as he felt comfortable. Formation flying in cloud was tricky even in the most benign warm front.

They switched radio frequencies and contacted Mont Apica GCI who vectored them east to 10,000 feet.

Michael Nixon

"I hope Lou knows what he's doing," Duckwalker thought. He'd never participated in a formation takeoff into cloud while in the number-two position and the near collision on the takeoff run pushed his heart into his throat. He could tell the formation leader was smooth, and they adjusted to Rhubarb One's climb rate and settled down. Wherever Don and John went, so did they.

He ticked off another box on his checklist.

Duckwalker lit up his radarscope and started a sweep in the direction of the target. He'd figured John had done the same, and gave him a tick-mark on his kneepad that he'd designed to facilitate different tasks, folding up to a paperback size on his right knee. A bottle of Wiser's rye to a machinist had created a piece of functional art.

When they passed through 8,000 feet, he did a personal safety equipment check. Several crews had been killed flying the CF-100 due to hypoxia. Oxygen-deprived brain matter exhumed from the crash sites told the tale. A disconnected oxygen tube was the usual culprit.

Duckwalker heard Lou's erratic breathing and sensed why.

'Check your oxygen mask connection, Lou. Your breathing sounds a little funny.'

Lou fumbled around, mumbled thanks, and checked his oxygen flow regulator. The blinkers responded on every breath.

'Everything seems okay up here,' he replied. 'My microphone crystals must have frozen up. Let me know if you hear any change in my voice.'

He owed Duckwalker. His hose had been disconnected. He never made those types of mistakes. He tightened his straps and checked the quick-release on his parachute. It was in the safe position. He tapped his mask to loosen the crystals, then further tightened up to Rhubarb One. "Might as well give the gimp in the back seat a little more confidence," he thought.

They leveled off at 10,000 feet and burst into sunshine. Duckwalker winced at the intensity of the light and buried his face into the scope. Lou informed Rhubarb One that they were disengaging from the formation and would observe the intercept from a distance.

'Good hunting Rhubarb One.'

Their target was forty-five miles to the east, climbing to 8,000 feet. Duckwalker switched his radar to long range and picked the B-25 up on the scope.

'I can't believe this guy's put himself in such a vulnerable position,' he remarked, 'especially after what you briefed me on at the Operations Center last night.'

'Don't be fooled,' Lou responded. 'He's got some tricks up his sleeve.'

Rylander's mission had no chance of success.

'PAN-PAN-PAN. This is Badger Two, ten miles north of Sacré-Coeur. We are iced up and have lost instrumentation. We have radar and attitude instrumentation, but no airspeed or altimeter indicators. Request assistance from any Rhubarb aircraft and Mont Apica GCI.'

Pete was not having a good day. He'd added climb power and turned away from the river, allowing the aircraft to ascend in a trimmed attitude that he maintained with the touch of his fingers. Without an airspeed indicator, he had to rely on the balance between the added power and the trim. He needed to find the eye of the storm and clear air. The two pilots focused on their attitude indicators, looking for any difference in the two. If they didn't harmonize, it was time to hit the silk.

The on-board radar would keep them safe for now, but sooner or later they'd have to land. If his recollection of the weather was correct, his options were limited. He went through a weather problem-solve that had him baffled, and decided to take the high road. If the ice didn't melt from the tip of the pitot tube and the static vent, his only chance to land successfully would be to formate on one of the interceptors, and have them do a UHF-DF homing and let-down with GCA pick-off into Bagotville.

"Lou Fender hadn't even been in the fight and he still won," he thought.

Pete added power, initiated a slow climb, and ordered parachutes on. Their situation had compound problems that could only be solved with airmanship and electronics. The disabled instruments would be replaced by radar, and Dan would provide air speed and direction. Pete would fly the beast, Dan would navigate, and Fred would communicate. Classic teamwork.

'Dan, I need that wizardry you're so hot on to get us the fuck out of here. The second any of those Rhubarbs comes on screen, let me know. If you can give me any ground reference, that'd be much appreciated. I'm declaring an emergency.'

'PAN-PAN-PAN, this is Badger Two.' Pete estimated his altitude and leveled off. Time to give up the fight. He turned west to Bagotville and waited for contact.

'Badger Two this is Rhubarb Two. Update your status.' Lou's transmission had a neutral coldness of superiority.

Pete felt humiliated and vulnerable. With the sheepishness of a wayward hound, Pete explained his situation, concluding with the suggestion that his best option of landing safely was to have one of the CF-100's do the instrument approach in cloud, with him tagging alongside. He'd flown formation with the CF-100 at a couple of air shows, and knew he could keep up with one. Approach speed was another matter. An aircraft in its landing configuration in cloud was as vulnerable as a snake on a highway.

'Rhubarb One, this is Rhubarb Two. We're heavy with tip tanks, so you'll do the penetration turn and the GCA. We'll follow you in behind, Badger Two. If you lose contact with Rhubarb One, climb out on heading and we'll pick you up for another try.'

With Duckwalker on the scope and Lou nipping the clouds with the tip tank, they orbited in the brilliance of the storm's eye, listening in as Rhubarb One and the GCI controller at Mont Apica teamed up to intercept the intruder.

Duckwalker put another tick mark on his checklist and scribbled 'good crew.' So far, the status report on 440 Squadron was favorable. He'd never submitted a favorable report and he felt relief. If the B-25 had been a Russian bomber, there was no doubt that it would have been destroyed. The system had not only worked, but he'd discovered aspects of the radar that opened new avenues of application.

Duckwalker's kneepad and radarscope became his palette and canvas. They'd been scrambled to observe the interception only to see the interceptor change roles from killer to savior. There was an irony in it that would take him a while to grasp. Search and rescue lay in the hands of the helicopter back at the base, but it would have been useless in this situation. They'd solved the problem before the chopper was needed to search for aircrew lost in the reaches of the Saguenay Valley.

Duckwalker watched the gold blip disappear from his radar screen as the two aircraft descended.

"There's a problem that needs solving," he thought. Look-down radar to track a low-level threat was something he'd get involved with.

A single controller manned the GCA shack, so they were forced to wait until Rhubarb One and Badger Two had landed. Lou asked Duckwalker if he could do a few aerobatics to loosen up.

'I've never had the chance to play with this thing. I understand you don't get airsick.' Without thinking things through, Duckwalker grunted approval. His thoughts were elsewhere. He'd scribble notes and diagrams while Lou showed off. The man knew how to fly, but then again, he'd seen this sort of shit before.

After his re-enlistment, Duckwalker completed the navigator course in Winnipeg and was seconded to A.V. Roe at Malton to liaise on the design of electronic components for the CF-100's radar. It was there that he began to doubt the effectiveness of the gun-laying radar and gun sight for the conventional pursuit-curve attack. For attacks against a Second World War-type bomber, it was effective, but for the faster, high-flying jet bombers that the Russians were expected to develop, a different method of attack was needed. This was to be the lead collision method. The US Air Force had adopted the system for their F-89 and F-94 interceptors, so installing it in the Mark 4 CF-100 only made sense. Adapting it to a different aerodynamic configuration was right up Duckwalker's alley.

If he'd managed to keep his attention on radar instead of the chief administrative officer's wife at the base, he would have lasted longer at the job.

The affair started as they all did. A mothering woman, intrigued by the brilliant crippled bespectacled baby-faced brat was captivated, then captured, in a spider web woven from years of maternal liaisons. A rendezvous at the Royal York Hotel was followed up by a weekend at a cabin in the Muskokas, which was followed by a bitter divorce that ruined the career of the chief administration officer, who was forced to resign from the Air Force. Duckwalker had been named in the divorce, but his plea of immaturity under such circumstances, and his lover's insistence that she had been the aggressor in the affair, led to a heavy rap on the knuckles. He was transferred to the navigator's school in Winnipeg, where the base engineering officer's wife initiated a scandal.

Three transfers in one year and the need to keep him in the service had the Air Force earmarking him as one to put on a leash. A wise personnel officer at Air Force Headquarters who'd researched his wartime history posted him to the Standards Division in Ottawa to keep him on the move. Wherever he went, someone was responsible for him, and when he landed, the orderly officer had his orders.

'Keep an eye on Flight Lieutenant Jones.'

He'd been on the job for six months and had flown with

pilots who'd relished making his experience in the back seat as miserable as possible, but the harder they pushed, the more he toughened up. Lou Fender was no different. Like the others, Lou would soon give up and admit defeat, the price being a TGIF of free drinks.

'How the hell can you stand it back there?' they'd query. 'Your head's in the scope, you never see the horizon, you never know when I'm going to pull G. I can tell by your breathing that you never black out or puke. Where does that come from?'

Duckwalker would puff his chest and stand on tiptoe, and with the strength of an enraged bantam rooster he'd proclaim his disdain for all pilots.

'You assholes think that because you have that hard shaft between your oh-so-sensitive fingers and legs that you rule the fucking world.' His outbursts were out of frustration and resulted in a sheepish retreat. His secret was his weakness.

Too often, he'd turned away from 'derring-do' conversation involving a 'pilots only' understanding. Navigators had a single creed.

'Feed them as required. They keep us aloft.'

Duckwalker did not feed them as required. His disdain was disguised by his disability. Little did they know he'd experienced aerial trauma far beyond anything they could imagine.

With a tug on the control column, Lou initiated the start of a vertical maneuver. Duckwalker shook his head in disbelief and decided to halt the proceedings. It had nothing to do with his comfort; that would never be the issue.

The aerodynamic stress on the wings with tip tanks prohibited rolling 'G.'

'Did you read up on the operating instructions regarding aerobatics while sporting tip tanks, Lou?' He was direct and assertive; a simple question requiring an immediate answer.

When they'd returned to the ready room after their tarmac inspection, he noticed that Lou hadn't read up on the flight characteristics of the aircraft when equipped with tip tanks. When he requested performing aerobatics, he had to step in to stop the proceedings.

'Is there something I should know about, old sport? Can't take the stress? A little woozy are you?'

Lou leveled off, pulled back the throttles, and the aircraft entered a cave in a mountainous cloudbank, swallowing them into a cement mixer of turbulence, wind shear, and hail.

Duckwalker was stunned by Lou's response. This was not a pilot in control. Since Met briefing, he'd made mistakes that could have wrecked their whole day.

'Well, old sport, as you put it, aerobatics with tip tanks are prohibited. You don't want to break this beautiful machine do you? Don't want to add another caterpillar to your collection?'

'Negative to both,' Lou replied.

Lou was furious. In less than an hour the gimp had called him out on two life-threatening aspects of his command. The disconnected oxygen hose and his lack of fundamentals on the aircraft he was in command of were serious miscalculations. Then there was the near collision on the takeoff run. He knew the reason why. Darlene Muncie was in his head.

She'd been on his mind from the moment they'd parted. He'd stealthily followed her to her barracks to see her safely home. If the military police had picked up a soaked, half-naked transient pilot skulking around the women's barracks at four in the morning, the CO would not be pleased. At Met briefing he'd had a hard on for her and hadn't lost it until he heard the words 'turbulence' and 'icing' from the Met briefer.

Except for the odd indiscretion during the war, he'd never flown with pussy on the brain. Monotonous trips over the jungle had produced the odd fantasy, but he'd never been caught like this before, not at 18,000 feet in the eye of a dying hurricane. His concentration was broken by the recollection of the errors of his ways.

He prided himself in knowing everything about the aircraft he flew. He hadn't taken the gimp's advice and read up on the tip tank specs while they waited to get scrambled. Instead, he'd played lip service to the standby crew, all the while concentrating on thoughts about Darlene. Standards pilots didn't bend aircraft. If he'd initiated any rolling 'G,' he could have ripped the tip tanks off.

At an inquest, he'd thank Darlene Muncie for that.

During the takeoff roll, he'd relied on the rudder too early and they'd gotten frighteningly close to Rhubarb One. The control tower had reported the altimeter setting and strength of the crosswind, but he had other things on his mind. He heard Duckwalker let out a groan of disdain as he re-engaged the nose wheel steering to get them back on track. During the climb to altitude, he thought he'd have to break formation from lack of concentration, but he'd managed to count on the leader's skill to keep them together.

The disconnected oxygen hose was the most distressing fuck-up. He may as well have sucked on the tailpipe of an idling car; the results would have been the same.

Flying the aircraft had become instinctive. He was a good pilot; some would say a great pilot, but that wasn't so. He was a great flyer, but that didn't make him a great pilot.

Events like not connecting an oxygen hose and other career near-misses were the reasons they'd never made him a test pilot. A few too many holes in the ground weren't assets in his R-211 dossiers.

The positive aspect of the fiasco orchestrated by the storm was that Pete Rylander had missed his chance.

Darlene and Pete had become issues for concern, issues that he suspected would change many lives before church on Sunday. He needed to get his brain back into the cockpit, to re-establish command of his aircraft and command of his life. There was nothing like a GCA approach in turbulence and hail to tune him up. "Time to go into the heart of danger," he thought as he pressed the transmit button.

'Bagotville tower this is Rhubarb Two requesting a UHF-DF homing and let down with a GCA pick-off-----Over.'

'Rhubarb Two, this is Bagotville tower, no need to contact GCA. The front just passed through. We should be full VFR by the time you finish your penetration turn. Maybe you can give us a fighter break. It's been kind of dull down here.'

CHAPTER 15

Saturday 1:00 PM 1700 GMT

L incoln had run out of memories. His plan had been thrown a curve and he was grateful for the delay of their departure. He'd finally erased the tape that was "her." No more hidden moments of their life together to intensify the guilt. The 'Novocain' had been flushed from his pores. From this moment on, everything was about the mission. He was back.

'Ding-dong, first call for dinner, Major Crisp.' Lincoln bolted upright after the third knock. It was Arnie "the Kraut." His twilight sleep had been interrupted every twenty minutes by the run-up and takeoff of each B-36. The bomber stream was heading for home.

He'd revised the plan to compensate for the delay, and discovered that it had improved his chance of success. His aircraft now needed to be the last to leave. By the time it arrived over Labrador, the GCI controllers and interceptor pilots would be exhausted.

Disappearing into the northern sector of the collapsing hurricane over Québec would be a cinch.

'Thank you, Lieutenant. I'll see you at seven.' He completed his ablutions like a surgeon about to amputate, then headed to the Operations Center to check in with Briggs on the status of the loading of the bomb, and get the updated weather report. Timelines were merging from diverse regions of geography, and the coordination needed to be fine-tuned.

'Well Linc, it looks like you'll be tail-end Charlie on this run. We've done our best to disguise the fact you're carrying a hot one, but the rest of the squadron has been chomping at the bit to get home, so I let them go.'

Colonel Malcolm Briggs was the commandant of the American out-station at RAF Base Upper Heyford. Only Briggs, Crisp, and two British officers knew the bomb being loaded was the real thing.

'If you want, I can get you out in an hour or so.'

'I don't want! My crew's rusty so they'll be performing a few extra checks before takeoff. It's a big airplane. I want to know what's happening at the ass end. I never get back there. When we carry a hot one, I require that the gun turrets are armed. I need to know if the stinger in the tail is ready for action. Who knows when a fucking MiG is going to jump us over the Atlantic at 40,000 feet?' He laughed at his joke.

'I'll have the wheels in the well by 2300. Then you can go to bed. Ever want to fly one of these houses again?' He was referring to the first test pilot who'd flown the B-36 who'd referred to it as 'sitting on the front porch and flying your house around.'

'No fucking way! I'm waiting for the B-47. It's jets and speed for me. For the misery of this posting, they'd better give me a whole fucking squadron of them. By the way, are you okay? You're a lanky bastard at the best of times but you look a little gaunt. And the grey hair, where the hell did that come from? A young buck like you shouldn't look that old. Still pining for her I suppose. What's it been, over a year now?'

Malcolm hadn't set eyes on Lincoln since Alana's funeral. The Lincoln Crisp that he'd hunted with was the same man, but the man he'd entrusted his Beech Staggerwing wasn't. His physicality and movement had become those of a rattlesnake looking for a reason to coil and strike. The layover had offered them a chance for an impromptu grouse-hunt on base and an evening of drinks. With every conversation, he sensed that Lincoln was holding back something, but he'd attributed it to grief.

'How's the Beech? You still getting lots of pole time in her?'

'I fly her to the coast to pick up lobster for the guys, and I've taken her up to the farm in Québec a couple of times. She awaits your return.'

'I appreciate how well you've taken care of her, Linc, especially after all that's happened. It can't be easy flying the aircraft that killed your wife.' He shook his head. 'The fucking hand brake, of all things. In all the time I've owned her, I never had a problem with it. What exactly was the problem again?'

Lincoln squirmed. The question haunted him.

'Loose cable. A screwdriver and a five-minute fix. That's all it took. I should've looked into the problem when I landed in Albuquerque. Hell, I had all day, but she wanted to take me shopping. What can you say? When I got into the cockpit that morning, it had completely slipped my mind. I fired it up and was going through my pre-taxi check before I realized the chocks were still in. Last thing I wanted do was do a shut-down. Alana had done such a good job of pulling them out the day before. Then there was the flicker vertigo thing. If I'd had any inkling she was pregnant I'd have done everything different.'

Hopefully, the answer was to be his last.

Malcolm had broached the subject only once before, and then he'd been drunk. As it was his aircraft, he'd been given a copy of the accident report, but to bring up the topic at this moment was unnerving. He'd spent the last day flushing the memory and guilt away and Malcolm had filled the toilet again. It was time to put the issue to bed.

"You're right Colonel," Lincoln thought. "It's cold-blooded of me to be flaunting my murder weapon, your airplane, but that's the whole idea. Nobody would believe so hideous a crime. What murderer walks with impunity, still holding the bloody knife or smoking revolver? Me!"

Lincoln studied the weather pattern over Labrador and made mental notes on the storm's progress. Malcolm sidled beside him and placed an arm on his shoulder. 'I'm sorry to bring it up, old boy. Whenever I think of her, all I see is what I imagine. She was so beautiful.' He lit a cigarette.

'The hurricane that came up the coast a couple of days ago was sure a doozy. Looks like it's headed into Québec. Good thing the squadron's over here and not hunkered down at Loring. Getting out of town was a smart idea. Good cover for our delivery service, huh?'

Lincoln needed separation.

'I'm heading to the mess, Sir. You coming for chow?'

'Naw…. I'll be here with coffee and cigarettes 'til you get away. Seeing you're the last to go, I might drop over to see you off. Spin your props to get you going.' The propeller remark stabbed at Lincoln but he held his cool.

Malcolm couldn't let the subject die.

'I still can't believe my airplane killed her. Even still, you know I can't get rid of "Mike Yankee Mike." She's my sweetheart.'

'It's okay Malcolm, let it go. I have.' He shook hands and left the room.

Lincoln felt the pang of paranoia as he walked to the mess. The remark about spinning the props on the B-36 was in bad taste. He knew it was a slip, but then again maybe it wasn't.

Ten minutes before he'd been clear of mind and purpose. He'd spent his time in the sweat lodge and he deserved its torturous reward. He'd been cleansed, freshened, and ready to go. That was ten minutes ago.

Had Malcolm seen through him? Were his intentions written on his face and movement? Was he subconsciously sending signals? Was he that obvious? Doubt suddenly became his enemy.

He hustled to the bathroom in the mess, doused his face in cold water, and was pleased with what he saw. It was Mr. Hyde, the killer. He grinned at the apparition and it grinned back. He would stay Mr. Hyde until the deed was done. Fuck doubt. Fuck Colonel Malcolm Briggs. Fuck them all!

Lou, Don, Pete, and their navigators were ushered into the briefing room by the orderly officer. When it came to flying, briefing and debriefing were a ceremonial constant. They stood to attention as the CO and OC of 440 Squadron strode to the podium. The orderly officer was dismissed, and the crews were invited to smoke. The click of lighters and muffled coughs of inhalations was followed by an unnerving silence. Lou sensed this was more than a debriefing. Too much shit had happened. Heads were about to roll.

Duckwalker sat in the front row, reviewing notes on his kneepad. Lou and Pete sat at the rear of the room with Dan Lacey as a buffer. They'd not set eyes on each other and, for the foreseeable future, had no intention to do so. Don and John sat behind Duckwalker, their flying suits damp from perspiration, the impression from their oxygen masks carved into their faces.

The OC of 440 was the first to speak.

'I wish to commend the crew of Rhubarb One on their professionalism. Flight Lieutenant Jones gave me a quick briefing on their contribution to this morning's operation's rather interesting sequence of events. We're fortunate not to have lost a perfectly good airplane and a few crew members. Since you're still the ready crew, we're discharging you to the showers and a fresh set of underwear. Good work Don. Good work John.' With a nod of approval from the CO, they butted cigarettes, zippered up, and departed.

The CO stepped to the podium. Silence fell as the executioner raised his axe.

'At midnight last night, I was summoned from my bed. At eleven this morning, I was interrupted from a birthday party for my daughter. You, gentlemen, are the reasons why. Twelve hours ago I didn't know you existed, and now you're ruining a perfectly good weekend that was supposed to be a base stand-down. What's most disconcerting is that you seem to know more about what the hell's going on than

I do, and I'm the fucking CO of this base! Maybe Flying Officer Fender and Flight Lieutenant Rylander can fill me in. Except for you two, the rest of your crews are dismissed.'

Sensing a drubbing was about to take place, Duckwalker and Dan Lacey exited, with the OC of 440 Squadron in pursuit. The OC needed to corral Duckwalker about his appraisal of his squadron and of the evening's social event. The orderly officer had informed him of Duckwalker's messing restrictions.

He caught up with him outside the hangar.

'Flight Lieutenant Jones, I need a few moments.'

'Sir?'

'Thanks for the update on my crew. I needed first-hand information that only you could provide. In thirty seconds or less I want a thumbnail sketch of Flying Officer Fender, up-to-date and to-the-minute. The CO has issues that he wants addressed.'

Duckwalker was taken aback. He was there to evaluate the squadron's efficiency, not his own pilot's.

'I've only flown with him twice, Sir. Seems like a good guy.'

'I want to know how he does up there.' He pointed his cigarette skyward. Duckwalker opened the pad and read his notes.

'You mean you evaluate everybody, even your pilot?'

'Everything and everybody, Sir. That's my job. And by everybody, I mean everybody.'

Behind dark glasses, Duckwalker took pleasure in staring down the senior officer, waiting for a twitch of the eye. The OC twitched.

'I hope your evaluation of me isn't quite so detailed.'

'Suffice that this was information you required,
Sir. Is there anything else I can help you with?'

The OC stroked his chin.

'I've been informed by the orderly officer that you're required to stay away from the Officers' Mess during mixed social events. I hope you will confine yourself to barracks this evening.'

Duckwalker was stunned.

'I'm sorry Sir, but I don't understand.'

'Certain aspects of your past have caught up with you, Jones. I'm required to keep you at bay and out of the way. I'm sorry I have to do this.'

Duckwalker thought for a moment.

'Sir, tonight I'm to be the guest of Squadron Leader Gerard, the chief nurse. She's putting together an outfit for me to wear to the Sadie Hawkins dance this evening. I can't put her out like that. I give you my word that I'll be on my best behavior. I'm sure she'd vouch for me.'

The OC looked down at his reflection in the sunglasses and felt a twinge of sympathy. How could this strange, bespectacled waddling man-child be a danger to the social hierarchy of the Air Force?

'I don't want to know about your past indiscretions, Jones. All I know is that you've made a few social blunders along the way, but you gave my boys a good report, and you've provided what the CO needs on Flying Officer Fender. For that, I'm grateful. I'm putting the responsibility for your actions this evening in your and Squadron Leader Gerard's hands. Treat our Florence Nightingale with respect, or you'll never be allowed on this base again. One more thing, if I see you drinking booze at the dance tonight I'll throw the book at you.'

'Yes Sir. Thank you, Sir.' They saluted.

The OC gazed skyward.

'Who'd believe we're in the eye of a dying hurricane? If a B-25 can't fly in this shit, how the hell are the Russians supposed to get here?'

'I've wondered the same thing a few times myself, Sir.'

Back in the briefing room, Lou repeated his story from the night before, omitting the part about his past association with Pete. The CO listened intently, looking for changes in his testimony. He recognized the omission. He nodded thanks and made notes.

When it came time for Pete to take center stage, he made no reference to having any association to Lou Fender, past or present. He explained his mandate and the terms of reference for his mission, thanked the ready crew for coming to his rescue, and offered the CO a telephone number in Ottawa to verify his facts.

This did not sit well.

'Flight Lieutenant Rylander, you're in no position to play cat-and-mouse with me. There's animosity between you and Flying Officer Fender. I don't care what caused it, but I won't have it played out at my base, in the air, or on the ground. Is that understood? There's fuel for your aircraft and services on base for your crew. Weather permitting, you will depart at the earliest.'

Pete stubbed his cigarette and rose to attention.

'I've been ordered to fly up the coast and eavesdrop on the Yanks flying from England to Loring Air Force Base, Sir. I'll be out of your hair by seven o'clock tomorrow morning.

I don't think the icing caused any damage, and I've already ordered the refueling. The crew hasn't slept in a decent bed for a week, so you won't even know we're here. Let me finish by saying that your command was attacked, or dare-say infiltrated, at a vulnerable time and as Flight Lieutenant Jones reported, responded admirably. By all rights, my crew and I should be hunkered down in a lean-to in the bush waiting for the storm to pass and getting diarrhea from tainted survival food.'

He nodded in Lou's direction.

'As for Flying Officer Fender and me, all I can say is that we'll smooth things out over a few beers at the mess. It's been a while since we've talked. Yellowknife, I believe.'

'Let's make that as few beers as possible Rylander,' the CO responded. 'No hangovers, for you or your crew. You'll stay dry. I'll have a talk with your boss in Ottawa to get my pound of flesh. I didn't appreciate his sneak attack, so to speak, not at this time. The squadron's only just been formed. I realize you were following orders, but I want to get to the bottom of this. I want you out of my hair by tomorrow morning. You will stay dry after your afternoon tea with Flying Officer Fender. Understood?'

'Understood, Sir.'

The OC of 440 Squadron returned to the podium and for several minutes of hushed conversation, conferred with the CO. They broke huddle, and Pete was dismissed.

Lou sat alone. The CO tapped the podium with his Zippo, waiting long enough for the beat to stir him upright.

'Well, Flying Officer Fender, we are down to you. This morning, you omitted certain information that you gave me last night, information concerning Flight Lieutenant

Rylander and yourself. You mentioned a vendetta. Did this information, or lack thereof, have any bearing on the exercise this morning? I understand you had a few minor mishaps that could have jeopardized the safety of your aircraft and crew.'

Lou felt an uncomfortable twinge.

'You understand that from whom, Sir?'

'Your navigator felt you were distracted somehow, and that you might want to visit the flight surgeon for a chat. Have you issues that you need addressed? You can speak freely here.'

Lou paused long enough to enhance his shrug.

'Not that I'm aware of, Sir.'

Except for the issue of his craving for Darlene; except for the issue of Wilding and Rylander and their vendetta; except for the issue of a navigator who was nothing more than a stool-pigeon; and most of all, except for the nightmare of Rangoon.

He yearned for the Prairies, leading an aerobatic team over some small farming community, responsible only to himself. It was all he ever wanted. It was simple then, one man in one machine. Bad timing had fucked his career as the lone wolf. Now he had to be a team player. In the end, there he was, in front of the school principal with no defence against hearsay.

'Look, Fender, I'm not here as judge and jury. I can ground you here and now. Your navigator did you a couple of favors this morning, favors that probably saved Her Majesty a very expensive aircraft and maybe your life. I suggest you have a pow-wow with Flight Lieutenant Rylander and clean this thing up. If I hear of any conflict between the two of you over this matter, I will follow through on my threat. Understood?'

Lou rose to attention.

'Yes Sir.... Thank you Sir.'

'Very good. Dismissed.'

Lou made a bee-line for the mess to confront Duckwalker. The son of a bitch had broken the rules. They should have had it out between themselves. When the wheels touched Mother Earth what happened in the air stayed there. His conscience had always been his chastiser, which was why he'd gotten away with more than he should have. Which was why he'd planted five aircraft into terra firma.

He found Duckwalker in the Snake Pit reviewing notes. The bar was closed and the tables empty save for the orderly officer and the helicopter pilot playing cribbage. He sat opposite Duckwalker, peeled back his flying suit and lit a cigarette, the snap of his Zippo lighter getting his attention.

'Okay D.W., it's time for another chat. First of all, who the hell are you, what the hell is your name, and what gives you the authority to go crying to momma? If I'm going to get castrated, I deserve to know what the name of the knife-wielding son of a bitch doing the cutting is. And second of all, where do you get the authority to go fucking up my future? Do you realize what your blabbering has done? The CO was ready to ground me for Christ's sake. My R-211's going to have red flags all over it because of you.'

The response was slow in coming. Duckwalker folded his kneepad, lit a cigarette, and stroked his chin. Things had changed since last night. Things he'd exposed to Josette, things he could address, things he'd suppressed for too long. What he'd divulged about his physical limitations would stay in the vault, but certain aspects of his past were now open to disclosure.

'My name is Dwayne. You don't need to know the second. I have a degree from MIT in advanced electronics, I did half a tour as a bomber pilot during the war, and I'm the most qualified CF-100 navigator in the Air Force. At present, you might say I'm doing research. Everything I see, everything I encounter, and everything about what we do is documented and transferred on to the powers that be at Standards. In a year, I'll be a squadron leader and you'll have to address me as 'Sir.' Does that give you a fair update on who I am?'

'You're going to report this morning's misadventures to our boss?'

'In general terms, yes. Look Lou, most of the pilots I've flown with haven't had your experience, but the issue here isn't flying, it's teamwork. My report's not going to get into the specifics of whether you read, or didn't read a manual, or that you had a disconnected oxygen hose, or that your head was somewhere else. My concern is that you don't play well on a team. It's not you personally that I'm criticizing. It's pilots like you. Canada is going to build six hundred CF-100's over the next five years. We need to know what type of pilot is needed to fly them. As an ex-pilot, I have the experience to make a judgment call. You are not suited for this type of flying.'

Duckwalker's sunglasses hadn't moved an inch.

Lou had never been berated in such a fashion. The crispness of his delivery and the coldness in his voice accentuated his authority. He wanted to reach across the table, rip off the glasses, and punch whatever face emerged. But that would have been the end of him.

'Not suited for this type of flying? You mean driving around with a panting bloodhound in the back seat, looking for prairie dogs that pop their heads up. You mean that type of flying?'

The sunglasses didn't move and the reply came in a near whisper.

'The very nature of your response tells the tale. I suggest you contact your career counselor and get yourself transferred to a Sabre squadron. Or perhaps you should go back to instructing. I understand you're good.'

'And where did that information come from?'

'Speaking of groundhogs popping their heads up, as you put it, I bumped into your esteemed Mitchell pilot friend in the can. He speaks highly of you. Said you were the best pilot he ever flew with, taught him everything he knows. Says you've flown more aircraft types than anyone in the Air Force.'

'Everything except four engines.'

'Well I got you beat there. He contradicts me a bit, doesn't he, my report that is.'

'Must have been a long piss.'

'Last night I met a pilot named Doc Hunter who referred to you as "Caterpillar Fender." Care to tell me why?'

Lou answered the question with a question of his own.

'Last night I overheard conversations where you were referred to as "Duckwalker." Care to tell me why?'

Dwayne shook his head, but Lou hadn't finished.

'So I'll do you one better, "Duckwalker." I earned my four caterpillars the hard way.' The emphasis on the word

'Duckwalker' sent a twinge down Dwayne's spine. 'My flying record is well documented. It's just something I don't talk about. I hope you never have to abandon an aircraft. Having been a pilot, you should know that. It's a sign of failure. I also pranged a P-51 Mustang into the trees. So that makes five. That's a whole lot of failure in this man's Air Force. None, and I mean none of the crashes were attributed to pilot error. I do a couple of trips with you, and, boom, I'm nearly grounded!'

'Is the scar from the Mustang you used as a chainsaw? It was something I heard at Standards HQ.'

Lou snickered.

'I wondered if you had the balls to get to that. Looks like we both wear our little miscues for the world to see, pushing up daisies being the big miscue, that is. That Doc guy you talked to last night knows what I'm talking about. I bet he wonders what he fucked up. And you know what, in the end it was the fucking aircraft that fucked up. This machine we're flying is brand new. Never tried. When I did the conversion course at North Bay, I flew one that had a baseball bat for a control column, for Christ's sake! The real interceptor, the Mark 4, is the airplane they're counting on. This thing we're flying is just the test bed. They'll be putting a control column in the back seat and converting them into trainers within two years. For now, we're supposed to shoot down high-flying bombers with them. Shit no! The performance we witnessed this morning on an obsolete soup can is a testament to that. I don't think the Russians are going to radio for help when they come calling, do you?'

Duckwalker was taken aback by his candid outburst.

There was more to Lou's background than he'd given him credit for. Maybe he was an agent for the manufacturer, like the rumor said. He'd need to do a little more digging for that.

After a pause to light cigarettes it was time to open up.

'My posture and limited vision are something that I don't talk about. My job makes me few friends; that I'm willing to accept.' With that, he opened his kneepad, ripped out a page, rolled it into a ball, placed it in an ash tray and lit it.

'The morning has been erased. We start fresh.'

'What about the glasses? Do you ever take them off? You look like a fucking dragonfly.'

Duckwalker pushed them into the bridge of his nose and grinned. 'Only when I lick pussy. Now let's have a nice trip to Ottawa tomorrow, shall we? It may be our last together.' He let the flame die and pointed to the ashes.

'On that, we'll call a truce.'

Duckwalker rose awkwardly and offered his hand. Lou responded with a firm grip. The hatchet had been buried. One problem solved.

Lou refreshed their coffees and they sipped and smoked in silence. The hangar doors were closed. He fumbled in his pockets, found Darlene's telephone number, and looked around for a house phone. He needed her now. His sudden addiction to her had overridden the only power he possessed, the power of flight. It was time to change partners and dance.

'Don't leave, Dwayne. I need to make a phone call and we have to talk about this silly dance tonight. I need a little help in the social department. I understand that you and the nurse set the whole thing up. So brief me.'

A sly grin creased the dimples on Duckwalker's cheeks.

'And it's my understanding that you and the teacher set the whole thing up. And, if you please, I prefer to be addressed as D.W. It makes me feel taller.'

'Not Duckwalker?'

'Definitely not Duckwalker.'

They broke out laughing.

CHAPTER 16

L incoln had the officers in his crew rounded up in the mess for supper and a briefing. They organized tables in conference formation and sat in order of superiority. As with King Arthur and his knights, spit and polish formality was the order of the day. Once assembled, Lincoln discharged them to the buffet for their food. Nobody ate until all had returned and grace had been said.

Lincoln perused his crew. Lieutenant Wright, the newly arrived weapons officer with a Howdy Doody freckle-faced innocence, sat mute. Nobody in the crew had seen him before and nobody asked what function he performed. At the moment, Kenny Wright didn't know what function he performed.

Lincoln had excluded the bombardier on this trip. Too many questions could be asked. Arnie Stonehawker would sit beside Lincoln in the copilot's seat, and the second copilot was to be relegated to the aft compartment. He'd send Stonehawker down to the navigator's compartment when the time was right.

Lieutenant Hartwig, the second copilot, would occupy the rear compartment with the gunners for a reason: one less obstacle for the success of the plan. Lieutenant Hartwig was a re-coursed ROTC graduate who'd flunked out on fighters and, as with the navigator, had been recruited by Lincoln for his lack of experience. His constant stammer magnified his insecurity and he appeared nervous and in awe of the team that he'd joined. Asked to introduce himself, he did so with the timidity of a rabbit.

'My n-n-n-name is Lieutenant Hartwig, Sir. I c-c-came over to England with another crew. I understand that you asked specifically for me?'

'That's correct, Lieutenant. You're new to the wing. I thought we could use you for a sensitive bit of skullduggery on this trip. Do a little acting, so to speak. Are you up to it?'

The young pilot's cheeks flushed at being singled out from the group. 'Th-th-th-thanks for the opportunity to f-f-f-fly with you, Sir. I'll do my best.'

Lincoln introduced him to the crew, and then gave him his marching orders.

'Lieutenant Hartwig, on this trip you'll be stationed in the rear compartment to observe the gunners. You'll note how they pass their time and how they respond when they're called into action. If you observe them removing their parachutes or jeopardizing safety in any way, you can pull rank. You'll pass yourself off as a passenger deadheading home. Bunk down and make yourself inconspicuous until things start happening. The gunners don't know it yet, but they're going to get some realistic action. You won't get any pole time up front on this trip but I'll make it up to you later. I want a detailed report when we debrief at Loring, so make sure you document everything.'

'Yes Sir, th-th-thank you, Sir!'

'Gentlemen, our return to Loring isn't going to be a milk run for home. I'll be testing everyone with realistic emergencies and combat scenarios. I'm breaking with protocol by informing you that the GCI and interceptor boys are going to try to intercept us and document their success with gun cameras. We're not going to let that happen. There's some interesting weather we may be using to fool the interceptors. To fool them all.' He looked to Stan Gidley and winked. The navigator's cheeks flushed. He had taken the Major's hint, and it was going to pay off. He knew the weather pattern over Québec by heart.

Lincoln shifted his focus to each member of the crew, extolling their virtues and how, as individuals, they were critical to the team and the success of the mission.

The briefing finished with coffee and cigarettes. "This is their last supper," he thought. "Mine too." He finished with the locker room speech he'd rehearsed, but as with every speech imagined beforehand, it didn't come off as rousing or poetic.

'Gentlemen, remember, we are all a part of the Strategic Air Command, flying the most destructive weapon system this planet has ever seen. Let's do this thing right. Let's show Uncle Sam that if we can beat a way through his wall, we sure as hell can kick down the Russian defensive line. You're the best-trained aviators in the world, and it's your skill and dedication to duty that makes America the safest freedom-loving country in the world.'

He gestured and the crew rose to attention.

'Lieutenant Stonehawker will brief you when to assemble under the wing. I suggest you have a crap and check your oxygen masks. Let's go to war! Now who will lead us in prayer?'

He shifted his gaze from one to the other, then focused on the one person in the crew who he'd let in on the secret.

'How about you, Lieutenant Wright?'

Lou Fender never felt more fucked up in his life. "A good thing happens, and all it does is churn up the past." Darlene had hooked him, and he liked being hooked. For the first time, he had something to gauge love by. His feelings for her went well beyond those that he'd felt for Francine and the nurse in Yellowknife.

"If that was love, then what the hell is this?" he wondered. It was a sensation as bewildering and overwhelming as any he'd ever experienced. What was most intoxicating was that it concerned someone he'd met less than a day before.

He needed her more than just for someone to love. He needed somebody to share intimacy with. He couldn't contain the nightmare of Rangoon any longer. The guilt from his cowardice was eating at him like a malignant cancer, and it had to be cut from its host, or his future was lost.

Darlene would be his savior.

She knew it was him the second the phone rang. He'd come home safe and sound. She'd attended officers' wives "night flying" bridge parties, and never understood how they could concentrate on their cards. When an aircraft passed overhead, someone would stare skyward with the look of widowhood.

On one occasion, during a serious bout of bidding, there'd been a telltale "boom" followed by sirens. The hand, albeit with shaky grips, was played out. With apprehensive goodbyes, the wives raced for home, waiting for the knock on the door. On that particular occasion, the pilot had bailed out, and at the next session of "night flying bridge" a new queen was crowned.

Darlene agreed to meet Lou at three o'clock at her quarters or at the mess for a martini. His choice. Either way she needed to give him a fitting for his costume.

'Can't do the martini thing, boss's orders, gotta stay sober. We're at war, you know. I like your first idea, but I may just want to talk. I'd come to your boudoir now but you don't want a stinky aviator clashing with whatever scent you've got coming from that makeup vanity of yours. Besides, I need an hour of shuteye.'

'Come to my place for a talk? Louis Fender, if I had a dime for every time I heard that line, I wouldn't be up here in this godforsaken place.'

'Again, why are you here?' He needed to let her know that he remembered the sensitive portion of her conversation from the night before.

The phone went silent. A throaty whisper broke the pause.

'I have to go. I've an hour to finish these costumes. Then, I have a date at three.' She rang off.

Lou returned to the table to make plans for the dance.

'I thought Sadie Hawkins days were in November,' he commented. 'Is this weekend out of phase or something? I don't know whether to shit or wind my watch.'

'It's compressing time for me too,' Duckwalker chimed, 'if that's what you mean. My tailbone tells me things aren't about to slow down.'

'Yeah, too much is happening too fast.' Lou growled.

'I've been here less than twenty-four hours and my life is never going to be the same. Not only that, but gutting myself in front of total strangers is not my style. That's not me. I'll see you at the dance tonight. Are we still in high school or something? It feels like it.'

'Aren't you supposed to smoke a peace pipe with your old buddy, Badger Two, this afternoon?'

Lou was taken aback.

'Where did you hear that?'

'I told you it was a long piss. What the hell has this guy got on you anyway? You made it obvious to the CO last night that he had some sort of vendetta against you. I understand that the subject came up again this morning. Care to elaborate?'

Lou ran his fingers over his brow then massaged his chin. What could he divulge that would placate his inquisitor? Or should he divulge nothing? He'd give him the basics.

'My association with Rylander goes way back. We ended up in the Far East at the end of the war, flying Beaufighters. The war in Europe was over and by the time I got there, the Burma campaign was wrapping up. There was a Canadian contingent seconded to the RAF: reprobates and Johnny-come-latelies, like myself. We were no more than taxi drivers by that time. We ferried aircraft to Rangoon and escorted transports that dropped supplies.' He paused for recollection. History had a way of changing over time.

'Pete and I met two months before Rangoon was liberated. By that time, the monsoon season had arrived and the air-to-ground action was limited to sporadic encounters with Jap forces that had been bypassed. The new Labour government in England under Attlee promised that any Brit who had more than three years away from jolly old England could be repatriated. Christ, half the aircrews there were eligible. The RAF needed pilots and navigators to top up the ranks so they scrounged up as many Commonwealth crews as they could. Pete and I were thrown together with a Limey squadron leader by the name of Wilding who ran the forward air control operations for the south of Burma. This guy knew the territory and without him, we wouldn't have gotten out of that godforsaken place alive.'

'I met Pete when Mandalay was liberated. I found out pretty quick that he wasn't a great pilot, but my instructor instincts toughened him up and he became relatively proficient. He flies well in nasty weather. Probably the reason he's got the job he has. It was monsoon season so we spent a lot of time in clag and he passed along a lot of goodly gen on how to handle weather. He had an instinct for it. I owe him for that. When the war suddenly finished, we shipped home on the same boat. We parted company in Vancouver on what I thought were pretty good terms. We ran into each other in Yellowknife a couple of years later and it was this reunion of sorts that got me back into the Air Force. Another thing I owe him for. You'll have to ask him what his beef with me is all about. Let me know if you find out what the hell it is? See you tonight.'

Lou made a beeline for his quarters. The thought of Darlene pushing her way through the door and heading for his bed had usurped the morning's disasters.

———•◦•———

Rylander felt lucky. He'd gotten away relatively unscathed. The disaster over the river had been his fault and he would pay for it from The Voice from Ottawa. He'd had no choice but to go begging for help. It was the closest he'd ever come to losing an aircraft and crew. Reading and aviating inclement weather was his strength, but in this instance his strength was not enough. The saving grace to his shattered ego was that Lou Fender hadn't been the one to escort him in on the GCA. That would have been too humiliating.

He organized his crew's messing and sleeping accommodations and went for lunch. As he entered the mess, Lou passed by without a glance of recognition. A pow-wow over a beer was definitely not in the cards. He sidled up to the buffet, filled his tray, and sat opposite the cripple with the glasses who he'd conversed with in the can. They ate in silence until a mutual uneasiness forced him to speak.

'So you're Standards chief scout and tattletale. I've heard about you. You're supposed to know everything there is about our state-of-the-art defence against the Russian Air Force.' Duckwalker raised his head in acknowledgement and slid his kneepad to the side. Snide remarks from whatever origin raised his hackles.

'So you're Wing Commander Stone's prairie dog who pops up from out of nowhere. The one who likes to stick his nose where others won't.' Pete had never heard The Voice from Ottawa referred to so openly, and he felt like a spy who'd had his cover blown.

'Or can't,' Pete responded sarcastically. He needed that understood. Their mutual rank allowed for an open duel and Pete was not about to give ground.

'Lou told me you flew together at the end of the war. Care to elaborate? I'm also curious as to why an experienced interdictor such as yourself made such a boneheaded mistake in not taking into account the water temperature when you picked the river to facilitate your attack. I knew you were fucked at Met briefing this morning.'

Pete picked away at a bowl of aspic contemplating a response that wouldn't contradict anything Lou might have divulged about their past. He knew the big secret was intact, otherwise the question would never have been asked.

'Whatever he told you, I'm sure it was all that he intended. It's personal, and it's really none of your business. What's it to you anyway? You met the guy only a couple of days ago. I smelled his farts for four months.' Pete saw his reflection in Duckwalker's glasses and it irritated him.

'By the way, when I'm being interrogated I like to look into my inquisitor's eyes. Care to take off the shades?'

'Sorry, no can do. Doctor's orders. Anyway, nobody said you had to sit there.' Sensing Pete was about to leave, Duckwalker offered a cigarette to soften the tone of the conversation, his peace pipe.

'Look Pete, I need answers. When the aircraft commander is willing to risk what you risked today over some past incident or misunderstanding, and it involves me personally, then I'd like to get to the bottom of it. Remember, I'm up there too. The best pilot you ever knew was not at his best today. The CO chewed him out, and I chewed him out. If you and I hadn't had our conversation in the can, there was a good chance he'd be grounded. I was willing to let the incidents slide, but only on your say-so. Like you, I report to a higher power. Is there anything, any little tidbit you can divulge about Lou Fender that I can work with?'

Pete took a drag and focused on Duckwalker's lenses.

'All I'll say is that Lou Fender is not what he seems. And that's all I'll say. Now, if you'll excuse me, I have a bed with my name on it, and I intend to claim it. You have greater luxuries than me. How often do you have to sleep in your aircraft?'

He butted his cigarette, grabbed his duffle bag and headed for the foyer. The notice board caught his eye and he focused on the poster announcing that evening's Sadie Hawkins dance. He felt for the empty vial, and his penis stirred. He'd packed jeans and a plaid shirt in his duffle bag. He had a party to go to. Somebody would bid for him. After all, he had the face of an angel and the eyes of a demon. What woman wouldn't want him?

He'd go into action drug-free, new territory. Next time he'd account for the temperature of the river.

———————

Duckwalker phoned Josette, couldn't make contact, and headed to barracks. A strange overcast heralded the advance of the trailing edge of the front. Part two of the weather system was about to envelope them. The system would dissipate by the time they flew home the next day. No flying for at least eighteen hours. He had a dance and a date, and for now, that was all that mattered.

The episode of the morning and his report on 440 Squadron's performance were Monday's problem. The issue of Lou Fender was dead. Once they returned to Ottawa, he would deep-six his files and never fly with him again. He'd be as diplomatic as possible, but that was that. The issue of the relationship between him and Rylander was none of his business and he'd keep it that way. They were big boys; they'd work it out.

He bumped into the orderly officer outside the foyer. Fred Malone had been excluded from the morning's debriefing and was eager to find out what the scuttlebutt was all about. Duckwalker gave him the basics but didn't elaborate on specifics. He regarded officers without wings as little more than clerks and treated them as such.

'What do you do when you're not the orderly officer?'

The orderly officer, a Joe-job that came out of rotation was, on occasion, doled out as a punishment. To have it on a weekend was usually the latter.

'I'm a nurse. You met my boss last night. She caught me gambling with a patient and gave me the weekend and this arm band to think things over.' He pointed to the two red zeros. 'She doesn't think the Air Force is suited to my lifestyle.'

'Tell me about her. I'm escorting her to the dance tonight.' Fred regarded the question with suspicion. Anything negative about her could bite him in the ass.

'As the chief nurse and hospital administrator there's nothing negative I'd comment on. She's a pro.' He lowered his voice and checked for eavesdroppers. 'Rumor has it that she has an appetite for young men, and women. I haven't first-hand experience mind you, but the two nursing sisters who work with me alluded to such. You met her last night; what do you think of her?'

'She's never opened up to you? I thought you nurses had a coven, like witches.'

'Do I look like a witch to you? A warlock, maybe. They don't even regard me as a nurse, for fuck's sake. I had to let them know I was fucking a Pepsi broad in Chicoutimi, so they didn't think I was a fucking fairy.'

'What's a Pepsi?'

'It's slang for French Canadian. They can't say Coca-Cola, so they only drink Pepsi. Anyway, as a male nurse I'm ostracized by you flyboys as a Nancy boy. I've been here four months, and all I can do to prove that I'm not one is to take other people's money. It's my way of extolling my masculinity. So far I've done pretty well.'

'I noticed you playing crib this morning. I take it you don't just play poker?'

'If I was guaranteed that I'd make as much money and have the security of a steady job, I'd quit this racket and head to Las Vegas.'

'It looks to me like you have the best of both worlds here. I wouldn't do anything rash. You're on duty for the rest of the weekend, so why don't we meet after breakfast tomorrow for a couple of hands of crib? Looks to me like you need some action. That's if you're not teaching Sunday school, of course.'

'I play for a dollar a point.'

'Serious stuff. Sounds good to me.'

'When I gamble I like to see my opponents' eyes, but that's not going to happen, is it? I had a chat with that Rylander fellow after this morning's briefing. Seems he's interested in some cards later in the afternoon. You can join in if you want. He's interested in medicine. Said he'd been trained in the pharmaceutical field. I might make a few bucks wiling away the weekend. If you can't make it, I'll see you at the dance tonight. If you happen to get blitzed, I'll be the sober one in uniform wearing the arm band.'

'Didn't the OC give instructions that I wasn't allowed any Kickapoo joy juice?'

'Just checking.'

Duckwalker gazed skyward and with a half-hearted salute, he bade Fred farewell. He needed a shower and a nap. He needed to power up for Josette. Who knew what was in store for the evening?

———•◦•———

Pete had found a source for his elixir, and after washing up returned to the mess to hunt down the orderly officer. A nurse had access to the hospital's drug lock-up, and a source of chloral hydrate to replenish his vial. He found Fred in the Snake Pit playing solitaire. He bought two Cokes, picked up a cribbage board at the bar, and sat down opposite him.

'You said a buck a point. That's pretty steep.'

'Only if I skunk you, and I intend to skunk you.'

They played two hands before he broached the subject.

'You have access to the drug lock-up, don't you?'

'I do. But why would that interest you?'

'With this crazy job of mine, I have a hell of a time sleeping. I have a prescription for chloral hydrate. You wouldn't have access to any would you?'

'I have access, but two keys are required to open the drug cabinet. How much do you need?'

Pete pulled the vial from his pocket.

'Not much. This thing filled will last me a month. I've been using chloral hydrate for a couple of years.'

'You know it's addictive, don't you?'

'Can't you tell that I've a non-addictive personality? I've

been on the run for two weeks, and the clock in my head's so fucked up that I don't know what time it is. I'm playing crib when I should be sleeping. The toughest part of our mission is still ahead of me. I've got eight hours of pole time tomorrow. You ever been in a B-25?'

The question caught Fred off guard and he miss-pegged a move.

'No, I can't say I have. Why do you ask?'

'I fly the most souped-up, technically advanced, medium bomber in this man's Air Force. We've got a radar system that can pick up a flock of geese.' It was time to set the hook. 'You ever been interested in aircraft?'

'I've never had a problem gambling with money. I do have a problem about gambling with my skin. Especially when it comes to flying. It's a mother thing. Her brother was a bush pilot. He was killed flying a Norseman, and from that moment on, there were to be no more flyers in the family. Whenever the newspaper had an article about some crash somewhere, she posted it for all to see. She was hell during the war. I find the confines of an aircraft's cockpit reptilian, like the innards of some mechanical creature. I've never been able to shake the sensation.'

'You, my son, are about to face your demons for the last time. When we finish this hand, we're going to the flight line. My dragon awaits.'

Pete paid Fred twelve dollars in winnings and they headed to the bomber. The overcast had intensified and the wind was freshening. The bomber had been chocked and tied down. Pete checked the control locks and was satisfied that any amount of wind would keep them stable. He ushered Fred up the ladder and into the belly and was satisfied to find nobody sleeping there. Fred bumped his head twice, cursing his awkwardness. "Large soft men do not make for tight confines," Pete thought.

They worked their way up to the pilots' compartment, where Fred sat in the left hand seat, gripping the control column and caressing the throttles. 'So this is where you make a living. It looks very complicated. Then there's the smell. I find it overwhelming.'

'Except for the radar attack-scope there, nothing in the cockpit has changed in twenty years,' he explained. 'It's the navigator's station that's changed the most.' He escorted Fred to Dan Lacey's lair, and sat him in the ejection seat. Pete unhinged the radarscope.

'This is where the future of our interceptor program lies. Without this shit, there isn't a pilot out there that can do his job. Intercepting Russians, that is.'

Pete had Fred crawl through to the bombardier's station and showed him the two 50-caliber machine guns.

'We keep everything as real as possible. The vibration of the guns on the radar can be significant. The Mark 3 has eight of these little buggers. We have to use real slugs because nobody makes 50-caliber blanks.'

After one too many enthusiastic 'wows' from Fred, they descended the ladder and bucked the wind back to the mess.

'That wasn't so bad was it?' Pete remarked as he held the front door and ushered Fred inside. 'You didn't seem claustrophobic or intimidated. You should get a private pilot's license. Learn to fly. If I wasn't returning to Chatham tomorrow, I'd see if you could come along for a ride.'

Fred hadn't felt this buoyed and heady in years. The guts of the monster had digested him, and he felt fine.

'Let me buy you a beer, Pete. I'll keep it hush-hush.'

The Saturday afternoon patrons in the Snake Pit were grouped around two speakers blaring crowd noise and the play-by-play of a football game. Fred poured their beers into coffee mugs and they retired to the lounge where they were shooed away by the officers' wives decorating for the dance, forcing them up to the dining room.

Pete needed a quiet place to weave his web. He'd forged enough of a bond with Fred that he felt he could ask him a favor.

'Damn it Fred, the clock in my head is all fucked up. I don't know how I'm going to pull off the trip tomorrow if I don't get any shut-eye. Is there any way you can help me?' He produced the vial and placed it on the table.

'I'm sure a little bit of this shit won't be missed.'

Fred stared at the bottle long enough to drum up his gambler's courage. The thought of allying himself with an accomplished pilot to fly a mission benefitting the greater good of the Air Force made him a player. He took the vial and tucked it into his cigarette packet.

'I can't promise you anything. If I come up with the goods, I'll be at the dance tonight.'

'I'll be early,' Pete replied. 'The earlier the better. Then I can get back to barracks and get some sleep.'

'Like I said,' Fred replied, 'I'll do my best.'

A deal had been made, and they finished their beers in silence. The tables were being set for that evening's buffet, and the kitchen help gave them the evil eye to vacate the premises.

'When you said you'd be here early,' Pete asked, 'how early did you mean?'

'Don't push too hard, Pete. I'm not guaranteeing anything.' Fred felt the power of the pusher and he wanted to keep it that way. His compatriot with the evil eyes was convincing in his need. Pilots were stupid when it came to alcohol, but Fred had never met one that had a chloral hydrate addiction. When it came to aircrew, alcohol was an accepted part of Air Force life. The war had spawned that.

'We could meet around six-thirty. It's not going to be easy. There's a nurse who owes me a favor. It's time I checked in with the Operations Center. The base is on stand-down for fuck's sake, and I must still make the rounds. I might break rotation and make the hospital my first stop.' He winked at Pete. 'Who knows what I'll discover there.'

L ou ran his fingers through his crew cut and meshed in enough hair cream to keep him honest. The scar looked uglier than ever, but the eyes seemed brighter and there was a smirk that hadn't been there since Rangoon. He was happy. He'd fucked up today more than he'd care to admit but it wasn't basic flying skills—it was her!

He waited for her knock on the door, and when he opened it, she breezed past, beaming and carrying a coat hanger on high.

'Well Li'l Abner, here's your outfit.'

For the next ten minutes, Lou was forced to endure the indignity of a mannequin as Darlene fussed with needles and straight pins. He felt an uncomfortable stirring whenever her fingers approached his crotch. What was to be his moment of monumental disclosure had turned into a farcical pantomime, but when his costume was complete and he saw his reflection in the bathroom mirror, there stood Li'l Abner.

'How the hell did you do this in such a short time?'

'I come from a large family, and when there are hand-me-downs you learn how to make quick fixes. Your pants came from a radar technician who thinks he loves me.'

'If I'm Li'l Abner, then you must be going as Daisy Mae.'

'Now, do I look like Daisy Mae? You'll see what I come as when you pick me up at seven.'

She came to him with want. He'd never embraced her standing and was surprised at her frailty. She raised her face and kissed him with a deep immobile tongue. She wanted him to search.

'What do we do about my scar? Li'l Abner doesn't have a scar. Will you use some makeup?'

'I'll never hide your scar. The scar makes you brutally handsome, Louis Fender. It's your scar that makes me want you more than I've ever wanted any man I've ever known. It's your scar that made me fall in love with you.'

Lou stood stunned by her admission and he wanted to respond with the admission that he had fallen in love with her, too, but he needed honesty and to have her accept his past. Only with her acceptance of it would he feel the comfort of completely giving himself to her.

Sensing his urgency, she hung up his outfit, helped him into a dressing gown, then pushed him into a tub chair.

'I think you have something to tell me. Now what is it you want to talk about?' Lou offered a cigarette, lit one himself, and exhaled loudly.

'What I'm about to tell you must never leave those beautiful lips of yours. My future, our future, depends on it. I've held a secret that, until I met you yesterday, I'd pretty well buried. Now, it's tearing me apart. Events that occurred last night and this morning opened a tear in me that only you can sew up. If you can't, I'm doomed. Something terrible happened in Burma at the end of the war, and what I did has haunted me ever since.' Lou stood, went to the window, and stared into the rain.

'The weather was the same as this, only warmer and wetter.'

He arrived in Rangoon in early May 1945, via Egypt, India and recently captured Mandalay. A month in the devastated city of Mandalay introduced him to the ravages of war, and he regretted being there. What he thought was going to be a combat tour turned out to be no more than escort work for squadrons of DC3 transports supplying ground forces working their way south to Rangoon. What was worse, the monsoon season had arrived, grounding air operations. The British 14th Army battled on, and after Burma's liberation, he was transferred to Rangoon.

'I'd never smelled anything like Mandalay or Rangoon. I can smell them to this day. When I wasn't in the cockpit, I was trying to stay healthy. There was a lot of disease and death, and believe me, death stinks, especially in the trop-ics. In Mandalay, I was housed with a certain Squadron Leader Wilding, who ran the forward air control opera-tions. He introduced me to a Canadian pilot named Peter Rylander. A real sprog. How this Rylander guy ever got to a combat theatre, I'll never know. He alluded to having some kind of political connection, but I never found out what it was. Anyway, over the next month, we flew from airstrip to airstrip, replacing aircraft and escorting the transports to drop zones. The flying was great when the weather cleared, and I took to saving Pete's skin as a side job.'

'When the weather socked in, he was the master of the air. After a month of spending money on brothels and booze, we became inseparable. When we took Rangoon in early May, Rylander and Wilding introduced me to a get-rich scheme that had Trouble written all over it.' He paused and lit a cigarette.

'How could there be a get-rich scheme when there was nothing to get rich on?' Darlene asked. 'Surely anything of value was already reaped, raped, or destroyed.'

'Oh, there was gold in them there hills. Only, it wasn't gold the two of them were after, it was airplanes, Jap airplanes.'

'Why in the name of God were Japanese aircraft of any value?'

'That was my first question precisely.'

The bar in the Strand Hotel had become a watering hole for a mixture of every uniform, head gear, and skin color in the Far East. With the port of Rangoon open, a steady supply of liquor, cigarettes, and quinine rejuvenated the most disillusioned jungle fighters. Seasoned officers and enlisted men broke protocol and drank together. Singapore was the next objective, and who knew what the outcome of that operation would be?

'I was in the bar at the Strand Hotel on a Friday evening, just like tonight, when Wilding and Rylander put a proposal to me. Like the idiot I can be at times, I got sucked in. Wilding was a cunning salesman.'

'Fender, this war will be over sooner than we think,' Wilding commented. 'If we're lucky, and that's a big if, the three of us will have nothing to show for it but our skin and a kiss goodbye. Even that's doubtful. It's going to be tough back home after we're demobilized. A man could use a little cash.'

He turned and pointed.

'There's an American colonel sitting at the bar who

approached me with a business opportunity, so to speak. He's a dog-robber for a movie company from Hollywood who's scouting the area for a war movie. It's a flying story. He says they won't have any trouble getting aircraft from us, but he wants to use real Jap aircraft for authenticity. Up to now, all the flying movies made about the war have been using models for Jap aircraft. He's willing to pay big dough if we can scrounge a half-dozen flyable Jap aircraft that have been captured or surrendered. He needs two experienced pilots who can fly in shit without the use of navigators. The two of you fit the bill. All you have to do is escort the aircraft here, no combat, no risk, big payday. What do you say?'

Lou looked into Pete's eyes hoping for a shake of the head, but all he saw was greed. The Cabbagetown pilot was already an eager partner. He exploded in rage.

'How the fuck are we going to hijack six Jap aircraft? And once we've got them, where do we store, then transport them to? Further to that, who's going to fly them? Japs? I'm sure as hell not, and my compatriot here hasn't got the skill. Where the fuck are they anyway?'

'Right now they're in Singapore.'

'Singapore! You said they'd been captured. By my recollection, and I'm only going from the newsreels, we don't own Singapore. Not yet anyway. Not only that, they'd have to refuel three times and have two shits before they got here. The logistics would be a nightmare. Whose idea was this?'

Wilding did the most Oil Can Harry twist of his mustache.

'The Colonel says they captured some high-ranking

Jap who'd got hooked on the movies when he visited Hollywood before the war. He says he knew there was a bunch of disillusioned fighter pilots in Singapore that, for a few yen, might be persuaded to defect.'

'And make a few bucks playing Jap pilots in the movie flying their own planes.' Pete interjected. 'They're paid separately.'

'They'll fly their aircraft here,' Wilding continued. 'You intercept them three or four hundred miles out, like good little fighter pilots, and I bring you home. Rylander says you're good in cloud. You'll escort them to an airfield north of Rangoon that I managed to quarantine. They think the runways are booby-trapped. What really saves our asses is that you come in formation with either one of you leading. The Jap aircraft are twin engine Ki-45's. They look a lot like a Beaufighter, so anyone on the ground will think they're one of ours. The Colonel will disassemble them, whisk them to the port, and ship them out. After a hefty cash transaction, we're out of the picture. We'll bring them in pairs, hopefully over three days. What do you think?'

Wilding and Rylander took swigs of beer and lit cigarettes. Lou leaned back in his chair and looked to the Colonel. 'I'd like to speak to the one who's paying.'

Wilding motioned to the Colonel to join them.

Colonel Eggerton was not as U.S. Army Air Force as his uniform indicated. He had the look of one who'd never seen combat but would tell a good story. Lou disliked him from the moment of introduction.

'Lou Fender, great name for a flying hero. Mind if I use it in a movie some day?' Lou looked into the face of a carnival barker and knew this was a dangerous man. There was nothing worse than a hustling Yank out to make easy money. It was always at somebody else's risk, and the partnership had little loyalty. He'd trained Americans during the war, and their attitude and insincerity grated on him.

But, the prospect of going home with a wad of cash intrigued him and he decided to hear him out.

'I'm willing to offer you gentlemen twenty-five thousand Yankee dollars for every Jap aircraft you deliver to Rangoon. You don't have to fly them, just keep them safe and sound 'til they get here. We'll take care of the planes and pilots once they're here. There's an abandoned airfield well outside Rangoon that Wilding has secured. I need at least six aircraft in decent shape to make the movie, so the operation could take up to a week. I know it's monsoon season, but Wilding tells me you're experienced in all types of weather. If anything goes wrong, you'll have to take whatever action you need to save your skins, but you won't get paid for what you don't deliver. You'll receive the cash on each arrival. Wilding will command your end of the operation and will act as the forward controller. He'll receive the funds and dispense them accordingly. If our Japanese associates defect when the weather's nasty, you'll have to escort them in cloud, so there's an element of danger, but then, that's why you'll be making the big dough.'

A buffoon's bravado, Lou thought.

'What's your risk?' he asked.

Eggerton shifted uneasily, thought of an answer, but came up with nothing. Lou's head felt like it was going to explode. What was proposed amounted to an act of treason, aiding and abetting, collusion with the enemy, and any other of a dozen charges that they'd throw away the key or shoot you for. There was still a war on.

Fifty thousand dollars per man was a great deal of money if the operation came off. Zero dollars and years in the pokey if it failed. Then again, who knew if they were going to get out of South East Asia with anything at all, especially with their lives?

'What happens if I say no?'

The Colonel looked to Wilding and grinned.

'Rangoon's a dangerous place, Fender. The jungle's swallowed up more men and machines than the RAF's willing to admit. Weather changes, mission profiles change. Isn't that right Squadron Leader Wilding?

'You are correct, Sir.'

'Christ!' Darlene exclaimed. 'They were blackmailing you with your life. They'd find some way to kill you.'

'They still do to this day.' He paused to light a cigarette. 'The plan was set in motion. I didn't deal with any of the back-rooms stuff. I was just a high-paid delivery boy. The weather was socked in pretty good, so Rylander did the intercept on the first two. Eggerton and Wilding extracted two Jap aircraft from somewhere up the Malay Peninsula, and sure enough, they turned up. Rylander escorted them to the abandoned field then landed back at our base. His dysentery had flared up, and he was hospitalized right away. The Jap bastards had the colossal gall to land fully armed. It didn't seem right for them to do that, but a buck's a buck, I guess. Since Rylander was out of the picture, the rest of the operation was up to me.

'I took off the next morning and headed out over the Gulf of Martaban on what was to appear on radar as a routine shipping patrol. That's what it was supposed to look like. It was the first time I'd flown over water for a long time, and I remember that I'd forgotten my Mae West and life raft. Wilding and I had our own UHF frequency, and he vectored me over the Gulf toward Tavoy on the Burmese isthmus. I was in and out of cloud for an hour before I got word that two enemy aircraft were approaching thirty miles ahead. That's when I got scared.'

'Scared!' Darlene exclaimed. 'You've got me petrified.'

Lou picked out the two Japanese fighters busting in and out of cloud, and formatted on them as lead with an aircraft off each wing. He acknowledged his purpose with hand signals and set course to Rangoon. His IFF/SIF was set to allow safe passage, and he settled in to deliver the goods. Having two armed enemy aircraft sitting to each side and behind him made him uneasy, so he signaled line abreast. Who knew what a disillusioned Jap was capable of?

As with the two aircraft already delivered, these two were also armed with 500-pound bombs under each wing. A foreboding overwhelmed him, and he pulled back into a slot position. Suddenly the radio crackled, and a panicked, upper crust, nasally British accent blasted into his headset.

'Reaper Three this is Reaper Two…, over.'

'Reaper Two, this is Reaper Three…, go on.'

'Reaper Three, the aircraft you're escorting are hostile. They're being flown by kamikaze pilots. They mean to do us harm! You're to shoot them down immediately. GO BUSTER! GO BUSTER!'

'The two Japs who'd flown in the day before had committed hara-kiri during the night, setting off a mad scramble to check on the aircraft being disassembled and crated up. The Colonel had his own entourage of mechanics, but by the time he got to the abandoned airfield, it was too late. He was about to do a cursory inspection on the first crate, when he was blown to smithereens. The second one went off fifteen minutes later. It took an hour for word to get to Wilding, and the asshole needed another half hour to figure out how he was going to save his ass. If I didn't get rid of the two Trojan Horses I was escorting, who knew what havoc they'd create. Escorting the enemy to bomb your own position is pretty well hanging material.'

Lou shook his head and let out a deep sigh of resignation. 'What did you do?'

'When you're told to go "buster" and are given five seconds to react, use four of them to think, and one to act. That's all the time I had, five seconds. I armed my guns, pulled back on the power and slid in behind the starboard aircraft. I gave him a good five-second burst, and the right engine started to burn. I thought I saw the pilot bail out, but there was so much debris breaking off, I had to get out of the way. The second guy knew the jig was up, and he dived for cloud towards Rangoon. I got him four minutes later, but not without the help of Wilding. He picked him up on radar and vectored me to him. I got him at low level. Poor bastard didn't even know I was there. After the nasty deed was done, Wilding agreed to meet me at our airdrome. We needed a pow-wow to cover our tracks and determine our course of action, but when I landed, he wasn't there. I've never heard from him since.

'What about the money for the first delivery, the fifty thousand? What about Pete Rylander? What about the other two Japanese aircraft waiting to come?'

'Wilding disappeared, and Rylander stayed in the infirmary for a week. Or so I was led to believe. He never knew what I'd done, though I've always suspected he did. I heard that a reconnaissance flight a day later discovered two Jap aircraft at an isolated jungle strip down the isthmus, and destroyed them. It seemed too coincidental. Wilding was into the scheme a lot deeper than just being a radar controller. There had to be someone else besides him and the Colonel. I had a tough time dealing with it. Still do. What I did was cowardly in every way. I shot down two fighter pilots who thought they were surrendering. I never should have joined that fucking pack of jackals in the first place, and I never should have been put in a position where I had to murder so as to not face a firing squad. If what I've done ever comes to the light of day, my career in the Air Force is over.'

'Have you ever tracked down this Rylander fellow? Surely he must have some answers.'

'Track him down! He's tracked me down. Twice! He's here on base this very moment. He's the aircraft commander of the B-25 sitting on the tarmac. He's here to finish a job he was meant do when he tracked me down seven years ago.'

'How did he find out you were here?'

'From Wilding.'

'He knows where Wilding is?'

'Wing Commander Chauncey Wilding commands the whole GCI system from the Great Lakes to Mont Apica. He and some asshole in Ottawa are Pete Rylander's puppet masters.

'How did you find out about all this?'

'Remember I said I thought there had to be somebody else? Well, he found me. Seems more money had been pre-paid for the aircraft than I was led to believe. Pete ended up holding the purse. When the shit hit the fan, Wilding conveniently had himself repatriated back to England under Clement Attlee's election promise, leaving Rylander with the job of getting the loot out of Burma.'

'Wilding is British?'

'British as they come, and as big a bounder as there ever was. He immigrated to Canada, joined the RCAF, and with his credentials, ended up where he is now. He tracked down Rylander and put a gun to his head.'

'With all that money, why didn't he just stay in England and have Rylander deliver it to him?'

'It was American cash. He'd have had some awkward explaining to do. Anyway, the cash was here in Canada. Pete had smuggled it in on our return trip. It was in our cabin the whole time. I didn't discover this until I was contacted by the very pissed-off Japanese businessman who'd initially set up the sale, but who'd been duped by Wilding. Seems his six lost sheep were not suicide pilots after all. Wilding had the first two murdered and made it look like suicide. He somehow planted the charges, and then set me up. Poor Eggerton got caught in the middle. Apparently I was next to go; still am.'

'This is the most preposterous story I've ever heard. The permutations and combinations of circumstances that brought you here together seem mathematically impossible. How could something that happened in Rangoon almost ten years ago culminate in this part of the world? You're pulling my leg, aren't you?'

'I wish it was so. But it's not. I've been expecting that, sooner or later, my past would catch up to me, only I didn't think it would happen here, especially this weekend. Obviously, Wilding set the whole thing up, but I don't think he was counting on Rylander screwing up. Rylander didn't account for the weird weather. With me out of the way Wilding only had to deal with Rylander and Tamaguchi. Tamaguchi wants his money back. I wouldn't want to cross a nasty Jap.'

'I wonder where it is?'

'I think Rylander has it stashed in the B-25.'

'Are you and Tamaguchi in cahoots?'

'Let's just say that if he gets his money back, I'll be handsomely rewarded.'

'How did he find you, anyway?'

'The same way Rylander did.'

'So what's your next move? Where do you go from here? Where do we go from here? You've put me in the picture, and you can't paint me out.'

'I need to confront Rylander ASAP and have it out. I've got a better hand to play, now that we're in the same cage. He's a slippery bastard, that's for sure. I just wish I had something I could use against him.'

Lou kissed Darlene long and hard, then escorted her to her barracks. There'd be no hanky-panky this afternoon. His secret was out and it was time to attack. The storm was strengthening and he hustled back to barracks. Pete Rylander was about to find out he had a new partner.

CHAPTER 18

Arnie Stonehawker felt uneasy, and when a German feels uneasy, he goes on the attack. He'd asked for an audience with Colonel Briggs at the Operations Center, and was about to gamble his career.

Things about Major Crisp just didn't seem right.

Colonel Briggs sat behind a clutter-free metal desk, sipping from a heavy coffee mug and holding a receiver away from his ear. The voice emanating from the telephone did not seem pleased, and the Colonel winced every now and then.

The young lieutenant stood rigid, waiting for an acknowledgement to stand easy, but it was a long time coming. He eyed the flow-chart and noted that his aircraft was the only one that hadn't been crossed off. The estimated time of departure was written in as 2300 GMT. Eleven o'clock—four hours away. Excluding him and the Major, the crew would be going through their pre-flight checks and taking stock of their personal survival gear. It took four hours to get the B-36 airworthy.

He'd reluctantly passed on his copilot's pre-flight responsibility to Lieutenant Hartwig, but it was worth the gamble if his audience with the Colonel paid off. He'd face the ire of Major Crisp if Hartwig fucked up, but that was the risk he had to take. He'd make up some excuse if it became an issue.

Colonel Briggs hung up the receiver and lit a cigarette.

'What can I do for you Lieutenant? Shouldn't you be supervising your crew? 2300's approaching pretty fast.'

'Permission to speak frankly, Sir.' Briggs knew that 'frankly' spelled problem, and with one aircraft left to deploy he didn't need any 'frankly' at this juncture. The bomb was loaded and headed for Loring and that was to be the end of that.

'Permission granted, Lieutenant. Stand easy. What's the problem?'

Arnie had composed a perfect presentation, but was suddenly tongue-tied. One did not question the judgment of a top aircraft commander without accepting the repercussions. Jumping over Major Crisp in the hierarchy of command was a serious breach of protocol, but his instincts about the Major's mental state couldn't be stayed.

'It's about Major Crisp, Sir.'

'What should concern you about Major Crisp, Lieutenant?'

'I think he might not be well, Sir.'

Briggs eyed the lieutenant and shook his head.

'What makes you think he's not well, Lieutenant? I spoke with him only a couple of hours ago, and he seemed quite healthy to me.'

'I don't mean he's physically unwell, Sir. There's something about the way he's acting that just doesn't seem right. I wouldn't be here putting my career on the line if I didn't believe what my gut tells me.'

'And what does your gut tell you, Lieutenant?'

'Sir, I think the Major is close to having a mental breakdown.'

Briggs clenched his fists and banged them on the table, rattling the floor. Arnie knew he'd made the mistake of his life.

'Lieutenant Stonehawker, do you have any idea what you're alluding to? What do you know about Major Crisp? What do you know about his war record, his post-war record, his personal misfortune, his contribution to the Strategic Air Command? What do you know about psychology when it comes to leadership? This isn't "The Caine Mutiny," and we're not dealing with a Captain Queeg here. I've known Major Crisp for seven years. You've flown with him what, maybe twice?'

'Three trips to the Pole, Sir, then this one over here.'

'On the basis of that, you're willing to throw caution to the wind and destroy two careers. His personal life has never affected his duty. Unless you have concrete evidence to back your claim, this conversation is terminated.'

Briggs was furious with himself for his own judgment being usurped. He'd suspected Lincoln was brushing over some hidden agenda, but had no evidence of what it was. Weight loss and premature greying were not something you could attack a man for, especially one who'd gone through a horrendous tragedy. He smiled and softened his tone.

'So what have you got, Lieutenant? Does he roll ball bearings in his right hand, chastise the crew for leaving their shirt tails out, look for strawberries that aren't there?'

The Colonel was using the premise of a novel to make his point, and that whatever form of evidence he had on the Major wasn't nearly as damning. Instinct had little weight in a court martial.

'Well, what have you got?'

Arnie stood rigidly to attention, his unwavering eyes focused on the wall behind Briggs. He couldn't continue to go eye-to-eye with the Colonel without giving away the weakness of embarrassment.

'This officer wishes to retract his accusation, Sir, and accept the Colonel's reprimand, whatever form it takes. My judgment in this issue was wrong, and I beg for leniency. I am truly sorry.'

Colonel Briggs thought long and hard. There was more to this than he was willing to accept, but his instincts about Lincoln paralleled the young lieutenant's to some degree. He butted his cigarette with the deliberation of a judge banging a gavel. The sentence was handed out.

'Lieutenant Stonehawker, you will proceed to Loring as planned, but it will be the last flight you'll make with Major Crisp. Further to that, you will be seconded to the Air Force Academy in Colorado Springs, where for six months you will lecture on military protocol. I will put your transfer in writing and there will be no record of this meeting. Your age and inexperience shouldn't be a factor in your future. What you did here today was wrong, and you recognize that.'

He felt a wave of relief. The Colonel was a just man.

'Yes Sir, thank you, Sir, I'll never let poor judgment on my part tarnish a highly esteemed member of the United States Air Force again.'

'Lieutenant Stonehawker, you're dismissed.' With that,

Arnie snapped a salute, did an about-face, and left the room.

Colonel Briggs lit a cigarette and poured a coffee. His hands were shaking and he had trouble dialing the telephone.

Arnie picked up his kit in the hall. He felt lightheaded and headed for the can. Within ten minutes, his life had changed. His punishment was acceptable but his ambition to become a captain on the B-36 would never be realized. Why hadn't he used his evidence against the Major? Why hadn't he been forthright about what he'd overheard? The Major's ranting during the night and that afternoon had his ear to the wall. Most of what he'd heard had been gibberish but a few key phrases had set chills up his spine. What was going through the Major's mind? Whatever it was led him to his audience with the Colonel, and look what happened there, a career nearly thrown away.

He hitched a ride to the aircraft to relieve Hartwig of the copilot's responsibilities and get up to speed. The bomber was bathed in spotlights and the diminutive figures scrambling about cast darting shadows on the magnesium and aluminum skin of the cigar-shaped fuselage. He was in constant awe of the bomber's enormity, and still couldn't imagine that he himself could fly it up to 50,000 feet and carry two nuclear bombs thousands of miles.

Fuel trucks sat under the wings, pumping their contents up into the wing tanks with enough fuel to keep the monster aloft for sixteen hours. The flight engineer slid down the massive landing-gear strut with the skill of a logger, jumped off a tire of the four-wheeled landing gear bogie and was wiping his hands as Stonehawker was dropped off.

'What's up, Sergeant?'

'Fixed a small oil leak in number three, Sir. A couple of circuit breakers popped on the way here, but that's about all I found. I'm getting too fat to be crawling inside wings.'

'How was Lieutenant Chatterbox? Did he t-t-t-t-t-talk your ears off?'

'Surprised me a bit, Sir. Knew what he wanted addressed and how fast he wanted it. Sort of inversely proportional to his speech.'

'Anything else I should know about? Anything the Captain may have told you?'

'I haven't seen the Major since we landed; unusual for him. I've been his flight engineer on the last dozen trips he's flown, and this time he hasn't hounded me about nothing. Shit happened on the way over that he could have stomped on me for, but he never said a word.'

Suddenly, the side of the aircraft rippled as headlights strafed the forward fuselage and left wing.

'Here's the Major now.'

J osette clasped her hands over her mouth in disbelief, stifling a sneezer's urge to burst out laughing. If she had, she sensed she could kiss the dance goodbye. Standing before her and having no inkling of what her amazement was all about, stood Pappy Yokum wearing aviator glasses.

He waddled to the mirror for a look-see.

'What do you think? With your glasses on, I can never see expression in your eyes. You have to tell me, what do you think?'

'I look like Pappy Yokum for God's sake.'

'That's who you're supposed to look like. It's a Sadie Hawkins dance. Your waddle, err walk, looks cute.'

'Enough about the waddle; when can I take this bloody thing off?'

'I have to make a few adjustments.' Josette toyed around his ankles then adjusted the inside seam of his pants, working her way up the inside of his thigh, brushing the tip of his penis.

'I see you dress to the left.' She saw an instant response and slowly slid the back of her fingers from tip to scrotum. She pulled a pillow from the bed, kneeled on it and exposed the full length of his penis.

'I've not seen it head on in daylight. In all my years of

nursing, I've never seen a specimen as large and perfect as yours. Circumcision does you proud.'

She closed the blinds and removed her glasses. He stood transfixed as she removed her blouse and brassiere. She moved to her vanity and massaged oil between her breasts. She kneeled in front of him and looked up.

'I'm going to make love to you with my breasts, and my mouth. That's all. I'll tell you when you can ejaculate. If you disobey, you'll be punished. Close your eyes. I'm going to remove your glasses.'

She blindfolded him and had him stand to attention. He knew she was inches away, and the ache in the head of his penis told him that he was pumping blood towards it at a prodigious rate.

'I can't stand it; I'm going to go off.'

'You will stand it, and you won't go off.' She squeezed his testicles until all he could think about was pain.

'See, you're still in control.'

She raised herself, pointed his penis skyward, then pressed it between her breasts, grasping his buttocks and forcing herself into his belly. She squeezed her breasts with her upper arms, buried his member, then began rhythmic vertical thrusts, sending Duckwalker's vision into Technicolor.

She controlled him by tuning in on the intensity of his breathing. His urge to grasp and envelope her was overwhelming, but he'd been ordered to stand at attention and there he'd stay.

Duckwalker had never been taken to the edge and held there by fear, pain, and pleasure. Flying, yes, but sex, no. With an imagination on afterburner, he looked down and imagined her in color and light. Her hair was blond, then red, then chestnut brown, her finger nails fire-engine red. He saw the head of his penis emerging with each of her vertical thrusts. He wanted to rip the blindfold off.

She rose and kissed him, driving her breasts into his chest. He thrust into her with his pelvis but there was no response. There was to be no contact below her navel. She went down on her knees and took him in her mouth, and when it was time, she squeezed no more. She kissed him and he tasted himself.

She slipped up his strides as she rose, then turned away and dressed. Duckwalker was tongue-tied and his legs quivered and quaked.

'Keep your blindfold on and stand at attention,' she commanded.

'Holy shit, Sir, err Ma'am, what did you just do to me? I know what morphine did to my head, but it sure as hell wasn't as potent as that. I'm wiped. You're going to have to give me some nourishment, or I'm not going to be able to do my Pappy Yokum thing tonight.'

Josette produced a small bottle of cognac and lay back into a pile of pillows she'd arranged. She raised her skirt and dribbled cognac onto her panties.

'Dwayne, there's something I want you to do for me.'

The last time he'd been called Dwayne by a lover, it had come from Doris' lips. Her face became a vision, but as he pulled aside the crotch of Josette's panties, searching with his tongue for the taste of musky cognac, Doris Kemper's face and ten years of guilt and pain vanished.

Rylander had done his best to avoid Lou Fender, but with the advent of their forced confinement he knew the inevitable. He was lying on his bed, smoking and conjuring. There was a rap on the door, and he thought it was Lou Fender beating him to the punch. His heart shot to his throat but he was surprised to see "what's his name," the orderly officer, grinning like a Cheshire cat. With a quick look up and down the hall, he ushered him in.

'I've got the stuff for you. Your medicine.' The inflection in his statement was one of a pusher, not a nurse.

'How did you get the other key? To whom am I indebted?'

'You're only indebted to me. Two keys are required for the narcotics storage. This stuff isn't in that category. There wasn't much there, so this is all I can give you.'

Pete grasped the vial and felt relief. The sleeping bag in the B-25 might just get some action before the night was through. Rain pounding on aluminum was intoxicating to an intoxicated lover.

The orderly officer wasn't about to leave; a bellhop waiting for a tip. 'Thanks err, um.'

'It's Fred, Fred Malone.'

'Thanks, Fred. This means more to me than you know. You took a sizeable risk, and I'd like to pay you back somehow. If there's anything I can do for you, just let me know.'

Fred jumped in with uncharacteristic glee.

'I want to fly with you tomorrow. I'll see my boss tonight at the dance, and if she gives me the go-ahead, I'll make my way back from Chatham on my own. There's always some transport coming through. She shouldn't object. She really likes me. Aviation medicine is an emerging practice in the Air Force, and first-hand knowledge is critical in nursing. That's my sales pitch.'

Pete lit a cigarette, offered one, but Fred declined. He'd seen a few lungs from heavy smokers, and the thought of inhaling made him gag. Pete took a couple of drags, coughed, and contemplated.

'Okay,' he replied. There was just enough reluctance in his inflection to make his decision seem more valuable. 'But if she says no, then all bets are off. We'll be even. Head down to the equipment stores and rouse a safety tech. Get winter flying gear, an oxygen mask, parachute, and a survival pack. Have it all ready by the time we leave, and we'll welcome you aboard. But first, I have an orderly officer job for you.'

Fred flushed, grinned, and pumped Pete's hand.

'Thanks, Pete. This means a lot to me. What can I do?'

'I want you to find Flying Officer Fender and request that he meet me in the lounge at five this afternoon. Give him this; he'll understand what it means.'

With that, he passed Fred an American one hundred-dollar bill.

'If he says no, tell him he can keep it.'

As he was about to leave Fred turned and in earnest sincerity exclaimed, 'I won't get airsick, I promise.'

Pete arrived at the lounge early to stake out his lair, but Lou had beaten him to the punch. He hadn't spoken to him since their meeting in Yellowknife, and the man he now encountered looked vastly different. The scar was new, the eyes more hooded and the cheeks more creased. He'd thought Lou a brutally handsome man, and still felt intimidated by his look. Gone was the beaten pilot he'd last met and gone was the look of envy he'd tried to hide when they'd last parted.

Lou stood and they shook hands with the manner of two boxers meeting in center ring, eyeing the other to gauge who was the more uncomfortable.

'Lou Fender, as I live and breathe.'

'Those were the very words you used the last time we met,' he reminded sarcastically. They sat opposite in easy chairs, and each proceeded to light cigarettes without offering. For several uneasy seconds, no one spoke. The lounge was occupied by patrons enjoying the traditional Saturday cocktail hour, and Pete was satisfied they were out of earshot.

Lou set the one hundred-dollar bill on the coffee table, sat back, and folded his arms across his chest. He let the image of the bill steep long enough to make Pete squirm.

'The orderly officer said you wanted to see me. I suppose it has to do with that.' He pointed to the bill, and eyeballed Pete with an aggressive stare.

'Is that part of my share, or is that all that's left of my share? I reckon you and Wilding have decided to finally put the Rangoon fiasco to bed. Couldn't kill me, so you decided to ante up. Is that it?'

Pete took a deep drag and composed his pitch.

'To be perfectly honest Lou, I haven't any first-hand knowledge about what transpired between you and Wilding after I was hospitalized. I delivered the goods and then I got the shits. Whatever happened after that is a mystery to me. I have my suspicions, but they've never been verified.'

'Don't give me that shit, Rylander. The Colonel got blown up, the whole operation went sideways, and I was forced kill two innocent Japs. You and Wilding concocted a double-cross, and you put me in the crosshairs. You must have known what had happened, when all that was left of the operation were the remnants of one American colonel and two Jap aircraft. Didn't Wilding let you know?'

'Wilding disappeared. I suspected something was up when your demeanor did a one-eighty. Top secret, bullshit! I thought you were tougher than that. My hard evidence came from you ranting and raving while you slept on our trip home. You were delirious when you slept.'

'That was from lack of quinine and guilt, you asshole. Why didn't you bring the topic of Rangoon up when you ran into me in Yellowknife? Why is this happening seven years later? If you're making some attempt to get me out of the picture, why didn't you do it then? Why am I so important to you anyway? You and Wilding have the loot. What's my connection?'

'The shit hit the fan after Eggerton handed all the payoff money to Wilding for safekeeping. All two-hundred thousand, the whole kit and caboodle. His henchmen found out what the payout was, and apparently didn't think their risk was being rewarded enough. I only found out about this when Wilding contacted me after the war. He said that you had double-crossed us, and had organized the booby trap that killed the Colonel. He said you shot down the two aircraft to hide your involvement.'

'What! You've been tracking me all these years based on a lie. Wilding must have given you some type of proof.'

Pete pointed to the bill on the table.

'Wilding says you were paid my share before he made his disappearing act. Says you double-crossed us, and that our chances of getting anything from you were so remote that the only satisfaction we'd get is to kill you off. He's the one who set me up in this operation.'

Lou let out a deep sigh and shook his head.

'Your math's a little off.'

'How's that?'

'Six aircraft at twenty-five thou apiece comes to one-fifty. Who owns the other fifty?'

'Did I say two hundred?'

'You fucking asshole! You mean the whole set-up this weekend was to put me out of the picture so I wouldn't claim my share?'

'Yours and Tamaguchi's. His was the other fifty.'

How the fuck were you going to do it?'

'I was going to shoot you down.'

Lou let out a loud "what?" turning heads in his direction.

'I'm flying the most advanced interceptor in the world and you're flying a beat-up old bomber, and you're going to shoot me down? That's ridiculous.'

'Not so ridiculous if you realize that my aircraft is sporting lead attack radar and we're armed with two 50-caliber machine guns. In cloud we're equal.'

'This is the most convoluted bullshit I've ever heard.' Lou shook his head in disbelief. 'I'm willing to bet that one hundred-dollar bill there that you're packing around Wilding's share, your share, my share and Tamaguchi's share in that B-25 of yours. And I'm willing to bet Wilding is shitting bricks right now because you didn't have the brains to figure out that the weather conditions at low level on the Saguenay were going to do you in. I don't believe a fucking thing you've said. And for the record, I don't want, or will not accept one dime of your ill-gotten booty. You were a friend once, and I did my best to keep you alive, but as far as I'm concerned you're slime.' With that, Lou extracted himself and headed into the storm.

A sarcastic grin creased Pete's face.

'Now why did I think he would get suckered into believing that story? Wilding had to come up with a better one than that. He pocketed the bill and felt for the vial in his breast pocket. It was good policy to keep a weapon at hand. If he couldn't kill Lou Fender in the air, he could do it on the ground.

CHAPTER 20

The bomber was lit up like a night game at Yankee Stadium. Lincoln slipped from the jeep before it stopped and returned an overly dramatic and uncomfortable salute from Arnie Stonehawker.

'The aircraft's ready to fly, Sir. All inspections are complete. A couple of circuit breakers had to be re-set and a minor oil leak in number three's been patched, but that's about it.'

'Very good, Lieutenant. I'm going to do a little trouble-shooting on my own before we fire up. We're about to play war and I want this aircraft to complete its mission with impunity. We're going to see what Uncle Sam can throw at us. When I'm finished, you can assemble the crew for the usual chat. Have the engineer take my chute and bag to the cockpit.'

'Yes, SIR!'

Lincoln doffed his parachute and duffle bag and proceeded to the tail. He'd rarely visited the aft cabin and needed a refresher. He poked his head up through the hatch and smelled a combination of sweat and burnt coffee. The hours of boredom endured by gunners who rarely got to fire their 20-millimeter cannons would be shattered this night.

'Aircraft commander on deck.'

The gunners sat to attention at their battle stations. The quarters were cramped and Lincoln could only imagine the claustrophobia they'd experience when they were required to wear their parachutes while the bunks were in use. He inspected the toilet for cleanliness, complimented them on their teamwork on the flight over, and reminded them that they might be spending a portion of the flight on oxygen. As he backed against the auxiliary radio, he twisted the tuner dial, snapped it off and slid it into his pocket. He opened the hatch of the tunnel to the forward compartment and lay down on the trolley.

'Crew meeting on the tarmac in fifteen minutes with chutes on.' Hand-over-hand, he propelled himself through the tunnel, checking for stress-points in the skin. Satisfied with his discovery, he proceeded to the forward compartment. Sneaking in the back door was a clandestine approach to a snap inspection. He popped the hatch and slid out.

'Aircraft commander on deck,' a pimple-faced kid barked.

'Carry on with your checks. I'm just doing a little snooping.' He moved to the nose and placed a hand on the navigator's shoulder.

'Things may get a little tricky later on, Lieutenant Gidley. Don't be intimidated by uncertainty. You've been well trained or you wouldn't be here.'

Hartwig, kneeling beside the navigator and holding a checklist, backed into a circuit breaker panel and bumped his head.

'Make sure you didn't pop any of those, Lieutenant. Wouldn't want Stan here to miss his target.'

'S-S-S-S-Sorry, Sir. I'm kind of new to the job. This is my last station check. L-l-l-l-l-lieutenant Stonehawker l-l-l-l-let me finish the rounds. I'll be sitting in the back on the way home, so I'm grateful he l-l-l-l-let me spend some time up here. I haven't had a lot of pole time on the 36.'

'Follow me upstairs, Lieutenant. You can sit in on my pow-wow with the flight engineer. He's the one who really makes this monster fly. Without those R-4360's turning, this airplane won't move an inch.'

Hartwig sat in the commander's seat while Lincoln and the engineer conferred. Excluding the jet engines out at the ends of the wings, power changes were first applied at the engineer's station. The six throttles between the pilots' seats slaved to the engineer's station and were manually manipulated in sensitive weather.

He caressed all six throttles. It had been a while since his conversion course, and he felt inadequate and over-whelmed. Fuel for the stutterer. His visit was interrupted when Arnie popped up from below.

'Time to vacate, Lieutenant. Five gunners await at the ass end.'

Hartwig squeezed past and descended to the lower deck, relieved that the dolly in the tunnel was there. He lay on his back and propelled himself hand-over-hand through eighty feet of darkness. He wanted to pull the same stunt on the gunners that the Major had just pulled on him, but thought the better of it. He popped the hatch, pulled down a bunk and lay down. He outranked the five gunners, but they spotted a sprog in an instant. Green lieutenants were grist for the mill.

The gunners were dressed in full flying gear, with oxygen mask hoses flopping around like elephant trunks.

'I'm-m-m L-Lieutenant Hartwig. P-P-P-Please go about your d-d-duties.'

'Sorry, Lieutenant, but you'll have to vacate the premises. Muster's in five minutes. Full flying gear required. Remember to bring your chute.' One by one, they descended to the tarmac.

Hartwig felt a flush of humiliation. He fumbled in his kit for his oxygen mask, dragged his parachute from its stowage, awkwardly descended the ladder, and dropped his checklist. The complement of the crew had lined up at the nose and were checking each other's parachutes as he joined in. Lincoln approached him, made two tugs on Hartwig's parachute straps, and gave him a thumbs-up.

'There you are, Lieutenant, ready for action.'

'Th-th-thank you, Sir.'

The crew stood in two ranks, and Lincoln gave his pre-flight briefing. Teamwork and professionalism were repeated several times. They'd heard it all before.

He raised the bar.

'The flight to Loring is going to be conducted as if we were heading to the Soviet Union. You'll be on alert at all times, and you'll respond to any situation the interceptor boys and I throw at you. Gunners will be vigilant, the flight crew will be vigilant, and the aircraft may be pushed harder than you are used to. There's no pretense here. Lieutenant Wright, the weapons officer, will be evaluating all of us.

That includes me. Let's go flying. Lieutenant Stonehawker, dismiss the men.'

The crew split into two sections and disappeared up into the nose and tail hatches. Lincoln looked down the length of the fuselage and checked the fit of the bomb-bay doors as the rear ladder disappeared. Satisfied all were aboard, he ascended to the flight deck and strapped in.

For the next quarter hour, pages of checklists were ticked off and banks of vacuum tubes began to glow. The order was given to start engines, and one by one, the massive propellers churned the night air with exhaust gas and thunder. Lincoln received taxi-clearance, released the brakes, taxied to the end of the runway, and ordered Arnie to start the jets.

This night, they'd need all the power and runway they had.

'Aircraft commander to crew, prepare for takeoff.' He turned to the flight engineer. 'Give me full power, Sergeant.'

The engineer slowly advanced his six throttles and after fifteen seconds of agonizing engine checks, Lincoln released the brakes and the bomber began its inexorable roll.

Lieutenant Hartwig, braced in his crash position in the rear compartment, could only focus on the gunners huddling with their backs against the bulkhead. The plane slowly picked up speed.

Hartwig felt the floor fall away as the aircraft began its takeoff rotation. After what seemed like minutes, the aircraft lifted off, settled, then lifted off for good. Several thumps resonated through the fuselage as the main landing gear retracted into the wings. He felt the aircraft lift into the climb, and wished to God he was at the controls. His ears plugged as the compartment pressurized and he felt he was more in a submarine than the largest flying machine on earth.

'Wow. Th-th-that was an experience.' He yelled above the roar.

'You've never been in the back on takeoff, have you Lieutenant? You've never seen how the other half lives?'

They waited for his answer with jackal's grins.

'N-N-N-No, I haven't. It's q-q-q-q-quite an experience.' He rose to full height, banged his head again, and then lay on his cot. He was in hell, in a sardine tin, and Loring was a long way off.

Lincoln and the flight engineer tuned the engines for the climb and the vibration receded. He tapped his copilot on the shoulder.

'You have control, Lieutenant. Put on your mask, and take us up to 40,000. Lieutenant Gidley, Lieutenant Stonehawker requires a heading for Gander. He needs it in ten minutes or less.' He checked his watch and noted the time: 11:10 local. Ten minutes behind schedule.

It was time to crack the whip.

CHAPTER 21

Saturday 6:00 PM 2300 GMT

Duckwalker, Lou, and Pete had the misfortune of arriving for dinner at the same time, and as gentlemen, sat at the same table. They were dressed in civvies they'd extracted from flight bags stuffed with dirty underwear and socks, and looked as unsavory a lot as could be found, garnering stares like subjects in a sideshow. The dwarf, the strong-man, and the barker.

They complimented each other on their mutual sobriety, and promised they'd not mention the war, their injuries, the morning's cluster fuck, or their evil. They were gentlemen, speaking as gentlemen, in a gentlemanly manly way. Duckwalker broke the agreement between dessert and coffee.

'So you two were on Burma, huh? Now there's a theatre of war I'm glad I didn't have to fight in. How did you manage to get out alive? If the Japs or disease didn't get you, then a snake probably would. Or you'd end up marrying a Burmese beauty. Give me the good old European theatre any day, with its milk-white British maids, and a pub on every corner. What kind of action did you see?'

Lou and Pete glanced at each other.

'I thought we agreed, no history.'

'Come, come, gentlemen, how can three pilots, and one navigator I may add, not talk about the only thing we know anything about? What damage can be caused by that?'

Lou decided to say all he wanted and end the probe there.

'Pete and I flew Beaufighters in Burma at the end of the war. We never saw action and we never had the glorious privilege of killing any of our Japanese counterparts. We ferried aircraft and did a little escort duty for the supply drops. I was there for six months, and then the war ended. I was hoping for combat but it never materialized. That's about it. Pete?'

Pete offered cigarettes and a lighter.

'The only reason I was there was because I was sick of flying out of Tofino on Vancouver Island. I was a second-dickey on a Catalina. They used to make us fly in shit that a maggot couldn't crawl through. I just wanted to fly VFR and see what the war was all about. Low and behold, they send me to the monsoon capital of the word. I couldn't fly worth shit 'til Scarface here took me under his wing. I couldn't have cared less for action; bit of a chicken when it comes to that sort of thing. Flying in cloud's my strength, except you wouldn't have known it by my stupidity this morning. And that's all I'll say about that. Now what's your story? You don't look like a shining beacon of masculinity.'

Duckwalker had dodged the question of his stature and sunglasses more times than he could remember, and the lie had become so much the truth that he had begun to believe it himself.

'I was on 433 Squadron flying Lancasters out of Skipton in the spring of '45. A motorcycle that had been passed around the squadron came up for grabs. I bought it off a pilot who'd finished his tour, and I used it to meet a lady I was hot for. She'd come from up from London and I'd meet her halfway. I was on my way back to base when I met with an accident. Blackouts are a bitch when you have no headlights. I convalesced in England and was repatriated in early '46.'

'If you were a pilot, why the hell would you want to be a navigator?' Pete inquired. 'What's that all about?'

Duckwalker reeled off the history of his post-war education and re-enlistment, pausing to answer queries about his ability in the back seat, and what the effectiveness of the next generation of the interceptor's radar would be. Pete expounded on the virtues of the MG-2 fire-control system that equipped his B-25.

Lou sat mute, wishing he was in bed with Darlene. He smoked and sipped coffee and let the two of them jabber on as visions of her blanked out any interest in the topic at hand.

"What the hell has she done to me," he thought, "and where does it go from here?" He checked his watch and rose.

'As Groucho Marx said, "Hello, I must be going." I'll run into you tonight at the dance. I'll be the one dressed as Li'l Abner, if you want to say hello.'

'You haven't a thing on me,' responded Duckwalker. 'Pappy Yokum is at your service. Will you be there, Pete?'

'I might show up. I hear there's a couple of nursing sisters who have a penchant for Scotch. It's going to be tough having to stay sober, but the law's the law.'

Lou and Duckwalker departed, leaving Pete to confer with his navigator and copilot.

'There's a social event here tonight, boys, but I'm ordering you to bed. Dan, you've got the shits, and Archer, you need the rest. Tomorrow's a big day. We're heading up the coast to eavesdrop on our American brethren, and I need you to be sharp. Wheels in the well by eight. I might need our steed tonight, so nobody's sleeping there.'

They shook their heads in disbelief.

'Captain, for God's sake, let us in on your secret!'

Duckwalker tore the envelope stuck to his door and phoned Josette. Her tone was authoritative.

'Flight Lieutenant Jones, you will accompany me to the dance tonight as we agreed, but I will not be in any position to bid for you in the auction. It would be inappropriate for a senior officer to show an interest in a junior officer, especially one who is new on base. One of my subordinates will bid on my behalf, so don't be too alarmed. We'll hook up at an appropriate time.'

Duckwalker felt the unease of being used.

'Ma-am, I agreed to accompany you on the basis that we'd spend the evening with Lou and Darlene. Is that still a given?'

'Of course. I just can't be seen as cavorting with strangers.'

'Yes Ma-am.'

'Was that a hint of sarcasm in your voice, Flight Lieutenant?'

'Yes, Ma-am. Shall I meet you at the mess, or shall I escort you from your quarters?'

'The mess at seven-thirty, Flight Lieutenant Jones.'

Duckwalker knew he'd never touch her again. There was no way she would even be caught dancing with him. She'd be humiliated. She'd made a perfect exit. Like the rest.

All except Doris.

If Josette was off limits, that left some horny senior officer's wife as a target, but the second the orderly officer caught him ten feet from one, it was off to the hoosegow. He reminisced about the last day. They'd made love once at night, and once in daylight, and that was that.

He looked at the outfit hanging on the door and burst into laughter. Genuine laughter. Knee-slapping laughter.

"What a crazy fucking weekend. It's all over the place. The storm. Josette. The revelation. The intercept. The sex. All to end up looking like Pappy Yokum."

He put on his outfit, waddled in front of the mirror, and cracked up so hard he nearly crapped his pants.

Lou did not intend to dress in costume and parade through the storm to the mess like Frankenstein's monster. The whole dance thing was new to him. Everything social was new to him.

All there'd ever been was flying and fishing and hunting. His father had been a bush pilot, and Lou learned to fly by the time his head came above the instrument panel. Schooling was by correspondence and any form of social life was a hundred miles away.

His father gave him a 30:30 hunting rifle and a shotgun when he was twelve. He'd asked for a BB gun for Christmas and was rewarded with a couple of cannons. He hunted moose, ducks, and prairie chickens in the fall, and shot skeet from his rudimentary range year round. Those who knew him said he could shoot professionally, but his father was his life, and until it was time to leave he was his best friend.

His mother never existed. Not to his memory. When he was nineteen he joined the Air Force, more to get out of northern Manitoba than to help win the war. He'd magically matriculated and was selected for pilot training.

'You're nineteen and you've logged two hundred hours,' the recruiting officer had exclaimed. 'Sign here, boy.'

Lou was as hick as Li'l Abner, which was the irony of the outfit. Women had always been ones to fear. His mother had abandoned his father when he was two, and his previous two loves had abandoned him, and every relationship thereafter had ended with a door slammed in his face.

'You don't know how to love, Lou Fender, and you never will,' had been their bugle call of retreat. There was sex when it was purchased, but intimacy was never part of the act.

Then, in a thunderstorm in Québec, he falls in love and nearly kills himself. All this within a day.

He knew that Darlene was one not to be feared. She'd stroked his scar with a touch of anointment. He would be with her until his grave.

But there was a bond greater than love: the bond of blood. What he hadn't disclosed was that there was Métis on his mother's side and for the first time in his life he felt the instinct to mate.

He'd hunted deer and moose during the rutting season, and he knew that bucks were at their most vulnerable because they went stupid. He gathered his costume and beat his way through the storm to the mess. Darlene was waiting.

Pete arrived at the mess early, setting up a blind to vet the incoming flux of characters. Wives had invested time and material on outfits that befitted their husbands' physicality and rank and he recognized the CO, the OC of 440 Squadron and the crew who'd guided them in that morning. The lounge had been transformed into Dogpatch, and a band played hoedown music. A rotund master of ceremonies dressed as Marryin' Sam heralded each couple as they entered, and the clapping grew in intensity as the lounge filled up.

Suddenly the room went silent.

Li'l Abner and Daisy Mae entered arm-in-arm, and as if coned in a searchlight pattern. Lou froze in his tracks as a hush came over conversation. Following close behind was a waddling Pappy Yokum on the arm of a voluptuous Stupefyin' Jones. The crowd rewarded the two women with cheers and applause as they were escorted to their pigsty.

Pete couldn't take his eyes off Darlene. She moved with aristocratic grace and emoted with a familiarity that triggered déjà vu. With Lou as her escort, she'd be off limits and he concentrated on two young women dressed as Moonbeam McSwine and Sadie Hawkins. They had to be the nurses, and he focused on Moonbeam McSwine and her stuffed pig.

She was his target.

He felt the vial and the rush in his loins that preceded the hunt. He slipped out the back and headed to the Snake Pit for a smoke and a Coke. What he wouldn't give for a

Scotch and soda. Dan Lacey and Fred Archer were into a poker game, and he found an empty corner where he could plan his hunt.

By 8 PM, the men were being auctioned off, and every now and then he'd hear cheers and applause as a wife paid for her husband. He was about to peek in on the proceedings when a wet Fred Malone rushed breathlessly towards him.

'I got all the flying gear you suggested, Pete. Here's hoping my boss will let me go.'

'You did all that without getting her okay?'

'No use getting the go-ahead without a parachute.' He grinned. 'I'll find some way to twist her arm.'

Pete looked into the lounge and spied his target.

'What can you tell me about the one holding the pig?' Fred scanned the room and spied his colleague.

'That's the hot one. She's a nurse straight out of Central Officers' School; still thinks a corporal outranks her. She's a great nurse but a little loose when it comes to you know what. I tried to date her but she says she has a boyfriend. She's been here three months and I've never seen her so much as wet her whistle with anything weaker than a glass of wine at dinner. She's as cute as a bug's ear. I couldn't get anywhere with her, but then again, I'm not a pilot.'

Like a vampire smelling blood on a bare neck, Pete began to salivate. The weekend was not a total bust. He had the locale, the prey, and the ammunition. It would be like shooting fish in a barrel.

———————

M i c h a e l   N i x o n

Darlene paid thirty dollars for Lou, and he was relieved to be taken off the market. He became uneasy as each bid for him went higher, and strange voices kept pushing up the price. The one dressed as Sadie Hawkins was the most aggressive, and he kept looking to Darlene with want after each round of bidding, hoping she would up the ante. When it became obvious that there was a bottomless pit of money backing him, the potential purchasers backed off, and Darlene claimed her prize.

Lou stepped from the stage weak-kneed and acknowledged the crowd's applause with a sheepish resignation of one who'd been captured and hogtied. Next up to the guillotine was Duckwalker Jones.

Duckwalker waddled onto the stage, and was captured by the spotlight. He shied from the light and struck his highest pose. Those who knew nothing of his affliction hooted and cheered at his ability to stay in character. With his false chin beard, heavy rope belt, lace boots, and aviator glasses he became the spectacle of the evening. He looked for Josette but she was gone and when the bidding started only the two nurses were left. To his horror, Sadie Hawkins was the successful bidder.

She introduced herself as Bonnie Hart. He escorted her to their lair, where he proceeded to explain that his waddle and sunglasses were not part of his costume. He evaded the usual questions, and discreetly looked for Josette. He needed an explanation of why he'd been discarded, and where he was to go from there. He knew the intimacy of their relationship was dead, but like a freshly weaned puppy he needed her maternal companionship to keep him in his comfort zone. Young women frightened him, and he was tongue-tied for conversation.

At first glance, Sadie Hawkins had all the characteristics of her namesake, but on closer inspection, he realized that she was a well-disguised cutie who had the confidence to mock herself. She hailed from Victoria, where she'd received her training at St. Joseph's Hospital. She'd joined the Air Force in hopes of seeing the world, but had ended up in northern Québec on her first posting. Their conversation was awkward and disjointed at first but she put him at ease with soft-spoken assertiveness that all nurses seemed to possess.

Bonnie's partner, dressed as Moonbeam McSwine, smoked, drank and peppered Duckwalker with questions about his sudden appearance on base, and why he looked the way he did, forcing him to ask Bonnie to dance. The band had struck up the resemblance to "Some Enchanted Evening" and he escorted her to the floor, holding onto her with the trepidation of an art curator receiving a Ming vase.

'I'm not a dancer, but I needed to get away from her. Questions that can't be answered have been a part of my life for years.'

'Marie can be a bit of a gossip, if you let her go on,' she whispered. 'Thank you for asking me to dance. I can see it must be difficult for you.'

'No, thank you for buying me. I don't think I could have stood the whole evening with her. May I ask you a personal question?'

'Of course.'

'Did your boss put you up to this? Buying me, that is?'

She pulled him in, and let the moment and the music frame her answer.

'Yes, and I'm grateful she did. She said you were brilliant, that you had a flawed body, and that you had the most wonderful personality. How could I not respond to that? I meet all kinds and they all have the same objective. Officers can only date officers and I'm rather picky. Now, my nursing sister partner sitting over there has a different point of view. Marie is the nurse that every male fantasizes about. That's not me.'

'What else did Squadron Leader Gerard tell you about me?'

'She said that if I used my training, I might find out why you wear those sunglasses all the time and why you walk the way you do. She wouldn't say what she knew, only that if I discovered the reason for your appearance, I would most likely fall in love with you. First, you have to take off that ridiculous beard.' He winced as she stripped it off.

'There, now I can see what you look like.'

'My God. You women pass around the goodly gen, don't you?' The music stopped, and they waited for the next piece but it turned out to be a jive. With a look of resignation, he escorted her back to the settee.

Marie resumed her banter, nervously casting the gaze of a wallflower looking for a suitor. The stranger with an angelic face and piercing eyes who she'd passed by on her way to the ladies' room was staring at her from the lobby. She turned away and felt flushed as she sensed his imminent approach.

'Excuse me, Miss McSwine,' Pete interjected, 'but I understand that your social status in Dogpatch is rather dubious. I myself come from Hogtown, some call it Cabbagetown, so we have something in common. My name is Peter Rylander. May I buy you a drink?'

Fred Malone felt he'd become the catalyst in a great drama. He'd altered the speed of the social intercourse being played out, but was himself unchanged. What Squadron Leader Gerard had meted out as punishment placed him center stage in a play that had no definitive course of action. His position as orderly officer gave him a playwright's role and he was about to exercise it.

The two crews who'd arrived out of thin air had become the central characters of a drama on a weekend that he thought he'd been sent to purgatory. It had been far from that. He had the goods on his boss and he was about to get payback.

He discovered Josette alone in the dining room, nursing a coffee. He filled a cup from the steaming urn and she didn't look happy when he asked to join her.

'I have a request of you, Ma-am.... I'm hoping you'll say yes.'

Josette looked out of place in her costume and he felt a stirring as he stared into her cleavage.

'What is it, Malone?'

'I've a chance to fly with the crew who flew in on the B-25 this morning. They're heading east tomorrow to do some skulking, then returning to Chatham. I've been given the okay to go with them, provided you find somebody to take my place, and that I have the appropriate safety equipment. Now, all I need is your okay.'

'My okay! Now what would make me change my mind and rescind my order? You deserved your punishment. You might want to get help with your addiction to the turn of a card or the flip of a coin. You're a good nurse, but if you gamble for money, one day you'll gamble with somebody's life. I won't stand for it, not in my hospital.'

'Your message was received and understood, Ma-am. I promised you that it wouldn't happen again. Your punishment was out of line. The orderly officer should be aircrew, not a nurse. I'm a fish out of water. There's been stuff going on that I haven't a clue about, and I feel like a fool.'

'What could be going on in this weather that puts you out of place or makes you feel awkward?'

'You know what's going on, Ma-am. We've been visited by two strange crews who we know nothing about, and suddenly things have changed for all of us. Miss Muncie and you included. The orderly officer gets to see and hear things that others might not notice.'

Josette felt a twinge of vulnerability, masking it with a deliberately forced stare into Malone's eyes. Was the gambler bluffing? Did he know about her relationship with Darlene? Did he have a winning hand?

'So you've unearthed a few secrets, have you Malone? Secrets that give you an upper hand. Secrets that you could blackmail me with. Do you know what accusations against a senior officer can get you?'

'It can get me what I want, Ma-am.'

'It can get you booted out of the service, that's what it can get you.' Malone had heard enough and decided to show his hand.

'Ma-am, I'm a nurse, just like you. I have rank, just like you. I don't fly, yet I'm a flying officer. You're a squadron leader, but you don't lead a squadron. Seems kind of silly doesn't it? If I get the boot for my lack of protocol, I'll still be a nurse, and a good one by your standards. I gamble, and you have other interests that this man's Air Force frowns upon. All the same, we're nurses, and that's what really counts. You run a tight hospital and I bow to your experience, but don't you think it's a little hypocritical that I'm being punished for what's going on this very minute in the Snake Pit? The navigator and copilot from the B-25 are cleaning out two Sabre pilots who haven't a clue they're being cheated.'

Josette began to tear up and Fred offered her his handkerchief. She shook her head and took stock. Alone, wearing a provocative outfit while being blackmailed by a junior officer was not what she envisioned for the evening. She had set in motion a plan to have Darlene and Lou to herself, in bed and private, and the only way she'd be able to fulfill it was to grant his wish. She'd find an excuse to discharge him of his duty, then find his replacement.

'It seems you have me at a disadvantage, nurse Malone.' Her emphasis on the word "nurse" put him at ease. She was addressing him as an equal.

'You'll continue your duties until 2359, at which time you'll report to the infirmary where you will lance a carbuncle on a child's abdomen. Once you've completed the procedure, you're free. I want you back at the hospital no later than 0800 on Tuesday. If you're not here by then, you'll be considered AWOL, and our deal is out of my hands. Don't ever try this tactic with me again. Now get the hell out of my sight!'

'Yes Ma-am, and thank you, Ma-am.' He headed to the

lounge to find Pete and give him the news. He was going flying in the morning.

Josette dabbed tears and composed herself. If Malone knew of her indiscretions, then who else knew? She thought she'd covered her tracks, but the dalliance with the cripple had been a mistake. He'd only been a puzzle meant to be solved, but when she'd sneaked into Darlene's room this morning, she'd been careless. Had Malone seen her or did he already know? Girls talk.

It was the other one she'd been attracted to: the one with the scar and the brooding eyes, the one who Darlene had fallen for, the one she sensed was broken far worse than Dwayne Jones. From the instant his grip had steadied her in the lobby she couldn't believe his resemblance to the only man she'd ever loved, the man who she'd arranged charred pieces together and escorted to his place of burial. She'd marched the slow march, his hat sitting on the wet Red Ensign that draped his coffin. Only she could see what others could imagine. Dead pilots were only whole in memory.

She'd managed to dump the cripple on Bonnie, and had set things up with Darlene for a late-night rendezvous. "Stupefyin' Jones" was not just a costume for the dance; it was the image she wanted to evoke, for him, and for her.

Pete was at the bar ordering a second set of drinks when he was confronted by Fred Malone. 'The boss has given me the okay, Pete. I'm with you 'til Chatham. When do we take off?'

'How the hell did you pull that off?'

'I told you she liked me. I have to be back here on

Tuesday. That should give me enough time to pick up a flight back.'

'Hey, a deal's a deal! If it's okay with her, it's okay with me. Wheels in the well by 0730. You got your gear?'

'It's in the operations room. I'll go and stash it in the aircraft right away.'

'Don't go inside the aircraft. That's an order. Leave your gear wrapped in a tarp underneath, and I'll get a crewmember to store it. Sometimes crewmembers sleep there, and I don't want them disturbed. We don't get enough sack time as it is.'

'Thanks Pete, this means a lot to me. And I promise I won't get airsick.' He gave Pete a wink, and headed off.

The vial in Pete's breast pocket was unopened. He hurried to the lounge with his Coke and Marie's second double Scotch. Her first double had been drained before he could administer his potion. How many drinks she'd consumed before their introduction was speculative, but by all accounts she could handle her liquor. If she was a boozer, what effect would the Mickey Finn have on her? He'd always dealt with virgin drinkers who'd succumbed to the same dosage. At this juncture, what he would need to get her into the B-25 was speculative. She slurred a hello as he sat down, and he made a mental calculation on the dosage. The sleeping bag in the bombardier's tunnel awaited.

CHAPTER 22

Lincoln was humming the musical score from the movie "The High and the Mighty." He'd turned down the lights in the instrument panel, and drank in the universe. It had a different intensity this night, and he surmised it was what all doomed men see when they gaze skyward for the last time. Battlefields had a billion final visions of the heavens that only God had access to.

Arnie and Stan had taken them at altitude and on course with only a moderate amount of fuck-ups. At this altitude, the aircraft had the density of a balloon and with the potential of a rivet-pop, a rapid decompression could occur, so one pilot was always on oxygen.

Lincoln had given Arnie the gears throughout the climb and made him don his oxygen mask so he couldn't curse without being heard on the intercom. Lincoln knew all the tricks.

The domed greenhouse canopy of the bomber gave the illusion of being in a planetarium, and the true navigators relished plying their ancient trade with a crystal-clear universe to work with. The aircraft flew slowly enough, so as to allow the diehards to match their skills against the technology of the day.

There were too few true navigators plying the heavens

these days, he thought. They'd become bombardier and interceptor navigators. They'd learn a little of celestial navigation in their training, but it would be quickly eclipsed by the electronic marvels of the age.

Their current track was a great-circle route that would take them over the North Atlantic, Newfoundland, the Cabot Strait, with a descent over New Brunswick and into Loring Air Force Base. The chatter from the GCI sites and the interceptors attacking the bomber stream ahead of them was sporadic due to the atmospheric ionization, so he had difficulty gauging the success of the exercise. The throb of the engines and the subdued banter from the crew pacified Lincoln into a calm, reflective melancholy. The first half of the flight would be uneventful. They were a weapon platform advancing towards a target, alone, unreachable, and lethal.

Lincoln turned to the nuclear officer sitting in the jump seat, and pointed to the hatch leading down to the radio room. It was time to talk.

'You're the boss Arnie. Lieutenant Wright and I will be below for a while.' Arnie nodded, and Lincoln followed Kenny below, ordering the two gunners and the radio operator to the rear compartment for a coffee and bathroom break. After the trolley had whisked the radio operator down the tube, they were alone and secure.

Lieutenant Wright was bursting with curiosity.

'What the hell are we carrying, Major? I didn't get whisked over here under cover of darkness for no good reason. I'm a nuclear officer. The squadron's carrying dummies, aren't they?' Lincoln pulled the young lieutenant nose-to-nose by his lapels, and with the voice of doom, laid out the situation.

'We're not carrying a dummy.'

'Not carrying a dummy, Sir? What the hell are we carrying?' Lincoln released his grip.

'What do you know about a nuclear test the Limeys had last year at Emu in Australia?'

Wright gazed out the gunners' observation bubble, and recalled the film and briefing on the incident.

'You're referring to Totem One. I recall it was a twelve kiloton blast that didn't come off too good. The Brits wanted to test plutonium from their commercial reactors to see if they could make their bombs cheaper. The plutonium-239 was contaminated with more plutonium-240 than they thought, but the test worked.'

'Then you know what the results were?'

'The fallout, so to speak, wasn't what they expected. The test was put together too quickly, they picked the wrong weather, and the radioactive cloud drifted over an Aboriginal settlement, causing considerable sickness and blindness. The cloud was so hot they had to scrap the aircraft that flew through it to measure the fallout. It was a disaster all around. But what's that got to do with us?'

'We're carrying one of the bombs they built using the shit-grade plutonium. We're the trash man. We're taking it to the nuclear storage facility at Loring for a checkup, then you and I will escort it to Carswell. What they do with it after that is no concern of ours.

'Why the hell is it going Stateside?'

'They need to explode it in a different locale with different meteorological conditions. Plus, we've got more experience in blowing the fucking things up. The Brits weren't satisfied with the measurements they got, and the Australians had enough of them polluting their turf, so they kicked them out.'

'So that's why there was so much difficulty loading the bomb bay. I thought it was strange that I wasn't allowed near the aircraft 'til the bomb bay doors were closed. How'd they make it fit?'

'Their bomb is the same shape and size as the one we dropped on Nagasaki, but a few minor adjustments had to be made. Have you ever had to change the oil in a British sports car? You have to practically drop the engine out. Not to mention their electronics. You were brought over in case there was a problem, but the Brits were able to slip it into the bomb bay without too much hullabaloo. Any time we transport a hot one we're obliged to have somebody like yourself along. You obviously know your shit.'

'So that's why our call sign is Trashcan. Does anyone else on the plane know about this?'

'No, we brought a Mark IV over so the Limeys can have a full complement. Maybe they'll learn from our simplicity. The nuclear officer who flew with us on the way over is staying with it. The Brits have only a couple of A-bombs, and they were counting on the one we're carrying to keep themselves dangerous.'

'So what's the status of the one we're carrying? Surely it doesn't have any electronic triggering attached?'

'We've been assured that it's been rendered inert.'

'It's inert unless something catastrophic happens to it on the way home. You know what happened over the Queen Charlotte Islands when 075 was lost in 1950. They thought the fucker had crashed into the sea, but no wreckage was found. There should have been at least something floating about. They found it last year on a mountain-top fifty miles south of the Alaska border. Luckily, they had a Mark IV bomb on board with a removable core. Without the core inside, they were able to detonate the explosive shell before it hit the water. Risky business we're in, Sir.'

'I know all about it. I also know that weather was the major contributor to the loss. I fly these things, Lieutenant. The engines let them down, not the crew. Thank God they were smart enough to bail out over the island. When the carburetors ice up, the engines run rich and burn like a blow torch.'

Lincoln knew everything about the crash in British Columbia. The loss of the bomb was not the first Broken Arrow. The removable plutonium core had saved American and Canadian asses on a half-dozen occasions. The core of the bomb they were now carrying sat in the center of a high explosive hemisphere thirty feet behind them in the freezing vacuum of 40,000 feet.

'What can I do to help with the mission, Sir?'

'You can go to the rear compartment for a shit and some sack time. Send the dolly back for me. I want to do a structural inspection in the tube. Nothing serious. I thought I saw a rivet pop when I slid through this morning.'

Lincoln helped Wright into the tube and watched until he reached the far end. The rear compartment bulkhead door closed, and within a minute, he pulled the trolley back. He entered the tube feet first, and with flashlight in hand, worked his way back to the center of the tunnel. There, he found the overlapping seam in the skin. He chiseled the two pieces apart with his survival knife, and soon the nasty hiss of escaping air heralded the breach. Satisfied the rate of loss wouldn't cause any further separation, he tugged himself back to the forward compartment, cut the cord that propelled the dolly, and closed the hatch. Within minutes, an alarm would signify a pressure loss in the tube, isolating the rear compartment. It made little difference. Without the trolley line, mobility between the compartments was near impossible. "Divide and conquer," he thought to himself. Ten crewmen were cut off. He had only to deal with the three forward crewmen.

Lincoln ascended to the flight deck and strapped in. He'd disposed of four forward crewmen with a magician's sleight of hand, and felt smug.

Arnie Stonehawker broke the spell.

'We've got a pressure loss in the tunnel, Major. I noticed it a couple of minutes ago, but I thought it was because of the differential pressures in the two compartments with the bulkhead doors opening and shutting at different times. Both doors indicate they're sealed but there's still a drop. It's definitely a leak, a slow leak; either way you look at it the tunnel's out of service 'til we're below 12,000 feet.'

'Aircraft commander to crew. The tunnel's U.S. Repeat, the tunnel's unserviceable.'

Lincoln was satisfied of his sabotage. The rate of discharge in the tunnel was slow enough to keep his plan intact.

'Good eyes, Lieutenant. If it becomes a problem, we'll decompress and I'll send you back with a mouthful of Double Bubble to patch the hole.' He looked ahead into the dark.

'You're helming a true and steady course, Stonehawker. Moments like this are what make you. You're a good pilot. I'll take over in an hour, and you can head to the basement to have a look-see over Lieutenant Gidley's shoulder. I'm going to throw him a few knuckleballs.'

At the rate Marie was drinking Scotch, Pete couldn't determine the amount of chloral hydrate he'd need to control her. He didn't want to drug her too early. Vacating the premises with a drunk early in the evening had pitfalls for both parties. It had happened once, and it would never happen again. Too many questions were asked on that one. For now, it was a wait and see. He asked her to dance, so he could take stock of her physique, and was pleased with the results. Firm and full-figured. He attempted a few feels of her derriere and she didn't flinch. She wasn't wearing a panty-girdle so he attributed it to numbness from booze, but she was too steady of foot and voice, and so he began to fear her.

They danced and she yakked on about nursing.

'The surgeon is an asshole and the head nurse is a bitch and an out-and-out lesbian.'

'Whoa there mister!' she exclaimed as his probing became too free. 'We just met.' Pete pulled away with an apology.

The band struck up another slow dance, and he invited her to keep the floor. She melted into him, grasped the back of his neck, and pulled herself up and into him.

'I like you, but I don't fuck on the first date. It's the

nurse in me. Take care of me tonight and I'll take care of you tomorrow. You're staying for a while, aren't you?'

'No, actually, I'm heading up the coast and back to Chatham early tomorrow. This isn't one of those "I'm off on a mission and maybe I won't return" excuses, but I do have to fly in the morning. Who knows when I'll get back here?'

'Too bad, but your sincerity will get you no sympathy. We weren't destined to be lovers. You're a great dancer, so we can always have a little fun on the dance floor.'

The music stopped, and they joked about needing to visit the restroom at the same time. They passed Lou arm-in-arm with an alluring Daisy Mae. Pete and Darlene made eye contact.

A sudden look of horror came over her, and in a flash, she collapsed into a faint.

'Cherie, mon Dieu!' Josette screamed from the staircase. Lou picked her up and carried her into the ladies' room where he placed her in a lounge chair.

'Out, Flying Officer Fender! I'll take care of her now.' She wet a towel and bathed Darlene's forehead and neck.

'What is it Cherie, what's the matter? You look like you saw a ghost.'

Darlene's eyes darted to and fro, and her touch was cold and clammy.

'It's him!'

'It's who? What are you talking about? Who's him?'

'It's him, the one with the eyes. The one I've been hunting for.'

'The one who raped you?'

'It's him, I know it!'

Josette settled Darlene with soothing applications of touch and encouragement. She'd known about Darlene's quest from the start of their affair, but she'd secretly questioned its validity. Her reaction had more than enough strength to back her claim.

'Did he recognize you?'

'If he did, he'd be gone by now. See if he's still there. If he is, I want Lou to take me back to barracks.'

'What about Lou? What should I say?'

'He's never to know. Say that my blood sugars are low.'

Josette emerged from the ladies' room to find Lou pacing and smoking. Pete Rylander, loitering about and holding a set of drinks, gave Lou a wink and a nudge.

'Wearing too much aftershave old boy? It can have that effect on a country girl.' Josette stared Pete down and he retreated into the lounge. She turned to Lou.

'She's okay, Flying Officer Fender. This weekend has been a little overwhelming for the dear thing. All she's been doing all day is talk about you and sew, sew, sew. She hasn't eaten anything since breakfast. I want you to escort her to the dining room. Make sure she eats. No more alcohol for her tonight.' She returned to the ladies' room to comfort Darlene.

'Cherie, you have to be strong. The officer in question is still here so it looks like he doesn't remember you. We have the upper hand. Lou is going to take you for some dinner. I'll keep an eye on whoever he is.' When she emerged, Lou gave Darlene a squeeze of encouragement, and escorted her up to the dining room.

'You're lucky to have a friend like her, Darlene. She

takes good care of you. Now, I want to take good care of you.'

Darlene felt torn apart and she sat in a stupor as Lou put a plate of food in front of her.

'Josette says you're to eat or it's off to bed. You don't want to ruin a couple of great costumes do you? I hear we've been nominated for best couple. This is one time I'm not afraid of being in the limelight.'

Darlene's food tasted like sawdust and she half drained a pitcher of water to ease it down. Years of searching were over. Her prey resided no more than a hundred feet away and only she and Josette knew his identity.

Her objective was to keep it that way. She'd decided that a confrontation was out of the question. There had to be a way to extract her revenge without blowing her cover. First and foremost she had to make sure that nobody at the dance was in his sights.

'Have you seen the nurse with the pig? The one dressed like Moonbeam McSwine? Her name's Marie. I need to talk to her.'

'Eat up and we'll go on a nurse-hunt.' As Darlene forced down her food, Lou took stock of her physique. She seemed too vulnerable and disjointed for somebody with hypoglycemia.

'Is something bothering you, besides the fact that your sugars were in your boots? Like maybe I'm coming on too strong. I'll pull back if you want. Take things a little slower.'

'Oh no, it's not you. I just had a small fainting bout from a lack of nourishment.'

'I know what you mean. I went face-first into the tarmac on a couple of Wings Parades. I was a natural fainter. It was usually from an empty stomach and heat. Don't feel bad. Take your time and we'll go find your friend.'

Pete decided to strike early. Who knew how drunk Marie would get as the evening progressed? He picked the drinks off the bar, hurried to the bathroom, and took the vial from his pocket. He felt the rush as he dripped the correct amount for her weight and alcohol intake. He added an extra drop for good measure, and headed back to the lounge. It would be her last double Scotch of the evening. The sleeping bag in the B-25 would see action on this night.

As he passed Lou in the lobby, a furtive glance in the direction of Daisy Mae induced a feeling of déjà vu. Her sudden collapse startled him. A smart-alec comment to Lou and a scold from Stupefyin' Jones hastened him to his target.

Marie was on the dance floor with Marryin' Sam, and Pete waited impatiently as she cavorted through two dances. She bounced off pairs of dancers on her return, sat down with a plop, took a swig of Scotch, and fanned her flushed face. Pappy Yokum and Sadie Hawkins were still on the dance floor, making it a perfect time for their escape.

'Whew, I'm getting a little hot and a little drunk,' Marie slurred. 'I think I should get some air. Drunk nurses have been known to get themselves into trouble.'

'It's probably a good idea. The night is still young. Let's finish these drinks, and I'll take you outside for a breather. I wouldn't mind a smoke. By the way, have you ever been inside a Second World War bomber? We could go for a walk in the rain and I could show you my office.'

'Take me to see your etchings is probably more like it.'
She drained her glass and stood awkwardly.

'I'll borrow a couple of raincoats from the cloak room.'
He gripped her, and she bounced off him a couple of times
before gaining some semblance of balance as they weaved
through the throng of dancers.

'Easy pickings,' he muttered as they exited the mess.
'Easy pickings.'

Lou scoured the lounge for Marie, and Darlene checked
the ladies' room, but she'd disappeared.

'I need to find her, Lou. She's probably drunk and when
she gets drunk she gets silly. If she's gone outside in this
weather, who knows where she'll end up.'

'Is she with anybody? Maybe she's gone outside for fresh
air and a smoke.' He cornered Duckwalker and Bonnie on
the dance floor, but they hadn't seen her leave.

'The last we saw her, she was with that Rylander fellow.
She'd definitely had a few.'

Lou was willing to throw in the towel and relax, but he
could see genuine worry on Darlene's face when he told
her that she might be with Pete Rylander.

'I'll have the orderly officer check her quarters,' was the
best he could offer. He wasn't enthusiastic about ruining
the evening just to look for a drunken nurse. He found
Fred Malone in the Snake Pit playing solitaire.

'Fred, I need you to check on one of your sisters. Seems
Marie has flown the coop, and Darlene is quite concerned.
Could you check up on her? See if she made it home safely?
It's important to me. I'll owe you one.'

'No problem. I was about to head to the Operations

Center. Going flying in the morning. I'll let you know what I find. Missing nurses are my specialty.'

Fred searched the cloakroom for his raincoat but ended up settling for a moth-eaten greatcoat at the bottom of the lost-and-found. It was rather oversized, so he wrapped himself in it like a blanket.

He was about to leave when Josette confronted him.

'Leaving the scene of the crime a little early, aren't we, nurse Malone? I said twelve o'clock, not nine.'

'I'm still on the job, Ma-am. Hunting for a sister. I'll be back in half an hour. By the way, have you found my replacement?'

'No, but I will.'

Fred hustled into the storm and beat his way to the women's barracks. He knocked on Marie's door, found it unlocked, and peered inside. She wasn't there. He headed to the Operations Center to pick up his safety gear to deposit it underneath the B-25. The operations room was empty save for one of the B-25 crew snoring away. He sweated under the heavy greatcoat as he shouldered the duffle bag out onto the tarmac towards the three aircraft glistening in the rain. He deposited it under the hatch of the bomber and was about to leave when a ladder dropped from the fuselage. Pete Rylander descended to the tarmac.

'Thank fucking heaven!' Pete exclaimed when he discovered that the interloper was Fred Malone, the nurse. 'I need your help. There's a woman inside and I don't think she's breathing.'

Fred's instinct and training clicked with an instantaneous assessment.

'It better not be Marie, Rylander—and it better not be

because of that shit I got for you this afternoon. Where is she?'

'In the nose.'

Fred followed Pete into the black bowels of the aircraft and ended straddling the body of Moonbeam McSwine. He slapped her twice for a reaction but there was none. He listened for her breath and checked her pulse. She was alive, but barely.

'How much did you give her? How much chloral hydrate did you administer, you fucking asshole?'

Pete pulled out the vial and shone a flashlight on what was left.

'You gave her that much? I saw you picking up drinks at the bar. It looked like she was drinking doubles. A two-year fucking pharmacy course and you're a drug administer. Done this a few times before, have you?'

He checked her airways.

'Get me an oxygen mask and pressurize the system. When you've done that, I want you to run as fast as those fucking feet can take you and get Squadron Leader Gerard out here. Fast!'

'Can't we keep this between us?'

'Look Rylander, there's a good chance my sister here is dead already. Now get that oxygen flowing!'

Pete scrambled about, and returned with an oxygen mask attached to a small bottle. Fred forced the mask over Marie's face and pulled the activation cord. High-pressure air filled the mask, and Fred began a regime of breathing assistance.

'Come on Marie, you can do it. Breathe for me!'

'The bottle's only good for a couple of minutes, Fred.

I'll get you a better supply.' He fumbled for the navigator's hose connection, and when the bottle ran dry, made a quick connection. 'That will keep you going. Are you sure we can't keep this between us?'

'It's pretty hard to keep rape and murder in a fucking bomber quiet, you asshole. I'll do everything in my power to keep her alive. Now get the fuck out of here and get Squadron Leader Gerard.'

Fred worked on Marie in desperation. He'd never been the savior of last resort, and he had no intention of losing his patient. A nurse saving a nurse. He hoped Josette's experience would be enough to bring her back from the brink.

Her vital signs began to improve, and she retched bile-tainted Scotch. "A good sign," he figured.

'Come on Marie, you can make it, you can make it,' was all he could encourage her with.

'Where the hell is Gerard?'

Josette and Pete arrived to find Marie with her eyes open and drunk as a skunk. She had no idea where she was or what had happened. The two nurses helped her out of the aircraft and into a waiting staff car. Fred was to accompany her to the infirmary for a check-up and a purge.

'It's a night in the hospital for you, Cherie. I'll come by in the morning. You take care of her, Fred. No doctors. Just say she's had a bout of something and that I want her monitored.' She turned to Pete. 'I don't think Flying Officer Rylander is going flying in the morning.'

As they were about to drive off, they nearly collided with a Service Police vehicle that Josette had summoned from the guardhouse.

Josette put Pete under arrest, and escorted him to the lockup in the guardhouse. She wanted answers.

'What drug did you administer to Flying Officer Lamb?'

'Chloral hydrate.'

'Where did you get it?'

'I have a prescription for it.'

'Why?'

'I need it for sleep.'

'How long have you used it?'

'Since I started this job. We move around a lot, and I never get much sleep.'

'Do the rest of the crew take it as a sedative?'

'Not that I'm aware of.'

'Have you used it before, like you did tonight?'

'Never!'

'Flight Lieutenant Rylander, you're a liar. I'm going to see to it that you never fly in the Royal Canadian Air Force again. If it proves that you raped Miss Lamb, I'll see to it that you're punished to the full extent of the law.'

'I didn't rape her.'

'There was a pair of panties hanging from the hatch. She wasn't wearing any when I examined her.'

'Those weren't hers. You'll find hers in her purse. She took them off in the ladies' room before we left the mess. The panties hanging below the hatch were a signal for the crew to stay away. Sometimes they sleep in the aircraft. It's a guy thing.'

'You're saying it's a guy thing to drug a woman for sex.'

'Like I said, I only did it once, and obviously it was a huge mistake.'

'That's the second time you lied to me. I have proof that this was not an isolated incident.'

'What proof? We only met twenty minutes ago. What could you possibly know about me?'

'I know full well that you damaged a young woman many years ago, and by all accounts what I've seen and heard, you've probably damaged many more. I want to know where you got the drug.'

Pete was grateful that he'd transferred the chloral hydrate to his own dispenser. The vial that Fred had given him would have implicated the nurse and added fuel to a court martial.

'Give me the drug.'

Pete pulled the vial from his pocket and dropped it at her feet. The instant it hit, he crunched it into crystallized sand with the sole of his boot. Josette stared at the liquid oozing in the grout of the tile. Nothing was recoverable and the demonic look emanating from his eyes sent a shiver up her spine. "The man is pure evil," she thought.

'Looks like a large portion of your case just ended up going down the drain, Ma-am,' he remarked with a sneer.

Josette knew she'd lost the high ground.

'Sergeant, I want Flight Lieutenant Rylander escorted to his quarters. I want a guard posted outside his room.'

She looked at the smug pilot sitting casually opposite her.

'This isn't finished, Mister. If you've damaged that young lady you'll feel the full wrath of the medical fraternity, the Air Force, and me. Once I start looking into your past, I'll find your trap line. Even a cold, calculating, despicable creature like you has a history that can't be totally covered up.'

Darlene and Lou were hailed as the couple of the night. Her subdued exuberance was out of character, and acquaintances stopped by to ask her if she was okay. 'I just had a little fainting spell,' she'd explained.

Josette returned and escorted Darlene to the ladies' room, where she explained the reason for her absence. She detailed the circumstances of Marie's disappearance, and assured her that the 'Bastard of Moose Jaw' had cooked his own goose.

'You don't ever have to worry about him involving you, Cherie. I'll find some way of putting him out of your life. You'll never see him again.'

'It's Lou I'm worried about. What if he finds out? He'll dump me and be gone forever.' Tears welled and Josette kissed her.

'If he loves you like I think he does, then you won't have anything to worry about. Let's not worry about the past. You discovered a missing piece of your history tonight, and you've faced it with a strength I always knew you had. In the last twenty-four hours, you've fallen in love and I envy you for that. Before we part as lovers, I have one request of you. If you agree, I'll set you free. No recriminations, no history.'

Darlene nodded her acceptance. Josette had been more than a lover. She'd protected her from indiscretions and social miscues like a big a sister and mother. Their love-making sessions had been no more than tenderness of touch and tongue, and Josette had saved her for the one that counted.

'Anything you want.'

'I want to be with you and Lou tonight. I want to make love with both of you, and I want it to be wonderful. When tomorrow comes, we will act as if it never happened. I promise as an officer, a nurse, and a gentlewoman.'

Darlene was not surprised at the inclusion of Lou. Except for the scar, he had a strong resemblance to the photograph on Josette's nightstand.

Reports of Josette having affairs with young pilots had never been proved, so she was forced to find a lover in her own barrack block. Last night she'd been discovered, and now she had to pay the price. She needed a man to jump-start her change of brand. That man was Flying Officer Lou Fender.

'What if he objects?'

'What red-blooded man would object to a dalliance with Daisy Mae and Stupefyin' Jones at the same time? He'd meet Virtue and Sin and fall in love with both of them.'

Lieutenant Hartwig had been staring out of the starboard gunner's bubble, piecing together constellations he'd studied during his wings course, when he noticed that two galaxies weren't where they were supposed to be.

He'd wanted to be a fighter pilot, but brilliant grades and natural talent were trumped by his stammer. He was shunted to the inglorious position as a copilot on transport aircraft, where the radio operator took care of all the transmissions.

Copilots sat mute and did what they were told.

Heavy arm-twisting and a political shove got him transferred to Carswell and the B-36 program, where he received top marks in everything except you know what. To become a captain, one had to be a reasonable public speaker, but though he'd taken elocution courses, he'd failed every one.

He'd been a second copilot for two years and only received pole time when he had to get recertified. He'd sat in the left-hand seat on long flights while the captain was having a piss, but most of the time, he was relegated to the lower deck of the forward compartment.

This flight was different. The aircraft commander had directed him to the rear compartment, and it didn't get any lower than that.

He did a final mental calculation, and decided to voice his discovery.

'Did you kn-kn-know we changed course?' He spoke loud enough to catch Kenny Wright's attention. The bunks had been in the middle of a shift change when he thought he felt a slight tilt in the floor. The gunner had traded places with him on the cot, and he was delighted to stick his head out into the observation bubble to study the heavens. That had been half an hour ago.

'Changed course? We're supposed to be flying direct to Loring. A great-circle route. What makes you think we've changed course?'

'Well, if-if-if my rudimentary navigation training taught me anything, it-t-t taught me that the North Star is where North is. We should be tracking southwest. We're going almost due west. Not only that, we're over land.'

Lieutenant Wright felt a chill. Somebody had just walked over his grave. The trip home was to be quick and dirty, and get there as fast as possible. If the Major had a problem with the aircraft why hadn't he informed the crew?

'Are you sure we're not over Newfoundland? Maybe we picked up a tailwind.'

'N-N-N-Not with the weather pattern I studied at Met briefing this morning. If anything, with the weather pattern over Québec we should be fighting a headwind. D-D-D-Do you think I should ask the Major what's up?'

'You've got more balls than me if you do. I wish they'd find some way to pressurize the tube. It's getting kind of chummy back here. Let me have a look.'

Wright stared into the heavens and at the earth, but he couldn't make a positive observation to back up Hartwig's claim. 'I can't tell where the fuck we are or which direction we're going. All I know is that this here airplane is supposed to be on a direct route. Wouldn't we be able to feel it, if the plane changed direction?'

'Not if it was a sl-sl-sl-slow coordinated turn. Your inner ear can be easily fooled. That's why you always believe your instruments. During my instrument training, m-m-m -my instructor ripped off the hood when we were upside down. It was at night, and I thought the stars were the earth and the lights on the prairie the stars. Climbing became descending and descending became climbing. It was only when I checked the altimeter and vertical speed indicator that I realized what he'd done.' For the first time in years, he'd put full thought and voice together.

Wright plugged into the intercom and switched to the private line to the aircraft commander's station.

'Major Crisp, this is Lieutenant Wright. Have we altered course?' He repeated the question several times, but there was no reply. He felt a pang of alarm and opened the master intercom.

'This is Lieutenant Wright in the rear compartment. The Major's intercom seems to be snafu. Could somebody up there inform the Major that he's disconnected?' He repeated his request, but heard only static. He faced Hartwig and shrugged in dismay.

'There's nobody home.' He woke up the radio operator. 'We need your skills, Corporal. Can you patch us in?'

Lincoln sat alone in the vastness of the night, contemplating his next move. He was about to descend into the top of the cloud layer that he'd targeted for the last hour. Slumped behind him was the body of the flight engineer, the victim of a gunshot wound to the head. Arnie Stonehawker was either dead or dying on the lower deck. Alana's Walther and silencer had seen to that. He'd dumped cabin pressure and was on oxygen. As for Lieutenant Gidley, he assumed the guy had succumbed to anoxia.

The opening to the lower level was a gate he controlled. Whoever was alive would be an idiot to stick his head up. Arnie had, and he was out of action now. He thought his headshot had been a little off, but blood and a bit of bone confirmed a hit. His plan had worked to perfection. Arnie Stonehawker had been the key to the disappearing act.

Lincoln had tapped his copilot on the shoulder. 'I'll take over now, Arnie. I have control.' Arnie nodded, removed his mask, rubbed the crease on his face, and requested a piss break. 'The relief tube's plugged up.' Lincoln had kept him at the control column for an hour longer than promised. No autopilot for him. He needed to wear him down. Hand-flying the bomber wasn't difficult, but it could be taxing.

They were approaching the outer limit of the Goose Bay GCI radar site, and he'd taken the bomber up to 42,000 feet. They'd fly directly over the radar site, and nobody would be able to reach them. Once overtop, he'd make a course change, drop some chaff, and throw the whole East Coast radar system into chaos.

'I want you to head down to Lieutenant Gidley's compartment, Arnie. I'm going to play with him for a while, and I want you to give me an assessment of him when we get back. You and I are going to do a lot of flying together. I like a man who can take shit.'

As he descended to the lower deck, Arnie felt a twinge

of guilt for doubting his captain's sanity. He pushed by a bank of electronics and entered the monstrous bubble of the aircraft's nose. Gidley was focused on his console and when he recognized Arnie he let out a sigh of relief. Things had not been going well.

'How's things going, Stan? Having a good time are you? I sure like the view from here. You realize, of course, that you're the first one to C.B.D. when we hit Mother Earth.'

'C.B.D.?'

'Crash, Burn, Die!'

'I never really thought of it that way. Christ, on this plane I'd be dead for ten seconds before anyone in the ass end got it.' They laughed and lit cigarettes.

'The Major says he wants to play some games. If you get flustered, feel free to give me a wink. I don't know if I'll be able to help, but I'll back you up. I have an in with the Major. Now what's this doo-hickey for?'

Lincoln had Stan calculate a direct route to the Goose Bay GCI site, and ordered the flight engineer to add climb power. He fired up the jets for extra boost. The GCI site had a one-hundred-fifty-mile radius at 40,000 feet. Anything above that altitude gave him impunity. If he could sustain 46,000 feet carrying a plutonium bomb, so could the Russians. He'd sail overhead of whatever interceptor they'd send up. A point had to be made.

'Pilot to navigator, when we pass over top of the Goose Bay GCI site, I want a heading to Chibougamau. Then, I want you to set up for a simulated bombing run on Montréal using the K-1 radar bombing system. You'll finish the simulation using the optical bombsight when we hit the initial point.'

Gidley looked to Arnie in disbelief.

'That's a tall order, Arnie. I know where Montréal is, but where the fuck is Chibougamau?'

'I think it's in Québec. Labrador hasn't a town bigger than an Indian camp.' They scoured the aviation chart and whooped when they found it.

'Holy shit!' Gidley exclaimed. 'It's north of Lake Saint-Jean. Why the hell is he taking us there?'

'Remember, the Major said we're going to attack the States like it was for real. He's got something up his sleeve. Ours is not to reason why. For all I know the only reason he sent me down here was to help you find the fucking place on a map.'

Gidley revised their heading, adjusted the bombing system for a course-change once they reached Chibougamau, and then linked it to the autopilot. Lincoln nudged the bomber to starboard. At their altitude, every course-change required added power and he adjusted the throttles from his console.

'Arnie, you need to change the radio frequency to the GCI site. The radio operator's stuck in the rear, so you'll have to take over. Let's hear what's going on.'

Arnie moved back to the radio compartment and dialed in. Soon the chatter between the radar station and two American Starfire interceptors rattled in their headsets. As they approached Goose Bay, the radar operators and the interceptor crews were at odds over their attack procedures, and they were called back to base. Lincoln had assessed their response to "tail-end Charlie" correctly and the bomber soared over the radar site without being touched. The dominoes were falling in order.

'We gave them the easiest target possible and they still couldn't touch us Arnie,' Lincoln gloated. 'How's that new heading coming, Lieutenant Gidley?'

Gidley worked the numbers, and Lincoln shut down the jets. He could make out the receding storm front hundreds of miles away by the flashes of lightning, and he requested a power reduction. It was time to begin the long, slow, descent.

First, he had to drop chaff.

A bombardier had been left absent from the crew list, so Lincoln ordered Arnie to the empty post and to activate the chaff dispenser, which he'd control from his cockpit.

'Then I want you to turn off the IFF/SIF. Let's not let them know where we are.'

The Major had brazenly let the GCI site know he was coming, thought Arnie—what gonads! He shook his head in bewilderment. The Major was pulling out all the stops on this one.

'Drop enough junk to make it look like we've disintegrated in midair, Arnie. That should fool them for a while.'

The scopes in the GCI site would light up like a pinball machine, and alarms would ring from Goose Bay to the Pentagon.

Trashcan One, carrying a plutonium bomb, had gone down.

"No turning back for anything or anybody," Lincoln thought. "I have to kill again."

Lincoln extracted Alana's pistol from his flight bag. He attached the silencer, flicked the safety, and shot the flight engineer behind his left earphone. His head jerked forward, and as he was strapped in, looked asleep. When they recovered his body they wouldn't be looking for a bullet hole in the head.

Arnie was next.

'Arnie, I need you on the flight deck.'

The instant Arnie stuck his head up through the hatch, Lincoln squeezed the trigger. Arnie screamed, grabbed his forehead, and fell back into the radio compartment, smashing into the radio with the force of a linebacker.

Lincoln depressurized the forward compartment. If Gidley didn't recognize the symptoms of anoxia, he'd be unconscious within a minute. He waited ten minutes, then called Gidley for a status report but there was no response. What he couldn't fathom was the shallow breathing over the intercom that originated from below. Somebody was alive.

Lincoln needed a cigarette, but it was impossible to smoke. He'd attempted to kill three men in the space of five minutes, but had succeeded with only two. The flight engineer was dead, but what had happened below was a mystery.

"Who's still alive?" he pondered. The rest of the crew in the aft cabin may as well have been stranded on the moon.

A half an hour passed before Wright came over the private line from the rear compartment.

'Major Crisp, this is Lieutenant Wright. Have we altered course?' Lincoln ignored him, and heard the snap of a switch for the master intercom.

'This is Lieutenant Wright in the rear compartment. The Major's intercom seems to be snafu. Somebody in the forward compartment better inform the Major that he's disconnected.' The sound of breathing from two oxygen masks was all he heard before the line went dead.

CHAPTER 25

Saturday 11:30 PM 0430 GMT

Colonel Briggs shot upright from a dead sleep, checked his watch, and answered the telephone. It was the hotline from the Pentagon.

'This better be good,' was all he could mumble.

'Trashcan One's gone down, Sir. It passed over Goose Bay a half hour ago, then disappeared off radar. The GCI site says all indications are that it may have broken up in flight.

Briggs was stunned. 'Send a car right away.'

Colonel Briggs arrived at the Operations Center ten minutes later to find two senior British officers and the representative who'd supervised the loading of the bomb. For the next half hour, they were patched into the Pentagon and the Goose Bay radar site, running through differing scenarios of what had gone wrong. All that was known was that the bomber had brazenly flown overhead, lit up the radar site, altered course, and was last seen proceeding in a westerly direction.

'God damn it, we've got another Broken Arrow over Canada.' The incident over British Columbia and another over the Gulf of St. Lawrence the same year had been embarrassing enough. Now, it seemed, they had to deal with a new one.

'Have they found the wreckage?'

'That's the weird part. They diverted a couple of

interceptors to the general area, but there wasn't any sign of wreckage. No flames, no distress.'

'Any large bodies of water on the aircraft's track?'

'None.'

'What does the Pentagon say?'

'They're in the dark, too.'

'Well I'll be God-damned, Lincoln Crisp screwed the pooch.' He poured coffee and lit a cigarette. 'Funny thing, I was just talking with his copilot before they took off. Seems he was concerned about Major Crisp's demeanor. Thought Crisp wasn't quite in his right mind. I spoke with Lincoln just before dinner and he seemed okay to me. He's gone through a lot in the last year, losing his wife and kid, and all that. Now, he's gone, too. Well, there isn't much we can do here. I'm going back to bed. This whole issue with your crappy bomb will have to wait until morning.' He dumped his coffee and butted his cigarette.

'You seem rather cavalier about the issue, Colonel. One of our nuclear weapons has just gone missing over our closest Commonwealth partner's territory. How are we going to explain that one?'

'Leave it up to Uncle Sam. We're getting pretty good at buffaloing our northern neighbor.'

Briggs conferred with the Pentagon for the next ten minutes, but realizing that he was isolated and out of time sync, he headed back to bed. He'd get the full story in the morning.

"Lincoln Crisp," he wondered as he tried to sleep. "What the hell happened up there?"

'Something's happened up front,' Lieutenant Wright informed. 'The red light flashing over the hatch means the forward compartment's been depressurized. Something catastrophic must have happened.'

'Remember the briefing,' Hartwig replied. 'The Major said he was going to pull out all the stops. I think it's part of th-th-the test.'

Wright knew differently.

'Gentlemen, this is no test. This aircraft is carrying a Mark III atomic bomb. There's no way we should be deviating from our flight plan. The consequences are incalculable if something happens to this aircraft.'

The complement of the crew focused on the two officers. The radio operator was the senior NCO and felt obliged to state their case.

'We're cut off without access or communication Lieutenant,' he piped. 'We don't know what the fuck's going on. Take a look at the altimeter. We're descending, albeit slowly, but we're descending. We're in the fucking caboose, Sir, and we don't know if Casey's on the throttle.'

Hartwig ordered parachutes on, but when the three from the forward cabin realized they'd left theirs, the atmosphere became testy.

'Mine's up there, too,' Kenny reminded them. 'I'm in the same boat as you.'

'L-L-L-Let's not react too quickly,' Hartwig stammered. 'We're descending, but it's slow and the wings are level. It looks to me l-l-l-like somebody's flying this thing.'

'Is there any way we can get somebody forward to find out what's up?' the radio operator asked.

'For now, no. But if we descend through 12,000—and

it's a big if—we should be able to open the hatch and send Hartwig through. He's the only one here who can fly this machine. Now get on the radio and see if you can get some answers.'

With the realization that Hartwig might be their only salvation, a murmur of dissent bantered between the gunners.

The radio operator warmed the set, but when he went to dial-in the emergency frequency, he discovered the tuning dial had been sheared off and was missing. He stuck his finger into the recess in an attempt to turn it, but could find no purchase. They looked for any tool that would do the job, but nothing worked.

'I'm going to have to use the frequency it's stuck at, Sir. It's the best I can do.' He put on a headset, put the microphone to his lips, and the two officers nodded for him to proceed.

'PAN-PAN-PAN, this is Trashcan One on 142.5. If there's anyone monitoring this frequency, please respond. Over.'

The crew waited in silence for a response, but after a dozen requests, the radio operator slid his headset to his neck and shook his head.

'All I'm getting is static and some weak gibberish in French, Sir.'

'K-K-K-Keep trying, Corporal. S-S-Somebody out there might p-p-p-pick us up.'

Wright focused on Hartwig.

'Don, you know how to fly this thing. We've got to find some way of getting you forward. I don't intend to perish back here in this grossly overrated soup can. How the hell are we going to do it?'

Six parachutes for ten men had mutiny written all over it. Hartwig felt the rush of responsibility, and grabbed his writing pad. The dynamics of the situation required a one-chance-only opportunity, which would need to be conducted with operating-room efficiency. The main obstacle was the depressurized tunnel. If he could make passage through eighty feet of tunnel and bust through the air lock, they might have a chance. What was beyond it would only be disclosed at that moment. Without pause for a stammer, he sat at the rear gunner's console and took control.

'Let's talk about it, Lieutenant Wright. You must have some ideas, you being a physicist and all.'

───────

Lincoln tightened his mask and engaged the autopilot. Their rate of descent would have them at 35,000 feet by the time they reached the cloud top and the wind that would fling them south. He pulled the clipboard from his flight bag and flipped through the various target scenarios he'd planned. A direct route would have him in the Detroit-Chicago area, but that was now out of the question. The winds of the storm had seen to that. He reviewed his maps and came to a conclusion. The greater Montréal area of Québec would suffice. He'd pass to the west of Lake Saint-Jean, and let the storm carry him south. The target didn't have to be in the United States. Canada would do.

He was unnerved by the breathing sounding over the intercom. Something was amiss. Gidley or Stonehawker was alive, and whoever it was posed a threat, but with the compartment depressurized, he couldn't descend to the lower deck without oxygen.

Repressurizing to check his handiwork made sense, but it was time-consuming. It also made him vulnerable. Who knew what to expect in the basement. Arnie couldn't have survived the gunshot to the head, but even if he was still alive, surely couldn't pose a threat. Gidley could be the breather, but he would have made contact over the intercom by now. Lincoln began to worry.

Arnie thought he heard a church bell ringing, and it brought him back to consciousness. It took a minute for his memory to return. What had transpired was attempted murder. He saw the Major point something at him, and as he turned his head to see what the Major was pointing at, a brilliant flash of red exploded and he felt the force of a baseball bat hit him in the right eye. He'd been out cold for thirty seconds, and he instinctively grabbed for an oxygen mask when the drop in cabin pressure made his ears throb in pain.

He was sitting upright with his back against the radio. He took several gulps before he settled down his breathing.

"The Major meant to kill me," he thought. "I was right." He felt his wound and was shocked when his fingers had entered his skull. Where once there was an Aryan blue eye, there was now a cavity, spewing blood down his cheek. He cupped the wound with both hands and chuckled. 'Never try to kill a German by shooting him in the head.' He lost consciousness as he was about to call Gidley for help.

The rear crew sat in a circle like Boy Scouts around a campfire. The lieutenants were in the process of planning Hartwig's escape and holding back a mutiny. Each man had a suggestion.

'Let's plug the hole in the tube.'

'How do we find the leak, and how do we seal it?'

'Can't we open the hatch and use our pressure to shoot the lieutenant down the tube?'

'And when he gets to the other end going head first? What happens to him then?' There didn't seem to be a safe solution.

Wright's plan was the one eventually agreed upon.

'We share what oxygen masks we've got, decompress the compartment, open the tube, and pull the trolley back. Lieutenant Hartwig here was lucky enough to pick out a fighter-pilot's parachute, which just happens to have a high altitude emergency oxygen bottle attached. He'll have enough oxygen to get there, open the hatch and patch into the intercom and oxygen. He'll pack three chutes and masks on the trolley and we'll pull it back.'

For the next five minutes they put their house in order. Two pairs of gunners shared masks, and all were ready when the cabin began to decompress. 'Force your mask against your face and blow like hell,' Hartwig ordered. 'That'll save your eardrums. You know the drill.'

Wright opened the hatch and felt the rush of frigid air. The radio operator pulled the trolley to the throat of the tube and yelled, 'The fucking rope's been cut, Sir! It will only work one way. Lieutenant Hartwig won't be able to propel himself.'

'What do you think Don? Can you propel yourself without it?'

'I'll use up all the oxygen if I do.'

Don and Kenny had been sharing a single mask until it was time to go, and their buddy-breathing and conversation had become almost comical. Hartwig looked at the slow unwinding of the altimeter, then down the tunnel.

'Let's let gravity do the job. Ease me down with the rope.' He lay on the trolley, and pulled the toggle on the oxygen bottle. A blast of high-pressure oxygen shot into his lungs.

The shallow inclination of the aircraft stalled the trolley twice and Hartwig clawed at the sides of the tube to increase his speed, but the cold and exertion had him gulping for breath. Halfway along he heard the rush of air and guessed he'd found the breach. When he reached the forward hatch he knew the bottle was nearly empty, and panic began to set in. He banged on the hatch in desperation, then found the latch under a blinking red light.

The hatch swung open, and he scrambled into the radio compartment to search for an oxygen outlet, only to discover Lieutenant Stonehawker propped against the shattered radio panel, bleeding and unconscious. Several gulps from Stonehawker's mask had Hartwig thinking straight, and he plugged into a gunner's outlet. He found three parachutes and two masks, slid them onto the trolley, and tugged twice on the line. The trolley disappeared and he closed the hatch.

Lincoln noticed the hatch light go from red to green to red, heard a second set of breathing over the intercom and knew he'd lost some of his advantage. He cocked his pistol and readied for a head to pop up.

Hartwig revived Stonehawker with a couple of slaps, and stabilized his bleeding with an improvised bandage. A pleading single eye and chalk-white skin were signs that he might have little conscious time left. Arnie put his finger to his mask to indicate silence, grabbed for the radio operators log and scribbled. "Don't speak. The Major shot me. Don't go up."

Hartwig scribbled "Why?" Stonehawker shook his head and nodded off, the blinkers on his oxygen flow indicator the only confirmation that he was still alive.

Hartwig scurried to the navigator's station and found Gidley slumped over. He found his mask, forced it on his face and waited for some form of revival, but if it was to happen, it would be a long time coming. He returned to the radio compartment and switched on the intercom feed to the rear compartment.

'This is Lieutenant Hartwig from the radio compartment. I made it forward okay. Not to be alarmed back there. The forward section is controlling the aircraft. I'll report back when I can get you some answers. You can go ahead and repressurize.' He switched off the intercom.

'Wow,' he barked. For the first time in years, he'd uttered complete coherent sentences without a stammer.

Lincoln heard the transmission, and assumed that the speaker wasn't the copilot he'd stashed in the rear. Stuttering was something one couldn't just cover up. He did a quick review of the flight status, and was pleased. The crew he'd picked to "not count upon" had done just that. Killing the flight engineer had been easier than he thought. Unconscious in sleep, then unconscious in death. There was no sport. With Arnie, it was a different matter. The splattering of blood and bone had all the similarities of Alana's murder. He'd peeked overtop of the access to the lower deck, and observed a pair of flying boots, but he wasn't about to test his luck with a full look-see. There was that breathing. Who'd made it forward?

He checked his rate of descent, and decreased it with a touch of power to the inboard engines. He needed to fly just over top of the approaching cloud. Penetration into it would come at the end when the time came to complete the mission. First, he had to make contact with the interloper, whoever it was.

He isolated the intercom. No use letting the back end know what was happening.

'This is the aircraft commander speaking. I am ordering those below to identify themselves. I repeat.'

He repeated it five times, and knew he had a game of cat and mouse on his hands. He held the high ground and a weapon. Without a working radio forward, the radio operator was of no value. The gunners were of no consequence. That left the nuclear officer, but that did not seem to be his voice. Curious?

Satisfied that there was little threat, he tightened his straps for the inevitable turbulence they'd encounter overtop of the storm. In less than three hours, it would be over and a new world would emerge. He'd loved Québec and he'd loved Alana, but both needed to be sacrificed for the good of mankind.

Hartwig cowered in the access to the navigator's compartment contemplating his next move. Arnie was still alive and the navigator's oxygen flow indicator blinked weakly. What condition he'd be in if he ever regained consciousness was dubious. The Major didn't seem to know who was shuffling about below him, and it gave him a feeling of immense power. He'd say nothing, do nothing, and plan. He'd made it this far. The aircraft's controls were only a few feet above him. He'd find a way.

CHAPTER 26

L ou and Darlene turned their backs to a squall on the way to her barrack block. They'd danced, she drank, and they received the accolades that competition winners were entitled to. The evening had more than exceeded his expectations. As midnight approached, they were both eager for the evening's reward. With adieus to all, they slipped arm-in-arm into the night. They staggered through the storm with Lou grasping her with the intensity of the catcher in a trapeze act.

'I want you to come to my lair,' Darlene insisted. 'I feel too exposed in the men's dorm. You don't want me to look like a one-night stand, do you? Anyway, I've got a surprise for you.'

Lou was not about to resist and as he sneaked into the lobby, she assured him that there wasn't a matron on duty.

Darlene had Lou lie on the bed while she stripped off her Daisy Mae costume. She removed her blond wig, and Lou pulled her close.

'I'm in love with you, Darlene. I don't know why or how it happened, but I want to be with you forever.' She stroked his scar and kissed it.

'Would you feel the same about me if I couldn't have children?'

'Of course. But what makes you think you'll never have children?'

'Years ago I was hurt, and my doctor said it was doubtful that I'd ever conceive.' Lou enveloped her and switched off the table lamp.

'There's something else I need to open up about. It's about Squadron Leader Gerard. I love her.'

Lou was stunned

'What do you mean you love her?'

'I love her like a sister, like a mother, and like a lover. She's part of my past. I've agreed that we spend a night together. You, me, her. Tonight. She wants to, and so do I.'

'You mean she wants to be with us, in bed?'

'Yes.'

She stripped Lou and curled up beside him.

'You have to know that I was never attracted to a woman until Josette saved me from a life of promiscuity and alcohol. If you'd met me under the same circumstances a year ago, you would have dismissed me as a slut. I still have a problem. That remark I made when we first met was the type of mouth I have when I drink. Josette and I have a similar appetite for sex. We joked many times of having a ménage à trois and when you made that rather callous remark about how you got your scar, I just blurted out the first thing that came into my head.'

'It was the most brazen thing a woman has ever said to me. It was also the moment I fell in love with you.'

'It wasn't really me that said it. It was the woman I'd become.'

'What made you turn to Josette?'

'I didn't. She came to me. She could tell I wasn't a whore

at heart. She comforted and supported me with tenderness and honesty. I usually stay for one school term at a time but I've been here for a year and a half. When I went home to Manitoba in the summer, Josette and I stopped in Toronto and Montréal. She has no one close. Her fiancé was killed in a training accident during the war and she's been true to her upbringing ever since. She's never had a man since, and she wants you to start the fire.'

'How do you feel about it? Me being with another woman, your best friend.'

'I'll find out when the time comes. For now, I'm okay with it. When she makes love to you, I may feel completely different.'

'Where is she now?'

'She's checking up on Marie. A locked door to my room signals that you're not in a participating mood. What should I do?'

'It means that much to you?'

'It means that much to me.'

Lou kissed her softly and cupped her left breast. Her heart was pounding and he knew the answer she wanted.

'Then we best leave the door unlocked.'

Minutes later, he heard the click of the door latch and the rustle of clothing being discarded. He glimpsed the silhouette of Josette's breasts and belly in a lightning-flash, then smelled the heady combination of liquor, perfume, and body heat.

Josette pulled back the bedding and slipped in beside him.

'Well, Louis Fender,' she whispered. 'It seems you have us at our mercy once more.'

She kissed his ear, and was about to descend to his erection when a violent pounding on the door and a booming voice shattered the moment.

'Flying Officer Fender, this is Sergeant Lucas. If you are in there, the orderly officer orders me to escort you to the Met briefing room. The base is on full alert. Something big is going down.'

Lou quickly dressed in his costume, kissed Darlene, gave Josette a wink, and slipped out into the hall.

'Something big you say? CO, huh? What the hell's he up to now?'

Darlene and Josette said nothing as they lay with the slowly diminishing impression of Lou between them. Darlene slipped her hand under the sheet to feel what was left of his warmth, then snaked over to find Josette.

'I didn't think everything would end like this.'

'Everything Cherie, what do you mean?

'Hold me. I've got a bad feeling about this Sunday.'

'I can't, Cherie. You heard it. We're on alert. They'll be looking for me. I have to ready the hospital.' She slipped on her bra and panties, wrapped herself in what was left of her costume, opened the door and faced a grinning Fred Malone, who was about to knock.

'Thought I might find you here, Ma'am.'

———————

Duckwalker and Bonnie slipped into the darkest reach of the lounge. Marie had disappeared into the evening with the suave interloper, and after several dances, he felt more comfortable than usual. Sobriety had its virtues. Their cavern became isolated as the partygoers left, and as midnight approached, all that were left were single officers snoring on couches, and a couple fighting about who said what to whom.

'Remove your glasses, so I can see your face. You have to give me that consideration.'

Duckwalker was on the horns of a dilemma. He didn't have a clue how to talk with a woman this young. When called upon, the removal of his glasses was a tool of seduction, and only then were the painful consequences overridden by whatever happened next.

'Bear with me. Light is pain. Without them, the glow of your cigarette sears my retinas. It's a long sad story that's not worth wrecking our evening over.'

'Josette said I'd figure it out, but you haven't given me anything to work with. Your strange posture and your glasses. What's a girl to do if you can't be honest?'

'I'm very awkward around women. Shy even. I thought I was in love once, but that's turned out to be a fallacy. I've always kind of been mothered, and I liked it. I like you, but I'm at a loss for the comfort of conversation. I can talk blue in the face about my professional side, but when it comes to anything personal, I'm hogtied. It's a story for another time.'

'Then why don't we talk about what we know best? For me it's nursing; for you it's flying. Now what in heaven's name do you do?'

For the next half hour, Duckwalker transfixed Bonnie with tales of derring-do, and she hung on his every word. She responded with tales from the operating and emergency rooms.

'I was in on an open heart surgery a year ago. It doesn't

get much more intense than that. Then there's bones. The rest of the body turns to mush, but bones shatter like china.'

'I did surgery on myself once,' he piped as he shot forked fingers towards his glasses. 'As you can see, the surgeon should be shot at dawn.'

He was about break down and spill the beans for the second time in twenty-four hours, when he was interrupted by a figure entering the gloom wearing an armband.

Malone!

'Flight Lieutenant Jones, you're not going to believe this, but the CO wants you in the Met briefing room in five minutes or less.'

'Not again? I promise I haven't had a drop or so much as looked at a married woman. Your nursing sister here can attest to that. Anyway, look at the way I'm dressed.'

'All kidding aside, Jones, something big is going on. The base is on full alert. The scuttlebutt is that the Russians are sneaking one over.'

———— • • ————

Pete Rylander chain-smoked and longed for alcohol. The loss of his elixir meant a sleepless night, and the doom that awaited in the morning had him scrambling for ideas on a way out of his predicament. He'd been cut off from communication, and his reliance on The Voice from Ottawa magnified his vulnerability. The weekend had become a nightmarish farce. Wilding was at the GCI radar site at Parent, waiting to do a victory dance, and he was holed up in a barrack block with no means of escape.

A simple plan is never simple. Especially if that plan gets a nasty weather pattern thrown in. Like Rangoon!

Wilding's format was simple. Catch Rhubarb Two in cloud, use Dan Lacey's state-of-the-art lead-attack radar, and accidently arm and fire the twin 50-caliber machine guns. There'd be shit to pay, but there'd be one less partner to worry about.

Wing Commander Chauncey Wilding, his puppet-master, was getting antsy for his money. Pete had the money, but Wilding had the control. He knew of Pete's addiction and criminality. Strong leverage. He couldn't remember if Lou knew too.

The topic hadn't surfaced at their reunion in Yellowknife or that afternoon, and he surmised Lou had forgotten about it. Now, it seemed everybody knew about it. Squadron Leader Gerard's accusation that she had further evidence to the evening's fiasco had him running faces and places across the screen in his mind. Suddenly, a violent knock on the door jolted him out of his thoughts.

'Flight Lieutenant Rylander, the commanding officer requests your presence in the Met briefing room immediately.' Pete opened the door to find the sergeant of the guard standing at attention, a holster dangling from a Sam Brown cross-belt that held in a hefty chest.

'Get dressed right quickly, Sir, there's big goings-on.'

Pete was hustled to the Met briefing room expecting to find his accuser wielding an axe, only to discover the same players who were at the afternoon's debriefing. His indiscretion that evening was obviously not the topic of conversation. He sat down, did a look-see, and spied Lou and Duckwalker looking at him and shrugging.

"Marryin' Sam" stepped to the podium.

'Flight Lieutenant Rylander, have you been drinking

this evening?' Pete couldn't fathom how such a question was pertinent at one o'clock in the morning.

'No Sir, I have not.'

'Is that so, Flying Officer Malone?'

Fred, festooned in full regalia, snapped to attention. 'Yes it is, Sir. I never saw him take a sip and the bartender's backed me up.'

'Then you're able to fly on a moment's notice, Rylander?'

'If my aircraft's fueled and ready to go, Sir. I'll need my flying gear, an APU, and I'll have to round up my crew.'

'That's been taken care of. When the time comes you'll be second to take off. Your crew's doing the pre-flight as we speak.'

The CO focused on his audience.

'Gentlemen, we are about to go to war. What you hear is top secret.'

He signaled for darkness and the screen lit up with a map of southern Québec and Labrador. He picked up a pointer and tapped the screen.

'Gentlemen, we have a situation that's as serious as this country's ever seen. Fifteen minutes ago, I was informed by the United States Air Force that a B-36 carrying a nuclear weapon is flying north of Lake Saint-Jean with the possibility that there isn't anyone in control. The GCI sites at Mont Apica and Parent haven't picked it up, and they may never will. Right now, the bomber's heading west towards Chibougamau, and for all we know, it could head in the same direction 'til it runs out of fuel. That's if it doesn't end up somewhere near Detroit. The Americans can take care of anything down there. We've been entrusted to plug up the stretch between Chicoutimi and Toronto. The Met officer informed me that if the bomber hits Chibougamau anywhere below 35,000 feet, it'd be whisked southward by the northern portion of the storm. The aircraft could be flung in any direction. The indication so far is that it's slowly descending. It may be that the aircraft's out of trim because there's no one in control.' Hands went up. 'Later, later!'

'We're fortunate in that we have two sober crews capable of making contact with the intruder if he happens to come our way. And there's a good chance he will. Could you identify yourselves please?'

Li'l Abner, Pappy Yokum, and Evil Eye Fleagle snapped to attention.

'When I finish the situation briefing, I'll brief you on our plan to intercept the bomber, a plan that includes the option of destroying it before it gets to be too late.'

Gasps and cigarette chokes reverberated from the dark.

'Here's what is certain. A B-36 on its way from England to Loring went off course and appeared to have broken up in flight and crashed in Labrador. Two hours after the incident, a ham operator in the boondocks picked up this signal. Turn on the tape recorder please, and turn it up as loud as you can.'

Crackling out of the speaker came the hoarse voice of someone about to give up.

'PAN-PAN-PAN, this is Trashcan One on 142.5. We're a B-36 descending through 38,000 feet on a southwest heading. The flight crew does not respond. Repeat, the flight crew does not respond. Ten of us are confined to the rear compartment, and we're trying to find a way to get to the forward section. Five crew members may be bailing out, I repeat—PAN-PAN-PAN.' They listened to it twice more.

'So there you have it, gentlemen. The bomber did not crash, and there are ten crewmen isolated in the rear compartment with no way of knowing what's happening up front. I don't know why they're isolated or what the status of the flight crew is. What's important is that we prevent another Broken Arrow.'

A door opened and a note was passed to the podium.

'Flying Officer Malone, you are to report to the infirmary immediately.'

Pierre LeSeach had run through the dials on his UHF radio with slow deliberation. Click, click, click. It was time to let the fire die down and snuggle between the dogs, but he went for one last sweep. He'd been splitting and stacking wood for the last week, and as he twisted the dial with his chapped fingers, his earphones picked up a strange voice on an obscure frequency. He heard it again.

'PAN-PAN-PAN, this is Trashcan One on 142.5. Over.' He listened to it again and again, but he couldn't understand its meaning. It was like that for all the flights he monitored. He attempted a reply but could only respond in French.

'Tabernac!' he swore. 'I've got to learn some English.' He checked his radio manual, and when he discovered the meaning of the word "PAN," he contacted the radio station at Sept-Îles. Within minutes, powerful UHF direction-finding devices determined the bomber's track, but by the time they were able to speak with the radio operator, his transmissions were inaudible. Radio fixes had determined the aircraft's track and rate of descent before the batteries faded.

'That's all we know,' the CO informed. 'I'll answer questions now.'

'Is the bomb armed?'

'I don't know.'

'Why can't the rear crewmembers get forward?'

'I don't know.'

'Do they think the flight crew has anoxia?'

'I don't know.'

'How much time have we got?'

'I don't know.'

'Why don't we scramble two aircraft right away?'

'We don't have the resources. We've been on stand-down since noon. Besides, we don't know exactly where they are. Gentlemen, you now know as much as I do. All we can do is wait for a GCI site to pick up the intruder, and we'll respond as best we can. What I can tell you for certain is that we have formulated a battle strategy that involves one of our squadron's aircraft and the B-25 that flew in this morning. Squadron Leader Carson will now take over the briefing.'

The leader of 440 Squadron stepped into the beam of the projector.

'Flight Lieutenant Rylander, you'll take up station south of Parent GCI at as high an altitude as possible in this weather. I understand that your aircraft's fitted with lead-attack radar, and armed with two 50-caliber machine guns. You're going to act as a goalkeeper, our ace in the hole so to speak. We're hoping you won't have to come into play but if the primary mission using our squadron's CF-100 doesn't pan out, you may be our last resort.'

Pete nodded and winked at Dan Lacey. He'd already imagined a scenario where he and Lou might end up being directed by Wilding himself. It was far-fetched, but plausible.

The OC addressed Lou and Duckwalker.

'You two will be flying the same aircraft again. She's being armed and fueled. The tip tanks have been left on for range and altitude. I want you in the cockpit, ready to go, the same time Rylander's Mitchell departs. If the B-36 turns south and GCI sites pick it up, you'll intercept them for a look-see. If there's someone alive in the cockpit you'll communicate using hand signals and flashlights. Maybe even make radio contact. Morse code should work. If there's nobody home, you'll try and contact the rear compartment, and have them bail out. Once they've vacated the premises you'll be officially ordered to destroy the aircraft. I'd have one of the squadron's crew do the job, but with the evening's festivities only just winding down, you two were the only sober crews to be had. Your experience is also vital to this operation. Questions?' Duckwalker rose to all of his five foot six.

'I was talking to the crew we flew with this morning, Sir. I've never seen a B-36 up close, but the information I gleaned from them was that it looks like it could be a tough bird to bring down. Then there are a lot of "what ifs." What if our 50-caliber machine guns can't do enough damage? What if they don't get the picture and decide to fight back? And what if the damn thing blows up in our face during the attack? Will that trigger the bomb? Finding it's going to be the easy part. Shooting it down is another story.'

'I don't have a single answer, Jones. Perhaps Flying Officer Fender can give us some insight?'

Lou had assessed the situation and felt the discomfort of the Rangoon fiasco. He couldn't shoot down another aircraft, but then the situation presented here was much more serious. He felt squeamish at being singled out, and in the ensuing seconds he took to respond, a battle plan came together. It relied on the Met officer, the aircraft, and Duckwalker Jones.

'Sir, if I get above the bomber, the chances of getting more than one pass are good. That'll allow for at least one identification pass and a setup for a kill, if the decision is made to shoot it down. With this weather, I'll need all the fuel I've got to get above him. If I use too much, I won't have enough to sustain the altitude and make a couple of interceptions. It'll take more than one interception to get results. They won't be ready on our first attack, so we'll get away unscathed. Our second attack will be against at least three twin turrets of 20-millimeter cannons. That means we won't be around for a third.'

He turned to the Met officer.

'If I'm able to use thermals and updrafts on the edge of the storm, I can save a shitload of fuel. That's if the weatherman here can point me in the right direction.'

The Met officer rose into the beam, casting a silhouette.

'Please project the latest weather chart.'

The slide was inserted and a giant swirl of isobars and frontal patterns lit up the screen. He stuffed his pipe in a pocket, picked up the pointer and directed it at Lou.

'Sir, that is the most ridiculous and dangerous idea I've ever had the misfortune to comment on. Turbulence, gust loading, precipitation, wind shear, they'd tear your aircraft apart.'

'I'm not asking permission to attempt it, Sir. I'm asking if you can find locations along the potential flight path of the B-36 where the conditions exist that Flight Lieutenant Jones and myself might take advantage of such a phenomenon.' He looked to the OC of 440 Squadron for support. Duckwalker interjected.

'Sir, as it stands right now we have a B-25 that in this weather might get to 15,000 if he's lucky. He's going to be bucking shit all the way. I wouldn't want to be in that washing machine. I've seen first-hand what the CF-100 will do in turbulence, and it's not going to break apart. It's a tough bird. The weather can give us the upper hand, if we're allowed to use it.'

The Met officer looked to the CO, and shook his head. 'I don't believe that's a prudent course of action, Sir. We have one chance to catch this guy, and I don't believe it'll be in an unstable air mass. If the bomber descends into the frontal system it'll be affected worse than our interceptor ever will. My instincts tell me that if the bomber is descending, and for whatever reason heads in our direction, the storm will cause its destruction.'

Pete had heard enough and decided it was time to come up with plan B and take a swing at Lou.

'Sir, we don't know if the intruder is even coming our way. I think Fender and Jones should climb to altitude prior to any GCI contact, set the aircraft up for range and endurance, and wait. If he shows up, he shows up. If they flew the Queen's coronation films from Goose Bay to St. Hubert nonstop with tanks on, surely these guys can loiter at 30,000 for a while.'

'But what if it's at 40,000?'

'Then I'd say that its rate of descent is low, and if that were so then the Americans can take care of it when it crosses their border.'

The lights snapped on and the CO's pointer shot skyward.

'Up there, there is no border. The Americans don't have an interceptor base in this vicinity. Bomber bases, yes; fighter bases, no. Like I said, we're the only interceptor squadron that can plug the leak. If it gets by us, somebody downstream is going to pay a pretty heavy price.'

Pete, standing at ease, pointed to Lou and winked.

'I have total faith that Flying Officer Fender will render the threat inert, Sir. I have first-hand knowledge that he successfully carried out similar tactics while serving in Southeast Asia. He's also a very good instrument pilot. He can get out of a flick roll in cloud if he has to. My sympathy to Flying Officer Jones.'

Pete had Lou and Duckwalker's attention and each understood his smirk and the wink that followed.

The two senior officers and the Met officer conferred in a pow-wow. A tapping of the pointer on the podium broke the silence.

'Rylander's plan will be the order of the day, gentlemen. The strength and direction of the upper winds in conjunction with the bomber's speed and rate of descent estimates that Mont Apica or Parent will pick them up in an hour if they come our way. That means they'll be at 150 miles or so and coming fast. That means we've got to get into the air pretty quick. Fender will be Banshee One and Rylander Backstop One, the B-36, Killjoy. I'm Bricklayer. Fender and Jones will be driven to barracks to change into flying gear. Rylander, I want a word with you. Gentlemen, I never thought I would utter these words in peacetime—let's SCRAMBLE.'

The room emptied, and Pete came to attention as the CO approached. He was offered a cigarette and the suspicion that news of his arrest had made it to the upper echelons was confirmed.

'Squadron Leader Gerard made some damning accusations against you, Rylander. The sergeant of police, whose ass I had to kiss to get you released, informed me of this. This is serious stuff we're talking about.'

'I swear it's all a misunderstanding, Sir. It'll never happen again. I used poor judgment.'

The CO looked at the bleached weather map on the screen. Without this man playing goalie, the game could be lost. Quid pro quo.

'It'll never happen on this or any base I happen to command or Squadron Leader Gerard happens to be posted to. Count yourself lucky this B-36 issue happened, or things would be much more grave. When you leave here you'll not return, not for any reason. If anything happens to that young lady lying in the hospital, I'll make you pay. Capisce?'

'Yes, Sir.'

'Now get the hell off my base. And by the way, good hunting.'

Pete found Dan Lacey in the Operations Center packing two flight bags and satchels stuffed with goodies he'd pinched from the mess.

'Well Captain, getting woken up at one in the morning and being told we're going to war wasn't what I'd bargained for when I signed up, but it sure gets the heart racing. That was some briefing. What was that with you and the CO? You been a bad boy again?'

'Yeah, something like that. Does the crew know what's up?'

'Not until you tell them. I got Jake Brown to check that the whole nine yards of 50-caliber ammo was in the machine-gun magazines. He was pretty excited about that. Do you think we have a chance against this fucking thing?'

'Only if we kamikaze it.'

'Give me a chance, Pete. Our radar and fire control system can set us up for a lead attack. Starfires in Korea have had good success. All we have to do is be in front and off the beam. The bugger doesn't fly that fast. We're an even match when it comes to speed. Think of the data we gain.'

Pete stared him down and shook his head in disbelief.

'Navigators!' Dan needed a reality check.

'We're not going to get much above 20,000, Dan. What B-36 in its fucking mind is going to be at that altitude in this fucking weather?'

Pete gathered his crew around the hatch and spelled out their mission. Fred Archer nervously wiped his glasses. The rest of the crew were handpicked volunteers and relished the mission, but he did not. There was a telephone in the Operations Center. His uncle needed to know. He could kiss goodbye any influence his uncle had on his future if he missed this opportunity.

'I've got to take a shit, Pete. I know you said not to touch the rations but I took a chance on some biscuits. There's a shitter in the Operations Center. I'll be back in five minutes.'

Pete pulled him aside and whispered raspily.

'So you can go and tell uncle what's going on? No fucking way, Archer. This is a top-secret operation. You get your ass into the right-hand seat. I don't care if you shit your pants. I want the pre-start check completed by the time I strap in.'

Pete had dodged a second bullet in an hour. The Voice from Ottawa needed to be kept in the dark. Wilding would be in the center of the action if the B-36 came into Mont Apica or Parent's radar range. If something did come of the operation, Fred's uncle would learn about it soon enough. Exposing the quisling changed the game anyway. Archer would get his payback with blackmail. The weekend had become a rollercoaster ride from hell, and the highest and steepest arches were still ahead.

Duckwalker waddled to the aircraft feeling lucky: called to duty, sober, and infatuated. Bonnie had wished him happy landings and kissed him goodbye. The taste of youth from her tongue still lingered. The taste in his mouth had been different when he'd last gone into danger. What lingered then was the kiss of death. Doris Kemper had seen to that.

What was fortunate about the mission was that they'd been briefed on the characteristics of the B-36 less than a day before. They had a sporting chance. "Lou said he'd get me up there, but the rest is up to me," he reminded himself. "Said that all he had to do was adjust the gun sight and pull the trigger."

Duckwalker jokingly suggested they do a JATO takeoff to save fuel but Lou failed to see the humor.

'The extra fuel from the tip tanks and the higher Mach

number we'll get at altitude should allow for three passes. That's if we're above him to begin with. That was a good call on the tanks. I won't do anything crazy up there. We can't at that altitude anyway.

Lou offered the ladder to Duckwalker and followed him up. He stood on his seat, turned to the B-25 and caught sight of Pete going about his business. The two pilots were caught off-guard as they made eye contact, neither one wanting to be the first to turn away. Pete snapped a sinister salute, which Lou replied with "the finger." The game was still on.

A bugle call to the joust crackled in the headphones as they started the engines and snapped on electronics. Duckwalker pulled down the radarscope and checked the circuit breakers. They closed the canopy, received taxi clearance and headed to the button of the runway. Duckwalker turned on the radar's master switch and waited patiently for the antenna gyros to stabilize. The aircraft came to a halt at the end of the taxiway and Lou came on the radio.

'Bagotville tower, this is Banshee One, ready for takeoff, over.' The voice of the CO replied.

'Banshee One this is Bricklayer. You are cleared for take-off. Contact Mont Apica GCI through five thousand, over.'

'Banshee One is cleared for takeoff.' Lou swung the aircraft onto the runway, spooled up the engines, released the brakes, and the aircraft began its roll. Duckwalker noted that the gyros had stabilized and the radar antenna had begun to sweep its sixty-degree cone. With the full fuel and ammunition load, the aircraft was at its maximum takeoff weight and accelerated sluggishly. The confirmation that they were safely airborne came with the clunk of the undercarriage and within seconds they were enveloped in cloud and rain.

Duckwalker tightened his straps and stared along the edge of the wing to the tip tank that vibrated with an alternate rhythm. 'We've got to keep the maneuvering speed within tight parameters, Lou, or we're going to lose the tanks. Without them we're fucked.'

Lou, focused on the instrument panel, grunted an acknowledgement. Duckwalker took this as an "affirmative" and focused on his scope. It was his third takeoff with the 'Undertaker.' He was the third man on the match.

CHAPTER 28

Hartwig cowered in the lower passageway, taking long slow intakes of pure oxygen, shivering and confused. Arnie Stonehawker, sporting a Germanic grin, had turned white and expired. There was no last gasp or call for momma, just a one-eyed aviator getting his angel wings.

His and the Major's breaths echoed over the intercom.

He'd devised a plan to force the Major's hand, but needed to fuel his strength. The action was to be short and violent, requiring physical exertion. Physicality was not in his nature. When one was bullied for a speech impediment it was not through physical and verbal altercations, but through subtle layering of humiliation. He'd wished he'd had the wherewithal needed to fight, but he'd always backed down.

Arnie had been staring skyward for ten minutes when the idea of using his body as a prop germinated. The light bulb went on when the aircraft made a turn to port and Arnie's torso shifted, startling him and setting his plan in motion. He checked his watch. He'd completed five minutes of deep hyperventilation and it was time to act.

Arnie lay propped against the radio desk and Hartwig wormed his way under his torso to get behind and beneath him. He removed Arnie's helmet liner and brushed hair over his eyeless socket.

Arnie Stonehawker was about to become a puppet.

Lincoln, oblivious to the cold, was lost in glee. He held his breath for a half minute and counted the breaths emanating over the intercom. One man was alive in the forward compartment beside himself. He moved to the right-hand seat to view the opening to the lower deck, and laid the pistol on his lap. The groundhog would stick his head up and the three bullets left in the magazine would finish the job. Then he'd pressurize the compartment and heat the place up. He hadn't counted on the cold.

The K-1 bombing system had been locked into the electromechanical computer and the impact-point of the bomber had been programmed in.

Lincoln's giddiness came from a sense of accomplishment. He'd pulled the whole plan off. He'd taken advantage of the Canadians, and they'd pay the price. Alana's death would be vindicated. The conception of their child had been in Québec and there he'd go to die. He'd come full circle, and couldn't have asked for more.

He focused on the slowly unwinding altimeter. The cross on the top of Mount Royal in Montréal was at 800 feet. That's when the altimeter and time would run out. For several minutes, the slow deep breaths coming over the intercom had become an irritant. Were they ones of incapacitation or concentration?

'I got to kill the groundhog,' he began to mutter. He leaned over and looked below. Movement. His heart began to race. He'd have to kill again. He readjusted the autopilot to compensate for the winds, and as the aircraft turned further south he punched in a final heading to Montréal, calculating the impact-point by decreasing the rate of descent. With six turning and a 70-knot tailwind, the aircraft was moving over the ground at 350 knots an hour. Impact was only an hour and a half away.

He concentrated on the stairwell.

Suddenly, two hands reached up and gripped the opening. The ghostly grinning face of Arnie Stonehawker shot up through the opening screaming, 'Major, don't shoot! Major, don't shoot!'

Only it wasn't his voice.

Lincoln aimed his pistol at Arnie's forehead and squeezed off two rounds. The torso reacted to the impacts, falling back into the radio operator's compartment and overtop of Hartwig. Hartwig fastened his mask and disengaged the intercom lead. Arnie lay face-up, and that's where he'd stay. If the Major needed proof of the kill, there it was.

Hartwig had his answer. How many bullets the Major had left, and why he he'd killed the forward crew was speculative. There was no attacking through the hatch; Arnie had seen to that. His only chance to get control of the aircraft was to cut off the Major's oxygen supply before he could repressurize the compartment.

He worked his way over the navigator and under the flight deck. He found the lead to the right-seat oxygen supply and cut it with his survival knife. Major Crisp would be unconscious in minutes if he didn't recognize the symptoms of anoxia.

Hartwig rummaged through the navigator's survival pack and found a distress mirror. He'd wait five minutes then take a peek. Shivering uncontrollably, he worked his way back to the ladder. He'd need heat soon, or he'd expire from hypothermia.

Lincoln had one bullet left. He hadn't missed Arnie that time. The silence over the intercom confirmed his quarry wasn't breathing, but he'd wait five minutes before checking his kill.

Soon Lincoln's reality slowly turned to fantasy as oxygen deprivation depleted his faculties. Giddiness became hallucinations that turned to confusion. Only then did his last vestige of reason have him recognize that he'd been duped.

Hartwig focused the mirror on the copilot's station, looking for movement. He couldn't discern what he was seeing until the reflection of the chest and head of the Major slumped onto the throttle console came into view. He ascended to the flight deck just as the Major was about to shoot himself in the head. Upon recognition that it was the stutterer who had put him in checkmate, Lincoln made a futile attempt to kill him, but the shot went wide, shattering a portion of the canopy over Hartwig's head.

He wrenched the pistol from Lincoln's grip and threw it down the hatch. The shattered pane, wailing in the slipstream, meant pressurizing and heating the compartment was out of the question.

Lincoln's unconscious body was slumped over the center console, and Hartwig was forced to lift him upright to access the throttles. He was still breathing, and the thought of him regaining consciousness led Hartwig to tie his wrists to the back of his seat with an intercom cord. He plugged in his oxygen, turned up what heat he could muster, disengaged the autopilot, and leveled the aircraft a thousand feet over the cloud top. He'd fly visual. He snapped on the intercom to the rear compartment.

It was time to check in with the caboose.

He conversed with Kenny Wright for five minutes in clear, cohesive sentences.

'All the radios are dead up here. The Major must have sabotaged them. Sooner or later, they'll pick us up on radar and our interceptors will escort us to the closest SAC base. All I have to do is stay on a heading and keep the engines running smooth. We're heading south, so eventually the front will dissipate and clear skies will allow me to descend to warmer air. It'll make for an easier approach and landing. I can't descend into the shit below us. Remember, there's only one of me.'

'Should I come forward?'

'To guard Wild Bill Hickok sitting here all tied up? That, and set up a morgue for the flight engineer and the two bodies in the basement. I wasn't expecting to break into prison and kidnap the warden when you sent me here. I definitely could use some help, but we've got the same problem we had when I was back there; there's just somebody different driving the engine. I'd be mighty grateful if you can find a way here.'

Hartwig felt confidence he'd never experienced. The success of their survival and the security of the bomb depended solely on him. He did an instrument crosscheck then examined the Major. He was deep in slumber and faint of breath. "No revival for him," he thought. "What would cause him to do such a thing?"

Suddenly, streaks of tracer shells slashed overhead, followed by a fleeting glimpse of a contrail. An unidentifiable fighter aircraft banked in front and climbed away. The silver flash of a salmon emerging from the depths came to mind and Hartwig felt the same rush. He pressed the intercom.

'This is Lieutenant Hartwig! Did any of you back there see what I just saw?'

'Don, this is Kenny. I think we just got shot at. We heard strikes on the vertical stabilizer like we got hit with buckshot. What the fuck's going on? We've got a nuke on board for Christ's sake!'

Hartwig did a quick assessment and came to a conclusion. The Major had gone mad, and the powers that be knew it. They were expendable.

'Order the gunners to open fire if we get attacked again. The aircraft that attacked us isn't one of ours. Must be a Canadian. If it is, treat it as the enemy. They don't know we're trying to save this bird.'

The tail gunner activated his radar and began sweeping the night sky. Two gunners mounted their perches in their observation bubbles and activated the turrets of the 20-millimeter cannons that popped out from hiding places within the fuselage. Kenny reported that the gunners were ready.

'If it attacks us again, it'll be from the rear, Kenny,' Hartwig directed. 'If it's using 50-cal. ammo we should be able to survive. This is a tough turkey. If the gunners get him, well so much the better. Christ, what the hell's going on?'

Colonel Briggs had been entrusted to deliver the news to the Canadians. There was a rogue intruder with the potential to do them harm, and it needed to be stopped, preferably on Canadian soil. Major Lincoln Crisp had overstepped his mandate and become a serious liability. The think-tank boys at the Pentagon had used their computer to filter through the thousands of scenarios presented and had come up with the most probable solution.

Trashcan One was on a suicide mission, targeting its homeland.

The saving grace was that the bomb was incapable of a full atomic detonation. If it went down with the aircraft the radioactive mess would take years to get cleaned up, but it would be localized. If it went down in an urban area, the loss of life and the humiliation of the North American defence system would be incalculable.

Lieutenant Stonehawker's gesture to fall on his sword when he presented his case about the Major's state of mind had been pooh-poohed by him, and he would pay for it if it ever came to light. He'd kept his mouth shut on that one, but if Stonehawker were to testify at an inquiry, his goose was cooked.

He was patched through to the commanding officer of a Canadian Air Force Base in Québec. Orders were straightforward. Destroy Trashcan One before it reached any populated area.

'If the aircraft comes your way, use whatever means are at your disposal to impede its flight path. Blast it out of the sky with dispatch.'

The CO felt cornered.

'What makes you think we can stop him? So far we haven't had much luck intercepting the damn things.'

'Ottawa and Montréal and all points in between are within its flight path. The storm's seen to that. If the bastard manages to make it across the border, then this conversation never happened. You're in the best position to determine the threat to your citizens.'

'Our record against the B -36 is dismal. The gunners nailed us every time. You got any suggestions?'

'Force him down into the storm. The aircraft's vulnerable when it's in turbulence and precipitation. The engines ice up easily and the mildest wind shear turns it into a bucking bronco. That new interceptor of yours is supposed to be "all weather" isn't it?'

'It's still in the development stage, and hasn't been fully tested. The vibration from the guns is prone to break radar tubes. If we get more than one pass without a breakdown, we'll be lucky.'

'Can't you send up more than one?'

'We've got a second aircraft in the air if he gets lower, but it's a long shot. We're on stand-down because of the storm, and I'm afraid we had only two crews with flying status.'

He'd decided it was prudent not to mention the vintage of the second aircraft.

'Well, two's better than one.'

'What about the radar sites? Are they on the job?'

'If it comes our way, Mont Apica and Parent will pick it up. They're GCI sites, and will vector our interceptor for a couple of passes. We've got experienced crews in the cockpits.'

'We want as little fuss about this situation as we can get. We need to keep it quiet like the Broken Arrow on the West Coast and the one in the Gulf of St. Lawrence. If this thing goes down where we think it might, all hell's going to break loose. Get the fucker for us, and we'll be eternally grateful.'

With that, Colonel Briggs signed off.

Pete was vectored southwest towards Montréal to take up station over La Tuque. They'd been in cloud since take-off, and the aircraft heaved and bucked as it worked its way to altitude in various intensities of hail and rain. As they passed through 10,000 feet he reminded the crew to take a bathroom break before they went on oxygen.

Within minutes, Jake Brown popped his head up into the flight deck. Paired with him was the grim face of Fred Malone.

'Look what I found in the rear compartment, Sir. We have a stowaway. I found him puking in the can.'

'What the fuck are you doing here, Malone?'

'You said I could come along, so here I am. A deal's a deal in my books.'

'Did your boss give you the okay?'

'With enthusiasm. Said you'd understand.'

'You were at the briefing. Don't you realize what's going on? You could put this whole operation in jeopardy. Get back where you were found and keep quiet. We're going on oxygen in a couple of minutes, so you better be through barfing.' Pete looked to Fred Archer and shook his head.

'I guess "uncle" is going to hear about this.'

Lou and Duckwalker broke out of cloud and into a brilliant night sky. They climbed to 40,000 feet and set the aircraft up for range and endurance. Mont Apica and Parent hadn't picked up the bogey on their screens and advised them to work their way north and maintain a holding-pattern between the two radar sites.

They flew in silence, perusing the northern sky for a bright moving star coming their way, hoping to pick it out before the sweep of a radar dish tattooed it on a screen. Duckwalker broke the spell.

'So what's the story, Lou? What's this Rylander fellow got on you? You've got my word that it stays between us old ladies. Tit-for-tat; you tell me yours and I'll tell you mine. Deal?' Lou thought long, and decided to come clean. His curiosity about the gimp's affliction seemed a fair trade. He went straight to the point.

'At the end of the war, I was ordered to shoot down two Japs who wanted to surrender. They were sitting ducks, and I've lived with the guilt ever since. Rylander was there and knows all about it. He's held an axe over my head ever since. It's fucked my life. I call it my Rangoon nightmare. The only way I can rid myself of it is to live as miserable a life as possible. It's a penance of sorts. I'm like that guy in Li'l Abner, the one with cloud over his head all the time. There's more to the story, but it won't be played out until one or both of us is dead. What's so strange about the last day and half is that here I am doing the same thing, waiting to shoot down a sitting duck…. I don't know if I can pull the trigger.'

Duckwalker adjusted the heater and emptied condensation from his oxygen mask. He pulled up his visor and squinted into the night. This was his time to fly. He lived in a world of shade and the night sky took him into his true realm of flight.

'This is no sitting duck, Lou. We're entrusted to save thousands of lives from a radiation disaster that could take years to clean up. You can't ask for more redemption than that.'

Lou went to the heart of the matter.

'I'm not after redemption. I just want to sleep in peace when I find happiness. What's your story?'

'A woman did this to me. I led myself down the garden path and made a bad decision: a self-inflicted wound. I gambled too much for perfection, and it bit me in the ass. Martin-Baker became my employer, and you can guess the rest. I had three hundred hours of right-hand seat time, and survived twenty missions. Then I traded ten seconds of life for two hours of heaven and nine years of hell.'

Duckwalker kept the suicide out of the story. No use pushing it. 'That's my Rangoon nightmare. My ass and eyeballs contributed to the design of the seats we're sitting in; yours truly's offer to the Gods of flight. I was the first Commonwealth human being to eject in flight. Things didn't quite happen the way they were supposed to. My chute hadn't fully deployed, and I hit the ground in a sitting position. I've been this way ever since. If I try to stand up to my full height, I feel like I have to take a shit.'

Lou ripped off his oxygen mask and broke into laughter. Duckwalker, oblivious to his mirth, continued his story.

'I was in the back seat of a modified Meteor. They wanted to experiment with rocket propulsion, and I was their crash-test dummy. When I pulled up the handles, the canopy didn't blow. The rocket in the seat shot me through it and I barely cleared the tail. The explosion buggered my eyes. That's why they designed it, so the blind is pulled over your face when it's time to go. The pilot didn't have an ejection seat and didn't get out. So I became a cripple. I met a couple of nurses last night who said there were advances in spinal medicine that might change things for me, but I don't hold much hope. I understand you've hit the silk a few times.'

Lou recounted his ejection from a Sabre, and his vow to never again be in a situation where he had to vacate the premises. 'Who knows what the hell's going to happen when you pull down the blind?'

Duckwalker reached overhead and gripped the ejection ring. Pull it down, and good old Martin-Baker did the rest.

'I know how you feel. If you ordered me to punch out, I've reservations about my success. So far, nobody in the back seat has successfully done it.'

'I've done enough for both of us,' Lou replied. 'You don't have to worry; we've got two engines, and like you said, this bird is built like a brick shithouse.'

They flew on in silence, scouring the northern sky, lost in thought. Suddenly Duckwalker's radio crackled.

'Banshee One, this is Bricklayer. The Americans have ordered us to stop Killjoy. You're to use all resources to bring it down as fast as possible. That's an order! Confirm you've received this transmission. Over.'

'Lou, Bricklayer just contacted us on the secure frequency. We've been ordered to dispatch Killjoy ASAP.'

Lou felt a pang in his gut.

'Let's hope the fucker doesn't come our way. I've a bad

feeling about this. You heard what Don and John said. If they've activated those 20-millimeter cannons, you may be the first to try out that seat you helped design.'

Lou did a slow one-eighty, and headed east to Mont Apica. Ten minutes later, he reversed back to Parent. 'Where the fuck is he?' He muttered over the intercom. 'Where the fuck is he?'

Duckwalker loved flying at night above cloud. His combat missions during the war had all been at night. With his visor raised, and wearing clear lenses, his dilated pupils sucked in light from the stars, magnifying them to the intensity of harvest moons: his realm, his daylight. He scanned the giant lens of clear air sitting on the northern horizon, his eyes moving in time to the sweep of his blank radarscope.

Then there it was, one star shining brighter than all the others.

'I got him Lou. Three o'clock level. The brightest star.'

'It's not moving.'

'That's because the bastard's coming our way.'

Wing Commander Chauncey Wilding paced behind two radar operators intent on their scopes. He was nervously twisting his handlebar moustache, hoping for a third blip to appear on the screens. The situation had become one of déjà vu. He and Lou Fender were back in Rangoon, and it was 1945 all over again. How ironic. The events unfolding gave hope to finishing him off for good. With him gone, all that was left to pick up his money was to meet up with Rylander and reap Rangoon's reward. Nine years was too long to wait for a payday. How many times had he spent the money? How many potential business ventures had been underfunded and vanished?

It had been a long wait for this weekend. The journey had been one of sacrifice. He'd had little difficulty in switching to the RCAF and keeping his rank. They'd even promoted him and given him control of four GCI sites. Battle experience, gleaned from his three years in Asia, had paid off, but that wasn't the true reason for immigrating to Canada. He needed the money.

Investing in a device that would eliminate electronic tubes in radios and radar would turn him into a millionaire, and he could kiss Canada goodbye. First, he had to get the cash; then he'd have to launder it. That's where Rylander earned his keep. Former associates in Toronto had been apprised of the situation and guaranteed eighty cents on the dollar. The current exchange rate on the strong Canadian dollar would give him another three percent.

Rylander had taken the money to Canada when he'd been repatriated, and held control of it ever since. He'd relinquish it when Lou Fender was dead and Tamaguchi had lost his partner. The evil of their pact had kept it secure but Lou Fender was the fly in the ointment. One word from him, and it was off to prison for the three of them.

The plan Wilding had hatched years before was to have culminated that Saturday morning, but the weather had thrown a monkey wrench into it. The only way he could salvage the plan was to mesh it into the Killjoy incident, and it was up to him to orchestrate it from the GCI site he was vetting. If Rylander couldn't bring him down, then Killjoy would have to do the job. If the B-36 appeared on the screen, he'd have the opportunity to arrange the chess pieces on the radarscope to make it happen. If it didn't, the wait for a next opportunity to dispatch him could be years away.

He needed the third blip.

'There he is, Sir. Right where we thought he'd be.' Wilding leaned into the scope and saw the strong signature return of the B-36.

'That's him.' Two sweeps of the dish confirmed its altitude and airspeed.

'He's a hundred and twenty miles out, and he's doing about three-fifty over the ground.'

Mont Apica came on the air.

'Scooter, this is Scabbard. We have Killjoy. Looks like he's coming your way.' Wilding relieved a controller and donned a headset. It was time to make things happen.

'Banshee One, this is Scooter. We have a bogey at your three o'clock about eighty miles. GO BUSTER! GO BUSTER!'

The unmistakable terminology and accent he'd last heard in Rangoon stunned Lou and it took him several seconds to fill in the blanks. "How did he get in on the action?" He muttered over the intercom.

'What did you say?' Duckwalker responded.

'Nothing. Thought I recognized the controller's voice.'

'That's Wingco Wilding, the best in the business.... We're in good hands if we've got him directing traffic. We have a target Lou. Let's go buster.'

Lou added full power and made a right turn to the north. Duckwalker switched his radar to long-range and buried his head in the scope, but couldn't find a return. With a closing speed of 700 knots, he frantically searched for the target.

'We can't waste a head-on attack, Lou. At our combined speeds, I can't guarantee any success. When I pick him up, I'll direct you off to his right and we'll do a starboard turn into a stern attack. We'll be coming in high so you'll have to adjust for our overtaking speed. Come in hot on your first attack so we can convert airspeed for altitude. Our next pass won't give us the same advantage.'

'Roger that!'

'Banshee One, this is Scooter. Your target is now at your two o'clock at sixty miles. You should be able to see him.' Lou made out a distinct moving star. Duckwalker's screen suddenly lit up with a strong return.

'I have the target at one o'clock, forty miles, Lou. It's moving pretty quick.'

"I've got it visually. Look at the contrails those props are churning! He can't be more than 2,000 feet above the cloud top.' Lou armed the eight machine guns in the belly pack and adjusted the radar gun sight. He was tempted to test the guns with a short burst, but opted for saving ammunition. It was going to take every 50-caliber slug in the arsenal to cripple the monster.

'Banshee One, this is Scooter. Your target is at three o'clock, ten miles.'

'Banshee One has it in sight. We're commencing our attack.' Lou banked the aircraft into a shallow starboard dive. Duckwalker called out the changes in their relative speed and position as they closed in over top of the six contrails.

'Holy shit, the fucker's big.'

'Can't see it, Lou; it's all up to you.'

Duckwalker concentrated on the huge blip approaching the center of his radar screen. 'Get in as tight as you can, Lou…. Remember what Don and John said. We don't want to break away too early. The closer we get the less drop and the more penetration we'll get from the fifties. Give it a good six-second burst.' Duckwalker held his breath and concentrated on the speed of Lou's breathing. It was a clear indication of his heart rate. His breath was slow and shallow.

The aircraft shuddered for four seconds, then climbed to starboard. Lou's breathing became erratic.

'Why the short burst, Lou?'

'I missed the fucker! Can you believe it? I missed the fucker.'

'How do you know?'

'The tracers were over top, and by the time it would take to steepen the bank, I'd waste too much ammo. It looked to me that I was a good twenty feet high all the way up the fuselage. My fault. I haven't done any live shooting since my Sabre days. Report in will you? Say the first attack was marginal. We know different.' Lou topped off his climb and headed in the opposite direction to the bomber.

'They weren't expecting us,' he informed. 'They didn't shoot, and they haven't taken evasive action. I'd say we have a runaway train down there. Makes me feel a whole lot better about taking my time. Set me up for the next attack.'

———•—•———

Lieutenant Hartwig had figured out the puzzle. The Major had been hell-bent on destruction. A whole lot of generals must have figured out the puzzle, too. The Canadians had been given the job of striking the first blow. He wondered what kind of interceptor they'd sent up, and how many? They were armed with 50-caliber machine guns with tracer, but that didn't bother him. As an ex-fighter pilot, he knew the bomber could easily take care of itself. He rummaged through Lincoln's flight bag and found the aircraft identification manual. He'd have to make it fast. He flipped it open to Canada, and there it was, the Avro Mark 3 CF-100. The gunners needed to know.

'Pilot to gunners, your target is a CF-100. It's a twin-jet interceptor armed with eight 50-caliber machine guns. We've had good success against them in practice. Our radar-controlled tail-cannons have the best chance. Drive them off, or we'll have to abandon this bird. I want to keep heading for home. Lieutenant Wright, if you can find a way, I could use a little help up here.'

Wright had beaten him to punch. Within a minute, he popped up through the hatch, kneeled behind him and plugged in.

'How'd you get here?'

'With saturation breathing and by holding my breath. The boys in the back gave me a shove and I clawed my way here. Eighty feet is a long way when you're on your belly and your breath's running out. That's quite a mess down there. Arnie Stonehawker took quite a pounding.'

He tilted back Lincoln's head and unhinged his oxygen mask. There was no breath.

'Looks like the Major's joined the others. Pretty good body count.'

'Kenny, I want you to bump the engineer out of his seat and sit at his station. I want you to monitor the engines. Another attack is on the way, and I need to concentrate on flying this thing.' Kenny unbuckled the engineer and slid his body down the hatch and on top of Arnie.

'What about the Major?'

'Leave him. I don't want to plug the hole with any more bodies. If we have to bail out, I want a clear path.' Wright strapped in and perused the bank of engine instruments. Hartwig pointed out the critical dials and explained the carburetor heat and mixture parameters.

'If we end up in cloud, the engines are our problem. They have a tendency to run rich and catch fire. I'm hoping we can stay above the cloud until we exit the front.'

'Rear gunner to Captain! I've picked up the bogey. He's three miles out and closing.'

'Captain to all gunners. Fire for effect. Shoot the bastard down!'

Duckwalker had set them up for a classic pursuit-curve attack. They'd lost the advantage of altitude and Lou was forced to approach level into swirling contrails. Their aircraft bounced and weaved in the bomber's wake as he concentrated on the erratic blip of his radar gun sight.

Suddenly, the tail of the bomber lit up with flashes of gunfire and the interceptor shuddered as the starboard tip tank was sheared off. The aircraft yawed violently and Lou rammed the rudder pedal in compensation. He squeezed the trigger, sweeping the bomber's wing from port to starboard with an eight-second burst. The tracers arced from wing tip to wing tip, deflecting off propeller blades and the top of the wing like a Halloween sparkler. He passed the bomber to starboard, pulled into a turning climb and felt a second hit.

'Where did that one get us? It feels like the tail.' Duckwalker loosened his straps and twisted around.

'The tip of the vertical stabilizer's gone. Is the aircraft controllable?' Lou released the rudder pressure, and the aircraft yawed violently.

'I've still got rudder, and enough ammo for one more pass.' Lou's breath had become erratic. 'If I can keep this bird flying, we've got one more chance.'

'We haven't enough airspeed to get back up to the bomber's altitude, Lou. All we can hope for is that he heads into the cloud.'

Lou nursed the aircraft upwards, but the drag produced by compensating for the missing tip tank allowed him to barely clear the cloud top.

Mont Apica and Parent watched the encounter, waiting for confirmation that the bomber had been dispatched, but all they saw was the large blip heading in the same direction and the smaller blip flying five miles off to its starboard.

Wilding was the first to spot an anomaly.

'The bastard is descending!' he yelled. 'Banshee One must have hurt him.'

Lieutenant Hartwig felt the vibration from the tail guns, and saw the erratic flight of deflected tracers whizzing overtop of the canopy. The interceptor passed to starboard and kissed the top of the cloud cover a thousand feet below. He watched it as it slowly climbed up to their altitude. "The front gunners would have got it," he thought, "but they weren't home."

He felt a difference in the hum of the engines and asked Wright to keep an eye on the tachometers.

'Three of the engines are running erratic, Don. It's like the propellers are out of balance or something.'

'I feel it too. The bastard hit the props. Probably chipped chunks off them. Ease back the throttles on the bad engines and we'll see what happens.' Wright pulled back slowly on the three levers and the vibration lessened.

'Still doesn't sound good,' Hartwig commented. 'The last thing we need right now is to have one of the R-4360's shake off its mount. We can't maintain this altitude with three engines at half power. I'm going to descend.'

'You're the Captain, Lieutenant.'

Hartwig re-engaged the autopilot on the original heading and trimmed the aircraft for a shallow descent. Within a minute they sliced into the cloud top, the vertical stabilizer disappearing like a descending shark's fin.

'I sure as hell hope we're going into a stable air mass, Kenny. This here aircraft doesn't perform too well in turbulence. That's the last we'll see of the Canadians.'

Hartwig vacated his seat and knelt behind Wright. He needed a first-hand assessment of the engine situation.

'With their rear configuration, the engines are prone to carburetor ice buildup. It happens in cloud. They run rich and fires start in the exhaust manifold. If the fire can't be put out, the engine has to be shut down and we'll have to abandon the aircraft. You know what that means.' Hartwig pointed back to the bomb bay and made a slashing motion across his throat.

'Kaboom!'

'Couldn't we land it now?'

'There isn't an airport within five hundred miles that's big enough to handle us, and we sure as hell aren't over the flatlands of the Midwest. That's mean country down there.' They waited through 5,000 feet of descent to confirm his suspicions.

'Number two's starting to run hot.' He pointed to the center of the right wing. 'Give me a shout if you see flame.' Hartwig disengaged the autopilot and took over manually. He'd hand-fly it from here on. It was his aircraft to save.

CHAPTER 30

Pete leveled the B-25 at 16,000 feet, and handed control to the copilot. 'This is as high as we're going in this shit,' he announced to the crew. He radioed the GCI sites to let them know the turbulence had become too severe and for now he had nothing else to offer in the way of altitude.

Dan Lacey, oblivious to the bumps and heaves, buried himself in his scope, fiddling with dials and conversing with the GCI sites. The B-36 was out of the range of his radar, but both GCI sites informed him that it was heading their way. Wilding's distinct British upper-crust nasal delivery let him know that big things were in the offing.

"The prick's orchestrating something," Pete thought. "He's working a friendly and a foe at the same time, and he wants to bring down both of them." He thought of the money stashed in the tail: his insurance. Wilding would do everything in his power to put the B-25 safely back on terra firma.

Suddenly, Jake Brown, paired with a grim-faced Fred Malone, stuck his head up into the flight deck. 'We've got a sick passenger in the back, Sir. By the looks of it, he hasn't got much left to puke up.'

Fred Malone was more than airsick. His nausea had reduced him to near incapacitation.

'You said you didn't get airsick, Malone. There's nothing I can do for you. Stay close to the center of the wing and don't lie down. We're going to be in this shit for at least two hours so you're just going to have to grin and bear it.'

Fred wished he'd never set foot inside the rattling tin can.

He found a jump seat and strapped in, but the stench of puke in his mask had him gagging. He removed his mask and gulped whatever thin air his lungs could glean, but the light-headedness of anoxia forced him back into the stench. He gulped down a half dozen deep intakes, removed his mask, and dry heaved. If this was what flying was all about, it was strictly for the birds.

What had started out to be a covert mission for his boss and an educational experience for him had turned into a nightmare of insecurity and embarrassment. His mission had not been self-serving. A clearly agitated Squadron Leader Gerard had ordered him to the hospital after the briefing. How fateful. He'd headed there thinking it was to follow up on Marie's condition, not realizing he'd end up puking his brains out in a World War II bomber in a storm, sitting in wait to shoot down the biggest bomber in the world.

When he arrived at the hospital, Josette had changed into her nursing outfit and her starched breastplate seemed to protrude farther than ever. What lay behind the stiff white apron had fueled his fantasy, and his subtle overtures of his desire to bed her had become more than a running joke between them. The proof of his suspicion that she had a fetish for women gave him power that her rank couldn't supersede. Quid pro quo. He'd hustled to the infirmary and made for Marie's room, but was ushered into her office.

'Fred, I'm not addressing you as a subordinate. You must live by the nursing fraternity and become warlock in the coven. One of our sisters was grievously violated tonight and it appears the perpetrator is going to get away without so much as a slap on the hand. You must understand that with regards to Flying Officer Rylander, we are dealing with a vile and repulsive criminal. You've seen what he's capable of doing. I have evidence that he raped her knowing full well she'd gone unconscious. She'd be dead if you'd not happened by. Who knows, he might well have dumped her body from 10,000 feet and nobody would have known what had happened to her. I wouldn't be forcing the issue if I didn't have further evidence of his treachery. He has to be stopped. I'm ordering you to fly with him. You're to stick with him until you have the evidence I'm looking for.'

She produced a vial of clear liquid and clasped it in his hand.

'What's this?'

'It's chloral hydrate. His weapon.'

'What am I supposed to do with it?'

'I want you to use it on him. It's the closest thing to a truth serum that I could get my hands on. I want information. Pick your time and place. You're a nurse. How you administer the drug is up to you. You'll need enough time for it to take effect and enough time to ask him these questions.' She handed him an envelope with a ballpoint pen inside.

'But most important, you must have a witness to

corroborate everything you hear. There's a document inside that you can fill out to make things legal. Do this and I'll let you fuck me. I'll do whatever you want. That's how important this is for me. Take what time you need. I'll cover for you. Here's my authorization.' She slipped him a second envelope.

'Return with the documents signed and sealed, and I'll give what you want.'

'I'll have to stow away.'

'You're a clever man, Malone. You'll find some way to do it.'

Fred commandeered a staff car, and sped to the flight line. He ran to the hatch of the B-25 as Jake Brown was about to pull up the ladder.

'I need to talk to Flight Lieutenant Rylander right away,' he screamed over the roar of jet engines. 'The CO sent me. I'll only be a second. I'll close the hatch when I leave. Just show me how.'

Jake gave instructions, helped him in, and scurried to his perch in the nose. He had guns and cameras to attend to.

Fred followed him to Dan Lacey's compartment, then did an abrupt turn and headed back to the tail where his flying gear had been stashed. He donned a flying suit over his uniform, slipped on a helmet and sat in the waist gunner's jump seat. Within seconds the vibration of the engines signaled there was no turning back. He was in.

Things had changed. His promise that he wouldn't get airsick had been a hollow one. The aircraft's nauseating circus-ride to altitude had him woozy and within ten minutes, he was shaking uncontrollably in fetal position. He found a makeshift toilet and for the next half hour wished he was dead. He recognized the effects of anoxia, donned his oxygen mask, then promptly puked in it. He choked, sputtered, swallowed, and ripped it off before he got a second heave.

Jake Brown discovered him washing out his oxygen mask with coffee.

'I just couldn't bear to piss in it,' was all he could yell over the din of the engines.

'What the hell are you doing here, Sir? You were supposed to see the Captain then leave. And where did you get the gear?'

'Go ask your Captain.'

'Follow me up to the flight deck.'

———•————

Duckwalker was in his element. He'd attacked the B-36 the same way the Junkers 88 had attacked him on his fifteenth mission.

They were returning from operations, targeting the rail yards outside Versailles when the two gunners spotted a German night-fighter attacking from the hindquarter. Six corkscrews later, and down to 7,000 feet, they broke free of their pursuer and made it back to Skipton. An unexploded cannon shell in the starboard wing tank fueled the booze-up that evening. The twenty-minute battle had been his zenith as a pilot. He'd shed the skin of a small man and he walked with a swagger until Martin-Baker made him a cripple.

'We're dead if we try another stern attack, Lou. They

hadn't even warmed up, and they still got us. Their tail guns have the same radar we have. We're even-Steven.'

'What's up your sleeve?'

'Instead of trying to rope him, I think we should head him off at the pass.'

'Tell me where to go.'

'We've got to get ahead of him, so you're going to have to speed things up. It's time to go into the soup.'

For the next ten minutes, teamwork and skill had them passing the bomber five miles to starboard on a parallel course. At the GCI radar site, Wilding could see the geometry in the three chess pieces converging on the screen, and formed a battle plan. To work it to perfection, he needed help from the Americans. They needed to drop chaff. He radioed the interceptor.

'Banshee One, this is Scooter. Killjoy is at your seven o'clock descending. What are your intentions?'

'What the fuck are our intentions, Duckwalker?' Lou groaned. 'My leg's cramping up.' Duckwalker hit the mike switch to let the team know the play.

'Scooter, this is Banshee One. Vector us for a lead collision-course attack. We want to be ten miles ahead of Killjoy before turning to attack. We've got enough ammunition to spray him stem to stern. If that's not good enough, then it's up to Backstop.'

Duckwalker had done the math. With an understanding of the radar he'd helped design for the Mark 4, the basics were the same. He'd have Lou shoot off the whole nine yards of 50-caliber bullets, seconds before they would collide. A sharp 6-G pull-up would avoid a collision.

'Is there any way you can dump the tank, Lou? We're

burning fuel like a bad thing, and we could use more speed. Isn't there some way we can shake it off?'

Lou had the answer.

'Hold on, I'm going to induce a violent yaw. With the tank sideways to the air flow, it can't possibly stay on.' Lou released the pressure off the rudder pedal and applied it in the opposite direction. Both had readied for the reaction and both had their eyes glued to the tip tank. The aircraft canted violently, vibrated and shuddered. The tank and the wing flexed out of sync. The tank tore away.

'There's an experience I never want to go through again,' Duckwalker commented. 'I thought the fucking wing was going to break off.'

'It may still do, if we go through anything as violent.'

'Does that include our breakaway?'

'That definitely includes our breakaway.'

———

Dan Lacey's head was buried in an empty scope. Communication between Banshee One and Scooter had been guarded, and he was in the dark as to the progress of the intercept. Suddenly his headset crackled.

'Backstop One, this is Scooter. Killjoy is at your three o'clock at fifty miles, and descending. Climb as high as you can.'

Pete picked up Wilding's accent, and knew the bastard was conjuring up something, though they both held a knife to each other's throat. Wilding held Svengali power over him. Some men were like that, alpha males for no discernible reason.

"Lou must have run out of ammo, or been shot down,"

he thought. Either way, it looked like they were mankind's last resort.

They'd been orbiting at 18,000 feet at reduced airspeed to minimize gust loading. The B-25 was built to dump bombs, not intercept the world's most advanced weapon system. The Yanks had used B-25's for everything, even launching a squadron of them from an aircraft carrier to bomb Tokyo. Now they were in an interceptor mode, armed with two machine guns and the best interceptor radar in the world.

First they had to get to altitude. Second, they had to set up for an intercept that had to be perfect. There was no catching the B-36 if it got by. He took control from Archer and advanced the throttles. He could get to 25,000 feet, but it would be a struggle. He activated the attack scope and tied it in with Dan's radar. When Dan got a positive lock-on, he'd pass the information to him, and he'd fly the attack. He wouldn't see the target and the target wouldn't see him.

Pete's mind was a swirl of disconnected mumbo-jumbo. The nurse puking his guts added to the pile of shit he'd have to dig himself out of. The things he'd traded for his potion. The biggest trade of all had been with Wilding. If he hadn't discovered his habit, the balance of power would have easily been in his favor. Rangoon again!

While convalescing with dysentery in a military hospital in Mandalay, shortly after his arrival in Burma, Pete chanced upon a sympathetic medic with access to chloral hydrate, whereupon an East Indian night nurse became his first victim. Unfortunately for Pete, the medic supplied a certain Squadron Leader Wilding with black market drugs and the nurse was the medic's girlfriend.

Wilding had Pete by the balls, blackmailing him into both the Rangoon fiasco and smuggling its reward back to Canada. The discovery that Wilding had manipulated both him and Lou about the Jap fiasco re-set the balance of power. What amazed him about Wilding was his management of the rigmarole. The steps Wilding had taken to return to today's Rangoon were as intertwined as the workings of a Swiss watch.

'What if we can't dispose of him?' Pete had asked.

'He has to go. The Jap, too.'

'What Jap?'

'Tamaguchi. The one who started it all; the one who wants his money back. I've a hunch he and Fender are in cahoots. It's just a hunch, but you know me.'

The conversation had taken place a year ago. Shortly afterwards he'd been recruited by The Voice from Ottawa.

What had become of Lou Fender? There was no indication from Wilding that he'd gone down. Lou Fender, the toughest bone to bury any old dog had to dispose of, was out there somewhere. Pete and Wilding had planned several schemes to kill him but neither one had the guts to resort to face-to-face murder. In front of a radar screen or in a cockpit, maybe, but with gun, knife, or poison, never. The morning's disaster had erased six months of planning, but within hours the same players were back at the table, ready to gamble with a fresh deck of cards. The storm had brought ill wind and renewal. This, time he would master the weather and put Rangoon to rest.

Dan Lacey came over the intercom.

'Pete, I've picked up Killjoy and Banshee One at forty miles. Christ, it looks like they're going to collide. Holy shit! There are four more blips on the screen. Either Killjoy's dumping chaff, or the bomber just blew up!'

With Hartwig at the controls and Wright monitoring the engines, they knew there was little hope of making it to the border. The security of the cloud against attack had been replaced by the engines' vulnerability to moisture and temperature. Within minutes the inevitable had happened.

'Number Two's on fire!' Wright screamed. 'It's a blow torch out there.'

Hartwig adjusted the mixture and they watched as the trail of flame was reduced to an ember's glow. The wings bucked and flexed in the turbulence as the bomber beat its way through churning cloud and lightning.

'Keep an eye on the cylinder-head temperatures, Kenny. Number Two's just a precursor. We've only just begun.' They flew in silence for five minutes, until they were jarred by the rattled voice of the tail gunner.

'Lieutenant Hartwig, I've picked up a bogey at five o'clock high, six miles out and closing fast!' Hartwig's hands began to tremble, and he felt his temples about to burst.

Worse news followed.

'Don, Number Two's acting up again and Number Six is on fire! What can I do?'

With an engine on each wing about to explode, and an interceptor about to unleash its weaponry, he knew he had only one option. He pushed forward on the control column, pulled back on the six throttles and lit the jet engines. The dial on the vertical speed indicator jumped earthward like a willow diviner, and the shrill of air through the bullet hole in the canopy increased by several octaves.

'Kenny, I'm dumping chaff, then I'll help you shut down Two and Six. Just do as I say!'

Suddenly a streak of tracers, followed by a thump and a grinding vibration in the rudder pedals, sent a shock up Hartwig's spine. The bomber yawed to the left and he jumped on the rudder.

'Fuck! We've been hit, Kenny! I don't think I can keep her straight.'

Hartwig fought the controls as the bomber insisted on maintaining a descent to port. Left to its own trim, it would turn through an eastward heading and return north. Add the sweep of the counterclockwise rotation of the winds, and the aircraft was destined to crash in the northern Laurentian Mountains.

Hartwig checked the altimeter.

'We're too high to bail out, Kenny. We'll stick with it 'til there's nothing more we can do.' He patched-in to the master intercom.

'Rear compartment, prepare to abandon aircraft! I repeat, prepare to abandon aircraft!'

Duckwalker had set them up for a 90-degree lead collision attack course. The future Mark 4 would fire a huge salvo of rockets and let the target run into them. The parameters would be different using machine guns, but the theory would be the same. Bullets were faster than rockets, so they'd have to get in close. The breakaway was the problem.

The sure-fire method of taking out the bomber was to collide with the behemoth and put everyone out of their misery, but the kiss goodbye from the nurse changed things. Besides, the kamikaze in him had already been used up.

The B-36's radar-return was large, clear, and ran a steady course. At 15 miles, Duckwalker got a positive lock-on and passed control to Lou's gun sight. Lou dialed in and picked up the pipper. Suddenly the radar broke lock.

'What the fuck just happened?' Lou yelled, 'I need a course and trigger time.'

'Christ, the bomber's either blown up or it's dropping chaff,' responded Duckwalker. 'If it's dropping chaff, then somebody must be in the cockpit. That changes everything. I can't tell which target to lock on to. We're going to have to do a stern attack. Turn to port forty-five degrees, and I'll keep him in focus using my hand control.'

Duckwalker switched his radar back to search-mode and found the stream of targets. Determining which was the B-36 was the puzzle. The progress of the lead blip was too enticing. He grabbed the hand control and locked on.

'She's all yours, Lou.'

The bomber released more chaff, and Duckwalker's radar broke lock again. As Lou was about to break away, a stream of tracers flashed by. The bomber, trailing fire from two engines, emerged from the cloud like a rising submarine.

'I see the fucker!' Lou yelled, but he was too close. With

a "what the hell" he bunted the nose down and squeezed the trigger.

The force from the negative-G shot Duckwalker up into the canopy, his crash helmet saving him from a knockout blow. Simultaneously, the canopy slid back, shot into space, and the roar of 400-knot air overwhelmed him, sucking his cockpit bare of anything not strapped down.

Lou, hunkered behind the windscreen and focused on the gun sight, was protected from the force of the slipstream. In the milliseconds he had to make the shot, everything about the moment was to put as many slugs into the bomber he could.

He raked the fuselage from tail to cockpit with his remaining ammunition. Only when he was about to break away did he sense the true proximity of the bomber, and the loss of the canopy. Suddenly, the razor's edge of the bomber's rudder scraped the belly of their aircraft, deflecting them into a climbing turn. Lou pulled back on the throttles, and let the aircraft bank into a descent.

'What the fuck's going on back there?' he screamed over the roar of high speed air. He'd heard nothing of Duckwalker ejecting, and surmised he was still there.

'Why'd you blow the canopy?'

'I didn't blow it,' Duckwalker screamed. 'My seat slid up the rails. It must have triggered it. It's fucking windy and cold back here.'

Duckwalker stowed his scope and forced himself into the instrument panel. He could feel the vacuum of the roaring slipstream tearing at his crash helmet.

'Get me down, or let me get the hell out of here! I can't last in this tornado.'

Lou knew their time was limited. He gripped the vibrating control column with the might of both arms, in an attempt to level off, but human strength was no match for the forces at hand. The aircraft was uncontrollable in any configuration.

'I can't keep her flying! We collided with the bomber. It's fucked the controls. Prepare to eject! Tell me when you've completed your checks. I'll be right behind you. I'll say it once. If you don't go, all you'll see is me blasting away!'

Duckwalker discarded his glasses, reset his visor and tightened his straps. He was going into the void once again, this time not by choice.

'I'm ready. Just say the words, Lou.'

'Eject! Eject!'

Duckwalker reached up for the D-ring with both hands but lost all sensation and strength as the force of the slipstream tore his arms out of the cockpit. He fought to bring them back inside but the power of the freezing wind had him defeated.

Lou reached up for his D-ring and was about to pull down the blind when he heard Duckwalker's rasping moan.

'I ordered you to eject. Now eject, eject!' Agonizing seconds passed.

'I can't! My arms are pinned back in the slipstream, and I can't move them. I'm helpless. You go!'

Lou understood. Without a windscreen, Duckwalker had no protection from the onrushing air. He'd have to slow the aircraft to a near stall to alleviate the forces pinning back his arms. There was one chance to save him, but only one.

'Listen Duckwalker, when I say go, use all your strength to bring your arms in and pull the ring! You got that?'

'Okay, Lou, but don't do anything to jeopardize your own safety.'

Lou slipped off his left glove, and placed it in the lee of the windscreen behind the gun sight. He eased back on the throttles and the control column, inducing the aircraft to the moment of stall. Thirty knots above the stall speed he bunted the nose and watched as his glove began to rise behind the gun sight. The instant it stabilized in space, he knew they were at zero-G and hanging in space.

'Now!' He screamed.

Duckwalker mustered his remaining strength and pulled his arms back inside the cockpit. He gripped his right wrist with his left hand, forced it over his head, grabbed the ring and pulled the blind over his visor. With a flash, he was flung into space, his last sensation before losing consciousness, that of a nightmare revisited.

'Mayday! Mayday! Mayday! Banshee One is at 20,000 out of control! My navigator's ejected and I don't know how long I can stay with the aircraft. Take a fix. Killjoy has been crippled. Over.'

With stick and rudder and two good engines, Lou vowed to stay with the aircraft. He had 20,000 feet and working instruments. Caterpillar Number Five would have to wait.

Dan Lacey patched through Lou's distress call to Pete. Lou Fender was fucked. Another caterpillar for the Grim Reaper, or maybe not. The student would have to make the coup-de-gras.

Dan Lacey had a habit of interrupting moments of joy. Like the time he caught Pete going at it with the CO's daughter in the cockpit at two in the morning. Did he know, or didn't he know? The question haunted him.

'It's up to us, Pete. Looks like Banshee One's done for.' His screen was lit up with six targets but he had little difficulty picking out the wheat from the chaff. The bomber's blip was strong, but the CF-100, meshed in with the chaff, was indiscernible until the returns hung in space, then dissipated like cooling embers, until two blips remained. Banshee One and Killjoy were still flying. Pete snapped to command and took control.

'Give me a heading, Dan! Pilot to crew, this is what we've been training for. Arm your guns and cameras. Jake, this is one you're going to show your grandchildren. You'll not give your film away easy on this one, I guarantee it!'

Wilding interrupted his pep-talk.

'Backstop One, this is Scooter. I'm passing you off to Mont Apica. It's up to you. Good hunting.'

Pete couldn't believe his ears. It wasn't like Wilding to give up the chase. The situation at hand was bigger than the Rangoon payoff. A renewed cry from Dan Lacey spun all thoughts of the money hidden in the tail.

'Something weird's going on, Pete. Either Banshee One's gone down, or he's formatted with the fucking bomber. Either way, all I'm showing on the scope is one big fat juicy target.'

Dan dialed in Mont Apica GCI who vectored them for a lead attack. It was new stuff for the GCI site and they fucked up a couple of vectors, until Dan straightened them out. The hunter and the prey were now at similar altitudes and the geometry played to the B-25's advantage. At twenty-five seconds to intercept, Pete's attack scope displayed a lock-on. The central ring shrank until the 4.5-second-to-fire indicator ring appeared.

The instant the rockets-gone signal slashed across his scope, Pete squeezed the trigger on the control column. Simultaneously, they broke out of the cloud into a clear night sky, the tracers from their two machine guns ripping into the fuselage of the bomber and deflecting off the top of its wings.

The fleeting sight that befell them, and the movie film later viewed by few and stored away in a Department of National Defence vault, was shocking. The bomber, trailing fire from one engine, was flying in formation with an RCAF Mark 3 CF-100.

'Holy fuck, do you see that?' Pete cried out.

Fred Malone, hunkered down beside the waist-gunner's window, caught sight of the bomber as they passed behind.

Suddenly, the bomber's tail spat glowing balls at lightning speed. With a mighty thump, two 20-millimeter cannon shells blew off the B-25's dummy tail turret—scattering aluminum, Plexiglas, and American greenbacks into the night.

This, Fred Malone did not witness. The gaping hole in the tail and the vacuum sucking at him had him scrambling to the cockpit, his airsickness losing out to primal fear. He emerged behind Pete and patched-in to the intercom.

'We've been hit, Pete! The ass-end's been blown off.'

'Are you sure? The controls feel okay. I felt a bit of a thump, but I thought it was wake turbulence when we passed behind the bomber.'

'I'm sure for fuck's sake! I nearly got sucked out.' Pete turned to the copilot.

'Get a heading to Chatham from Dan, Fred. I'm going back for a look-see. You stay here, Malone.'

'Why Chatham, Pete? Bagotville is only an hour away.'

Pete looked into the nurse's eyes.

'We're persona-non-grata there. That's all I can divulge. Chatham it is. Report what you just witnessed then take her down to 10,000 as fast as possible. I'm sick of wearing this fucking thing!'

He disconnected his mask, unstrapped and disappeared. If what Malone had reported was true, nine years of planning for a payday had been shot to rat shit by an American tail gunner.

Lou was alone in an open cockpit fighting to control an out-of-trim bucking bronco. There was little to update. He'd reported in and had become superfluous to the war at hand, an ejected spent cartridge that hadn't made it all the way to the ground. Duckwalker was hopefully hanging from a parachute, his position known. A search and rescue helicopter from Bagotville would be airborne in minutes. He'd be home for breakfast.

He dialed in Bagotville and got a homing signal, and decided that he'd make an effort to save the aircraft. He didn't need one more caterpillar. The black of the night, intensified by the density of the cloud and the freezing wind was pushing him to his limits. He'd been cold before, but not this cold, and he'd brought home crippled aircraft before, but not one as crippled as this. He needed to find clear air, fly visually, and figure out the aircraft's flawed aerodynamic geometry. He banked to port and headed east.

With the wind flowing in that direction, sooner or later he'd intercept the clear air of the center of the storm.

Minutes later he blasted into brilliant star shine. He'd chosen to keep as much altitude as possible, so he only had himself to blame if he froze to death. He made minor gyro and trim adjustments and discovered that his steed had indeed some semblance of control. With only himself to worry about, he settled in for the trip home, forcing himself under the gun sight and cursing that the good old RCAF hadn't provided them with some sort of goggles or visor. The gimp in the back used one, but that was so he could fly in daylight.

Lou did an outside head-sweep and instantly picked up a cigarette-glow of light from inside the cloudbank 2,000 feet below. A shake of his head and a more intense focus revealed that the glow was attached to the left wing of a B-36 emerging from the mist. The glow intensified, becoming a stream of fire trailing from the center engine on its left wing. When the rudder emerged, he saw the missing curve from its tip.

Three feet lower on his last attack and both aircraft would have been doomed.

The bomber was at his mercy, but without a single round of ammunition left, the only method he could use to bring it down was by ramming. The Japs and Germans had exercised that tactic, but it wasn't for him.

He'd find another way.

He eased his interceptor into the crook of the bomber's nose and right wing, and as its enormity came into scale the magnificence of its function had him in the same awe he'd experienced the first time a steam locomotive had rumbled by.

He concentrated on the bomber's bulbous canopy, and made out the silhouette of someone in the left-hand seat. Somebody WAS flying the bomber, somebody who had a shit-load of trouble to deal with. He snapped on his anti-collision lights, switched off his radio and IFF, grabbed his flashlight, and shone it on the bomber's cockpit. He wanted anonymity from his masters. He needed to work this one out by himself, for himself. He needed to assure his adversary that they had a choice. Within seconds, he had a return beacon.

Contact.

In rusty Morse code he flashed, 'FRIEND OR FOE,' twice.

In rusty Morse code, came a reply.

'FRIEND.'

"Things are getting interesting," Lou smiled to himself. "I know exactly what to do to make things right. I'll help land the fucking thing, and change history."

Hartwig and Wright were not expecting the third attack or the damage the bomber was enduring. Once again, it had been a stern attack and the tail gunner had managed to drive the interceptor off. With two engines feathered, and a third on fire, the cockpit resembled a Chinese fire drill. Hartwig moved from his seat to the engineer's station and back, pulling carburetor and mixture-levers, and checking cylinder-head temperatures. With two engines down and a third on the way out, he had the jets on the wingtips screaming at full power. Even then, they were in a constant descent.

They broke free of the cloud and into a starlit night.

'Fuck, I'm glad to get out of that shit!' Wright commented.

'Speaking of which, I need something to piss in.'

'Me, too. Slip off the Major's boots. I don't think he'll miss them.' They both laughed, but it was short-lived.

The cockpit was suddenly lit by a beam of light followed by the unmistakable flashes of an aircraft's anti-collision lights. Flying beside them was a large fighter aircraft without a canopy, its pilot huddled into the windshield, signaling in Morse code.

'Where the fuck did he come from?' Wright exclaimed.

Hartwig reached into the Major's flight bag, found a flashlight, and signaled back. It took several minutes to decipher the Morse code signal.

'He wants to know our intentions,' Wright said. 'Are we friend, or are we foe?'

'We need every piece of luck we can muster, old boy. This guy could probably clobber us.' In faltering Morse code, he replied.

'FRIEND.'

With an unexpected rattle, their bomber was suddenly lit up by deflecting tracer shells coming from their starboard.

'What the fuck's going on?' Hartwig screamed 'Where did THEY come from?'

Emerging from the cloud bank, spitting tracers, and on a collision-course, came the unmistakable silhouette of a B-25 Mitchell bomber.

'Christ, what else are they going to throw at us?' Wright screamed. 'We can't take any more of this shit.'

The B-36, riddled with punctures and dents from the hundreds of rounds of 50-caliber strikes, plowed on like a harpooned whale. The bomber's fuel tanks and hydraulics had been spared but its power plants hadn't, and without the ability to dispose of the bomb, its demise was a certainty.

The B-25 passed behind, and the rear gunner reported he was certain of a hit. Hartwig knew it wouldn't have the speed and maneuverability to catch them, and unless the Canadians had another ace up their sleeve, they were safe from any more predators. He helped Wright shut down and extinguish the fire of the burning engine and proceeded to contact the fighter by Morse.

'NEED HELP. BROKEN ARROW.'

Lou had the answer.

'FOLLOW ME.'

Duckwalker regained consciousness and found himself dangling from a parachute. He grabbed for the shrouds to get some semblance of control and tried to focus on the forest and hillside he was about to encounter, but the pain from his shoulders made steering ineffective. He'd lost his visor, and was blind without glasses, but the night and cloud were a godsend. He activated his Mae West and released his survival pack on its thirty-foot lanyard. If it was to be a water landing, he'd hear the splash. If it was to be a tree landing, he'd hear the sound of breaking tree limbs. He couldn't decide which he'd prefer.

His greatest fear was the advent of daylight and his vulnerability for near snow-blindness. At survival school he'd had little problem putting together his camp, but there he'd had his sunglasses and help. At daybreak, he'd need to blindfold himself. There were four hours left until sunrise, so he'd have to work fast.

In the final second of his descent, he heard the snap of breaking branches, and stiffened for what was to follow. His instinct to protect his spine had him grabbing for his derriere, and his arms took the brunt as he fell into a grove of birch and maple. He hit the ground on his side and rolled into a blueberry bog, the shrouds of his parachute enveloping him in a spider's web. He drew his hunting knife, cut his way free, and paused to collect his thoughts. Autumn leaves rustling in the wind and the unmistakable drone of the B-36 had him looking skyward. "Strange," he thought, "sounds to me like it's heading east." He checked his vitals, and except for abrasions on his forearms and a sore hip, he felt satisfied he was in reasonable shape.

"Well this is different," he thought. "Down in one piece and walking away. Not like the last time."

Except for the issue of the slipstream hindering his ejection, everything else had worked out fine. There'd have to be a modification to the navigator's cockpit, or there'd be a few dead ones; his first-hand experience would see to that. Quick thinking on Lou Fender's part had saved his life. He'd get a medal for that.

He pulled his parachute canopy out of a tree, made a lean-to tent, then set about gathering wood for a fire. It had stopped raining, but he was forced to search under deadfalls for dry fuel. He organized his campsite, limbed a spruce for a mattress, then opened the survival pack, yielding a sleeping bag, cooking utensils, hardtack, and Oxo cubes. Packed away was a breakdown .22 Hornet rifle. He shaved a dry branch into a pile, added fuel, shielded his eyes from the flame, and felt the heat as the flames intensified. He'd stoke it every half hour and sit with his back to it until daybreak.

The success of his survival was all about preserving his sight. He'd stowed his dark glasses in the cockpit, but forgotten them in the haste of the ejection sequence. He found a smooth granite rock, spat on it and began to sharpen the blade of his hunting knife. Satisfied that it was sharp enough, he embraced several birch trees, seeking one with the same diameter as his head. The mask he'd create needed to fit like that of the Lone Ranger's. Satisfied with his choice, he peeled off a large unblemished portion of bark and checked for snugness.

He worked at it for half an hour, contouring it to his nose and forehead, and increasing the eye-slits to allow a mild glow of firelight. Satisfied that he'd have protection at daybreak, he attached the mask with parachute cord, and laughed when he saw his reflection in his signal mirror.

"If Lou could only see me now." He looked skyward. The drone of the bomber had long since faded.

Had Lou ejected? He tried to remember the sequence of events once he'd pulled down on the ejection blind, but all he remembered was waking up, dangling from a parachute, wondering what lay below. His first bit of luck was that he hadn't landed in water. His second bit of luck was that he hadn't been injured when he busted through the trees. He hoped Lou's results were the same. For now, he'd stay in the back of the lean-to and wait for daylight, and the "whoop, whoop, whoop" of the Piasecki helicopter. He'd throw green boughs on the fire to create a smoke signal, and he could see the two of them having Sunday morning breakfast, listening to Pete Rylander's blow-by-blow account of how he'd shot down a B-36 bomber.

———

Lou's plane took two of Pete Rylander's 50-caliber slugs into the intake cone of the right engine. He felt the vibration of a turbo-jet out of balance, and pulled back its power to idle. Keep it alive; it might come in handy later on. He added power to the left engine, and cursed Rylander and Wilding. The fuckers had nearly pulled it off. Three feet forward and two feet up and they'd have got him between the eyes.

The objective of his mission was still intact. On the horizon was a landing spot bigger than any B-36 had ever landed on.

Lou signaled to the bomber. 'MAP.'

Hartwig scavenged through Major Crisp's flight bag and found an aviation chart that dealt with the Province of Québec. Inscribed on it was his complete battle plan. Except for the final target, the Major's mission was sketched out in precise detail. The map showed four targets: Montréal, New York, Detroit and Chicago. He was thankful they were heading east. Montréal could sleep easy tonight.

Hartwig signaled back. 'FOUND.'

Lou signaled. 'FOLLOW ME.'

For the next twenty minutes, the two aircraft were swept northeast, skirting the edge of the towering cloudbank and descending as they went. The two pilots switched to hand signals to speed communication.

Hartwig studied the map and saw what his savior knew. Fifty miles to the north was Lake Saint-Jean, the source of the Saguenay River, a perfect spot to land a B-36 carrying an atomic bomb. They were running on three pistons and four jet engines and had enough altitude to make it there. Hartwig signaled that he understood, set a course, and wished his escort Godspeed, but the interceptor held its position. The Good Samaritan was not about to leave.

'How do you feel about taking a little swim, Lieutenant

Wright? I'm going to ditch us in the middle of a very large lake. I figure if the bomb detonates on contact we minimize the fallout.'

'Let me see the map.'

Wright studied the extent of the Lake Saint-Jean and Saguenay River system. 'The lake empties into the ocean for Christ's sake! We might minimize the fallout but we could contaminate an enormous water basin.'

'It's either into the mountains or take a swim,' Hartwig responded. 'If it pops, the radiation is either into the air or into the water. Take your pick. If I land this thing the way I think I can, I might not so much as crack the egg. I'm getting pretty good on this thing. It's not a fighter, but at the lower altitude it responds well.'

'A water landing it is. Better give the caboose the good news. They'll have to bail out soon or stick with the Titanic. You're the captain; you make the announcement.'

The rear compartment opted for bailout, wishing to be clear of water and high enough to see the terrain and the location of the other parachutes in flight.

'Take as much survival gear as you can carry. If Lieutenant Wright and I don't make it, it might be a while before you're found. It's cold, so bundle up.'

One by one, the gunners exited the hatchway into the freezing Québec sky. The radio operator reported each exit, including his own, but he had other ideas. He donned a Mae West and strapped in to a gunner's chair. He'd bailed out over Europe and he was reluctant to do it again.

Lake Saint-Jean shimmered on the horizon. In the event of a detonation, Lou planned for the bomber to ditch nearest the center of the lake, but it became apparent that the two aircraft were approaching it downwind and were too high. They'd have to overfly the lake, reverse course, turn into the wind and exercise the forced-landing procedure they'd practiced at flight school: high key, low key, final key.

The B-36 pilot would know the parameters.

Lou peeled off as the bomber began its final turn. The two pilots gave each the 'salute' as they parted. He reversed course, watching the bomber descend until streaks of white knifed across the lake as it broke into pieces that skipped on the surface. He did a ten-mile orbit of the crash site waiting for an explosion, saw what was needed to be seen, turned on his radio and IFF, and called Bricklayer.

'Bricklayer, Bricklayer, this is Banshee One. Repeat, this is Banshee One. Killjoy's ditched into the middle of Lake Saint-Jean. There was no detonation. The aircraft landed under control. There may be survivors. I'm returning to base.'

'Banshee One, this is Bricklayer. Didn't know you were still in the ring. GCI lost you after you reported your navigator's bail-out. Thought you might have followed him. You must be freezing. Eject if you need to. GCI's got your position. Thanks for the help. See you at base, over."

———•◆•———

Hartwig had practiced simulated flameout and forced-landing procedures during fighter training until he could do them blindfolded. The only variable was the difference in the sink-rate between the two types of aircraft. The wing of the B-36 was like the wing of a glider: it wanted to keep flying, especially during round-out for landing. He'd compensate for the compressibility of ground effect.

He saluted his escort and briefed Wright on the cut-off procedure to the three remaining piston engines.

At the north end of the lake, he made a sweeping turn to the south and headed into wind. He estimated the wind speed at 30 knots from the wave pattern. The waves would be a help or a hindrance; it was up to the way he landed. He straightened for final approach and shut the fuel to the jets. They'd be the first to bust off.

'Call out the airspeed for me, Kenny. I've got my hands full trying to judge the altitude.' Wright pushed the Major aside to read the airspeed indicator but had a fright when he heard a wheeze of breath as the Major's head flopped over.

'The throttles are all yours, Don. I'm strapping in tight. You should do the same.'

Hartwig had one objective.

"I will not crack the egg, I will not crack the egg," he repeated to himself.

The horizon became a blur.

'I'll keep 30 knots above the stall-speed, and sooner or later, the bastard will have to touch down. I'll keep the nose high and drag the tail. That should slow us down. What happens after that is anybody's guess.'

He eased back on the control column, and the bomber hung in space until he felt the flutter of the elevators reacting to the stalling wings.

He let off the back pressure and felt a slight bump.

The bomber hit the water tail-low and bounced from its grip. There was no stopping a secondary stall. It pitched up, then plunged nose first into water hard as concrete, shattering everything back to the wings. What was left of the nose rose like a harpooned whale, broke away and sank, taking the six occupants with it. The rest of the aircraft broke into pieces that scattered over the surface of the lake. There was no fire, no secondary explosion. The tail section was the last to sink, but not before a life raft was ejected, and a lone occupant paddled away at high speed.

'There's a fucking nuke sitting under me,' became his mantra. 'There's a fucking nuke sitting under me. And I know the fucker's going to blow.'

P ete returned to the flight deck a humbled man. Two
    Freds sat in the cockpit and he was loath to have any-
thing to do with either of them. One was a quisling and the
other a blackmailer. It was the company he kept.

He patched in.

'You're right, Malone. Lucky for us, they didn't hit the
elevators or we'd be pushing up daisies. Pretty tough putting on a chute in a vertical dive. The radio room is yours
'til we land.'

Pete sensed this might be his last flight in the B-25 and
decided to hand-fly it to Chatham. No autopilot, just the
basics. What he'd witnessed in the rear of the aircraft and
in the sky during the intercept of the bomber had snook-
ered the Rangoon payoff. The money was gone, and Lou
Fender was a turncoat. The fleeting glimpse of him paired
up with the bomber was no less than the vision of a Phoenix.

He thought he'd seen bullet strikes on Lou's aircraft.
Jake Brown's gun cameras would tell the tale. When all
indications were that the bastard had gone down, how the
hell had he risen from the grave? Dan had reported that
once the chaff had cleared, there'd been two returns, then
one. Without a navigator, how had he managed to meet up
with the bomber? It had to be bullshit luck; there couldn't

be another explanation. When he saw the CF-100 in formation with the bomber, he understood the single return. Wilding wasn't going to be happy, and Wilding was going to be hunting him for answers.

He'd come away empty-handed on all accounts. No money in the bank and nothing to enhance a career. Three senior officers were about to wield axes over his head with Lou Fender holding a dagger for the coup-de-gras.

His hands began to shake and he felt nauseated. It was a three-hour flight to Chatham and he was in no condition to continue flying. Too many forces were pulling at him. When they landed, he'd have a chat with a flight surgeon. Maybe they'd give him a desk job. Maybe they'd give him the boot.

Maybe they'd put him in the pokey.

Gerard was his greatest fear. She'd alluded to having evidence of his past indiscretions. That sort of evidence carried a greater punishment than anything Wilding or Fender could inflict. Chill blades magnified his shakes and he released his hands from the control column. What was happening to him?

As they descended through 12,000, he informed the crew that they could remove their masks.

'Take over, Archer. I'm going back for a piss and a lie down. Put it on autopilot if you want. Give me a call if we need to do a GCA, otherwise the landing is yours.' He retreated to the waist station and sat facing Fred Malone.

'Well Malone, you experienced combat and lived to tell about it. What do you think?'

Rylander was distressed and Malone sensed his vulnerability might be exploited. Gerard's serum was ready, but finding the right moment to administer it was the challenge. He needed a good fifteen minutes for it to take effect and he needed somebody to corroborate her questionnaire. He could wait until they landed, but who knew what points of the compass they'd be scattered to?

Rylander was captive and at his most vulnerable. Malone eyed the coffee thermos and formulated a plan. Dan Lacey would be his witness.

Rylander opened a survival pack, extracted a sleeping bag and wrapped himself in it.

'You okay, Captain?'

'Do I look fucking okay, you bastard?'

'What the hell do you mean?'

'You know what I mean. The only reason you're here is because of that fucking nurse.'

'Which nurse?'

'Does it matter?'

———•••———

Lou dialed in Bagotville and clawed for height. The altitude he'd traded off to guide the bomber down to lake level needed to be reimbursed. There was weather and terrain to leapfrog. The right engine refused to spool up when he advanced the throttle and with a bang and a shudder, it seized up. Bagotville was below VFR limits, forcing him to set up for a UHF homing and letdown with a GCA pickoff. His fuel situation was near critical and he knew that a missed approach would mean a fifth caterpillar. After contacting the GCA controller, Lou intercepted the glide-slope, and commenced his descent to the runway, the droll monotone of the GCA controller and his instruments guiding him home.

'Banshee One, you are fifty feet above the glide path. Increase your rate of descent to….. Banshee One, you are to the right of the glide path, turn left to a heading of…. Banshee One, you are…….'

As the aircraft slashed through freezing rain, the windshield froze over, and Lou knew there'd be no forward visibility once he'd passed through GCA limits. He dropped full flaps and trimmed, but as the altimeter wound down, he sensed he was going to be forced do a missed approach and overshoot. Overshoot meant he'd have to eject. There'd be no fuel for a second attempt.

'Banshee One, you are passing through GCA limits, take over visually.'

There was no taking over visually. There was no runway. The windshield was a sheet of ice and he couldn't stick his head out the side for the blinding freezing rain. He added full power to the left engine and began a climb into cloud.

Suddenly, he felt the asymmetrical force of a split flap. The collision with the rudder of the bomber had weakened a hinge and a flap had broken off as he overshot.

Lou fought to keep the aircraft from rolling violently to port, but human strength couldn't stop it from rolling on to its back. With the realization that he had no chance of survival he had one last vision of Darlene, and thanked God for his time with her. He broke out of the cloud base inverted and saw the rush of the ground coming to greet him.

He made an instinctive grab for the ejection ring, but he knew he was beyond salvation.

Darlene heard the thud of an explosion then the wail of sirens. It had been a sleepless night. She rushed to Josette's room, only to find it empty. She dressed and ran through freezing rain to the base hospital. She had a bad feeling, and the bad feeling concerned the man she loved.

Josette was conferring with OC of 440 Squadron when she arrived and the grave looks she received made her heart sink.

'Did Lou's plane crash?'

'Yes.'

'Did he get out? Did he eject?'

'We don't know yet. They just got to the crash site.'

'What about his navigator?'

'He ejected near Mont Apica a couple of hours ago.'

'A couple of hours ago? How did Lou end up here?'

'He escorted an American aircraft in distress to a successful ditching in Lake Saint-Jean. He was attempting to bring his crippled plane home. Things didn't work out. All we can hope for is that he's hunkered down in the bush having a smoke….. Now, as this is strictly an Air Force matter, you must return to your barracks.'

Josette embraced Darlene and wiped her tears.

'There's always hope that he got out, Cherie.'

But Darlene had felt his loss the instant she heard the sirens.

The OC briefed Josette on the possible outcome of the crash, and she assured him she was capable of taking care of the details.

'If he didn't get out, you'll have your work cut out for you.'

'Don't worry. I've managed in these situations before.'

'You may have to go to the crash site to pick up the pieces.'

'I know.'

Pete Rylander, wrapped in a sleeping bag, couldn't stop shivering. It wasn't cold causing his symptoms. Along with everything else, he'd lost his nerve. They were an hour out of Chatham and he prayed they'd never get there. Conversation with Malone had been of a medical nature but it didn't alleviate his shakes.

'Let me get you a coffee, Pete. I saw a couple of Thermoses in Dan's cockpit. I'll get one for you.' Pete nodded weakly and Malone headed forward. He shook the thermoses for content, picked the one half-full, poured in the contents of the vial and tapped Dan Lacey on the shoulder.

'Dan, you know Pete pretty well. I think he's having a bit of a breakdown. I'm going to give him a coffee to perk him up. Could you drop back in a quarter of an hour to see what you think?'

Malone returned to the radio compartment to find Pete shivering uncontrollably. He poured the coffee and forced it between Pete's chattering lips. When the cup was finished Fred drained the rest and encouraged Pete to finish it all.

Within minutes, the chloral hydrate began to sedate him and probing questions confirmed it had taken effect.

Then the inexplicable happened. Rylander's babbling went off on a tangent and for five minutes he had Malone transfixed.

'I think you'd better get back here Dan,' Malone ordered. 'Pete's really fucked up. I think we might have to restrain him.'

Dan emerged into the radio compartment to find Pete babbling gibberish.

'Christ, what the fuck's happening? I've never seen him like this before.'

'That's because he's getting a taste of his own medicine. I need you to listen to every question I ask him and verify the answer he gives. Here's my authorization.'

Dan read Gerard's order and reluctantly agreed. He'd stuck by the Captain through thick and thin, but the implication that he was a serial rapist shook him to the core.

One by one, Malone probed Pete with inquiries about his past and one by one he spilled the beans. After each question was answered, Malone wrote the reply and had Dan initial it.

In ten minutes, the deed was done.

'Thanks, Dan. It must have been tough for you to hear all that, but he had to be stopped. He nearly killed a nurse a couple of hours ago.'

'No. Thank you. Pete's been walking on water too long. None of us could figure out how he got so much tail.'

'And none of the crew is ever going to know about this, or you'll be navigating the North Atlantic hunting Russian submarines. I want you to radio Chatham on a secure frequency and have the Service Police meet us on the tarmac. Our boy here is going to jail.'

'Fair enough.'

Dan returned to his post and Malone tended to his patient. For the next hour Pete sat in a catatonic stupor, oblivious to what had happened. They broke out of the overcast as the false dawn heralded Sunday morning and as the bomber touched down, Pete had the look of a hypnotist's subject who'd been snapped back to reality. As he was led to the paddy wagon he kept looking back at Malone, wondering what had happened and why a grin was slashed across Malone's face.

He understood.

'Gerard,' he muttered between clenched teeth. 'I've been done in by a coven of fucking nurses and an American tail gunner.'

Duckwalker was feeling antsy and neglected, suspicious that nobody knew what had happened to him or where he was. The GCI sites would have tracked their aircraft but an undersized navigator dangling from a parachute was not about to become a blip on their radar screens. All he could hope for was that Lou had put out a distress call once he'd vacated the premises. Then again, he might have punched out after him and was camped just around the corner.

Dawn broke and there were no rescuers; noon arrived and there were no rescuers. He opened a container of hardtack, and the smell had him chucking it into the fire. He'd starve before he'd eat that shit. He assembled the .22 Hornet, and sighted down the barrel through the slit in his Lone Ranger mask. There'd be grouse coming out of the trees at dusk to fill their crops with gravel, but that was iffy at best. He staked out a slough and shot a muskrat that he skinned and roasted.

At three o'clock, he heard the Piasecki helicopter.

He heaped boughs on the fire and within minutes, the chopper found a clearing large enough to land in. The two rescue technicians sent to retrieve him complimented him on his resourcefulness and Halloween mask.

'Anybody on board got sunglasses?'

'Don't think so, Sir. Hey, you're the guy with the glasses. The navigator. They've got a name for you.'

'Duckwalker?'

'That's it. Duckwalker.'

The trip to Bagotville with the mute rescue team was worrisome.

'Have they found Flying Officer Fender?'

The rescue techs weren't about to disclose the morning's events. By all accounts, Lou Fender had not been found.

'Can't say, Sir. I don't know.'

'What happened to the B-36?'

'What B-36?'

'The one we were sent to destroy.'

'News to me, Sir.'

Duckwalker chain-smoked in silence on the trip to Bagotville, aching for information. A Service Police wagon was waiting to take him to a debriefing. Both SP's wore side arms and very large sunglasses. His birch bark Lone Ranger mask was starting to chafe his ears, so rank was called into play, and he relieved a pair of top-line aviator glasses from a pissed-off sergeant.

On observing an empty flight line, he assumed the worst.

Looking disheveled and smelling of campfire smoke, he was escorted to the Met briefing room, where the CO and the OC of 440 were the only ones in attendance. The participants had been reduced to three.

Duckwalker was craving information.

'Have they found Lou, did he bail out?'

'Flying Officer Fender was killed this morning doing a

GCA. He missed the approach, and wasn't able do a go-around. He went in with the aircraft. We don't know why he didn't eject.'

'He saved my life.'

'He saved a lot of lives.'

'The bomber, did we get the B-36?'

'Yes. Thanks to Fender, it's at the bottom of Lake Saint-Jean…. There doesn't seem to be any problem with the payload it was carrying. At nine this morning the Americans flew some hot fighter over the crash site with Geiger counters on board. There wasn't any radioactive activity. Had some infrared gear on it, too. That's how they found the crew members that were alive.' The CO passed his cigarettes, waited for muffled coughs to subside, then continued.

'The B-36 pilot was good. He landed on the water with a nuke on board like he was flying a glider. The Americans will be arriving en masse to retrieve their lost souls, atomic bomb, and any sensitive material the bomber was carrying. It'll be a mad house around here. The bastards will leave the rest. A bunch of gunners and a radio operator managed to get out. I can't wait to hear their side of the story. First we want to hear your side. We can get you something to eat from the mess if you want.'

Duckwalker adjusted his glasses.

'No thank you, Sir. I've got a gutful of muskrat I have to process. Could use a coffee.' The OC 440 turned on an Ampex tape recorder.

'Tell us what you know and what you saw.'

Duckwalker recounted their mission from the moment the landing gear retracted. Questions about the aircraft and the GCI performance occasionally interrupted his story, but by and large, he was able to keep it in real time and in chronological order. He was complimentary of the combat performance of the CF-100, but took issue with its current weapon.

He'd always thought it would be the opposite.

'Fifty-caliber bullets won't bring down a bomber that size, Sir. We just got lucky. Maybe we did some damage and maybe we didn't. I'd say the bomber did as much damage to itself as we did. We made three attacks and used up every bullet we had. Not only that, but they nearly shot us out the sky. We'd better get the Mark 4 operational quickly or we're vulnerable.'

The CO corrected.

'Four attacks, Jones. The B-25 caused some damage.' The CO went on to recount the attack and the subsequent outcome.

'The B-25's on its way to Chatham. There'll be some interesting insight gleaned from their debriefing. Some poor asshole in Ottawa's going to wear it.'

Duckwalker jumped into the conversation with an item more dear to his heart.

'And speaking of vulnerability, Sir, let me go on record that if the navigator's cockpit isn't redesigned with some sort of windshield, there aren't going to be any navigators to recount stories like I just did.'

He recounted how Lou's aerodynamic trickery saved his life. 'I know he should get a medal for what he did with the bomber, but you have to add me to the citation.'

The reel of the tape recorder ran out and, while a new one was spooled through, Duckwalker waddled to the bathroom to clean up. He looked into the mirror and saw a man he didn't know. Then he began to cry. Not just a teary cry, but a full-blown sobbing wail. He couldn't stop.

The OC burst through the door.

'Are you okay?'

'No Sir, right now, I'm not okay.'

'When you hear about Flying Officer Fender's contribution to the war effort, I'm sure you'll feel much better.

———— ·•·•·—— ————

Malone was back at the blackjack table and was about to double down. What Rylander hadn't seen in his smile, when he was escorted to the paddy wagon on the tarmac, was that prior to Dan Lacey's arrival, he'd disclosed the complete Rangoon fiasco. His revelation came out of nowhere, and so fast that Fred had to have him repeat certain passages to be sure it wasn't bullshit.

He headed to the mess for breakfast and to digest the information he'd become privy to, information that could wield him a winning hand in another game at another table.

There was more to Rylander than just his nasty habit. The issues were rape and money laundering. He knew secrets that had been under wraps for a decade. He bummed a cigarette, sipped coffee, and relived the conversation in the bowels of the B-25.

The conversation had taken off on a tangent five minutes after Pete had ingested the chloral hydrate. He sat mute at first, shivering uncontrollably and smoking.

He began to babble, and nothing made sense until distinct words and phrases caught his gambler's ear.

'The money, the money. It's all gone.' Malone's ears pricked up.

'What money?'

'The money that was stashed in the tail. Where the turret use to be.'

'What about it?'

'It's gone. Tamaguchi's going to kill Wilding and me. Fender's free. They were partners.'

Pete rambled on about Rangoon. Malone took it all in, memorizing details with the expertise of a card-counting gambler. When times, dates and players in the scheme had been exhausted, he removed Josette's envelopes and called Dan Lacey to witness the inquisition.

Signed and sealed, the documents were ready for delivery, and the expectation of their payout had him checking the Operations Center for the next scheduled run from Chatham to Bagotville.

Squadron Leader Josette Gerard, the born-again virgin was his for the taking.

'There's an American C-54 coming through from Loring, Sir. They're picking up some film then they're on their way to Bagotville. Something big is going on there. We've been told a whole bunch of Yanks are headed there. I heard through the scuttlebutt that a CF-100 crashed there this morning, but I can't see why that would be so important to them.'

'A CF-100 crashed?'

'Yeah. A Standards guy augered in off the end of the runway. Why he was flying when the base was on stand-down is a bit of a mystery.'

'Killed?'

'So I heard.'

'Navigator? What about his navigator?'

'No goodly gen on him, Sir.'

Malone was heartbroken, and tears welled. It was Lou Fender. The money and a Rangoon interceptor were gone.

That left Wing Commander Chauncey Wilding, mastermind and puppeteer, and Pete Rylander, all around asshole.

Malone felt his deck grow cold.

"There must be some way that they atone for Lou Fender," he thought.

Where Wilding existed, or how he'd access him, was a mystery. And when he found him, what would be the net gain? There had to be some way to make money off him.

"Gamblers are natural blackmailers," he thought. He'd blackmail him anonymously and play him like a pike, exhausting him until it yearned to be gaffed.

"Rylander and I are the only ones who know where the money is," he thought. Let Wilding go after Rylander, even if he's in jail." It was going to be an interesting dance to sit out as a wallflower. The weekend as the orderly officer had been an education and life changer for all. One dead, one destined for the pokey, and one waiting to get his throat slit. Rangoon's blackjack table was on hiatus.

Malone boarded the C-54 and picked up the scuttlebutt. An American transport had strayed off-course and ditched in a lake up in the boondocks. Naval officers and diving equipment filled the forward section. He sat apart and took in the cross-section of skill that he was riding along with. He'd bet every one of them two to one that he was a nurse and clean up.

It didn't take him long to ascertain that the transport lying at the bottom of the lake was Killjoy.

He chuckled aloud.

'Johnny Canuck was on the job.'

He landed at Bagotville at four in the afternoon and headed to the mess for his Sunday night T-bone. He was back home and, in the grand scheme of things, wasn't the orderly officer anymore.

He was chomping away and recollecting when Darlene and Josette entered. Mourning women had their look. He turned his back. They'd meet, but this was not the time and place.

He'd never consoled the lover of a pilot who'd been killed, but felt he could do so now. He'd been up there as it happened, and they could never take it away from him.

As he got up to leave, he received an inquisitive glance from Josette and he patted his breast.

'I've got it,' he mouthed.

'Thank you,' she mouthed back.

He headed to the Snake Pit for a three-handed game of crib. Three players and a deck of cards had endless combinations.

EPILOGUE

'Make way gents, make way, coming through.'

Squadron Leader Duckwalker Jones parted the crowd like an icebreaker. His newfound mobility made him a formidable weapon around a crowded bar on a late Friday afternoon. Several students wished to throw accolades and seek his wisdom, but he was required by law to check in with his wife and report on his condition. They lived off base and Winnipeg could be a nasty place to drive in the winter if you were three sheets to the wind.

He was about to dial when he was struck by the graceful neckline of a woman sitting in the lounge. Darlene Muncie, holding a child on her lap, and more poised and beautiful than he remembered, triggered memories. He hung up the receiver and entered the lounge.

'I wouldn't be addressing Miss Darlene Muncie by any chance, would I?' Startled, she looked up, saw the sunglasses and smiled.

'I wouldn't be in the presence of, oh my gosh, Squadron Leader D.W. Jones, would I? Congratulations on your promotion.'

'And who might this young chap be?'

'This is Louis Fender Junior.'

Duckwalker could see him in the eyes, the shape of the jaw. The only thing missing was the scar. He was overwhelmed.

'Lou Fender and you? That weekend?'

'The very one.'

'You don't know how happy that makes me.' Tears welled, and she invited him to sit. It was question-and-answer time.

'I live in St. Boniface and teach grade eight. It's all in French.'

'And Josette?'

'Josette runs the hospital at Namao. We meet once a year at a women's retreat in the Lake of the Woods. She's showing a little grey, and since she's been out west, her accent is more French Canadian than ever. She does it deliberately.'

'I happen to think it's very appealing.'

'So do I.'

'What brings you here?' Darlene inquired.

'I run the CF-100 navigator school. I had spinal work done shortly after Lou was killed and I've managed to grow a couple of inches, although I still can't see worth shit. They still call me Duckwalker behind my back.'

'Married?'

'I married a widow. She's a little older than me and I love her dearly. Cracks the whip on me every now and then…. What brings you here?'

'I'm meeting my fiancé. Here he is now.'

Duckwalker rose to meet a tall bespectacled Squadron Leader wearing pilot's wings.

'Squadron Leader Jones, may I introduce Squadron Leader Archer, my fiancé.

Duckwalker rose and shook hands.

'Dwayne.'

'Fred. Pleased to meet you. Say—weren't you the CF-100 navigator involved in that thing that never happened a few years ago at Bagotville?'

'Yes, but how do you know about it and why would you ask? That's top-secret information.'

'I was up there too. Maybe we can talk about it over a few beers sometime. I'd like to hear the full story.'

'The full story is owned by Flying Officer Lou Fender, and a file buried deeper than any of us has rights and access to,' Duckwalker tersely responded. 'One day the story will be told.'

They both looked to Darlene and her eyes began to tear. Duckwalker offered to hold the child while she composed herself. He raised Lou's son over his head and felt his reaction.

'Tough little tyke. Looks and feels like a pilot to me.'

In a clearing off the end of a runway in northern Québec, a shattered crash helmet tattooed with the fading logo of the Grim Reaper slowly emerges from the ground, drawing a yearly return of the Mourning Cloak butterfly. Each year, the return is more prolific, and in spring the trees surrounding the site become festooned with millions of caterpillars, building cocoons to nourish wings that give them the gift of flight.

The End